DEAR READER,

I remember the day I discovered the Hapsburgs. After reading all of Mary Stewart's, Victoria Holt's, Phillippa Carr's, and Catherine Gaskin's books I discovered Evelyn Anthony. I was searching the stacks of the public library for more of her wonderful romantic suspense when I came across a book that changed my life. That book, *The Archduke* by Michael Arnold, was a historical novel written in the form of a diary kept by Crown Prince Rudolf of Austria-Hungary during the last year of his life, documenting the events leading to the tragedy at Mayerling.

I was ten years old and that wonderful discovery was the start of my lifelong romance with Rudolf and all things Hapsburg. I read everything I could find on the Hapsburgs, especially Rudolf and his parents, Emperor Franz Josef and Empress Elisabeth. But the Austro-Hungarian Empire was a distant memory and reading material was hard to come by. I persisted, learning to painstakingly translate German and French word for word with French–English and German–English dictionaries because the only material on the Hapsburgs I hadn't read hadn't been translated into English.

Three years after college graduation and marriage, I pulled out a notebook and began to write one. My first romance novel, *Whisper Always*, was born.

I've written five other romance novels since I wrote *Whisper Always*—all set in the American West during the 1870s and I sold all five of them before I sold *Whisper Always*. I built a reputation as an Americana writer, but I never forgot my love for the Hapsburgs or European royalty and history. My fascination with the Hapsburgs and my writing of *Whisper Always* made my American books possible. And now it's enabling me to tell the stories I want to tell—stories that take place in other times and settings on both sides of the Atlantic Ocean.

In *Whisper Always,* I wanted to tell the story of a man and a woman who fell in love and made mistakes in an unforgiving society. I wanted Rudolf to be part of that story because history has always regarded him as weak instead of a world-weary and disillusioned crown prince forced to wait until his father's death in order to do the job he'd been born to do. I wanted to show the human side of the crown prince. I used Rudolf to bring my hero and heroine together and he provided the opportunity for them to risk everything for love and to learn how to trust. I like to think that had they actually lived, Blake and Cristina would have done the same for him.

Had he lived, Rudolf would have ascended the throne in 1916 at the age of fifty-eight, and World Wars I and II might have been avoided. Rudolf's misfortune was to be heir to an absolute monarch who lived to be eighty-six and whose reign lasted sixty-eight years. Rudolf tired of the wait on January 30, 1889, at the age of thirty.

A small portrait of Rudolf sits on my desk and looks down on me as I write this. I hope *Whisper Always* has treated him fairly. He wasn't much for displays of sentimentality, but I think he would have liked Blake and Cristina and enjoyed the role he played in bringing them together. I hope you do, too.

REBECCA HAGAN LEE

June 1999

Whisper Always

REBECCA HAGAN LEE

JOVE BOOKS, NEW YORK

WHISPER ALWAYS

A Jove Book / published by arrangement with
the author

PRINTING HISTORY
Jove edition / October 1999

All rights reserved.
Copyright © 1999 by Rebecca Hagan Lee.
This book may not be reproduced in whole or part,
by mimeograph or any other means, without permission.
For information address: The Berkley Publishing Group,
a division of Penguin Putnam Inc.,
375 Hudson Street, New York, New York 10014.

The Penguin Putnam Inc. World Wide Web site address is
http://www.penguinputnam.com

ISBN: 0-515-12712-4

A JOVE BOOK®
Jove Books are published by The Berkley Publishing Group,
a division of Penguin Putnam Inc.,
375 Hudson Street, New York, New York 10014.
JOVE and the "J" design
are trademarks belonging to Penguin Putnam Inc.

PRINTED IN THE UNITED STATES OF AMERICA

10 9 8 7 6 5 4 3 2 1

For enduring and understanding my lifelong obsession
with the Hapsburgs,
for taking me to see the Lipizzaners every time they're
touring nearby, and for watching *Mayerling* over and
over again
without complaint.
For always believing I could do it and for making it
possible,
I dedicate this book to you, Steve.
With love.

Part One

Avarice, ambition, lust, etc., are nothing but species of madness.

—BENEDICT [BARUCH] DE SPINOZA 1632–1677

Prologue

Winter 1854
Everleigh, Sussex, England

THE BLACK-HAIRED WAIF huddled closer inside the blanket, staring out the window of her bedroom at the shimmering gabled roof and chimneys of the magnificent country house across the way. She often sat there in the early morning hours, dreaming of the day when she would live at Willow Wood. She hadn't yet worked out the way she intended to catch the eye of the heir to Willow Wood, but she would. She must. It wasn't enough to be the daughter of a country squire, she had to be something—someone—more. She moved back from the window so she could see her face reflected in the glass. At ten years of age, she already showed the promise of great beauty. A beauty she didn't intend to see wasted on a farmer or the son of a squire or any of the lower branches of the aristocracy. She was destined for greater things. One day she would be the marchioness of Everleigh. And her beauty would be her most valuable tool.

She tightened her grip on the blanket. She shivered in the

chilly air, but that couldn't be helped. Her bedroom was freezing cold in the winter and suffocatingly hot in the summer. Her father strutted around the village, pretending to be a powerful man, a force with whom to be reckoned in the district, but she knew better. Her father was a mere country squire. A country squire with a pitifully small income. Lord Everleigh was the real power. Everleigh, whose only son was a couple of years her elder. Everleigh, who had given refuge to his younger brother's widow and his nephew. She watched them from her perch in the window, watched as the two boys raced across the fields on finely bred horseflesh. She'd already met the nephew and begun weaving her spell around him. But at ten, she hadn't yet learned enough to control him. That's why she often sneaked out of her bedroom and carefully spied on the occupants of the room across the hall where her governess entertained her father every Thursday night. It thrilled her to watch and listen as plain Miss Franklin wheedled and cajoled her father into submission. He might rule the other rooms of the house with a beefy fist and a leather strap, but her father was just a quivering mass of groans, grunts, and sighs in the bedroom across the hall. And the fact that he surrendered his will to a governess every Thursday night gave her hope. She could see all the opportunities, the possibilities out of such weakness.

There was sweet satisfaction in knowing her father could be so easily controlled. And if her father could be controlled, so could other men—richer men, more powerful men. She stared at the boys. One day, she promised herself—one day she would have everything they had. One day she would own them both. She simply had to bide her time and watch and learn. Manipulation was the way of the world. The strong manipulated the weak. She was strong and she intended to do more with her life. She had no intention of being meek and mild like her mother, turning the other cheek while her husband fornicated with the governess beneath her very nose, or of bowing and scraping to ladies of the peerage.

Her aspirations went far beyond that. She intended to rule. And she was willing to hide in the wardrobe in a cold, dark bedroom every Thursday night to learn the necessary talents that would give her power over men. She had already learned a great deal, and she regularly practiced what she'd learned on Everleigh's nephew. Every day Jack surrendered more of his will to her. Eventually his cousin would, too.

She thrived on the thrill, the exquisite power of conquest.

If the heart of a man is depress'd with cares
The mist is dispelled when a woman appears.

—JOHN GAY 1685–1732

One

Spring 1878
London

"IS IT TRUE?" The tall blonde matron leaned over and whispered to the woman standing next to her.

"Is what true?"

"Don't be coy with me, Patricia." The blonde nodded toward the line of young women awaiting presentation to the queen. "The town's been whispering about the wager for weeks. And I couldn't help but notice poor Cristina's dress."

"Oh?" Patricia laughed.

The sound grated on the nerves of the man who stood directly behind them.

"Of course it's true," Patricia replied. "I wagered Cristina could catch the eye of the crown prince dressed in sack cloth and ashes."

"Do you really believe she can?" The words were annoying, spoken as they were in a malicious, conspiratorial whine.

"But of course," Patricia smiled. "If I could have presented her in sack cloth, I'd have done so." She shrugged her sleek, white shoulders. "As it was, her dress was the best I could do. Not that it will matter. The crown prince will notice her. That's to be expected. He's a connoisseur of beautiful women and Cristina is made in my image."

Lord Blake Ashford, ninth earl of Lawrence, shook his head. *When you were younger, perhaps,* he thought uncharitably, *but not now.* He glanced from mother to daughter. The girl waiting in line was exquisite—even dressed in that abominable creation.

The evening gown she wore ranked high among the most unbecoming garments Blake had ever seen on a woman. The dress was lavishly decorated. Overdecorated. The delicate silk was burdened with ruffles; bows; yards of wide, Belgian lace; and a multitude of hideous white satin rosettes. The rosettes clung to the bustle like lichen attaching itself to a rock, then extended in sweeping tendrils to cover the formal train. It was a horticulturist's nightmare in white silk and satin.

Blake gritted his teeth, remembering Patricia Fairfax's words. The deliberate fussiness of the gown made Cristina Fairfax look like an awkward child—a child caught playing dress-up with her mother's clothes. And judging from the set of her jaw and the belligerent thrust of her pointed chin, the young woman knew it.

"How much did you wager?" The eager question drew Blake's attention.

"I didn't wager money," Patricia replied.

"Then what?"

"You'll find out," Patricia said. "Once I've won the bet."

Blake scowled and focused his gaze on the daughter. Cristina. God, he hated women like Patricia! He pitied her absent husband and the young woman awaiting her formal debut. Women like Patricia Fairfax were Machiavellis in satin skirts. Beautiful, ambitious, and immoral. He knew the type all too well. He had spent a lifetime in their midst.

Disgusted by the women's talk, Blake moved away. He didn't want to hear the details. He didn't need to hear them. He understood society. He had learned the rules of the game years ago and he knew enough about those rules to realize that beautiful Cristina Fairfax was a pawn in her mother's nasty little schemes. Blake glanced at the young woman's profile. He wondered, suddenly, if she realized her mother was using her for amusement. Or if she cared.

Blake studied the girl, noting her proud carriage and the set expression on her face. She knew. Apparently she was powerless to do anything about her mother's scheming, but she knew and she cared. Cristina Fairfax seemed too proud, too innocent, and too aloof to be part of her mother's little wager. Blake took an involuntary step backward. The direction of his thoughts alarmed him. What did he know of innocence? His judgment was suspect where women were concerned, his instincts flawed. He had played the chivalrous knight once. And once was enough. He had learned from his mistake and vowed never to repeat it.

His instincts warned him to leave the reception while he had a chance, to forget what he had seen and overheard, but Blake didn't leave. He stood quietly and watched Cristina make her curtsey and felt an unwelcome surge of pride when the queen pronounced her, "a truly sweet and lovely girl."

He told himself he watched because he had a genuine respect for true courage. But he suspected the truth went far deeper than that. Blake pushed the bothersome thoughts aside. He didn't want to delve too deeply into unexplainable emotions. He didn't want to learn the results of Patricia Fairfax's wager or care what happened to her daughter. Cristina wasn't his concern and neither was her mother. So he waited for Cristina to back away from the queen, waited until she had rejoined her fellow debs, before he made his way to the opposite side of the room—as far away from the receiving line as possible. He had work to do.

Carefully blending into the crush of people, Blake mingled among his peers. He smiled to acquaintances, stopping here and there to exchange pleasantries, as his mind rapidly catalogued the faces in the crowd, searching for the unfamiliar.

Half an hour later, he nodded to his Austrian counterpart, then waited as the man answered his signal. Blake exhaled, relieved. The guests were all recognizable. There were no unknowns. He signaled to the Austrian once again, then slipped quietly out of the reception. He could relax in one of the small adjoining chambers until the dancing began. It was going to be a long night. He needed to rest while he could.

"PERDITION!" THE MUFFLED oath greeted him as Blake opened the door to one of the anterooms. He paused in the doorway and frowned.

Cristina Fairfax stood inside the door with the train of her gown clutched in her hand. He had spent the past half hour avoiding her only to find she had slipped away from the crowd to find a quiet private place to . . . Blake shrugged his shoulders, not really sure what she was doing. Or attempting to do. He watched her as she twisted her body at an unbelievable angle and single-mindedly cut the threads anchoring the mass of rosettes on her bustle.

Blake thought about keeping quiet and silently retreating from the little room, but impulsively decided to speak his mind. "I think it might be easier if you removed the dress."

Cristina whirled around to face the man leaning against the doorjamb, nearly tumbling in her haste. A guilty flush stained her cheeks as the gold embroidery scissors and a handful of artificial roses fell to the floor. Her green eyes widened in horror. She opened her mouth to speak, but words failed her. She stood silent, clearly embarrassed.

He smiled at her predicament. His dark eyes crinkled at the corners with amusement. "I agree. Something needs to be done about that god-awful dress. And I know desperate times require desperate measures, but taking a pair of scissors to a ballgown while wearing it seems—well"—he shrugged his shoulders once again—"a bit dangerous."

Cristina remained perfectly still and speechless as he closed and locked the door behind him before walking toward her.

"Turn around," he commanded. "It will take you all night to do it by yourself."

"Stop! Don't come any closer. I'll scream." Cristina had obviously recovered her power of speech.

"Don't be ridiculous." He spoke softly, but his deep voice held a note of warning. "I'm not going to hurt you. I'm simply going to help you finish whatever it is you're doing to your dress."

"I don't need your help."

"Perhaps not, but you cannot go back into the ballroom without someone's help, and I'm the only one available."

"But you can't—"

"Of course I can." He smiled down at her. "Now, be a good girl and turn around. Your roses need pruning. They're straggling down your bustle."

The corners of Cristina's mouth turned up in a smile, and she obediently turned her back to him.

Blake bent down to retrieve the scissors and began diligently cutting the remaining rosettes from her bustle and train. Stepping back to review his handiwork, Blake shook his head in dismay.

"I'm afraid the bows and ruffles will have to go, too."

Cristina twisted around to see what he'd done. "Are you certain?"

"Trust me," he said, as he knelt behind her once again.

Minutes later, the remains of white satin bows, ruffles, and rosettes littered the floor around Cristina's feet. The only adornment left on her gown was the wide, Belgian lace stretched across her abdomen and the row of pearl buttons that fastened the back of the dress.

Blake levered himself up from his knees then circled Cristina, slowly viewing the dress from all angles.

"Well?" Cristina demanded anxiously.

"Perfection," he said solemnly. "Simple, elegant perfection."

Cristina sighed in relief. "I don't know how to thank you for your help," she began.

"Seeing you this way is thanks enough. I was happy to relieve you of that monstrosity." He bowed slightly. "Now you can run along to your ball and enjoy yourself."

Cristina nearly blinded him with the brilliance of her smile. She took a step forward and found herself tangled in the mound of white at her feet.

"What should we do with all this?"

"I'll take care of it," he assured her. "This will be our secret. No one else need know."

Cristina smiled once more as she quietly slipped out the door.

Blake watched her go, then bent to pick up the refuse. He slipped a rosette into his jacket pocket. A memento of the unusual evening, he told himself, a memento of a unique situation—and a very lovely young woman. He smiled at the thought, then carefully stuffed the rest of the white satin decorations between the cushions of the sofas.

Lord, I wonder what fool it was that first invented kissing!

—JONATHAN SWIFT 1667–1745

Two

A WHIRLING MASS of white silks and satins filled the ball-room. Interspersed here and there were the colorful gowns of the older women and chaperons, accentuated by the scarlet, blue, green, and gold slashes of the military uniforms of the various regiments from countries throughout Europe and the ever-expanding empire. Their brilliant apparel served as a striking counterpoint to the elegant, black coat and tails of the other gentlemen.

In the center of all the gaiety, Cristina Fairfax stood en-thralled by the display, and almost overwhelmed by eager young suitors. Breathless from the previous dance, she balked when the music began once again and her young partner for-got himself long enough to tug on her gloved hand.

"The squares are forming for the quadrille, Miss Fairfax. If we don't hurry, we'll miss the beginning."

Cristina dug in her heels and pulled against him. "No, please, we must stop. I'm exhausted and parched. I must catch my breath before we go any further."

"But . . ."

"I'm sorry," she stated firmly, "but I simply can't walk

another step. A quadrille is out of the question.'' She flashed a perfect smile at the young man to soften the blow as she refused the dance, but the steely glint in her green eyes made it quite clear she was through dancing for the moment.

She was hot and tired and gasping for breath in long, un-ladylike spasms. She hated to disappoint her partner—knew she wasn't being fair to him—but Cristina had never fainted before and had no desire to start a trend by collapsing in the middle of her presentation ball. The eligible young men had crowded around her all evening vying for her attention as they waited for the chance to whirl her around the ballroom and she had met their demands. She'd spent the evening flirting outrageously, fluttering her silk fan and her eyelashes with aplomb, bestowing smiles on admirers, and breaking young hearts right and left. But now she simply had to rest.

Even remodeled, her ballgown was hot and heavy. The rigid stays she wore beneath it bit into her ribs and hampered her breathing and her dancing slippers pinched her toes.

She knew the ballroom was buzzing about her. But this time the whispers were anything but cruel. Cristina smiled as she remembered the look of astonishment on Patricia's face. Her mother hadn't expected her to enter the ballroom in a completely refurbished gown and the tight pinch of her dancing slippers had like seemed a small price to pay for an evening of triumph. But that was hours ago, and now . . .

Cristina turned to apologize to her partner. ''I'm sorry to disappoint you, Mr. Brown, but I know if I keep dancing I'll drop.''

Timothy Brown looked at her with adoring, spaniel-like eyes. ''That's all right, Miss Fairfax, I've been quite thoughtless. I should have realized you were tired. If you'll wait here a moment, I'll bring us some refreshment.''

''Thank you, Mr. Brown, I'd like that very much.'' Cristina thanked him with a genuine smile of gratefulness. ''I'll await your return over there.'' She nodded toward the far wall where the crowd had thinned, then made her way through the crush of people surrounding her while Timothy hurried off in the direction of the refreshment tables.

She reached the wall and leaned against a marble column, shifting her weight from one leg to the other as she wiggled her toes in an effort to restore the circulation in her feet. Cristina glanced around to see who might be watching. She was well aware that she was on display—presented into society for the sole purpose of finding a husband—and she couldn't help feeling like a box of Swiss chocolates in a confectioner's window, wrapped and waiting for someone to purchase and devour. She wondered which of the men she'd danced with tonight would call on her in the morning. Could she accept any of them if they did? She was bored by their talk of horses, hounds, and university life, and completely unimpressed by the not-too-subtle mention of titles and wealth. She yearned for romance and adventure, but all she found was the business of merging family bloodlines and increasing fortunes. None of those young pups were husband material, Cristina decided. Not one of them could keep her mind off the pain in her pinched toes.

She sighed, allowing her gaze to scan the room, searching. . . . Could anyone compete with the pair of penetrating, black eyes she remembered laughing at her in the antechamber?

Cristina looked around the room and found those same dark eyes glaring at her. She shivered as a mixture of trepidation and excitement coursed through her veins. He was devastatingly attractive. And when he smiled . . . His was a face one did not forget easily. It was a bronzed, lean face, molded with enticing planes and angles. She noticed that the whiteness of the starched shirt front and collar contrasted sharply with his face, lending it an exotic, almost foreign look. His eyes were keen, sparkling black like chunks of coal beneath straight brows. His nose was straight and aristocratic and his nostrils flared slightly as he scowled at her. Yes, she thought, he was a fine figure of a man from the top of his dark head to the tips of his polished shoes. His handsome, clean-shaven face set him apart from the multitude of men sporting sidewhiskers, beards, and huge hussar mustaches.

Cristina pulled her gaze from the mirrorlike shine on his shoes and looked him in the eye. Her emerald green gaze clashed with his simmering black one. She had the urge to pull away, to run and hide from his gaze, but found she couldn't seem to break the contact. She stared at him, fighting a battle of wills that made her forget about her aching feet and made her incredibly curious about the man who shared her secret. What had she done to make him so angry?

"I see you've finally captured every man's attention."

The sound of a voice at her ear startled her. Cristina turned.

A slender young man of medium build stood smiling next to her. He noted Cristina's questioning glance, discerned the reason behind it, and explained with a nod toward the other man. "He is a bit slow. I noticed you hours ago. As soon as you entered the ballroom."

"Pardon?" Cristina was still slightly bemused by his sudden appearance.

He repeated his observation.

"I don't know what you mean," Cristina told him.

"Don't be coy, Miss Fairfax," he said, his eyes becoming a warmer shade of clear blue. "You must know you stand out in the crowd like a ruby surrounded by diamonds."

His compliment embarrassed her and Cristina ducked her head, suddenly immersed in the patterns of streaks in the marble floor.

"You're blushing! It's refreshing to find someone who actually blushes these days."

Cristina looked up, taking the opportunity to study him. He stood ramrod straight in his British cavalry uniform. The rigid set of his spine made him seem taller than he actually was. He appeared to be about the same age as Timothy Brown, perhaps twenty or twenty-one. But his manner and bearing were that of a much older man. His light brownish-blonde hair was cropped close and there was a distinct accent when he spoke. A military man, Cristina decided, a well-traveled one.

"Why do you suppose debutantes wear white? It's so bland, so ghostly, so virginal."

His blunt statement stunned her. She covered her surprise by pretending a sophistication she didn't feel.

"I don't know why we're required to wear white unless it's to proclaim to all the gentlemen that we *are* virginal. Just as two ostrich feathers mean unmarried, and three, married. It's polite advertising." Cristina tipped her head forward to indicate the two white ostrich feathers held in place by a diamond clip fastened in her red curls. She shrugged her shoulders. "Then again, it may have nothing to do with advertising. Maybe Her Majesty prefers white gowns and ostrich plumes."

"Another royal whim," he suggested, "like her Indian servants, the Scottish ghillie, and her prolonged mourning. What a pity you could not wear green. You are lovely in white, but I should love to see you in green. And perhaps I'll have that opportunity at a future date . . ." His discerning perusal instantly reminded Cristina of the imaginary box of chocolates in the sweetshop window.

"I'm afraid you take entirely too much for granted. I spoke to you out of politeness because you spoke to me, but that doesn't mean I'll allow you to call on me." She delivered her haughty setdown and turned in the direction of the door when the young man caught her arm.

"Wait! I apologize for offending you. Give me the chance to make amends."

"I don't want you to make amends," Cristina insisted. "I want you to release me immediately."

"I don't want to release you." He leaned closer. "I want to apologize for my behavior and I insist you allow me to do so. Come dance with me," he whispered very smoothly into her ear. "I want very much to hold you in my arms."

"No . . ." Cristina began to protest, but her partner ignored her as he half led, half dragged her into the mass of dancers.

He surveyed the room and with a nod of his head, the orchestra broke into a lively Strauss waltz. The dancers parted like the Red Sea before Moses to allow them onto the center of the floor. As he swept her around the room, Cristina found herself wondering for the first time exactly who he was and how he commanded so much attention in a room full of dignitaries. Everyone in the room, including the Prince and Princess of Wales, was staring at them.

"Let go," Cristina ordered. "You're holding me much too closely. I don't imagine the queen would approve of this."

Her partner threw back his head and laughed at her rebuke. "Why shouldn't everyone stare at us?" he asked when he recovered from his outburst. "We make a striking couple. And it doesn't matter how tightly I hold you. The old queen isn't here and even if she were, she has no jurisdiction over me."

His boast astounded Cristina. While she knew Queen Victoria was greatly loved by her relatives and subjects, Cristina also knew many of them quaked in their boots when summoned for an audience. She had lived in the "upper ten thousand" all of her life and she'd never met anyone who was oblivious to the queen's opinion. The very idea was revolutionary.

As if reading her thoughts, he teased her, "Now, I've captured your imagination, lovely one. Intrigued you, aroused your curiosity."

She opened her mouth to deny his theory, but he cut her short. "Don't bother to protest. I can see the truth in your eyes. You must learn to hide your thoughts. Your eyes betray them."

His last observation was too much for Cristina, who had been trying to rein in her explosive temper since he had swept her onto the dance floor. "My thoughts are my own. You've no right to pry. I've never found dissembling necessary. And I've never met anyone so full of his own importance. I couldn't care less what you think you see in my eyes." Cristina lifted her chin in a gesture designed to show she didn't give tuppence for his opinions.

He laughed again. "You are far too impulsive for your own good. If I was someone of rank and importance, Miss Fairfax, I might be offended by your sharp tongue. But I forgive you your youth and remind you that your words may come back to haunt you someday."

"If they do, it won't be any of your concern," Cristina

retorted again. "I know you're not English. Your accent is German or Prussian, but that tells me nothing. There are always German relations at Court. Are you part of the family?"

Her artless question amused him and Cristina's blood began to boil at the sound of his laughter.

"I know it's rude of me to blurt out my thoughts, but it's even more rude to laugh each time I ask a simple question. I don't know you. We shouldn't be dancing together."

"Will your mother scold you?" he asked, successfully diverting her attention from the question of his identity.

"I very much doubt my mother is paying attention to me," she answered. "My mother has a flock of admirers. She can't be bothered by a mere daughter."

He frowned at the obvious bitterness in her tone. "I am acquainted with your lovely mother."

Cristina was surprised. "You've met my mother?"

"On several memorable occasions."

"Aren't you a bit young for her? Is that why you're toying with me? Are you thinking like mother, like daughter?"

His eyes glinted angrily as he stared back at her and his words were a cold rebuke. "You are rude and insulting, Miss Fairfax." He loosened his hold around her waist and came to an abrupt halt.

Knowing she was about to be abandoned on the dance floor, Cristina attempted a halfhearted apology. "I'm sorry . . . I shouldn't have—"

"No," he agreed, "you should not have. However, I will tell you what you want to know. I am dancing with you because it is what I wish to do. I find you very lovely, but also younger than I would have liked. Perhaps too young. . . ."

"I am not!"

"I'm not talking about your age, Miss Fairfax, I am talking about experience. Worldliness. You look like a woman, but you're a fledgling schoolgirl. Still, there is a part of me that would like to explore the possibilities of a more intimate friendship." He allowed his words to trail off into the realms of innuendo.

"That will never happen, sir," Cristina haughtily informed

him. "Our brief *acquaintance* is at an end. You'll never have the opportunity to know me—intimately or otherwise."

He remained undaunted by her harsh words. "I'll be in London for several weeks and I hope to persuade you to change your mind. I can be very persuasive when I want something." He sounded almost charming and definitely wicked. "You're not immune to me, Miss Fairfax, and given time, and the right incentives, I think you may come around to my way of thinking."

Cristina summoned all her courage, looked him straight in eyes, and challenged him, practically spitting the words in his face. "That remains to be seen, doesn't it?"

"Then we shall wait and see." He smiled at her, bowed low over her white-gloved hand, and kissed it. "Thank you most kindly for the dance, *mein fraulein*." He clicked his heels together in military fashion and strode quickly across the ballroom where he disappeared through a set of double doors.

Cristina was left stranded in the midst of a crowd of dancers with her former partner nowhere in sight. She was just about to fight her way through the dancers when a man took pity on her and moved forward to escort her off the dance floor.

"I'll say one thing for you, you're the most impulsive, bravest, or incredibly foolhardy young woman I've ever met, but even you can't think it was a good idea to challenge him. It's the one way to ensure his interest. Or is that your game?"

Cristina was taken back by the absolute fury she heard in the voice of the man escorting her. It reminded her of a pair of glaring black eyes. She tilted her head back to get a look at her accuser.

"You!" The words left her mouth in a rush as she faced those dark, glacial eyes.

He ignored her startled gasp and continued his accusations. "Whatever your intention, it worked. You intrigue him and he usually gets whatever he wants."

"So he said."

He ignored her sarcasm just as he had ignored her earlier gasp of recognition. "I would advise staying away from him if you've no intention of becoming his latest plaything or having your reputation ruined beyond repair. I realize the lure of wealth and power is impossible to resist, especially to a young woman about to make her mark on society, but stay away from him or you'll be hurt. He isn't the man for you." There was the barest hint of bitterness in his voice.

"You don't think highly of him, do you?" It was more of a statement than a question.

"On the contrary, I like him very much, but I'm not looking to be his mistress." His lean, tanned fingers surrounded the upper part of Cristina's arm as he ushered her away from the crowd. He was unaccountably angry at her for the surge of jealousy he felt toward Rudolf. "Now, if you no longer require my services as escort, I think I'll go back to my own amusements." He bowed low, turned, and started to walk away.

"Wait!" The cry sprang from Cristina's lips as she reached out to grasp his sleeve.

The touch of her hand on his arm burned through him. A flicker of some undefinable emotion crossed his face. "What is it? What do you want?"

Cristina froze and he barked again, impatient with her. Something about her disturbed him. She had the knack of shaking his unshakable facade.

"Who is he?" she whispered, cowed by his attitude.

"You mean you don't know?" Blake was genuinely surprised. "You must be the only woman in the room who doesn't know who he is."

"Then why don't you enlighten me?" Cristina snapped, impatient with herself for her own timidity, and equally impatient with him for mocking her ignorance.

"All right, since you demand to know. The man you were dancing with, my dear young lady, was His Imperial Highness, the crown prince Rudolf Francis Charles Joseph of Hapsburg-Lorraine, the ruling family of the Austro-Hungarian Empire."

Cristina's knees nearly buckled from the shock of his revelation. Her stomach began to ache and she swayed on her feet and silently prayed the marble floor would open up and swallow her. She had flirted outrageously, danced with, and been deliberately rude to a prince without even knowing it. Not just any prince, but the heir to a vast empire. She had issued an unmistakable challenge to his manhood which she had no intention of allowing him to answer. And she had insulted him. He would certainly demand satisfaction from her mother, and at the very least, an apology from her. Fortunately, her sex prevented him from calling her out to duel at dawn. But then, if she had been a man, none of this would have happened.

Blake watched the play of emotions on her transparent face. So she really hadn't known the identity of her admirer. Amazing. He wouldn't have believed it possible for Patricia Fairfax's daughter to be so naive where royalty was concerned, but he would bet his last shilling she wasn't playacting. The shock on her face was quite evident and she clutched the fabric of his sleeve as if it were a lifeline. Her face, devoid of all color except the startling green of her enormous eyes, reminded him of a cornered vixen. He could almost see the wheels turning in her brain as she sought an escape route. He could feel her rising panic and Blake half expected her to bolt and run for the door.

"Are you all right?" A stupid question, he berated himself as soon as the words left his mouth. He could see his revelation had stunned her.

"I don't feel very well." Cristina's tiny voice caught him completely unawares. There was no resemblance to the confident, almost haughty young woman of moments before. Her voice wavered with uncertainty and she stared at him like a bewildered child suddenly afraid to move. "Could I please sit down?"

He led her away from the ballroom back to the antechamber. Cristina noticed his ease with his surroundings and vowed to guard her tongue around him. Just in case . . .

"Feeling better?" he asked when some of the color returned to her face.

"Yes, much. Thank you. For a minute, I was sure I was

going to be sick, or faint, or both," she admitted.

He smiled at her candor, and a lopsided dimple transformed his usually serious features. "For a moment there so was I, Miss Fairfax," he replied.

"How do you know my name?"

"I was at the presentation tonight. Didn't you realize the young bachelors have been awaiting your official debut for weeks? You've been the talk of the town. Why do you think Rudolf sought you out?" His smile abruptly vanished and his clipped aristocratic voice masked any traces of emotion.

Cristina didn't care why the crown prince chose to single her out for his unwanted attention. She simply wished he hadn't. The chance encounter with the man in front of her was the only good to come out of the evening. He'd rescued her twice in one evening. Who was he?

"You have me at a disadvantage, sir. You appear to know all about me, while I know nothing about you, not even your name."

"My name is Lawrence," he supplied the missing information. "Blake Ashford, ninth earl of Lawrence."

"I'm in your debt again, Lord Lawrence. You've aided me twice tonight. Thank you."

"Your gratitude isn't necessary. I was only doing my job."

Cristina decided she was tired of all the mystery and forgetting her vow to guard her tongue, attempted to satisfy her burning curiosity about the evasive Blake Ashford with the dark, dangerous eyes. "I wasn't so busy dancing that I didn't notice you glowering at me from across the room, Lord Lawrence. What is your job? Spying on unsuspecting debutantes? Rescuing damsels in distress?"

"I'm in the diplomatic corps. My father recently retired from his post as ambassador in Vienna. And I've twice been posted there. As I'm well acquainted with the Austrian royal family, the Prince of Wales asked me to serve as guide to Crown Prince Rudolf while he's in London."

"What do you do?" Cristina persisted.

"Obviously, I guide."

His deliberate evasiveness irritated Cristina. "What do you guide?"

"I guide the prince's entourage about factories, banks, Parliament, London, et cetera."

"What about the crown prince? You said you were doing your job. What does touring England have to do with seeing me off a dance floor? I fail to see a connection."

"I am the connection," he told her. "Part of my 'unofficial' duty is to make sure the crown prince amuses himself with the right, or should I say wrong, type of woman. He is to stay away from innocent young debs with more curiosity than sense."

Cristina rose to face him. "You think that I . . ." she sputtered.

"Aren't you?" Blake countered. "You are a debutante fresh from the schoolroom, presumably still a virgin, out to snare a husband. Preferably a rich one."

"How dare you make such presumptions about me?" Cristina exclaimed.

"I dare many things," Blake told her, "including an honest reply."

"You're wrong."

"Really?"

"I don't have more curiosity than sense."

Blake laughed. "Then you are a rarity. Most women find the lure of a royal title and immeasurable wealth irresistible. It's considered a definite prerequisite for marriage." He recognized the anger glinting in the depths of her verdant eyes, but ignored the warning. "And I've learned that every woman puts a price on her affections. Some are higher than others, but all can be bought."

"By you?" Cristina scoffed.

"By anyone with money enough."

"I suppose that makes you feel very superior. Well, let me tell you one thing, Lord Lawrence, I am a free-thinking human being with the rights and privileges of any other British subject. I can't be bought by you, the crown prince, the tsar of Russia, or any other man at any price. I'll give myself to a man only when I choose to do so. And when that time comes, he certainly won't be a man like you!''

Blake calmly regarded the girl standing before him. Her firm, young breasts heaved against the silk of her gown after her angry tirade. Watching her, listening to her made him feel younger than he had in years. She was so natural—such an enchanting mixture of ideals and innocence, of fire and ice, of child and woman. He was almost ashamed of himself for goading her. Almost, but not quite.

''Bravo, Miss Fairfax,'' he applauded. ''You're as naive as you are rare. I admire your little independence speech. You've managed to include everything except 'God Save the Queen.' But, to quote the Bard, it's all 'sound and fury, signifying nothing.' This is a world run by males, and you, Miss Fairfax,'' he said with a deliberate perusal that raked her from head to toe, ''are most definitely a female.''

''Oh!'' Christina gasped in outrage and her hand flew up to avenge his insult.

Blake reacted swiftly, catching her hand before it could make contact. She struggled furiously against his hold. He grasped her flailing arms and imprisoned her wrists against his hard chest, effectively trapping her hands between their bodies where they could do no harm. His firm mouth curved into a mocking smile as he impulsively bent his head and kissed her. Thoroughly. Branding her lips with his, tasting her, tantalizing her until Cristina leaned against him, seeking more.

Blake's senses reeled at the desire sparking between them. He tore his mouth away from hers while he was still able to think and stared down at her. Her emerald-green eyes were half closed and dazed with longing. An almost overwhelming urge to kiss her again seized him. Blake forced himself to ignore the hot blood racing to his groin—forced himself to put an end to the madness.

''My dear Miss Fairfax, are you certain you won't choose a man like me?''

Cristina opened her eyes and stared at him for a full minute before his hateful words penetrated her brain. She plummeted back to earth with a thump, the harsh reality of his words and actions stinging her pride. Gathering the shreds of her dignity, Cristina pulled herself out of his arms and stood waiting for him to say something else—to apologize for his ungentlemanly behavior—or to kiss her again. But she waited in vain.

Blake stood immobile, unapproachable.

Without speaking a word, Cristina turned her back to him. She stiffened her spine and straightened her shoulders, pausing for a split second, before she walked to the door. She pulled the heavy paneled door open, then quietly stepped through the opening.

While Blake, ninth earl of Lawrence, stared at the door.

Alone once again.

I have seen the wicked in great power, and
spreading himself like a green bay tree.

—PSALMS 37:35

Three

"STOP!" BLAKE SHOUTED as the carriage passed the Georgian mansion. The driver pulled the coach to the side of the street, steering around a host of other vehicles crowded along the drive and along the street.

"What do you suppose is going on?" Blake asked the coachman as he opened the door. A crowd gathered outside Strathemore's residence.

"Looks like a big party to me, sir."

Blake nodded in agreement. It looked that way to him, too. "It was supposed to be an intimate midnight supper for a few members of the club." He muttered an oath beneath his breath.

The coachman whistled in awe. "Is this Lord Strathemore's idea of intimate?"

A variety of carriages lined both sides of the block. Several more inched down the street.

"No," Blake answered, "but, it's the crown prince's idea of intimate. Look." Blake pointed to the prince's borrowed coach. The prince might be traveling incognito but his coachmen wore the distinctive livery of the Prince of Wales.

It was half past midnight, but Blake knew he had plenty of time. He hadn't come for supper. He'd accepted Lord Strathemore's invitation strictly out of curiosity. Although he and Strathemore were both active in the government and members of the same men's club, Blake rarely attended Strathemore's social gatherings, and he had never attended his intimate midnight suppers. While he didn't actively dislike the man, Blake knew Strathemore's idea of amusement differed from his own. It was one of the reasons Strathemore's invitation to supper surprised him.

Seeing Crown Prince Rudolf's carriage parked outside Strathemore's house explained everything. Blake now understood the reason behind the invitation. Lord Strathemore had invited him because Rudolf was present.

Blake smiled as he entered the house. Strathemore was too much of a politician to exclude him.

"Good evening, Lord Lawrence."

Blake looked down. Lady Strathemore stood at his elbow.

"We didn't expect you this evening." Her voice was nasal, high-pitched.

Blake recognized it immediately. He'd overheard her conversation with Patricia Fairfax earlier in the evening.

"You don't usually attend our little auctions."

"Auctions?" Blake stared at his hostess.

"Yes. Sometimes we have card games but tonight we're having an auction." Her high-pitched voice grew even higher. "Tonight even gentlemen who don't normally attend our little soirees are here." She eyed Blake meaningfully. "Lady Fairfax insisted we invite everyone of wealth and importance. Isn't it exciting? I can't wait to see what she wagered!"

Blake started to turn away.

"You are going to bid, aren't you, Lord Lawrence?" Lady Strathemore looked up at him under the veil of her darkened lashes. "I'll be auctioned tonight."

Her straightforward approach startled Blake almost as much as it disgusted him. He'd heard about the so-called midnight clubs where the wealthy, jaded peers auctioned their wives and mistresses to other men for amusement. It was procurement and prostitution at its highest level.

A half-dozen replies to her suggestion flashed through Blake's mind, but he chose the least offensive one. Charlotte Strathemore had never been known for her intelligence, only her lack of it. "I prefer to be monogamous in my relationships."

"But you don't . . . I mean you aren't . . ." Charlotte stammered.

"Then I choose to remain celibate."

Charlotte stared at him, awed by his statement.

Blake regretted the words as soon as they left his mouth. Imagine telling a featherbrain like Charlotte Strathemore that he preferred celibacy. God knows what rumors would be flying tomorrow morning.

"Oh, you mean like a monk or something." Charlotte continued to stare, fascinated by his apparent abnormality.

"Or something," Blake said. "Now if you'll excuse me. . . ." He flashed her a winning smile before he turned away. He needed a breath of fresh air. The atmosphere reeked of overindulgence. He gathered his hat and cane and started for the front door.

"Lawrence, my dear fellow, surely you aren't leaving so soon?"

Blake gritted his teeth as the Prince of Wales called to him. He turned in time to see the prince make his way through the crowd, Rudolf at his side. "I don't recall seeing you at any of Strathemore's gatherings," the Prince of Wales remarked, clapping Blake around the shoulder.

"No, sir, this is my first."

"Rudolf's as well. Come, my boys, I'll explain the rules at supper."

The Prince of Wales occupied the place of honor at the dinner table. Rudolf sat on his right, while Blake sat on his left. Strathemore had graciously relinquished his seat to Blake when the prince announced his intention to explain the rules of the auction to the newcomers.

Gentlemen, married or single, could bid on the "slaves," but only married women could be auctioned, provided they were willing. Courtesans and other low-born women could only be auctioned at the gatherings if no society women were present. Low-born "slaves" could be married or unmarried, with virgins high in demand.

Society debutantes or spinsters could not participate. They were considered off-limits to everyone.

"To everyone?" Rudolf asked.

"Yes," the Prince of Wales replied.

"Even to us?" Rudolf persisted.

The fine hairs at the back of Blake's neck began to tingle at Rudolf's question.

The Prince of Wales smiled indulgently at Rudolf. "Even to us, my friend," he explained. "The young demoiselles are protected until they're safely married."

When they become fair game, Blake thought.

"No woman who isn't, or hasn't been married, is auctioned. All gentlemen abide by that rule." The Prince of Wales ended the subject.

After supper, the auction began in the ballroom. The excitement mounted as gentlemen "slave traders" displayed their "merchandise" on the raised dais set up in the center of the room. The bidding process astonished Blake. Wealthy, influential peers of the realm bartered the sexual favors of their wives in return for racehorses, carriages, jewels, money, even gambling debts. Blake tried not to think about the auction or its participants. He had no desire to know who was cuckolding whom. The leers on the faces of his colleagues and their sordid amusement repulsed him. He glanced at the Prince of Wales and Rudolf, hoping for a chance to escape without notice.

"You're not bidding," Rudolf chided him.

"Neither are you," Blake pointed out.

"There is nothing here that interests me," Rudolf replied with a small smile. "I've made other arrangements. What of you?"

Blake shook his head. "I'm working, Your Highness, and in any case, I'm possessive and very discriminating."

"The idea of sharing a woman doesn't excite you?" Rudolf asked with a lift of his brow.

Blake decided to be very diplomatic. "I prefer to choose my partner in a discretionary manner. I see no reason to give other men ammunition to use against me."

"Very wise," Rudolf said. "Very wise, and very dull, but I applaud your sense of morality."

Blake's reply was lost in the sound of catcalls and whistles as Patricia Fairfax stepped onto the auction block.

"I bid one thousand pounds!" called a voice from the back of the room.

Patricia laughed. "I'm not for bid, tonight, gentlemen. I'm here to announce the terms of my wager."

There were more catcalls.

"Ladies, and gentlemen," Patricia smiled. "I graciously admit defeat. I lost my wager. My daughter, Cristina, didn't catch the crown prince's eye in her original dress. He failed to notice her until she changed gowns." Patricia glanced at the crown prince, then at the women in the room. "Ladies, take note, the crown prince only has eyes for beautiful women, beautifully clothed. Therefore, I forfeit five hundred pounds to Lord Strathemore."

The crowd heaved a collective groan of disappointment.

"And," Patricia continued, "I abide by the terms of the wager and offer my daughter, Cristina, for auction to the highest bidder."

Silence filled the room. Everything halted. No one moved or spoke. Everyone waited. The unwritten rules of the club were explicit and no gentleman dared break them. Patricia Fairfax, however, was a woman who had dared the unthinkable.

"Madame, I protest this . . . this . . . breach," the Prince of Wales stuttered, shocked.

Patricia turned her most charming smile on the prince. "But, Your Highness, I'm doing only what's best for my daughter," she protested. "I'll conduct private negotiations. Cristina will go to the highest bidder," Patricia paused, dramatically. "Yes, ladies and gentlemen, the highest bidder wins my lovely daughter's hand," she announced, before adding coyly, "in marriage."

The Prince of Wales laughed. The crowd began to breathe again. Trust Patricia to turn the ordinary into the extraordinary. Trust Patricia to turn the most exciting wager of the season into a massive joke. The guests relaxed and began to laugh and joke at their gullibility.

All except Blake Ashford. He had seen the look that passed between Patricia Fairfax and Crown Prince Rudolf. He had seen Rudolf's almost imperceptible nod of reply.

HOURS LATER, CRISTINA watched as the rising sun brightened her bedroom ceiling. She climbed out of bed to close the heavy drapes, determined to find the sleep that had eluded her since her return from the palace. Her first court ball had been an unprecedented disaster. Oh, she had left her mark on London society as she said she would, but Blake Ashford had left his mark on her. He had attracted her and intrigued her with his arrogant manner, rescued her, mocked her, insulted her, and kissed her until she was breathless—all in one evening. She was confused and exhausted, but her mind insisted on replaying the evening's events, skimming over her faux pas with the crown prince in order to dwell on Lord Lawrence.

He was a mass of contradictions and he fascinated Cristina. He had kissed her forcefully but he hadn't tried to force her to respond. That had been her own doing. His lips had been so gentle. Cristina never imagined a kiss could feel like that. His mouth had been warm and coaxing and passionate and she had responded with a rush of feeling that frightened her. Could you lose your soul in a kiss? Had she? The effect of Lord Lawrence's lips on hers had been beyond belief. She hadn't anticipated his kiss or her response and that rush of uncontrolled feelings frightened her. Cristina had learned a long time ago that love made you vulnerable. Passion blinded you to everything except your own needs. She knew what to expect from love and passion. She had lived with the knowledge for years.

Cristina blinked away the memory that haunted her, forcing herself not to relive the pain of that night. But she couldn't prevent the sting of scalding tears each time she remembered her father's departure from Fairhall. Her mother had driven him away with her constant stream of lovers, her hateful words, and the awful lies. Cristina would never forgive her for those lies.

"Missy, wake up, your mother wants to see you right now."

Cristina huddled under the covers, ignoring Leah, her maid.

"Wake up, Miss Cristina, it's past noon already."

It couldn't be! She had just closed her eyes. And as her sleepy brain attempted to convince Cristina darkness dominated the sky, Leah pulled the drapes to reveal rays of sunlight.

"Hurry, she wants to see you right away," Leah urged.

Cristina slipped on a silk wrapper and slowly headed down the hall to her mother's room, dreading the coming confrontation. She reached the door, drew a deep breath, and knocked.

Patricia sat upright in her bed surrounded by satin pillows of all hues. Her chestnut hair spilled down around her shoulders and curled atop the coverlet. She wore an ivory lace bed jacket, a stunning emerald and diamond necklace, and nothing else. At thirty-seven, she was still a beautiful woman.

"Well, Cristina, do you like it?" There were no preliminary niceties before Patricia began the grill.

Cristina breathed a sigh of relief at the familiar question. "It's beautiful, Mother. All your jewels are beautiful." Her reply was mechanical and equally familiar.

"This necklace is different, darling." Patricia purred like some expensive feline and Cristina inwardly cringed at the sound.

"You must have bought it for yourself. Your taste is better than that of most of your admirers, who tend to lean toward gaudy vulgarity. But the necklace you're wearing this morning is truly beautiful and that's enough to make it different from your normal assortment.'' Cristina could not contain the bitter sarcasm.

"Oh this necklace is different, Cristina, but not for the reasons you suppose. It's different because you obtained it for me.''

"But I didn't. . . .'' Cristina was puzzled.

"Of course you did.'' Patricia's purring voice held a note of triumph. "You enchanted a certain gentleman at the ball last night. He sent a messenger over this morning with this little token of his esteem.''

Enchanted which gentleman? Cristina wasn't certain that "enchanted'' was the correct word. Intrigued, perhaps. Or incited. But not enchanted. She hadn't enchanted any gentlemen last night. She'd insulted one and angered another. Which one of them thought he could bribe her when she'd made it perfectly clear that she wasn't for sale? "You may send the necklace back to whomever sent it. I want no part of him or his jewels.''

"Are you crazy? I'll do nothing of the sort. This is just the beginning. He sent this to show his regard for you. Be nice to him and you'll have others like it.''

"Sending it back will show my regard for him,'' Cristina told her mother. "I wasn't nice to him last night and I don't intend to be nice to him in the future.''

"He offered this necklace in payment for your companionship, Cristina. It will make a lovely addition to my collection. Naturally, I accepted it on your behalf.''

"You can't.''

"It's already done. Don't you see, Cristina, this is my opportunity? What I always hoped for. This man is very important. He can open new doors for us and further our social standing.''

"I don't care about social standing.''

"I do,'' Patricia warned her. "I've been in a precarious situation with the queen since your father left. And, well, London seasons are expensive, as are engagement parties and weddings. When this gentleman approached me, I thought, why should I spend all that money to give Cristina away, when this man is willing to pay for her? All you have to do is be his companion. Go where he goes, dine where he dines, sleep where he sleeps. What could be better?'' Patricia waved a delicate hand in the direction of the door. ''Now, go back to your room. Leah will bring you a bite to eat. He's sending his carriage for you tonight, so you have plenty of time to rest. Run along, I have a great deal to do.''

''You *sold* me?'' Cristina refused to move.

''It was better than paying someone to take you,'' Patricia replied with her own brand of indisputable logic.

''I'm not leaving Fairhall with your gentleman, tonight or any other night.''

''You have no choice. You can't stay here in London without a chaperon and I'm tired of playing mother. A gentleman friend has offered me a month or two on the Continent with him and I've decided to accept. I'm closing the house until I return.'' Patricia's voice was coldly determined as she jerked the bellpull over her bed. Her bodyguard and sometime lover hurried to her side. ''Claude, take Cristina to her room and keep her there until it's time for her to leave. Oh, and tell Leah to take her breakfast tray back to the kitchen. She can do without food for the rest of the day.''

Claude grabbed Cristina by the elbow and escorted her out of her mother's bedroom to her own room where he shoved her inside and turned the key in the lock. Cristina rattled the doorknob with all her might, but it did no good. She could beat upon it all afternoon and into the night, but the door would stay locked until Patricia decided to release her.

Unable to withstand the urge, Cristina threw herself on the bed and hammered out her frustrations on the feather pillows, crying out her rage and humiliation in hot, bitter-tasting tears. She fell into an exhausted sleep and slept until the sound of the key turning in the lock once again made her sit up, muscles tense, nerves taut like tightly stretched wire. The door opened and Cristina relaxed, sudden relief washing over her pinched features as Leah entered the room.

''Another quarrel, Miss Cristina? Why do you keep arguin'

with her when you know she'll punish you?" Leah chided.

"It seems a small price to pay for standing up to her. She thinks she owns me just because she gave birth to me. I have to show her that I'm a person in my own right, not one of her possessions." Bitter gall rose in Cristina's throat, threatening to choke her.

"But your rebellion is all for nothin'," Leah pointed out. "It ain't done you a bit of good."

"It helps me preserve my self-respect. It reminds me that I'm my father's daughter, not hers."

"She's your mother, missy."

"She isn't a mother," Cristina lashed out. "She's an expensive whore my father purchased for a while. She brought him nothing but pain, then drove him away."

"Cristina!"

"It's true, Leah, and you know it. My mother has the morals of an alley cat prowling from one tom to another. She's a whore and she's trying to make me one."

"She wouldn't dare," Leah gasped, outraged. "Sir William wouldn't—"

"Sir William is off exploring Africa. He isn't here to protect me. I'm being sold tonight to a certain wealthy gentleman with connections who admired me last night. I fetched a handsome price—the emerald necklace around her neck." Cristina struggled with her emotions, trying to sound detached and uncaring as her declarations of the previous night returned to haunt her. She put on a brave front, but inside she quivered. "It seems I'm to follow in her footsteps and I've no choice in the matter, not even in my future lovers."

Leah wrapped her arms around Cristina and hugged her tightly. "Don't worry, missy, we'll think of something."

First say to yourself what you would be;
and then do what you have to do.

—EPICTETUS C. 55–135 A.D.

THE CARRIAGE CAME for Cristina at midnight.

A scarlet liveried footman knocked at the front door and waited patiently for his passenger to appear. Minutes later, the door opened and Claude ushered Cristina to the doorway.

Her face was pale. The dark green of her dress and the upswept mass of copper curls emphasized the whiteness of her skin.

The footman smiled reassuringly as he took her hand to lead her down the steps, but Cristina didn't respond. She stared ahead, seemingly unaware of his presence, failing to notice as he gripped her icy fingers through the fabric of her gloves and gave her hand a gentle squeeze. Or that he reached out to steady her as she hesitated before the carriage step. At the moment she was blessedly numb. Her world was shrouded in fog that blurred the edges of harsh reality and Cristina was grateful for that fog. The horrid, laudanum-laced tea Leah had poured into her eased the pain of the beating Claude had given her and Cristina was temporarily free from the pain in her backside and the agony of walking. The soles of her feet tingled, but she managed to step forward. The beating had convinced her to cooperate with the plan for her seduction, but Leah's medicine provided the soothing fog. She climbed into the carriage and closed her eyes, reveling in the blessed numbness that kept the pain at bay. Praying it would last the night.

She dozed during the ride, finally forcing her eyelids open as the vehicle turned down the winding drive that led to the Prince of Wales's London residence, Marlborough House. The house was ablaze with lights, evidence of the party taking place. Splendid carriages, waiting to drop fashionably dressed partygoers, lined the drive to the house. Her coach didn't stop with the others. It continued down the path around the servants' wing to a private entrance where a young maid waited to escort her inside.

They traveled a maze of passages before reaching the third-floor guest rooms.

"You're to stay 'ere, miss." The maid threw open the doors to a lavish apartment.

"There's been a mistake," Cristina tried to explain, but her voice sounded distant, unrecognizable, even to her own ears.

"Oh, no, miss, there's no mistake. I was told to bring you 'ere and see that you were taken care of until the gentleman arrives. You're to make yourself at 'ome."

"Thank you." Cristina spoke slowly and carefully, managing a tiny smile as she crossed the threshold into a chintz-covered sitting room. A welcoming fire warmed her, but she made no move to discard her traveling cloak.

"Rest 'ere, miss, while I fetch your dinner. You must be starved. I bet you didn't get a bite to eat before you left."

"I'm not hungry." Cristina smothered a yawn.

"You might get 'ungry later on and you might as well be comfortable while you're waiting. It'll be a long while before that party breaks up. 'Is 'Ighness's parties never end before five in the morning." The maid said more than she should have, but she felt sorry for this girl who couldn't be any older than she was. She wasn't one of the regulars. You could tell by the looks of her that this one was a real lady. "Let me go get you a bite. Beggin' your pardon, miss, but it looks like you could do with a bite to eat. And a nice pot of tea will work wonders.''

Cristina grimaced. The thought of drinking tea after swallowing Leah's terrible concoction was enough to make her retch, but the maid was going out of her way to be kind and Cristina saw no point in offending her. She remembered her manners and tried to return the girl's kindness.

''That's very good of you. I think I would like something to eat, but please, no tea. Bring anything but tea.''

''All right, miss. I'll be back before you know it.'' The maid bobbed a curtsey as she closed the door.

Cristina sat by the fire trying to focus her thoughts on finding a way out of her dilemma. She should try to escape while the other girl was gone, but she knew she couldn't go very far in her present condition. But once a bit of the numbness wore off . . .

The pain would be agonizing. She knew that. But she also knew she had to find some way out. It was too far up for her to jump from the window, but there might be another means of escape. . . . Cristina squeezed her eyes shut. If only she could think clearly. . . .

'' 'Ere you go, miss.'' The maid opened the door. ''I brought you some supper and two bottles of wine to wash it down.'' She hesitated. ''I 'ope that's all right.''

Cristina nodded.

''All right, then, let's get you all comfy and tucked into bed. You can eat your supper there.'' She put the tray on a table near the fireplace and started toward Cristina.

''No bed.''

''All right, just let me take your cloak.'' The maid spoke softly, slowly enunciating each word.

''No, I think I'll keep it on,'' Cristina clutched the folds of her traveling cloak closer around her. ''I don't want you to take my cloak.''

''Then why don't you come sit by the fire while I turn down the bed?'' The maid patted the seat of a brocade chair near the fireplace. "You can sit here and eat. You don't want your food to get cold."

Cristina sat down on the chair and picked at the food on her plate while the maid turned down the covers on the bed. Cristina glanced at the sheets. The bed was bigger than she'd imagined. She had read somewhere that one could make a rope by tying bed linens together. Forcing her brain to work, Cristina eyed the covers of the bed and the hangings speculatively. Were there enough sheets to make it to the ground from the third floor? Could she do it? She didn't know, but she knew she had to do something. When the maid left . . .

But the maid wasn't leaving. She settled herself into a chair in one corner of the room, leaned her head against the wall, and closed her eyes.

"Why don't you go to bed?" Cristina asked, smothering another yawn. "I'm sure I'll be fine. It must be late."

The maid opened her eyes. "It was nearly one when you got 'ere."

Cristina tried again. She had to escape before she became too sleepy to move. "You must be tired."

"I am. I start work at 'alf-past six in the morning."

Her answer shocked Cristina. "You mean you've been up since half past six this morning? And you're still working?"

"I've been up since six, miss. I start work at 'alf-past six."

"But it's so late. You'll be able to sleep in this morning and start work later?"

"Oh no, miss," the maid seemed surprised by Cristina's assumption. "I start work at 'alf-past six like always."

"That's only a few hours away. You must go to bed." Cristina's voice was firmer, steadier. Her eagerness for the maid to leave was tempered by concern for the girl's health.

"I can't go to bed. Beggin' your pardon, miss, my orders are to stay with you until you're settled in bed."

Cristina understood. How many times had Leah waited up for her postponing her own sleep until Cristina was in bed? She was very gentle as she spoke to the maid. "If you'll help me out of this dress . . ."

The girl rushed to do Cristina's bidding. She took the cloak

Cristina handed her, then went to work on the fastenings on the heavy green brocade dress. Minutes later, Cristina stepped out of the dress and the three petticoats she wore under it. The laces of her corset were freed and she took a deep breath. This was much better. The unrestricted breath helped clear her head.

"Do you want me to help tuck you in?" The maid asked when Cristina stood before her in her chemise.

"No, thank you. I'll manage," Cristina turned and climbed into the huge bed, settling herself against the pillows and pulling the covers up to her chin for effect. She smiled at the maid. "See. I'm all settled."

The girl returned her smile, then removed a bottle of wine and a glass from the supper tray and handed them to Cristina.

"I brought plenty. His Highness won't miss it and the wine'll help dull the pain when he comes," she told Cristina before hurrying out of the room.

Cristina slowly counted to one hundred, then scurried out of bed. She pushed the covers to the floor, and yanked the top sheet off the bed. She bit at the hem with her teeth, until she managed to rip a hole in it. Then Cristina grasped the sheet firmly in each hand and pulled. A loud tearing sound filled the room. She smiled in grim satisfaction, then removed the bottom sheet.

BLAKE'S HEAD BUZZED from the wine and cigar smoke. He feigned a grin as he accepted another glass of brandy from the Prince of Wales. The conversation had turned to racing, jockeys, and horses. Blake wondered if he could endure another hour. It was close to three in the morning and he had an appointment to see the queen at nine. It was time to make his move. Hoping Rudolf was too drunk to notice, Blake turned to the Prince of Wales.

"May I have your permission to retire, sir?"

The Prince of Wales looked up at Blake, his prominent eyes

watering. "So soon, my boy?" he glanced over at Rudolf. "We're just getting started."

"I'm afraid so, Your Highness. I have an early appointment with Her Majesty this morning."

Wales shuddered slightly at the mention of his mother's name. "I understand. Duty calls, my boy, duty calls. Go find your bed." He smiled at Blake. "It does seem a shame for you to miss all the fun, though." He clapped his hands and called for more cigars. A large man, he was full of energy. Keeping up with the prince was a job in itself.

"Thank you, sir." Blake stood up and bowed.

The Prince of Wales nodded.

As the door closed behind him, Blake heard the crown prince laughing at something the Prince of Wales was saying. Curiosity almost got the better of him, but Blake couldn't afford to waste more time by staying around to listen. He hurried through the rabbit's warren of passages through the servant's wing until he reached one of the back entrances. Opening the back door, Blake signaled his coachman. The vehicle halted in front of him. He snatched open the door and held his hand out to the passenger just as it started to rain.

"Hurry," Blake urged. "We haven't much time."

"All right, all right. Take it easy, guvnor." The cockney dialect coming from the lips of the beautiful woman startled him.

She was older than Cristina, but her carefully painted face made her appear younger. Her hair was brighter, a brassier shade of red than Cristina's burnished copper, but her eyes were green. Blake couldn't believe his good fortune. Her resemblance to Cristina was astonishing. But her voice could give her away.

"Don't talk," he warned. "The gentleman is sure to know the difference if you talk."

"All right."

"Don't talk," Blake warned again. "Just listen and nod your head yes or no."

Her head bobbed up and down to indicate she understood.

"Good. Now, are you certain you want to do this?"

She nodded vigorously.

"You can back out if you like," Blake told her. "I can find another means."

"It's all right, guvnor. I know wot I'm doing. It ain't like I'm a bleedin' virgin or anything. For fifty pounds, I'd sleep with the queen herself. You ain't corruptin' me. I've been corrupted afore this."

He clenched his jaw.

She patted his arm. "I'm shuttin' up. I just wanted you to know I appreciate 'onesty. And, I really don't mind sleepin' with a crown prince for a night. Cor', wait till I tell the other girls!" She made a motion as if to button her lips.

Blake lifted her down. "Then let's go."

"Right behind ya, guv."

Blake shot her a warning glare.

"All right, all right, I'm shutting it!" She buttoned her lips a second time. "For good."

Blake shook his head in exasperation. This whole scheme of his was too crazy to be believed and the worst of it was he didn't have the faintest idea why he was creeping around Marlborough House's halls in the middle of the night with a Cockney prostitute who couldn't keep her mouth shut. Why was he doing this? Why was he risking so much? It didn't make a damned bit of sense. Running to Cristina Fairfax's rescue like a damned knight in shining armor. He was mad.

"Slow down!" The girl beside him hissed the order.

He automatically slowed his stride, reached down and gripped her elbow, then propelled her along beside him. He took the first set of stairs almost at a run. When she failed to keep stride, Blake swung her up and over his shoulder.

"Now, wait a bloody minute!" She began as he placed one hand firmly against her rear end. "Ouch!" Her skirts cushioned the soft blow to her bottom. Her cry was one of surprise, rather than pain.

"I thought your lips were buttoned," Blake muttered more to himself than to her.

"They are!"

"Really? I hadn't noticed. It must be the grating noise coming from them that keeps distracting me."

"Are we there yet?" the girl asked when Blake came to an abrupt halt some minutes later.

"Yes. Sssh!"

"Put me down. I'm dizzy!"

"Be quiet." Blake crept to the door of the apartments Rudolf was temporarily occupying. A silver tray containing an empty wine bottle and one glass sat on the floor in the hallway in front of the door. He knew Cristina was inside. He just hoped to God she was alone. Stepping around the tray he grasped the handle on the door and silently eased it open. It yielded an inch or so, then refused to go any farther.

"Hurry before I toss up my dinner!"

"Don't you dare!" Blake hastily stood the girl on her feet, eyeing her with suspicion.

"Works like a charm." She smiled angelically. "Why don'tcha open the door?"

"It's blocked with something. Probably furniture."

The girl peered through the keyhole. "Looks like you're right, guv. She is unwilling, ain't she?"

"Naturally," Blake snapped, concentrating on widening the opening without making any noise. "She's a young lady."

Blake turned to look at his companion. "Can you squeeze through?" He stopped.

Her expression was belligerent. Her eyes, so like Cristina's, shimmered in the meager light from the lamps.

He realized what he'd said almost immediately and began to apologize. "I'm sorry, I didn't mean to imply that you aren't a young lady. You are."

"No, I'm not, guvnor." She brightened suddenly. "But it was nice of you to say so." She gave him a smile, then squeezed through the doorway.

Blake waited impatiently while she cleared the furniture.

"She ain't here, guvnor," the girl said as he shoved his way past the furniture.

"Then where is she?"

"Down there." She pointed toward an open window. A

crude rope of knotted bedsheets hung over the casement.

His heart almost stopped. "She didn't!"

"She sure did." The girl whistled low in admiration. "Cut up the Prince of Wales's bedsheets, she did."

"I don't give a damn about the bedsheets." Blake crossed the room in three quick strides. He kicked a half-empty wineglass as he reached the window.

The prostitute hurried to join him. "Do you see her down there?"

"Good God!" He leaned out the window and searched the courtyard below first, squinting against the falling rain and the darkness looking for a mass of red hair against the gray stone. The makeshift rope reached below the second-floor windows but he couldn't see her. An experienced climber might make the jump without serious injury, but a young woman? "Cristina?" he called in a low, urgent voice.

She heard him call her name and knew that one of the men she'd been trying to escape from had found her hanging for dear life, onto a rope made of bedsheets. "I'm here," she answered, afraid of what would happen when he rescued her, but more afraid of letting go of the rope.

Blake grabbed hold of the pile of bedsheets and jerked.

"Don't!" He heard the panic in her voice. "I can't hold on much longer. I'm slipping."

"Bloody hell, Cristina! I thought you said you had good sense. Just hold on. I'm coming."

"She ain't got a bloody lick!" The prostitute whistled again.

"Stay here," Blake said to the girl, "and don't let anyone into the room except me." He raked his wet hair out of his eyes. "Christ! I've heard stories of girls who prefer death to . . . to . . . this!" he finished, at a loss for words.

"'Appens all the time in my line of work. But not tonight. Not to your young lady, guvnor." She grinned. "We got 'ere in time to save 'er."

"Lord Lawrence?" Cristina called from below. "Hurry!"

"I'm on my way." He sprinted out the door and down a

flight of stairs, praying all the while that he would get to Cristina in time.

When he reached the second floor, Blake tried door after door until he found one that wasn't locked. He pulled the heavy velvet drapes open and spotting the white rope, quickly unfastened the window, swung it open, and glanced down. Cristina clung to the knot of sheets about two feet away.

"Cristina?"

She looked up and breathed a grateful sigh when she saw him. "Lord Lawrence."

"I'm going to pull you up," he explained. "Hold on tight."

Blake carefully pulled the line of sheets up the wall and over the window casement until Cristina Fairfax lay huddled on the floor. She wore one petticoat and her traveling cloak. A bare, shapely calf was exposed to his view and she was soaked to the skin. He struggled out of his coat and placed it around her, before he leaned forward to pick her up.

Cristina wrapped her arms around his neck in a stranglehold and buried her face against his damp shirtfront. She listened to the thumping of his heart and admitted, "I was more afraid of falling than I was of you."

"It's all right. You're safe," he said, inhaling the scent of her. She smelled of rainwater and strong wine and a floral perfume he couldn't name. "I've got some business to attend to upstairs," Blake explained, "then I'll take you home."

"No."

He saw the flash of alarm in her green eyes. "Don't worry. I'm not going to hurt you. I'm taking you someplace safe."

Too tired and wet and cold to do anything else, Cristina huddled against Blake as he carried her out of the room and back up a flight of stairs.

The young prostitute met him at the door to Rudolf's apartments. "Looks like she was bolstering her nerve a bit." She held up another half-empty bottle of wine.

Blake placed Cristina on the chair near the fire and tucked a lap robe around her. Cristina closed her eyes, too exhausted to fight any longer.

The prostitute followed him to the chair, then leaned in for a closer look at Cristina and whispered, "Cor! She looks almost like me!"

"She doesn't talk like you," Blake reminded her.

"I bet she doesn't do lots of things like me." She glanced pointedly at the empty bed, then licked her lips.

Blake ignored her flirtation. "In that case, grab those sheets—you'll need them."

The girl muttered beneath her breath as she hauled the rope of wet linens inside the window and carried them back to the bed. She untied the knots in the sheets, then flipped back the top covers. The mattresses were bare.

"These ain't going to do me no good," she said, showing Blake the halves of a monogrammed sheet.

"Give them to me," he ordered.

She tossed the sheets at him.

"Lie on top of the covers. Maybe he won't notice that there aren't any sheets."

The prostitute laughed seductively. "I can guarantee he won't notice if I'm on top of the covers." She flopped down on the bed and struck a classic pose. "Turn around."

"Why?" Blake asked.

"I've got to get ready."

"No, you don't," Blake decided. "I'll think of something else."

"A deal's a deal, guvnor," she said.

Blake turned to face her.

"Don't look!" she ordered.

"What's wrong?"

"Nothing's wrong, guvnor, 'cept I like you, you see. And I don't want ya comparing her and me." Her voice dropped to a whisper, before she regained her bravado. "Your ladybird might not measure up." She finished with a sad laugh.

"Are you sure you want to go through with this?" Blake asked again.

" 'Course I am. It's a pleasure helping ya out. Doing business with ya, so to speak. Wot's your name, guvnor?"

Knowing he was opening himself up to potential scandal

or blackmail, but somehow trusting this girl of the streets, Blake answered. "Lawrence. Blake Ashford, Lord Lawrence."

She tapped him on the shoulder.

He turned to find her encased in the coverlet, her hand outstretched.

"Frances Kilkenny," she told him. "My customers call me Fran."

Blake took her hand in his, but instead of shaking it, he brought her fingers to his lips and kissed them. "A pleasure, Miss Kilkenny."

Tears sparkled in her eyes. She brushed them aside. "You better get going, guvnor. From wot you told me, that royal gent could come anytime." She winked at the double entendre.

Blake scooped Cristina up in his arms. She was breathing heavily. Sound asleep.

Frances held up the bottle of wine. "No sense letting this go to waste."

Blake smiled at her. "If you change your mind . . ."

"And lose this golden opportunity to sleep with a real prince? Not a chance, guvnor." She opened the door for him. "I'll be just like bloody Cinderella."

Blake glanced at the hallway. Footsteps sounded on the stairs to his right. Unsteady footsteps. Drunken footsteps. He hoisted Cristina higher into his arms and turned to the left.

"Lucky girl." Frances Kilkenny took a drink from the wine bottle, then lifted it in salute, watching as handsome Lord Lawrence carried his lady friend away.

Was it a vision, or a waking dream?
Fled is the music:—Do I wake or sleep?

—JOHN KEATS 1795–1821

Five

CRISTINA DREAMED OF warmth pressed intimately against her and snuggled closer to the source, enjoying the novelty of sleeping nestled in between two warm arms. She dreamed of his gentle hands with long, strong fingers and the enticing roughness of knuckles decorated with coarse, black hair that stroked her body through the silk of her shift. She dreamed vividly of the man who had haunted her thoughts since the night of the ball, perfectly recreating his face in her mind.

She luxuriated in the sensual dreams as she allowed her long-dormant emotions to come to life. She pictured his black eyes burning into hers, his long legs nakedly entwined with hers and the feel of his dark hair, rough and crisp beneath her questing fingers. Her instant attraction to him was as confusing as it was overwhelming, but he had somehow become her dream lover. He was her fantasy and she was loath to give him up. Cristina strained, arching her back, moving even closer in her dreams to the lover waiting to fulfill her desires and make her his woman.

He responded to her body with an answering moan.

Cristina opened her eyes and recoiled in horror as she realized she was not alone in her bedroom. She fought to piece together the fragments of her memory—to separate the dreams from the reality.

Glancing down at the strong arm wrapped around her waist, she discovered that it was not part of her dream. It was real. She was in a bedroom in Marlborough House with the man selected to be her lover.

Cristina pushed back the covers, struggling with the insistent hands that pulled her body back into the circle of his warmth.

"Be still," he hissed. "I'm not going to hurt you. We can't leave until the party breaks up. And I need a little sleep."

Leave? She couldn't leave with him. Any more than she could continue to share a bed with him. Cristina turned and shoved him away.

He grabbed at her again, one hand reaching around her waist while the other caught the back of her camisole. "Lie back down. We'll leave just before daybreak. By then everyone else will have retired for the night."

"Let go of me. I'm leaving *now*." Cristina turned on him in fury, lashing out with her hands. Her clenched fist connected with the bones of his face.

He groaned again, this time in agony, instinctively releasing his hold on her as warm, sticky blood gushed from his nose. "You can't leave now. Dammit to hell, Cristina, I'm not after your bloody virtue. I'm trying to save it. But I need some sleep." He pinched his nostrils, attempting to staunch the flow.

Cristina slid off the bed and pressed herself against the wall as he rolled off the opposite side of the bed and got to his feet. She dared not breathe as she waited for his next move.

Water splashed in a basin nearby. She listened intently to the mutters and moans as he poured more water into the bowl. Cristina peeked around the bed hangings and stared in astonishment as her velvet cloak disappeared from the back of a brocade chair. She realized suddenly that she was in her underclothes. Her dress and petticoats had been removed. She tried to remember where she'd last seen them, but her head ached unbearably and she was unable to recall anything except the vague blur of her arrival and the vivid dream.

The splashing ceased abruptly. Cristina pressed farther back against the wall, scarcely daring to breathe. She listened to his footsteps as he left the basin and stumbled back to bed. She recognized a grunt of pain, a muffled thud, and the scrape of furniture against the floor. Colorful curses in a variety of languages filled the air. The brocade, Cristina thought, as the chair crashed to the floor.

She sucked in a deep breath at the sound of the mattresses creaking beneath his weight.

"Are you coming back to bed?" His words were somewhat muffled, but Cristina heard him.

She didn't answer, but remained pressed against the wall.

"Suit yourself," he said as he rolled over in bed and pulled the covers up around himself.

Cristina allowed herself a tiny sigh of relief when she heard him begin to snore. She would wait a little while longer, she decided, to be sure he slept and then she would make her escape.

She awoke with a start sometime later to find herself in bed, the covers wrapped firmly around her. Her memories of the previous night returned with a vengeance and she jack-knifed into sitting position, prepared to do battle with him once again. But she was alone. He was gone. She rolled from the bed and stumbled to her feet. Her queasy stomach rumbled in protest at the sudden movement and Cristina rested her head against the wall for a moment, willing her unruly stomach to settle down.

She raised her head and swallowed a new wave of nausea. Her head pounded from the effects of too much wine and Leah's concoction and her body ached in a dozen different places. But Cristina forced her eyes to focus in the dimly lit room before she made her way around the foot of the bed to the brocade chair. Her feet throbbed and her legs wobbled like the legs of a newborn colt. She used every ounce of her concentration to lower herself onto the chair. Gritting her teeth against the incessant pounding in her temples, she belatedly realized the folly of looking for courage in the bottom of a wine bottle. The wine hadn't helped at all. It hadn't steadied her nerves. It had given her only a colossal headache.

Forcing herself to her feet and moving as quickly as possible for a human being in her condition, Cristina began the arduous task of dressing herself. Her underclothes were torn and damp, but wearable. She could only guess at the condition of the rest of her clothes as she scanned the room in hopes of locating them. But the rest of her clothes were gone. She was left with the clothes she wore—her camisole and drawers—and a chemise, petticoat, and her cloak. And all of them were damp.

Cristina inched toward the velvet cloak. It lay in a heap on the floor beside the screen. She hated to wear it. She could feel the rough, matted spots where the blood from his nose had dried. He had used it as a towel, then kicked it aside. She pulled it around her, anyway. She had no choice. Dressed in her underclothes and wrapped in her traveling cape, she waited in the chair gathering her strength, preparing for her escape. A surge of nausea threatened her. She balled her cold, numb fingers into fists and jammed them into the pockets of her cloak. Her right hand touched the small glass bottle and she remembered Leah's insistence that the medicine would help her on the morning after.

Tiptoeing to the washstand, Cristina poured a glass of water, mixed the powder, and drank it down as Leah had instructed. Then she crept from the room without a backward glance.

She paused in the doorway studying the corridors before she made her decision. Turning right, she headed down the maze of passageways. Her satin slippers pattered against the marble floor.

Somewhere down the hall, a clock chimed six times. She had very little time. Soon the staff would begin their workday. She could not be seen leaving the house with her hair lying loose about her shoulders. She could not be seen leaving the house at all. Cristina stopped short, trying to get her bearings. She must have turned wrong. Where were the doors? She bit her lip, mentally cursing herself for not being able to concentrate when she arrived, and slowly retraced her steps. Her heart pounded as she spotted the doors at the opposite end of the hall. Through those doors lay the stairs. Three flights down and freedom. Down and down and down once more and then she was free.

Cristina emerged from the house and stepped out into a downpour, but she paid the rain little heed. She was free and that was all that mattered at the moment. She ignored the burning in her lungs, the pounding in her chest and the cold rain soaking her to the skin. Drawing a ragged breath of the early-morning air, Cristina mouthed a prayer of thanks to the heavens for allowing her to escape. And she prayed for the strength that would carry her down the long winding drive, on aching feet, to the streets of London and all the way to Fairhall if necessary.

The pink- and mauve-colored fingers of dawn streaked the misty horizon before she made her way to the end of the drive. Her wet slippers blistered her heels and added to the agony in her feet. She limped slowly down the drive until the blisters forced her to remove her shoes and walk barefooted.

A cabbie caught sight of her and pulled to a stop.

Cristina climbed into the comfortable cab, rested her weary feet on the opposite seat, and allowed her mind to wander at will. She would have to face her mother once she reached Fairhall, but the London morning traffic was heavy. She had a little while to rest before the confrontation. She didn't have to think about the coming battle. For as long as it took the cabby to negotiate the crowded streets of London, Cristina could close her eyes and forget.

*Those sweetly smiling angels with pensive looks,
innocent faces, and cash-boxes for hearts.*

—HONORÉ DE BALZAC 1799–1850

Six

"I WANT THE necklace." There was steely determination in the voice of the girl who stood dripping in the doorway. A determination that surprised the occupants of the room.

"Cristina, what are you doing here? I thought you'd be busy this morning."

"I came to collect my belongings," Cristina ignored her mother's other remark. "And I want the necklace."

"Darling, this isn't the time." Patricia glanced at her lover, then back at Cristina. "I thought I taught you better manners than to enter my bedroom unannounced. Why don't you run down to the kitchen for breakfast? We can discuss the necklace later."

"With you fluttering about somewhere in Europe? I don't think so, Mother. We'll discuss the necklace now." Cristina's gaze bored through her mother, noting the rumpled bed and the naked man lying next to Patricia. Yesterday she would have left the room in embarrassment, but Cristina had changed overnight. The sordid tableau before her angered rather than embarrassed her. "I want the necklace. It was sent to me and I mean to have it."

Patricia recognized the change in her daughter. There was a new strength of will about her that hadn't been there the day before. The night with Crown Prince Rudolf hadn't broken Cristina's spirit. If anything, the night with the crown prince had added to Cristina's strength of mind, given her confidence, made her more determined than ever to defy her. Patricia smiled nevertheless and tried to dismiss her daughter.

"Darling, all this quibbling over a necklace. Why don't we discuss this after you've cleaned up and eaten breakfast? When you are in a calmer frame of mind?"

"Stop it," Cristina demanded. "Stop your pretended concern for me. You don't care about me. Let's end the hypocrisy. You simply want to delay the inevitable. *We* aren't. quibbling over the necklace—you are. It was sent to me and I will have it. Give it to me."

"Cristina, you're making too much of this," Patricia began.

"Too much? Hardly. I don't consider being sold too much," she replied coldly.

"You would have been auctioned anyway," Patricia declared. "What do you think marriage is for people like us but a business transaction? It's all buying and selling."

"No, it isn't. Marriage is about choosing a mate because you can't stand the thought of living without him. It's a partnership, a sharing, and before I spent the night alone with a man, I should have had a ring on my finger, the blessings of the church, and all the rights that go along with being legally married."

"You can still think that after being brought up in this house? After viewing the sorry state of my marriage to William Fairfax?" Patricia laughed. "My darling, you are an innocent. A married woman has no real rights. Marriage for women of our status is a form of slavery. We are commanded and we must obey. For life, Cristina. When you marry, you're trapped until one of you dies."

"I don't believe that."

"Then you're going to be very disappointed," Patricia warned. "Love is an illusion, Cristina. It's like a fairy tale.

It makes a nice story, but nobody really believes it. It's what we're promised when we're young children, but I'm here to tell you that it's just a word. It has no meaning.''

"It may mean nothing to you, because even I'm aware you're very free with your favors." Cristina stared at Claude, who lay watching the mother-daughter confrontation with interest. "But it means something to me. I'm not like you."

"Yet you're demanding the necklace in payment for last night . . . ," Patricia mused aloud, fingering the emeralds and diamonds she still wore around her neck. "Perhaps there is more of me in you than you think." She smiled a decidedly catlike smile, arching her brow as if to pursue the thought more fully.

Cristina could stand no more. Anger welled up inside her and demanded release. "There is nothing of you in me," she said. "I'm not a whore."

Outrage and naked hatred gleamed instantly in Patricia's eyes. "You will regret that remark, Cristina."

Cristina masked the apprehension hidden deep inside her. Pulling herself to her full height, Cristina glared down at her mother. "I don't think so, Mother. I only wish I had had the courage to say it sooner. It might have saved me a great deal of grief."

Patricia was livid. She scrambled out of bed, raised her arm, and slapped her daughter with all her strength. She detested this stranger who stood before her refusing to quiver in fear or humiliation, refusing to look at her with those green eyes that had begged to be loved, refusing even to place a hand over her burning cheek, to show any sign of pain or regret. Cristina stood her ground and she reminded Patricia so much of William that she wanted to hit her again just to make her cry out.

"Claude, take Cristina to her room and lock her in. I'll deal with her later. In the meantime, you may punish her in any way you see fit. Give Leah the key to her room when you've finished." Patricia turned and began dressing.

Claude made a move toward Cristina, but Cristina stopped him with her words.

"Claude isn't taking me anywhere. I'm not leaving until you hand over the necklace." Cristina smiled at Patricia, then played her trump card. "It won't go very well for you if my 'gentleman friend' has to force you to surrender his gift." Cristina's heart hammered in her chest as she plunged ahead, weaving a fabric of half-truths, not daring to let them know just how alone and afraid she was. "You've made me a mistress, Mother, but I'm still a lady and a member of the peerage. My lover"—Cristina stressed the words—"would be shocked to learn I don't have his little token of affection. And, I'll tell him if that's what it takes to get my way. He was disappointed that I didn't wear his gift last night. Shall I tell him the truth and explain why I didn't wear the necklace? Is that what you want, Mother, to have the whole of London know you acted as procurer and sold your own daughter for less than a traditional wedding band?" Cristina began to tap her foot against the floor in a deliberate show of impatience. "Now, please. I've kept him waiting long enough."

Claude stepped to the window, ignoring his nakedness, and drew back the drapes.

Cristina was glad she had had the forethought to ask the cabbie to wait.

"There is a cab waiting outside."

"She's bluffing." Patricia jeered.

"That may be," Claude admitted. "But the driver is obviously waiting for her to come out. And we have an early train to catch."

Cristina copied her mother's purring tones. "Well, Mother, what shall it be? The necklace or the truth?" She held out her hand. Waiting.

"Take it!" Unwilling to risk her social standing with London society further, Patricia unfastened the diamond and emerald creation and flung it at Cristina. "Take it and be damned!"

"The feeling is mutual." Cristina caught the heavy jewelry against her body and squaring her slim shoulders, walked away from her mother and out of Fairhall into the blinding rain.

She didn't dare stay long enough even to pack a bag. The cramps had begun wracking her body during the confrontation and Cristina couldn't risk remaining a minute longer than necessary. She couldn't risk having them see how weak she was.

She slipped on the stone walkway as she trudged through the puddles on her way to the carriage and fell to her knees. The driver jumped down from his seat to help her inside.

"I hope it was worth the chill we're going to catch, miss," he grumbled.

"I hope so, too." She answered, stuffing the necklace into the pocket of her cape and climbing into the shelter of the cab.

"Where to, miss?"

Cristina hadn't thought about her immediate concerns, only about using the necklace to locate her father and join him. She had no money and no place to go. She couldn't even pay the driver unless she managed to sell the necklace.

"Miss, I ain't standing in this rain for nothing. Where to?"

"St. James," she answered. She would be able to find a hotel there and maybe someone would buy the necklace or at least loan her the money to pay the driver.

Cristina closed her eyes against the swaying of the cab. She was tired—tired of thinking—tired of everything. Reaction was beginning to set in. Her head hurt, her body ached. She was exhausted, doubled over in pain, and could not seem to get warm. She pulled the hood of her cloak over her wet hair. The hood was as wet as the rest of her but it helped block the morning light. Shivering, she leaned back against the seat and willed herself to sleep.

She was pleasantly drowsy when the carriage swerved violently in the street, sending her tumbling to the other side of the seat. The door flew open as the carriage came to a halt and a dark-coated figure agilely leaped inside, slamming the door behind him to escape the downpour.

He sat on the opposite seat. He wore no hat and the rain dripped from a lock of dark hair that hung over his high forehead. Cristina could see the sparkling droplets clinging to his lashes. He ran an impatient hand over his face to wipe away the rain, then slid his fingers hastily through his hair, combing it back into place. He had removed his coat and was stretching his long legs out in front of him before he noticed the bundle huddled in the corner of the opposite seat, as skin-soaked as himself. "Pardon me for grabbing your vehicle like that, miss, but my own carriage met with an unfortunate accident." He nodded toward the window.

Cristina craned her head to look out and saw an overturned vendor's cart and a damaged wheel on a shiny victoria. He continued making conversation.

"I have a meeting shortly and I've no wish to be late or drowned or both." He smiled ruefully.

Cristina sat very still. She had recognized him at once and was afraid of giving her identity away. She could hardly expect Lord Lawrence to be sympathetic to her plight after the night they'd shared. In fact, Cristina was quite sure that her early-morning flight had likely angered him. Her only chance was to keep her mouth shut, her face averted and pray he didn't recognize her.

Blake stared at his bedraggled companion, who was trying her damnedest to appear small and insignificant in the corner of the padded leather seat. Something about the way she tilted her small pointed chin defiantly and hid her face from his curious gaze tugged at the corner of his mind, imploring him to remember. He thought of Cristina Fairfax. He'd left her sleeping at dawn while he went downstairs to collect her dress from the kitchen where he'd taken it to dry and to get a pot of hot chocolate and some toast for her and some coffee for himself while he tried to figure out a way to smuggle her out of the house. He returned to find she had sneaked out of Marlborough House on her own. Blake shook his head. The girl across the seat from him couldn't be Cristina. Because Miss Cristina Fairfax had had plenty of time to make it home safe and sound. Still innocent, and apart from sharing a bed with an exhausted man for a few hours, none the worse for her little adventure. He peered at his companion a bit more closely. It couldn't be Cristina. But something about that cape and the stubborn set of her chin. Surely she had more sense than to sneak out of Marlborough House, then traipse around London all morning in her wet cape and underclothes. But then, she hadn't had the sense not to climb out a third floor window on the Prince of Wales's bed linen. . . . He bit the inside of his cheek to keep from smiling. Now that his fear for her had passed, now that he knew she was safe, Blake could smile at her impetuousness and her stubborn audacity.

Cristina huddled against the wall of the cab, utterly miserable. The sodden velvet cloak and her wet undergarments clung to her like a second skin, leaving her feeling cold and clammy.

She shivered visibly and drew her cloak closer around her.

"You'll never get warm that way. Your cape is soaked through."

Did nothing escape his sharp eyes?

"Why don't you remove it? I'm sure you would be much more comfortable without it."

He didn't know everything, Cristina thought uncharitably. She would find it impossible to be comfortable while sitting across from him wearing nothing but her wet underclothes. She ignored his suggestion and pulled the cape even tighter. Within minutes, her teeth began an audible chatter.

"Oh, for God's sake!" He exploded, his dark eyes menacing in anger. "Are you going to let your stubbornness make you a victim of pneumonia?" He didn't wait for her answer. Instead, he reached across to where she sat and yanked the velvet cloak from around her shoulders.

"Christ! It is you!"

Cristina heard him swear, but she couldn't hear anything else over the loud roaring in her ears, which drowned out all other sounds until blissful darkness claimed her.

But the bliss was short-lived. Her eyes fluttered open, then closed just as quickly, trying unsuccessfully to prolong the darkness.

"Open your eyes, Miss Fairfax," the hateful voice commanded. "And tell me what the bloody hell you're doing here. You left Marlborough House over an hour ago. You should have been home safe and warm by now."

"I've been home, thank you, and it wasn't safe or warm for me there. I'm going someplace else."

"Dressed like that?"

"Yes, and only a rogue like you would mention it." She slapped at his hands as he reached for her again. "Go away and leave me alone."

"As much as I would like to, I'm afraid that's not possible. I think you ought to see a doctor. You're not well."

Her eyes opened and widened in fear. "I was fine last night!"

Blake's face hardened. "You were sotted last night. And sleeping it off this morning. But you look feverish. I'm taking you to a doctor."

Her objection was instantaneous. "No!"

"What's wrong with you? Why are you afraid to see a doctor?"

He studied her closely and what he saw made him gasp in fury. She was very pale despite an obvious fever and there were heavy dark rings under her eyes. It looked as if she hadn't slept for days, yet he knew she had. He pulled the cloak farther off her shoulders. The creamy whiteness of her upper arms was marred by a succession of blue-black marks. He remembered their struggle the night before.

"Did I do this?" The idea sickened him.

He looked so appalled, Cristina couldn't let him take the blame. "No."

"Then who?" Someone had gripped her arms hard enough to hurt her and the knowledge disturbed Blake more than he liked. "Who did this to you?" he demanded, indicating the bruises. "Who hurt you? Tell me."

"It doesn't matter."

"Who was he? Tell me, Cristina."

"It's over. It won't happen again."

"Tell me his name." Blake gritted his teeth and reached for her shoulders. He wasn't used to defiance. He would get the name out of her if he had to shake it out of her. He was about to do just that when he realized what he was doing.

"Let go." Cristina demanded, trying to shrug free of him.

But she might have been an insect caught in a web, for the harder she struggled, the more entangled she became—in her long hair, her wet garments, and his arms.

"Be still, you little idiot! Do you want to overturn us? I didn't mean to hurt you. Calm down." He bit out the words in an effort to control the rage sweeping over him. His grip about her waist became viselike, forcing her to sit close to his side.

Cristina could feel the heat emanating from him. She wanted more than anything to relax in the warmth his body offered, but she forced herself to remain rigid.

"I'm sorry." His voice was strangely gentle when he spoke to her. "You might as well try to relax, Cristina. I promise not to harm you. But I'm going to take you home so you can be properly tended."

"No! Not home! Not there!" Cristina pulled out of his grasp and lunged for the opposite seat.

He reached for her and she threw her cloak in his face, hoping to blind him long enough to make her escape. The heavy emerald and diamond necklace came out of her pocket and Cristina watched in horror as a trickle of blood appeared on the bone beneath his eye.

"Bloody hell! First you try to break my nose and now you try to blind me!"

Blake caught hold of her arms, forgetting about the bruises there or the fact that he would make new ones, wanting only to protect her from doing further injury to herself and to him. "You will explain yourself," he told her furiously, holding her firmly as he rapped on the roof of the carriage and shouted directions to the driver.

"W-w-where are you taking me?"

"Home. To *my* home, where we will get to the bottom of this," he promised, holding the necklace up for Cristina to see.

She sucked in a ragged breath and stared—not at the necklace, but at the angriest pair of coal-black eyes she'd ever seen.

If to do were as easy as to know what were good
to do, chapels had been churches, and poor men's cottages
princes' palaces.

—WILLIAM SHAKESPEARE 1564–1616

Seven

"HOW IS SHE?" Blake asked as the doctor emerged from
the guest room.

"Right now she's a very sick young woman. She has a
severe chill, and a high fever that could turn into pneumonia
or influenza. She's also experiencing abdominal cramps and
blood loss. On top of all that, someone has taken a strap to
her. Thankfully, she's sleeping. That's best until her fever
breaks."

"How long will that be?"

"It's hard to say. It could break tonight or tomorrow or the
day after that. But if it doesn't break by then, she could be
in real danger. Blake, how well do you know this girl? Is she
a special friend of yours?"

"Don't you recognize her? That's the beautiful Cristina
Fairfax. Her mother is Lady Fairfax. I met her two days ago
at the last drawing room" Blake explained.

"What on earth was she doing out at this time of morning?
And in this downpour?"

"Running away from me."

"What?" Nigel Jameson was burning with unprofessional

curiosity. "I mean, debutantes don't usually run about London in their underclothes."

"I'm aware of that, Nigel. I'm bloody well furious about it myself." Blake raked his fingers through his damp hair. "If she'd stayed in bed until I'd returned she'd have been all right, but no, she had to try to escape. What next? What the hell next?" He rubbed at the bridge of his nose, then yelped in agony at the tenderness. Cristina Fairfax packed a mean punch.

"What?" Nigel thought his friend was joking for a moment before he realized Blake was completely serious and very agitated. "You spent the night with her?"

"I'm not that much of a reprobate, Nigel."

"But . . ." Nigel began to pace. "You said . . ."

"I know what I said." Blake sounded weary. "Let me clarify it. I shared a bed with the lovely Miss Fairfax very early this morning. It was completely innocent. She had passed out from the effects of the wine and I was half drunk myself. Too drunk to have amorous intentions. Completely disinclined after she punched me in the nose."

"She punched you? I wondered how you got it." Nigel laughed in spite of himself. "You're quite a sight this morning, my friend. As battered as a Queensberry fighter on Sunday morning."

"Thanks."

"Is that it?" Nigel demanded. "Aren't you going to tell me the rest?"

Blake looked at his friend, then at the floor. "It's a hell of a pickle."

Nigel smiled, glad to be of service. "I've got plenty of time this morning. We can talk over breakfast."

Blake nodded absently, then suddenly pinned Nigel with his gaze. "Have you ever been to one of Strathemore's midnight suppers?"

"No!" Nigel looked astonished. "That's not my cup of tea. You know that." He glanced at Blake. "I wouldn't say it's yours, either."

"Hardly." Blake snorted. "But I was there two nights ago.

I was there when Patricia Fairfax sold her daughter's innocence." Blake, realizing they were standing in the hall outside the guest room, took Nigel by the arm. "Let's go down to my study. I'll tell you all about it. God knows I need to talk to someone about this obsession."

Obsession was the only word for it, Blake decided once they were comfortably settled in the study. It was the only way to describe his sudden urge to go against his better judgment and try to protect Cristina Fairfax. She wasn't his responsibility. He didn't want her under his roof, and yet he couldn't seem to let her go. . . . There was something about her—something that appealed to him despite his better judgment.

To keep her in his home would be asking for trouble. He couldn't deny his attraction to the girl and he wasn't at all sure he could control it. Before meeting Cristina, Blake hadn't felt compelled to kiss a young woman at any function, much less a court ball.

He did not want the responsibility of Cristina Fairfax. He had to keep his distance.

Blake realized the folly of his plan to rescue Cristina from Rudolf as he outlined the details to Nigel. He recognized the fact that he had changed Cristina's future by whisking her away from Rudolf's bed and into his own, no matter how innocently. He should send her away. Send her back to her own home. Anywhere away from him and his sudden obsession. "Nigel, can you take her home with you?"

"Blake, she isn't a stray puppy. She's a young woman. And right now, I think she should stay where she is."

Blake stood up and began to pace before the fire. "I run a bachelor household. She can't stay here."

"Not indefinitely, I agree. And not unchaperoned," Nigel declared. "But surely she can stay a few nights until she's better."

"Nigel, I don't want her here. I want you to take her. She'll be better off with you."

"Nonsense. Beth is in the country visiting her family at the moment."

"But you're a physician," Blake reminded him.

"My being a physician matters not a whit if you wish to preserve the young lady's reputation. Haven't you an older female relation here in town?" He frowned, searching his memory of older widows and dowagers, trying to remember who was in town for the season. "There must be someone who can stay here with you while Miss Fairfax is in residence?"

"I don't want anyone staying with me. Especially an older female relation. That's the point, Nigel. I don't want Miss Fairfax here."

"Nevertheless, we would do better to leave Miss Fairfax where she is until she recovers from her illness." He snapped his fingers. "I've got it! How about your father's sister? The one who was one of the queen's ladies in waiting. Lady Wethering. That's it."

Blake groaned. "Aunt Delia? Lord, Nigel, she must be seventy if she's a day. And deaf to boot."

"She's perfect, Blake. Think about it. She's a highly respected and highly respectable widow who dotes on your father. She'll be thrilled at the prospect of doing you a favor." As far as Nigel was concerned, the matter was settled. "You can send a note around to her house right away."

"I don't want my life turned upside down," Blake insisted. "You take her—and Aunt Delia."

"Be reasonable, Blake."

"No, Nigel." Blake bit out the words. "I order you to take her."

Nigel was shocked, then outraged by his best friend's audacity. "You know what you can bloody well do with your orders."

"Threats, Nigel?"

"You know better than that. Dammit, Blake, I think you deliberately turn on your freezing glare just to ruffle my feathers." Nigel smiled at his old schoolmate. "Unless you want me to threaten you? Shall I run tattling about town with news of your latest amour?" The teasing words were out before Nigel could stop them.

Blake's face hardened. The warm glow of friendship left his onyx-dark eyes, replaced by the steely glint of anger.

Nigel realized his mistake at once and began to apologize for his teasing. "Blake, I didn't mean . . . You know I would never . . . run tattling to anyone about anything you do."

Blake held up his hand in a sign of surrender. "Enough, Nigel, don't apologize. I'm the one who owes you an apology. I'm to blame. You were teasing. I don't know what came over me. My head aches so much I can't think straight."

The tension instantly dissolved and with a shower of compassion, Nigel moved to place his hand on Blake's brow. "Well, you don't have a fever, so your soaking's done you no damage, but you do have a nasty bruise on your cheekbone to go with your swollen nose. And a small cut as well. Don't be surprised if your eye turns black in a few hours. Mind telling me how you got this wound? Did she hit you again?"

"It was an accident and it's none of your bloody business." Blake winced as Nigel disinfected the cut and slapped a dressing on it. "Ouch!"

"That should teach you to be nasty to a compassionate healer," Nigel commented as he finished. "There's nothing else I can do here except argue with you and I do have patients to see this morning. Miss Fairfax should sleep through the afternoon and probably into the night. I suggest you send a note around to Lady Wethering and go about your usual business. It should be interesting to see how you explain that black eye to your Home Office colleagues." The doctor smiled, ignoring Blake's muttered imprecations. He enjoyed seeing Blake in a prickly mood. His mask of cynicism was rarely removed long to allow anger to surface.

Nigel felt it was good to be reminded Blake hadn't lost all feeling. He was so efficient and so coldly unemotional most of the time, it was sometimes hard to remember he really was a very caring man.

Nigel Jameson was no fool. He had known Blake since they'd been in nursery frocks. He knew him well enough to know what caused the cynicism, the lack of feeling. He was also one of the few people who understood how it had all begun. Blake couldn't continue to live his life in a void, pretending he didn't need anything from anyone. He was an intelligent, sensitive man who needed someone of his own. Maybe that was why Nigel had insisted the Fairfax girl stay put when it would have been relatively simple to transport her to a hospital. There was something between them. There had to be. Blake hadn't shown this much emotion toward anyone in a very long time. It was good to see him lose his temper. The loss of control could be beneficial to him.

Nigel Jameson smiled to himself and whistled the chorus of a bawdy tune as he packed his medical instruments into his bag. He would check on Miss Fairfax's condition as often as possible. Lawrence House was going to be a lively place to visit while she remained in residence.

"STOP! STOP! YOU'RE hurting me! Go away and leave me alone. I'm not like you! I hate you! Do you hear me? I hate you. . . ."

The sound of anguished cries came from the guest room. Blake heard them from his bedroom down the hall and bolted from the bed with a start.

"Mackie, what is it? What the devil is going on in there?" Lord Lawrence demanded of his harassed housekeeper as he stood in the doorway of the guest bedroom and watched Mackie struggling to keep Cristina in the bed.

"Bad dreams. She was crying in her sleep, then she sat up and started wailing like a banshee," Mrs. MacKenzie answered, fighting to protect her face from Cristina's flailing arms.

"She's in pain," Blake said suddenly. "She's been beaten. Roll her over."

Blake hurried to help his housekeeper as Cristina continued to strike out at the arms and the bedclothes that imprisoned her. "It's all right, Mackie, I've got her now." He lay almost atop Cristina, holding the covers close about her body, forcing her to cease her thrashing about.

"Please, leave me alone. Let me go. Please." She twisted

her head to evade the strong hand stroking her damp hair as hot tears slid down her face onto the pillow.

"Ssh," Blake soothed, easing his weight off her. "I'm not going to hurt you. I'm only going to roll you over onto your stomach so you'll be more comfortable."

"Hot," Cristina whispered. "Too hot."

Blake nodded grimly as he moved to toss the covers aside. Mackie caught his arm. "But Master Blake, you can't. She's—"

"It's all right, Mackie," Blake said. "I've seen women in their undergarments before." He flipped back the covers and carefully guided Cristina onto her stomach.

He had seen *her* before, when he'd removed her sodden petticoats and put her to bed at Marlborough House. But he hadn't seen her like this. He hadn't seen the angry red marks crisscrossing her finely molded buttocks, the tender flesh of her thighs, her shapely calves, or the delicate arches of her feet. He hadn't seen the strap marks. Until now.

Mackie made a quick sign of the cross and rolled her eyes heavenward, whispering softly, "Sweet Mary, who would do such a thing?"

Blake sucked in a ragged breath. "A bastard of a jaded aristocrat," he muttered. "The lowest sort of life form."

"The poor child's anguish breaks your heart."

Blake's mouth tightened into a thin line. Tension strained every handsome muscle in his face. He remembered all too well the panic he'd felt when he'd seen the Prince of Wales's bedsheets flapping in the breeze. And the agony Cristina must have endured just hanging onto them. "She'll be all right, Mackie. We'll see to that. Miss Fairfax is strong. She wants to live. But for now she's hurt and she's tired. She needs someone to take care of her."

He raked his fingers through his disheveled hair. He didn't understand how he knew what was going through Cristina Fairfax's mind, but he did. And that made him very uncomfortable. He didn't want to share her private thoughts. Having her under his roof was bad enough.

"You're tired, Mackie. Why don't you go back to bed?"

"All right, Master Blake. I'll wake your aunt. She'll sit with Miss Fairfax."

Blake shook his head. "Let her sleep. She needs her rest, too." He smiled. "Besides, if Miss Fairfax's shouting didn't awaken Aunt Delia, your calling her isn't going to do it. I'm awake. I'll stay with her awhile." Three nights of sitting up with Cristina had taken their toll on Mackie and on his aunt. Mackie looked tired and worn and old and Aunt Delia had barely been able to keep from nodding off at dinner. Blake was filled with remorse. "Go on to bed," he urged. "It will be all right. I'll leave the door open for propriety's sake."

Mackie nodded an affirmative and hurried away in the direction of her bedroom, relieved and more than willing to let Master Blake watch over the poor girl.

Blake waited until his housekeeper left the room before he pulled a sheet over Cristina's bare back and tucked it gently around her shoulders. He shifted his weight to the edge of the four-poster bed and sat quietly, studying her features, almost memorizing them, until Cristina opened her eyes and uttered a single word.

"Please . . ." She grasped his hand and clutched it in her own sweaty palm.

"What is it, Miss Fairfax? Cristina?"

There wasn't a spark of recognition in the feverish depths of her green eyes as she spoke again. "I'm afraid."

Blake's voice was infinitely tender. "What are you afraid of, Cristina?"

"Dreams," she muttered. "My dreams."

"Ssh." Blake placed a finger against her parched lips. "I'm here. There's nothing for you to be afraid of. I promise not to hurt you and I won't let anything else hurt you." He lifted her hand with his captured one and brought it to his lips. "I promise, Cristina."

She smiled and closed her eyes.

Blake awoke as the pinkish-gray colors of dawn streaked across the sky. He stretched his cramped muscles and automatically swiped at the irritant tickling his face. The damp odor of jasmine and perspiration assailed his sensitive nostrils.

He opened his eyes, suddenly wide awake. He lay on his side, his body curved around the delectable form of Cristina Fairfax. His legs were intimately embracing hers and his arm rested lazily across her narrow waist. He sighed contentedly and Cristina stirred in her sleep, moving closer to the warmth radiating from his body until her baby-soft bottom rested familiarly against him.

Blake groaned aloud as the root of him instantly sprang to life, proudly erect, prodding her softness, seeking entrance. His brain flashed a sudden warning which told him he should leave while he still had the chance, but Blake ignored the warning. He followed his instincts, those marvelous instincts that urged him to pull her closer.

He buried his face in her hair, inhaling her scent as he ran his hand down her arm and over her side. He traced the outline of her ribs through the sheet, following her curves as he imagined her passionate response to his lovemaking.

God, but it would be heaven to kiss that soft mouth again and bury himself deep within her. Sheer heaven to wake up to her every morning.

Footsteps in the hall interrupted his passionate musings. Blake rolled away from her and scrambled from the bed with the agility of a panther. She was sick and hurt. He was supposed to be taking care of her and all he could think about was making love to her. Blake frowned. What kind of man was he? What kind of jaded aristocrat had he become?

There was a light tap at the bedroom door. Mackie peeked in.

"Still sleeping quietly, I see."

Blake swung around. Cristina was curled on her side and sleeping soundly when he half expected her to be pointing an accusing finger and staring at him as if he were a two-headed monster. He released a deep breath and brushed his hair off his forehead with trembling fingers. He didn't know if he was more thankful for the fact that Cristina slept undisturbed or that all evidence of his previous arousal vanished when Mackie opened the door. Either way, he decided, he had been lucky. Lucky and foolish.

"You must be tired, Master Blake. Why don't you try to get a few hours' sleep before your afternoon appointment? One of the maids can sit with her now," Mackie suggested, taking a good look at his unshaven face and the worry lines etched in his forehead.

Blake nodded in agreement, but he left the guest room reluctantly and as he climbed back into his own bed, he noticed how large and empty it was.

CRISTINA AWOKE THE evening of the fourth day after her arrival at Lawrence House. Blake was keeping vigil in the chair beside her bed when he saw her eyelids flutter open. Her fever had broken and she looked pale and tired. Her skin was almost translucent and there were purple shadows beneath the eyes. Blake watched her, waiting patiently for her to focus her gaze on him.

"So you're awake at last. I was afraid you had decided to sleep forever. How do you feel?" He whisked a cloth off a tray containing a steaming bowl of broth. "My housekeeper sent this up a little while ago. We thought you might be hungry when you woke up. You've been asleep for quite awhile." He kept up a steady flow of conversation as he spooned broth into her mouth. He was behaving foolishly by insisting on waiting for her to wake up and then feeding her himself when he had a whole house full of employees more than willing to do it. And if that wasn't foolish enough, he was chattering away like an infatuated schoolboy. He was a seasoned diplomat and he was acting like the biggest fool in London and he couldn't seem to control the impulse. He wasn't even all that sure he wanted to. "The doctor has been in to see you," he told her. "You'll soon be up and out dancing again."

"I don't think I want to attend any more dances," she said softly. "My last one turned out to be a debacle."

"Nonsense." His manner was light and teasing. "You were the undisputed belle of the ball."

"Right up until my confrontation with royalty," she replied bitterly. "And British diplomacy. Thank you for the soup, but I'm very tired." Cristina shook her head, refusing to open her mouth for the spoonful of broth Blake held for her.

Her open hostility burst his foolish bubble.

A small nerve on the side of Blake's mouth began to twitch as he clenched his teeth. He tightened his grip on the spoon until his fingertips whitened and the silver grew hot in his hand. When he spoke all traces of his earlier gentleness vanished. He became a cold, hard stranger once again. "If you want to be alone, Miss Fairfax, I'll be happy to oblige you. But as soon as you've recovered from your illness, I expect an apology and a feasible explanation for your behavior."

"I don't need to apologize or explain myself to you."

"As a guest in my home, you owe me some courtesy after turning my life upside down. I'll accept an apology and an explanation."

"That's very magnanimous of you." Her voice was soft and laced with sarcasm.

"I think so." Blake agreed. "You were alone in a carriage riding through town in the pouring rain at half-past seven in the morning wearing a cape and a petticoat and raging with fever." Blake knew he was being unfair. He knew why she'd been without her clothes. He knew why she was alone. What he didn't understand was why she had chosen to run from him when he had been the one to rescue her from Rudolf's amorous intentions. Didn't she realize how lucky she was? "Surely such extraordinary behavior from a first season debutante deserves some explanation. And if you don't care to explain that behavior, you might try explaining why you assaulted me with a necklace while I was trying to help you. Yes, Miss Fairfax, I think you owe me an explanation. Not to mention cab fare."

"Cab fare?" Cristina sputtered. "You'd dare to charge me for the cab fare after commandeering it for your own purpose?"

Blake smiled. A little color had returned to her face. He realized that he preferred the flush of her anger to the deathly white of resignation. "I thought you understood. I'm a man who dares many things. Good evening, Miss Fairfax." Blake delivered his parting shot and left her fuming.

Cristina stared at the bowl of broth, wondering if she dared fling it and the tray across the room. He had no right to treat her so high-handedly when he'd treated her so kindly once before. She hadn't asked to become his houseguest. She hadn't asked him to assume responsibility for her. She hadn't asked for anything except to be left alone. She appreciated the care he had given her during her illness, but she didn't need it any longer. She needed to be on her own and she had no intention of exchanging her mother's domination for Lord Lawrence's. She intended to use the necklace as her avenue to freedom. She would sell it. And once it was sold, she would pay Lord Lawrence for his dubious hospitality and use the remainder of the cash to join her father.

The thought of the cash the necklace would yield comforted Cristina. It meant she had the means to pay her way. It was reassuring to know she wasn't alone *and* penniless. Reassuring. Until she remembered that the last time she'd seen the necklace *he* had held it in his hands, demanding an explanation. His hands, not her own.

She had been asleep for a long time. The necklace could be anywhere. She had to get it back. And with that thought in mind, Cristina picked up the spoon and began to spoon the tepid broth into her mouth with grim determination.

My only books
Were women's looks
And folly's all they've taught me.

—THOMAS MOORE 1779–1852

Eight

HOURS LATER, MACKIE peeked into the sickroom to check on her patient and found Cristina curled up on the big bed. The girl was sleeping like an angel and Mackie couldn't help wondering what had happened to make Master Blake storm into the kitchen and demand his dinner be served in the library instead of in the sickroom with Miss Fairfax as planned. Nor could she understand why he'd gone into the library muttering blasphemies about "that ungrateful girl."

She shook her gray head. No doubt the strain of staying up and worrying about the young lady during the night and working during the day had taken its toll on Master Blake.

Mackie was mistaken. The strain of work and worry had very little to do with Blake's explosive frame of mind. For one split second when Cristina had stubbornly refused to take the broth, she had reminded him of Meredith. Unfaithful, deceitful Meredith, crushing his youthful dreams of love.

He stood staring into the flames that licked at the dry, seasoned logs in the fireplace, hoping to quell the unreasonable anger that surged through his body. He had lost control and allowed his temper to get the best of him and that was something that surprised him as much as it appalled him. He almost never lost control of his temper. Men in his position could lose everything they had worked so hard to gain simply by losing control of their emotions. Exposed emotions made a person vulnerable to his opponents and Blake had vowed never to be vulnerable again. He refused to let anyone have the upper hand over him and hiding his true feelings behind a mask of indifference that gave nothing away had become second nature. But that slip of a girl, not even old enough to know her own mind, had penetrated his stony exterior and caused him to lose control of his carefully guarded emotions. It infuriated him to know she could get under his skin without realizing what she was doing.

He turned away from the fire. The copper flames reminded him of the young woman who lay upstairs tempting him. Getting rid of the little vixen with her alluring body and her sword-sharp tongue would be a relief. The sooner he had her out of his house and out of his mind, the better.

As soon as she was on her feet again, he was sending her home where she belonged. But before he allowed her to leave, he intended to find out how she came to have that particular necklace in her pocket.

He tossed off another brandy and walked to the safe behind the portrait of his great-grandfather, the sixth marquess of Everleigh and restorer of the family fortune. Blake moved the portrait aside and spun the dial of the hidden safe. He pulled down firmly on the handle and the door of the safe swung open to reveal its contents.

The necklace lay nestled in a box lined with soft black velvet and alongside of it lay a matching bracelet and a pair of drop earrings. Blake had recognized the necklace the moment he'd held it in his hand. He had designed it himself and had it made for his bride. His bride. Meredith. His beautiful, faithless bride.

Blake rubbed the bridge of his nose with his fingers as the memory of his impetuous courtship and marriage returned to haunt him.

Meredith Brownlee had been the darling of Sussex. A spoiled, beautiful girl with an adventurous streak and a flair for riding to the hounds. Being the youngest of five children and the only daughter of an impoverished squire had left its mark. She was pampered, willful, and absolutely ruthless in obtaining her heart's desire. And despite her family's lack of wealth, she was the envy of every young girl in the village, the desire of every young man who was fortunate enough to glimpse her riding across the meadows dressed in a blue velvet habit with her long, ebony-black hair whipping in the wind.

Blake had seen her that way. He was home from Oxford and preparing to take up his post in Vienna when he caught sight of Meredith flying across the fields on a roan horse with all the fury of a modern-day Joan of Arc. His heart had pounded at the sight. And he'd decided then and there to have her for his very own.

The courtship was fast, furious, and so intense, Blake paid no attention to second thoughts. He was too enthralled by the breathtaking beauty of Meredith—too caught up in the dream of having her. He had never once paused to ask himself if Meredith returned his affections. He never wondered why she agreed to the courtship though she barely responded to his kisses. Blake didn't want to know why she agreed. He only cared that she had. He told himself she was shy, that she would learn to love him because he couldn't stand to think that she might not. He couldn't stand to think that his wealth might be more of an attraction for Meredith than he was. So he never asked. He never delved too deeply. He simply pursued her with single-minded determination to have what he wanted. And he won.

His four-week holiday flew by and at the end of the month, the little village of Everleigh was dazzled by the marriage of Meredith Brownlee to Blake Ashford, the ninth earl of Lawrence. The groom's father, Lord Everleigh, the marquess of Everleigh, had spared no expense for the wedding of his only son and the result was every young girl's dream of a wedding.

The bride was a vision of loveliness in her cream-colored satin gown, her black hair braided with sprays of orange blossoms. The groom, equally resplendent in an elegant, striped morning suit, stood tall and handsome beside his bride in the village church.

They made a handsome couple.

Everyone agreed. They were perfectly matched. Blake thought so, too, until he kissed his bride.

Their first exchange as husband and wife had been revealing. Too revealing. It was a greedy kiss, grasping and desperate, but devoid of love or tenderness. It was passionless. It was disgusting. It was faked. Meredith pretended overwhelming passion but she shuddered with disgust and a barely concealed tolerance of his touch.

It was as if a veil had been lifted from Blake's eyes. He had been so blinded by her beauty that he hadn't been able to see what was clearly visible. She didn't want him.

Nigel had seen it as had Beth, Nigel's wife, and his own parents. They had all tried to caution him not to be too hasty, but he hadn't listened to them.

Marry in haste, repent in leisure. The idle phrase ran through Blake's mind as he stared down at the emerald creation that had triggered the Pandora's box of his memories. He had repented and repented and repented. He had repented for six bloody years—until mercifully, the farce had ended.

Blake jabbed his fingers through his hair. Had there ever been a bigger farce than his wedding? He remembered brooding all through the reception following the wedding. He had stood in the midst of the celebration and gaiety accepting congratulations, and wondering how he would cope with the ugly realization that his wife—his bride—didn't return his affections, until Meredith interrupted him.

"Darling, I'm going upstairs to change."

"I'll go with you," Blake suggested.

"No." Her objection was hasty. Too hasty. She tried again, softer this time. "No, stay and enjoy the reception a while longer. I need a few minutes alone. To get ready." The words rolled off her tongue convincingly, but Blake was aware only of the fact that his wife was stalling—delaying her wedding night.

He told himself it was natural for a bride to be nervous, to dread the unknown, but a seed of doubt had been planted. He wondered about his wedding night. And, as he wondered, he ceased to look forward to it. He dreaded what he would find. A stone-cold wife. A wife who hated his touch. He prayed he'd be wrong, prayed he'd misread the situation. He hoped he was mistaken, hoped he'd find passion and love.

Blake had waited an hour, then half an hour more before he made his way up the stairs. He paused outside his bedroom then tapped on the door. He knew what he would find as soon as he heard the voices, the urgent, unmistakable murmurs of lovers. Still he had waited, delaying the inevitable, listening through his bedroom door like a thief or a spy—or a betrayed husband.

The jewelry box slipped out of his grasp and dropped to the tabletop and Blake squeezed his eyes shut, hoping for a brief moment that he could finally blot out the ugly image burned in his memory. When he opened his eyes again, he fixed his sight on the mantel, then walked over and poured himself another brandy, waiting for the pain to begin—waiting for the vivid, wrenching knife of betrayal to turn in his gut at the remembered sight. A snort of self-contempt for the boy he'd been escaped him. He had wanted so desperately to find Meredith consumed by passion. And he had.

She was so consumed by passion she'd risked discovery on her wedding night. The memory of that night and the voices assailed him.

"Goddammit, Meri, this was a stupid idea! He could walk in at any minute." The man snarled at her between grunts and groans. "Did you even bother to lock the door?"

"Of course not." She laughed. "The thrill of discovery has always lent a certain edge to the fun."

"You're crazy," he muttered.

"I always have been. About you. For as long as I can remember." She gasped in pleasure and a series of whimpers escaped her.

"If he walks . . . in . . . everything . . . is . . . ruined."

"Not necessarily." She paused to kiss her lover. "He might enjoy watching. Or even participating. A threesome might be enjoyable. I might even be able to bear his touch if you were here helping."

"The way you help with the serving girls?" They shared a laugh. A secret lover's laugh. And, on the other side of the door, Blake had clenched his fists in anguished impotence. He knew that voice. That laugh. He'd heard it many times before. He struggled to maintain control, agonizing between the need to see for himself and the desire to remain in the bliss of comparative ignorance.

"I can't help it." Meredith purred, "I'm so jealous of them. You've spoiled me for other men. I don't like it when you take other women."

"They're just a substitute for you. For when it's too dangerous for us to be together," he groaned.

"Truly?"

"Truly," he promised.

"What about your wife?" Meredith asked.

"She means nothing to me," he avowed. "Now open up, my beauty. Spread your legs for me. Let me in."

"Oh, God! Oh, Jack!" In the moment of supreme pleasure, Meredith cried out her lover's name.

And Blake quietly opened the door.

She lay on the huge bed, the bodice of her wedding gown open, her lush breasts exposed and glistening with the wetness of Jack's mouth. Her skirts were crushed about her waist, the satin crinkling in rhythm to the man pumping between her legs. Jack. Her lover.

His first cousin.

Blake fought to keep from retching at the sight of his bride with his cousin. The man who had always been as close as a brother was sprawled between Meredith's thighs. For the first time in his life, Blake wanted to kill. Both of them. "Get off." His voice was calm, his actions clearly restrained as he grabbed Jack by the back of his collar, pulled him from the bed, and flung him into the opposite wall. Jack howled as his nose smashed forcefully into the wall.

"Cover yourself!" he ordered Meredith, ignoring Jack's cry.

She ignored him. She continued to lie with the bodice of her wedding gown open and her skirts bunched up around her waist as the mark of his cousin's possession seeped down her inner thighs.

"Isn't this what you wanted? To be discovered. Isn't that why you didn't bother to lock the door?" Blake spoke in a harsh whisper. "You were hoping I'd walk in."

She smiled at him. "Of course."

"Am I the only one who rates a private performance of wedding day adultery or should I shout down the stairs and invite all of our wedding guests to come up and witness this?"

"Why don't you?" Meredith countered.

Jack paled. "Have you lost your mind, girl?" he demanded hoarsely. "My wife is downstairs. What if he does it?"

"He won't." Meredith was confident. She stared at Blake, daring him to invite the cream of London society to share, to witness—her wedding gift to him. Daring him to carry out his threat and expose his family, friends, and colleagues to scandal on the day of his wedding.

He wanted to. He wanted to call the guests to come see his adulterous wife. He wanted someone else to witness the unspeakable. His wife involved with his cousin. His married cousin. But that was the rub.

Meredith Brownlee was now his wife and any scandal that linked her with his cousin would hurt other people. Innocent people. Jack had a wife and two adorable children. A scandal would taint them as much as it tainted Jack.

Blake wouldn't risk the scandal. And Meredith knew it. He was too honorable, too ambitious, and too full of youthful idealistic pride.

The bedroom door was open. Blake waited until Jack crawled toward it, then slammed the door shut, turned the key in the lock, and pocketed it.

"Sensible, very sensible." Meredith leisurely fastened the bodice of her gown.

"What do you want?" Blake ground the words through his clenched teeth. He had been set up from the beginning. Neatly snared, like an unsuspecting rabbit.

"I have what I want." Meredith smiled at Jack. "We have what we want."

"And that is . . ." Blake gripped the bedpost as Jack fastened his trousers, wiped his bloodied nose, and moved to sit next to Meredith.

"Respectability. Land, position, servants, wealth. A mansion in London. I wanted a way out of Everleigh and a ticket into the cream of London society. And now I have it. I have what I've wanted all my life. Everything you took for granted. I'm the countess of Lawrence and one day, I'll be the marchioness of Everleigh. Nothing can change that."

"Except an annulment. Your tenure as countess will be the shortest in Lawrence history," Blake sneered. "I'll start proceedings in the morning."

"Too late," Meredith purred, placing a hand on Jack's crotch. "If all goes well, I should present you with the Lawrence heir nine months from today." She looked up at Blake. "As all good and faithful wives should do."

"Well, well." Jack smiled approvingly at Meredith. "And I thought you wanted to give me a farewell tumble. I should have known. You are a clever puss."

"Goddamn you!" Blake took a step forward, his fingers itched to curl themselves around her throat. "Any abomination—"

"Abomination! I take exception to that, Blake," Jack interrupted. "You're talking about a cousin fathered by me and I happen to make beautiful babies."

Blake ignored him. "Any abomination you deliver nine months from today won't be the Lawrence heir."

"Prove it. Prove it, Blake. Prove it in a court of law. Tell the world that I betrayed you. Deny your loving wife, deny your heir."

"I haven't touched you," Blake said.

"Can you prove that?" Jack echoed his lover.

Blake focused his attention on Meredith. "If you value his life, you'll keep him quiet." Then, he looked at Jack. "One more comment out of you and you'll be swallowing your teeth and holding your groin."

"I'm not a virgin. Any decent doctor can tell that. How will you explain my condition? Will you admit to being cuckolded in court?"

"That shouldn't be too hard to do," Blake retorted cynically. "Half the men in the village will probably admit to being your lover."

"But you're my husband. It will be your word against mine and I'll swear it's yours. I'll even swear you seduced me before the wedding."

"You'd be lying. No one would believe you."

"Oh yes, they would. I can be very convincing when I want to be and it's common knowledge around the village that you could hardly keep your hands off me whenever we were together. Then there is this hurried marriage. People are already whispering that I'm with child. I'll tell everyone I am. I'll confess to my parents and name you the father. I married you for your money and your position and I intend to keep both. You aren't going to cheat me out of what's rightfully mine without a huge scandal, the likes of which you've never seen. And think what a scandal like that would do to your diplomatic career and to your family name. Not to mention your mother's weak heart."

"You plan to blackmail me." Blake said. "What makes you think I'll allow it?"

"It's in your best interest." Meredith told him triumphantly. "You have pride, Blake. Too much pride. You're arrogant and ambitious. You would never do anything to bring scandal to your family or to hurt your promising career."

"An annulment of my brief marriage would not cause scandal," Blake reminded her.

"Maybe not," Meredith agreed. "But a divorce would and I'll make certain you're denied an annulment."

Blake had been neatly trapped by his own weakness and he knew it. He was tempted to throw everything away to be free again, but he knew deep down inside he would never be happy if he gave up the career he loved and had worked so hard to attain. A career that could be over before it had really begun. And he couldn't allow Meredith to hurt the people he cared about. He no longer gave a damn about Jack, but that didn't mean he was willing to stand by and allow Meredith and Jack to ruin the lives of Jack's wife and children. They were innocent. Blake shook his head. He'd been the fool. A blind, impulsive, stubborn, lusty fool and now he was about to suffer the consequences. "Suppose I agree to this idiotic farce . . . what do I get in return for not causing a scandal?"

"What you wanted to begin with. The perfect wife, of course. I'll take care of your households and be the perfect companion and complement to you and the perfect hostess for your friends and associates. And you'll have the right to do what you've been itching to do since we met."

Jack groaned aloud and Meredith gifted him with a brilliant smile before she reached over and patted his cheek. "It's only fair, Jack. You sleep with your wife. Why shouldn't Blake sleep with his?" She turned back to Blake. "You'll have the right to possess my body whenever you like and in return I'll give you your heir and a spare."

"I already have that right," Blake said bitterly. "The law and the church just granted it to me."

"And I won't object to your using it. I know you want children."

"Mine or Jack's?"

"Does it matter?" Meredith asked with a shrug. "As long as we keep it in the family."

"You expect me to accept Jack's leavings?"

"I prefer to think of it as sharing Jack's bounty," she smiled. "And I have no objection if you take a mistress. As long as you respect my position as Lady Lawrence, I'll gladly turn a blind eye to your infidelities."

"If I agree to overlook yours?" Blake responded sarcastically.

"Of course. That's the way the game is played, Blake."

"That's not the way *this* game is played, Meredith," Blake said coldly. "I don't care who you dally with from now on. As long as it's not *him*," he nodded toward Jack. "If I catch him in my house with you like this again, I'll kill him and sue you for divorce. And be well within my rights to do so. Adultery is grounds for divorce."

Blake meant it. And Meredith knew he meant it. "You thought of everything except one tiny little detail," he continued. "You've played me for a fool. I know that. And I admit that where you're concerned, I've been a fool. But no more. I may be a fool, but unfortunately for you, I'm a principled one. So, Meredith, you had better pray to whatever gods you hold dear that you are with child. Because if you aren't, there will never be a Lawrence heir and you'll be cheated out of part of the countess of Lawrence's rightful inheritance. Lawrence House, that London mansion you want so much, is entailed."

"She knows that," Jack snapped. "It's been in the family for centuries."

"Does she know how it's entailed, Jack? Is that why she's so eager to have your child and pass it off as mine? Did you tell her that Lawrence House was originally given to the countess of Lawrence by Charles the Second? He had it built for her, his mistress, because her husband, my ancestor, had threatened to throw her out on the streets when he found out the younger children she'd been passing off as his belonged to the king. Charles, kind and generous lover that he was, threatened to throw the earl of Lawrence in prison instead, but he eventually realized that imprisoning one of his noblemen for his unwillingness to be cuckolded—even by a king—could result in the kind of anger and retaliation by the House of Lords that had cost his father his head. After all, sleeping with the king's wife is an act of high treason. So Charles decided a wiser, and perhaps more fitting, course of action was to grant Lady Lawrence a separation from her husband, build her a house of own, and gift her with a tidy fortune that would belong solely to the countess of Lawrence, so long as she has borne the earl of Lawrence a recognized heir. Her fortune is to remain separate and apart from the monies and holdings of the earl of Lawrence for as long as the monarchy stands. The earl may add to the wealth, but he can't take anything away from it. The house is tied to the title, but the earl has no right to it or say over its administration. If there is no living countess or dowager countess or female heirs, ownership of Lawrence House reverts to the crown and the fortune is placed in trust until such time as there shall be a living countess, dowager countess or female heir. It cannot be appropriated by the crown or sold by the earl or his male heirs. It belongs to the mother of the heir. Unless you become the mother of the *recognized* heir, Lawrence House and the money that goes with it will remain in my mother's possession."

"What?" The gasp of surprise came from Meredith.

"That's right. The London mansion currently belongs to my mother. Because I choose to live in London and she chooses to live in the country, she allows me the use of it. But I don't own it and neither does my father, so it's impossible for me to inherit it through him."

"I don't believe you."

"It's true. The jewel in the Lawrence crown is on loan. And should I die without recognizing an heir—legal or otherwise—it reverts to my father's closest female blood relative, our aunt, Delia, or the crown." Blake glanced at his cousin. "I'm surprised Jack didn't tell you."

"I didn't think that it would matter," Jack stammered, staring at Blake. "I never thought there might be a possibility that you would not recognize any child born to your wife. I never thought you'd be capable of branding a child—any child—a bastard."

"You should have told me," Meredith accused Jack. "You should have explained all of this."

"God, Meri, you've got to believe me, I didn't think it mattered. I thought if Blake ever found out about us, he'd keep quiet for the good of the family."

"Blake is keeping quiet for the good of the family," Blake

said as he stared with unconcealed distaste at her exposed thighs. "*Your* family, Jack. So you'd better start praying, Meredith, because this is your only chance. Ironic, isn't it? The reason that Lawrence House came into being—the objection of an earl of Lawrence to being cuckolded—is the very same reason you'll never have the opportunity to own it."

"I wouldn't be so sure if I were you," Meredith taunted. "Jack has already proven his potency."

"Granted," Blake replied. "But you haven't."

Meredith's eyes narrowed and she sucked in an angry breath.

"You might try standing on your head," he advised. "To keep as much of Jack's potency as possible from escaping. Because I won't touch you. I refuse to grace your bed. I'll never give you the opportunity to bear the Lawrence heir. And if, after the nine month anniversary of our nuptials, you attempt to pass someone—anyone—else's bastard off as my child, I'll sue you for a divorce on the grounds of adultery and throw you, penniless, into the street."

Meredith nonchalantly shrugged her ivory shoulders. "You'll be the one to suffer, Blake. You'll be the one without a son and heir. . . ."

Blake smiled grimly. "Really? Why is that? No one would fault a man for adopting an heir when his wife is hopelessly barren. And certainly no one could find fault with a man for deeding his entire fortune to his heir—legal or otherwise—in celebration of his birth." Blake turned, and taking the key from his pocket, unlocked the door. He walked back to the bed, grabbed Jack by the collar once again, and hauled him into the hallway. Blake heard Meredith's shriek of fury as he locked the door from the outside.

"And, you, you miserable bastard," Blake shook Jack like a terrier shaking a rat. "You'd better pray you didn't leave a child behind. Because your life will be a living hell if you did. Do you understand me, Jack? I don't have to go public to make you miserable. I know how you live. I know about your reckless gaming—the debts you owe and the men you owe them to. A few well-chosen words in the right ears and you could be out on the street along with your mistress."

"What about Annalise? And the children?" Jack asked. "Would you throw them out on the streets, too?"

"How very ingenious of you to remember your loving, faithful, and wealthy Annalise now that you wish to hide behind her skirts. I'm very fond of Annalise, Jack. I've known her since we were children. Her parents are my godparents. Do you know that your father-in-law is listed to receive the Queen's Cross? I would hate to cost him that richly deserved reward by bringing scandal down around his head. And I have no intention of sacrificing my career or my father's good name and impeccable reputation to amuse Meredith. I've heard the whispers and the rumors regarding my hasty courtship of Meredith and I'm here to tell you that this is the end of them. I've provided all the gossip, all the amusement, all the titillation, and scandal I intend to provide for you, for Meredith, for the county, and for society at large. Do you understand that? Do you realize that my control is the only bloody thing keeping you alive? Can you begin to guess how Annalise's father would feel about what just happened here? Do you understand how he would view an adulterous son-in-law? I won't have to kill you or see that you're thrown out on the streets to fend for yourself if you hurt his daughter. He will." Blake dragged Jack to the top of the stairs. "Maybe I deserve punishment for being so damned arrogant, and so damned stupid, but there are other people involved who don't deserve to be hurt and humiliated. So heed my warning, Jack. I'm not going to kill you now. I'm not going to say a word. But I will kill you if I find you've been in my house again or sniffing around Meredith's skirts. And scandal be damned." With that final promise, Blake shoved Jack down the stairs. "Somebody take Jack home!" He shouted down behind him. "He's had too much to drink. I found him in my bedroom offering to help Meredith off with her dress!"

Jack paled, choked, then stumbled down the rest of the stairs when he heard his father-in-law's hearty laughter. "Boy, don't you know three's a crowd on a wedding night?"

But there was no wedding night. Blake spent the night in his dressing room. Alone.

The following morning, he unlocked the door to his wife's room. He greeted her cordially, accompanied her to the wedding breakfast arranged by his parents, and later boarded a train bound for Vienna. But not before arranging for Meredith to be observed and guarded at all times.

The pattern for their marriage had been set. The ground rules established. The earl and countess of Lawrence, like so many other fashionable Victorian couples, began married life as bitter antagonists who happened to share the same name, address, and very little else.

Their arrangement couldn't be called a marriage. It wasn't a relationship that even remotely satisfied Blake who wanted the kind of marriage his parents shared, but he tolerated it until he was mercifully released from it by Meredith's accident.

She was on holiday, fox hunting at Willow Wood, the Lawrence country estate, when her horse caught its foreleg on a fence rail. She tried valiantly to keep her seat, but the horse went down and she went with him. She screamed as she fell and her scream mingled with that of her mount as its leg splintered.

Meredith lay flat on her back, crushed beneath the weight of the horse.

Blake hurried to England from his post in Vienna, but by the time he arrived with his parents, Meredith was dead. Dead and hastily buried. Meredith's family had arranged it all, they said, to spare him the sight of her crushed body.

A log rolled from the andirons into the glowing embers, sending a shower of sparks up the chimney. Blake stared down at the jewelry box on the table. He had planned to give the jewels to Meredith as a wedding gift, but he hadn't. He had given the box to his father instead, and asked that it be locked in the safe at Lawrence House until he returned to London. The box had remained locked in the safe for years. Blake had never opened it again. He hadn't known the necklace was missing until four mornings ago, when he opened the Lawrence House safe and found empty the velvet spot where the necklace had lain for years.

He realized then that the necklace in Cristina Fairfax's possession wasn't a copy of his design. It was his. Stolen from safekeeping.

Blake smiled. He could easily imagine Meredith's rage when she discovered the intricately carved box inscribed "All My Love, Blake." And he knew without a doubt that Meredith had somehow gotten hold of the necklace and disposed of it. He felt it in his bones.

The crack of the crystal was so quiet that the pain took him by surprise. He looked down to find the brandy snifter shattered in his hand. Blake sucked in a breath, gritting his teeth against the sharp sting as the golden liquor seeped into the cuts on his hand, merging with the deep red of his blood.

He opened his hand, allowing the pieces of broken glass to fall on the tabletop, then fumbled with the silk tie around his neck. Blake tore the tie free and wrapped the delicate fabric around his fist to staunch the flow of blood. Mackie would scold him when she saw his hand. It was covered with cuts and faint white lines, scars from other cuts. Over the years, numerous brandy glasses had succumbed to his grip when memories of his wedding night overcame him. Blake slumped into his favorite leather chair. Meredith had been dead over six years and she still had the power to enrage him. He shook his head. When would it end?

He closed his eyes and leaned back against chair. It wouldn't end for a while. It couldn't. Not until he found out when Meredith had taken the necklace. Not until he learned how it had come to be hidden in Cristina Fairfax's pocket.

*Claret is the liquor for boys, port for men; but he
who aspires to be a hero must drink brandy.*

—SAMUEL JOHNSON 1709–1784

Nine

HE COULDN'T SAY what woke him. It might have been
some sixth sense telling him something wasn't quite right, but
suddenly he knew he wasn't alone. He opened his eyes. The
fire in the fireplace had burned out. The coals glowed reddish
orange in the grate, but gave off little light. Blake shifted his
weight in the chair, praying the comfortable leather wouldn't
creak and reveal his presence. He wasn't afraid. He'd detected
faint scent of jasmine and recognized his intruder.

Blake heard the scratch of a match, then smelled the sulfur
as she lit the lamp on his desk. He held his breath, waiting
for her to look up and find him sitting by the fireplace, but
her attention was focused on his desk. She hadn't seen him
because she was busy searching his desk drawers. She had
come with a spoon in hand in order to force the drawers of
his desk open, but it wasn't necessary. None of the drawers
was locked. His important documents were in the safe, as was
the household money. Everything of value in his office except
the paintings and the objects d'art rested safely behind the
marquess's portrait. Blake glanced down at the box on the

table at his elbow. Everything except the small fortune in jewels he'd left lying on the table.

"It has to be here somewhere," Cristina muttered. "Surely he has a safe. He's not stupid enough to leave valuables just lying around."

Blake winced at her words. That was debatable.

"Behind the portrait."

Cristina looked up at the portrait above her head. "I was getting to that," she said aloud before she realized she hadn't thought the words. Someone had spoken them.

Cristina whirled around so quickly her white nightgown fanned out around her. She clutched the spoon in her fist.

Lord Lawrence sat in a leather wing chair watching her. He nodded politely. "Don't let me interrupt."

Cristina nearly screamed in shock and in relief because the voice belonged to Lord Lawrence, not some housebreaker come to steal valuables. Guiltily she realized she was the only one trying to do that.

"What are you doing here?" she demanded, pointing at his chair with the spoon.

"I live here."

"I know that. What were you doing in here?" Cristina waved the spoon around, indicating the interior of his study. "The lamps were out."

"I was sleeping," Blake told her.

"I thought you slept upstairs. You're not supposed to be sleeping down here. Mackie said your room was down the hall from mine. I tiptoed past it." In her agitation, Cristina rambled on.

"I didn't realize there were house rules concerning my sleeping habits." Blake eased himself to the edge of the chair. "Do you mind finishing your search for whatever it is you're looking for, so I can go back to sleep?" He faked a yawn. "By the way, what are you searching for?"

Caught off-guard, Cristina forgot to evade his question. "My necklace. The one I had in the hansom cab. I couldn't find it upstairs. Can you tell me what happened to it and where I might find it?"

"You mean the emerald and diamond necklace you used to try to blind me?"

Cristina had the grace to blush as she nodded her head.

"In the safe." Blake left the ornate box full of diamonds and emeralds on the table and stood up. As steadily as he was able, he walked toward his desk and Cristina.

"The safe?"

"The one behind the portrait," Blake confirmed. "The one you were going to get to next."

Cristina's green eyes sparkled like the emeralds in the necklace. He was being so nice. "Will you get it for me?"

"I'd be happy to." Blake told her. "But I can't."

"Why not?" She knew there had to be a catch. He was being too nice.

Blake held up his right hand so she could see it. His palm was bandaged and the cloth wrapped around it was stained with blood, the dark brown of old blood and the brighter red of new, fresh blood.

"I can't turn the dial." Blake frowned at his hand and swayed a bit on unsteady feet. "I think I'm going to require a stitch or two this time."

Cristina rushed to his side. "This time? Do you cut yourself often?" She held his palm, trying to see the damage. He seemed completely in control, but Cristina was close enough to smell the brandy fumes. She groaned as he leaned on her.

"You're drunk," she accused. "No wonder you cut yourself."

"I've been drinking," Blake corrected. "But I'm not drunk. There's a difference."

"A minor point," Cristina reminded him.

"Not so minor," Blake responded. "The cut on my hand wasn't the result of drinking too much, but of not drinking enough to forget."

Cristina was intrigued in spite of herself. "Forget what?"

Blake shook his head. "About the necklace."

"What about it?"

"I can't turn the dial to the safe."

"I can turn the dial," Cristina assured him.

"No." Blake pulled his injured hand out of Cristina's grasp.

"Why not?"

"I won't give you the combination. Never trust anyone with the combination." He smiled at Cristina. "How do I know you won't try to steal from me?"

Cristina was indignant. "I'd never do that!"

"I didn't think so."

Realizing that even in his inebriated state he'd managed to trap her, Cristina stepped away from him, intent on locating the door.

Blake attempted to follow her, but light-headed from brandy and the loss of blood, he wobbled. Trying to steady himself, he reached for Cristina and grabbed a handful of white, lawn nightgown.

The fragile fabric came apart in his hands, baring her slim body.

They stared at each other in mute stupefaction.

Slowly, steadily, the light in Blake's eyes changed. Warmed. Smoldered.

He pulled her against his chest and covered her lips with his own in answer to his overwhelming need to feel.

Cristina stiffened immediately, expecting his lips to bruise, expecting his kiss to be hard, forceful. It wasn't. His kiss was exquisitely tender. He took his time, tasting, nibbling, learning the texture of her lips, the subtle contours of her mouth. Though his lips were cool, his kiss seemed to burn her skin with its fire and to run unchecked throughout the length of her body.

She was breathless from the force of emotion sweeping through her. She wanted to open her mouth and demand that he stop, and at the same time she wanted the intensely pleasurable feeling to go on forever. She purred with delight as his hand moved slowly and silkily up and down her spine.

His lips wreaked havoc on her fluttery pulse.

"Ah." Her breathless sigh reached his ears as his lips spread their trail of fire along the column of her neck, down the rosy peak of a breast.

Logic escaped her at this wondrous exploration. Cristina let herself be swept along on the crest of the intoxicating new emotions engulfing her. Her senses were acutely aware of him—the feel of his soft shirt pressed next to her uncovered flesh, the unique taste of his lips, flavored with brandy, and the intimacy of standing together, legs entwined. Cristina felt the play of his taut muscles, rippling with every movement, and the lean, hard length of him pressed urgently against her stomach while his hand and mouth roved over her, setting her nerve endings aflame.

"Kiss me, Cristina," Blake ordered, angling his good hand in her silky hair and wrapping the other around her waist to pull her even closer to him. "Kiss me back."

It was an order Cristina eagerly obeyed. She pressed her mouth to his and instantly felt his hungry, tangy-sweet kiss devour her. His tongue thrust against hers, an insistent, probing, relentless teacher. Her arms went around his neck and Cristina kissed him back, mimicking the actions of his tongue, restlessly searching the cavern of his mouth with all of her newly acquired skill.

He deepened the kiss and Cristina responded. She found the thick, coarse hair at the nape of his neck and explored it with her fingers. The feel of it excited her. She wanted to explore all of him, to feel the coarse hair that covered other parts of his body. The hair that teased the sensitive tips of her breasts where his opened shirt exposed his bare chest. She wanted to become as familiar with his body as he seemed to be with hers.

She existed for the moment and for this one man. She surrendered herself to him and stood quaking with emotion, waiting . . . wanting . . .

Blake understood almost immediately when Cristina decided not only to surrender, but to participate fully in what was about to happen. "Let me love you, Cristina. Let me teach you how to love me." He heard himself murmur the words and he couldn't believe what he was saying. The jasmine scent of her hair and of her body drove him mad. And the brandy was talking, making him maudlin. Yes, he wanted

her, but . . . What did he know of love? The one time he
thought he'd found it had been a disaster. He didn't know
love. He didn't trust love. Yet when he opened his mouth
romantic, loving phrases wanted to flow from his tongue. He
was forced to bite them back. Sex, he could teach, but love . . .

Blake broke the kiss. Every nerve in his body screamed at
him, calling him ten kinds of a fool, but he gently pushed
Cristina away. She was in danger. She could be hurt. More
importantly, he was in danger . . .

"Lord Lawrence? Blake?" She smiled up at him, waiting
for him to continue kissing her.

"Go, Cristina." His words were rough, husky with emotion. "Go back to bed. Now."

"Are you . . . is everything all right?" There was concern
for him in her eyes.

"I'm fine. But, you"—he ground his teeth together—
"you're in grave danger. Go upstairs, now, while you can.
And for God's sake, don't come back down here tonight."

Cristina stared at him. His eyes were closed, his teeth
clenched, his skin taut, his muscles trembling. She wanted to
stay, but she was frightened by the sudden change in him.
She picked up the pieces of her nightgown, and holding them
against her breasts, fled the room.

Blake opened his eyes in time to watch Cristina disappear
through the open door. Forcing himself to walk to his favorite
chair, he gingerly eased his body into the comforting depths.
He stared at the dying embers. There was no point in trying
to sleep. Not while his mind insisted on replaying Cristina's
exit. The sight of her tight, rounded buttocks and the slim legs
that seemed to go on forever—and the pink welts and
purplish-yellow bruising from the strap that damned barbarian
had used to try to impose his will upon her—would keep him
company throughout the rest of the long night.

My mind is troubled, like a fountain stirr'd;
And I myself see not the bottom of it.

—WILLIAM SHAKESPEARE 1564–1616

Ten

"NIGEL, YOU'VE GOT to take her," Blake insisted. "She can't stay at Lawrence House any longer. Not even with Aunt Delia in residence."

The two friends sat at a corner table in the lounge of the St. James Club, Piccadilly. Both were drinking coffee. Blake sported a white bandage on his right hand, a bandage that covered three of Nigel's tiny stitches. He was also nursing the remains of a monstrous hangover.

"I can't take her, Blake," Nigel told him. "You know Beth won't be back for another week. And I'm not admitting her to my hospital. If she can go rifling through your desk in the wee hours of the morning, she doesn't belong in a hospital."

"Then what the devil do I do with her?" Blake demanded of his best friend.

Nigel grinned.

"That's the bloody problem!" Blake admitted. "It's all I think about. Dream about. She's driving me mad. I can't eat. I can't sleep. All I can do is drink myself silly each night. But I can't function with these cursed headaches every morning."

"So what's the problem?" Nigel laughed as the frown between Blake's brows intensified. "Send her home."

"To be beaten again?"

"What other choice do you have?" Nigel asked.

Blake stared at his friend.

"Don't look at me. I've given you my reasons. And they're all valid. Besides, I'm not her legal guardian and neither are you."

"I know, but sending her home is out of the question. She doesn't want to go home and I won't force her. There has to be another solution." Blake took a sip of his coffee. "Besides, I called at Fairhall this morning. I was going to attempt to negotiate with her mother, to try to work out some arrangement to provide for Cristina and her safety, but the servants were closing the house. It seems Patricia has left for the Continent."

"What?"

"That's right, my friend." Blake signaled for more coffee. "Lady Fairfax has left London and her daughter behind without so much as an inquiry as to Cristina's whereabouts. The story the housekeeper told me was that Miss Fairfax's staying in the country with friends until her engagement is announced."

"What a crock!"

"Exactly." Blake lowered his voice as the waiter refilled their cups. "Especially when Cristina's maid is still at Fairhall. What young lady goes to the country without her lady's maid?"

"So Patricia thinks she's with Rudolf?"

"I doubt Patricia has thought about her daughter at all, but I'm hoping that's what she supposes." Blake drained his coffee cup.

"Where is Rudolf now?"

"When I left his rooms this morning, he was packing for the weekend at Sandringham with the Prince of Wales. I'm expected to join them in the morning."

"Did Rudolf say anything about his redhead? The young woman you hired to take Miss Fairfax's place?"

"He believes the story Patricia put about. It seems his little redhead disappeared before he woke up."

"Then you and Rudolf have a lot in common."

"I'm surprised she and Cristina didn't pass each other in the halls. He thinks Cristina's in the country and he's eagerly awaiting her return to London."

"And now you're trying to foist her off on me."

"Nigel, you've got to take her. She can't go home and she can't stay with me."

"I told you before, I can't keep her, Blake. Besides, you're going to Sandringham for the weekend. You won't be at Lawrence House for two or three days. Let her stay there until you get back. Maybe I'll come up with a plan while you're gone." Nigel had no intentions of coming up with a suitable plan. He was enjoying Blake's "little problem." He hoped it would continue, right up until they purchased a special license and rang the church bells. Nigel stood up. He had rounds to make at his private hospital and he wanted to include a visit to Lawrence House and Blake's fascinating house guest.

Blake nodded his head in agreement. "You're right. We'll think of something. God, I must have been mad to get involved. It wasn't any of my business if her mother auctioned her off. I should have ignored it and her. Damn those green eyes."

"Cheer up," Nigel told him. "If it gets too bad, you can always give her to Rudolf."

Blake's dark gaze raked his friend. Nigel could almost feel the fire.

"That's a hell of a thing to say. You know what kind of life she'd have as Rudolf's mistress. I didn't risk my neck and my reputation saving her from Rudolf just to give her back!"

"Then I guess you'll just have to keep her," Nigel shot back.

Keep her. The words echoed in Blake's mind a thousand times during the long afternoon. It wasn't such a bad idea. He'd already admitted he wanted her. And if her kiss was any indication, she wasn't immune to him. He could keep her. He could set her up in a little house somewhere close by. A discreet little house. It was done all the time. Instead of becoming Rudolf's mistress, she could become his. The idea had merit except for one tiny thing. If he did that, he was no better than her mother, selling her to the highest bidder. No better than Rudolf buying her . . .

~~~

CRISTINA CONFRONTED BLAKE as soon as he entered the front door of Lawrence House later that afternoon.

"I'm ready to leave."

"What?" Blake was in no mood for a confrontation.

"I said I'm ready to leave." Cristina repeated her words slowly as if he were deaf or simpleminded.

"I heard you," Blake told her. "It's out of the question." He walked past her into his study. Where had that come from? Hours earlier, he'd been practically begging Nigel to take her home with him.

Cristina followed him. "I don't think my staying here is a very good idea." She'd spent the day thinking about Blake's kiss. It was the second time he'd pushed her away. She didn't understand why he'd gone to all the trouble to buy her if all he intended to do was kiss her and push her away. Unless he had done it just to prove he could buy her—that she did have a price. And if that was the case, she didn't want to stay at Lawrence House a minute longer than she had to. "I really don't want to be your houseguest."

Stung by her frankness, Blake snorted. "I really don't recall asking you."

"Maybe I'd feel differently if you had," Cristina allowed. "But now, I'd appreciate it if you'll just turn my necklace over to me, so I can be on my way."

Maybe I'd feel differently if you had. He felt his chest tighten at her softly spoken admission. "Where do you intend to go? Your mother has left London for the Continent. Fairhall is closed."

Cristina sank down on a leather footstool. "She told me

that's what she was going to do and I believed her at the time, but somehow it doesn't quite seem possible.'' She knew her mother was capable of abandoning her—had in fact, sold her—but it hadn't seemed real. Until now. Fairhall closed? Where was Leah? Surely Leah hadn't abandoned her as well?

"It's true. I went by this morning." Blake hadn't meant to be so harsh when he told her, but then, he hadn't expected her to confront him with her desire to leave him. "But"—he looked down at the girl sitting almost at his feet and tried to soften the disappointment—"your maid was still there. Along with the butler and housekeeper. It seems your maid refused to leave without you. She stayed at Fairhall to wait for your return. I asked the butler to have her pack some of your things and I sent my coach for her late this afternoon. She should arrive any minute.''

"You sent for Leah?"

"Now that you're up and about, you'll need a lady's maid to help you. And as you can see, I don't have many running about.'' Blake smiled. "Although I'm sure Aunt Delia has been more than generous in sharing hers, I thought you'd like to have your own while you're here.''

"So you bought Leah, too," Cristina said, bitterly. "I suppose I should be happy about that?"

"Well, yes," Blake said. "I thought it would make you happy.''

"How much more am I going to owe you?"

"I can well afford to pay one lady's maid.''

"I don't doubt that, Lord Lawrence. I think you could probably afford to buy just about anything you wanted.''

Something about her tone of voice ignited the fuse on Blake's already short temper. "Is that why you were attempting to break into my safe last night?''

"I told you, last night I was searching for my necklace.''

Suddenly they were standing toe-to-toe, facing each other like pugilists in a ring.

"You mean *my* necklace," Blake said. "That necklace belongs to me.''

"It belonged to you before you sent it to my mother to buy

me," Cristina corrected him. "Now it belongs to me."

"Before I what?" Her words stopped Blake in his tracks.

"You heard me." Cristina flung the words at him before she began to pace the room.

"I couldn't have heard you correctly." Blake's voice was deceptively gentle. "Repeat what you said, please." The last, polite phrase he added on as an afterthought.

Cristina turned to face him, her green eyes glittering with anger, clenched fists propped on her hips. "I said the necklace belonged to you before you sent it to my mother. Now it belongs to me."

"You actually think *I* bought you?" Blake was incredulous.

"I think you're despicable," Cristina cried. "As despicable as she is." She turned away from him, trying to choke back the tears that threatened to overflow.

"I—" Blake started to defend himself.

"No, you're worse than she is," Cristina continued. "You bought me just to prove you could. At least she was honest about her reasons. While you—"

"While I what?" Blake waved his handkerchief over her right shoulder. Her anger was easier to cope with than her tears.

Cristina snatched the handkerchief from him. "You just did it to humiliate me. To prove all women can be bought for a price just like you said. You did this just to prove a point. You don't want me."

Blake shook his head in disbelief. Not want her? She was complaining about his not wanting her? He was consumed with wanting her. Obsessed with wanting her. Tormented with wanting her. But she was too damned much of an innocent to recognize it.

"You obviously don't understand the meaning of the word," Blake muttered. He reached out to touch Cristina's shoulder, encouraging her to turn around and face him. "I didn't . . ." He started once again to tell her that he hadn't bought her, but stopped himself. It was better for her to think he was the villain than for her to know the truth. It would hurt her far less to think he had purchased her out of a warped sense of pride than to know she'd been sold at a public gathering of jaded aristocrats.

"Do you really think I'd go so far just to prove a point?" Blake asked her.

"I don't know what to think anymore," Cristina admitted. "I knew you were angry at me, but I never thought you'd stoop to bartering with my mother or sending an anonymous necklace. I never dreamed I'd be sent to Marlborough House, then wake up and find myself in bed with you. I shouldn't have let you pull me in. I should have jumped when I reached the end of the sheets."

"You'd probably have broken your little neck," Blake reminded her.

"Maybe. But I'd be free."

Blake studied her face, the earnest gleam in the depths of her green eyes. The longing for something she needed. He recognized the longing. He knew what it was like to feel trapped, coerced, used by another person. He understood her need for self-determination. But another part of him was wounded by her lack of faith in him.

"Is that what you want, Miss Fairfax?" His voice was low, husky, full of emotion, his dark eyes compelling. "Do you want to be free of me?"

She wanted him to kiss her again. She wanted him to pull her into his arms and tell her he wanted her. She wanted the safety and security of his hard body. She wanted the something she saw in his eyes, but she couldn't name her feelings, couldn't put them into words. So she resorted to evasions. "I want to leave. I want you to let me go."

Her reply stung him.

"Fine." Blake whirled around and stalked to his desk. "You're free to go." He was tired of being maligned, tired of playing the hero for an ungrateful slip of a girl. Tired of wanting.

"Fine," she agreed. "Give me my necklace and I'll be out of your life."

"I'm afraid that's out of the question." Blake's face was

set in harsh, unyielding lines. He shuffled some paperwork around on his desk, pretending to give it his undivided attention. "You're dismissed. You may go."

"I'm not leaving without my necklace." Cristina's voice was firm.

"Then you might as well make yourself comfortable." Blake assured her. "*You're* free to go. The necklace stays here."

"But I need it for traveling expenses," Cristina tried to reason with him. "I don't have any money."

"I'll loan you money." He picked up his silver pen and dipped it into the inkwell on his desk. "I'll write you out a bank draft."

"I can't repay a loan."

"Fine." Blake looked up at her. "Then I'll give you the money."

"No." Cristina leaned forward and placed her hands on the top of his desk. "I won't take money from you."

"How much do you need? Five hundred pounds? A thousand?" He took a leather bound book from his drawer, opened it, and wrote out a bank draft.

"You can't soothe your conscience that easily," Cristina stated. "I don't want your thirty pieces of silver. I want the necklace."

"That's your misfortune."

"You gave me it to me."

"Gave, Miss Fairfax?" Blake raised one eyebrow. "Minutes ago you were accusing me of sending it as payment. Payment for services to be rendered, I believe."

"I rendered the service," Cristina informed him. "I spent the night with you."

"Did you?"

"You know I did. At Marlborough House. You owe me the necklace."

"We shared a bed, Miss Fairfax, nothing more."

"Well?" Cristina demanded, as if that were proof of intimacy.

"Allowing you to share my bed while you're in a drunken

stupor does not constitute payment for services rendered. Any self-respecting mistress knows that.'' Blake threw the insult at her as an afterthought to see what she'd do next. ''If you want the necklace, Miss Fairfax, you'll have to earn it.''

Cristina sucked in a breath, then released it in fury. ''You don't have enough money to buy me.''

Blake looked her right in the eyes. ''I thought I already had.''

He waited.

She looked as if she wanted to slap him, then thought better of it. Reaching across the top of his desk, she touched the small silver pot.

She wanted to throw it. Blake could see it in the depths of her green eyes. She wanted to bounce it off his chest. But she didn't. She looked him in the eye, then carefully and with great dignity settled it back into place on his desk and walked out the door.

Brilliant strategy, Lawrence, he berated himself. To push her into a corner like that. Now if she ever did come to him, he'd never know if it was because she wanted him or the damned necklace.

Christ, what a tangle! Blake cursed the necklace. He cursed Patricia Fairfax and Rudolf. And he cursed Meredith for her duplicity. But most of all, Blake cursed himself for always wanting what he could not have.

BLAKE WAS SITTING in his favorite chair beside the fireplace in his study deliberately polishing off a bottle of brandy when his Aunt Delia entered the room and announced in a voice loud enough to wake the dead, ''Perryman says that Miss Fairfax's maid has arrived and that she's asking to see you or Miss Fairfax, or both.''

''Tell him to show her to Miss Fairfax's room.'' Blake rose from his chair as his aunt entered the room. Although his aunt was hard of hearing, he tried very hard not to shout at her. He'd noticed that she seemed to understand what was said around her much better when she could look the speaker in the face, so he placed his snifter of brandy on the mantel and walked over to stand in front of her. He didn't like shoving the task of seeing Cristina's maid properly settled into the household off on his butler, his housekeeper, or his aunt without having first welcomed her himself, but he was in no condition to acknowledge her arrival. Not while he was still fuming over her young mistress's erroneous assumptions about him. Not while he was trying very hard to drink his thoughts of Cristina away.

"What did you do to the gel?" Aunt Delia asked.

"Why?" A vision of Cristina hanging from the upstairs window on a rope of slashed bedding flashed through his mind.

"Miss Fairfax isn't opening her door," Aunt Delia informed him.

He blanched. "I'd better send someone around back to check her window."

Delia narrowed her gaze in suspicion. "And why would you need to do that?"

"To see if she's still in her room," he answered automatically.

"She's there. She's threatening to brain anyone who tries to open the door, but she's still there."

"Good." The note of relief in his voice was unmistakable. He exhaled the breath he'd been holding. "She's upset with me, but she's forsaken the bedsheets."

Delia stared at her nephew as if he'd lost his mind. "Blake, dear boy, she's threatening to bash us over the head."

"With what?" Blake asked, more out of idle curiosity than out of any real concern.

"With a vase. She said to tell you it was Chinese porcelain, probably early Ming." Aunt Delia paused. "If it's the vase in the carved niche by her dressing table, I suspect it's a few decades older than Ming. But I'm not an expert. And Chinese porcelain is rather difficult to date at times because each generation of artisans tended to copy patterns of the previous generation. But the glazing and firing techniques did improve.

Still, I suppose the only real way to be certain about the date is to locate the household manifest and see when it was purchased or to allow Cristina to break it. The sand used in Ming porcelain is very, very fine. . . .''

Blake held up his hand. His aunt was an amateur antiquarian and prided herself on her patronage of the London Museum of History. ''Aunt Delia, please tell Miss Fairfax her maid is here and that if she breaks the vase, it'll go on her account for services owed.''

''Blake Ashford!'' Aunt Delia was outraged by the suggestion. ''You wouldn't!''

''No, Aunt Delia, I wouldn't.'' Blake stood up and followed his aunt as far as the bottom of the grand staircase, then fondly patted her cheek. ''But she doesn't know that.''

''Her maid is waiting in the front hall.''

Blake nodded. ''Aunt Delia?''

''Yes, dear?''

''Would you be sure to tell Miss Fairfax that cook is holding dinner for her? This household will not eat until she appears for dinner.'' He made the announcement loud enough for Cristina to hear.

He didn't have to wait long before the sound of her voice drifted down from upstairs. ''Lady Wethering, you may tell Lord Lawrence that I will be more than happy to dine with the rest of his household as long as he dines elsewhere.''

''Now, dear . . .'' Aunt Delia's words were lost as Perryman, the butler, ushered Leah into Blake's study.

Mackie followed close on their heels. ''Thank goodness you've come. I simply don't know how to handle the young miss.'' Mackie shrugged her shoulders in an eloquent gesture.

''Mrs. MacKenzie, I forbid you to take the Miss Fairfax's supper to her,'' Blake interrupted loudly. ''If she wants to eat, she can come downstairs and eat with me.''

''But Master Blake . . .'' Mackie stared at her employer and nodded her head in the direction of his study.

''Mackie.'' Blake stressed the housekeeper's pet name to let her know he meant business. He couldn't allow his softhearted housekeeper to circumvent his order. If Cristina continued to act like a naughty child, he would treat her as such.

He turned to Leah. "You must be from Fairhall."

"Yes. Your Lordship sent for me. I'm Leah and I brought some of my young lady's clothes," Leah explained, not quite sure how far into the bottle his lordship was.

"Your young lady?" Blake muttered suggestively. "She may be a lady, but right now she's not acting like one. Have you any idea the amount of trouble that young woman has caused me?"

Leah grasped the situation immediately. There was a power struggle going on in this house and both of the participants were determined to win. "I have a good idea, Your Lordship. You see, I've known Miss Fairfax from the day she was born and I know she can be a handful. She's given me many a gray hair in my head from worryin'," Leah told him, "but she can also be the sweetest, most lovin' girl in the world."

Blake leaned closer to Leah. "I haven't had the privilege of seeing much of her nicer side. "Apparently we bring out the worst in each other."

If he hadn't seemed so earnest, Leah was sure she would have burst out laughing.

"Why do you suppose that is?" he asked.

Leah turned to Blake and flashed him one of her rare smiles. "Well, if I were to really think about it, I would think it might be because you tend to be a wee bit overbearin'." Then seeing his shocked expression, she hastened to add, "Don't get me wrong. I think that's a fine quality in a man. A man should rule his household, but Miss Fairfax hasn't been around many men and she don't understand that. She's real sensitive, with a firm sense of right and wrong and it just goes against her grain for someone to try to force her to do somethin'. She reads a lot of books and she likes to make her own decisions. Of course, it's hard for a young lady in her position to accept that she's not going to be allowed to think for herself once she's introduced into society. It was all right for her to have all those ideas about emancipation when she was younger, but now that she's of marriageable age, she's got to learn to put those things aside. And the man who gets

Miss Cristina must handle her with a gentle hand. She has a terrible temper.''

Blake smiled, showing one tiny dimple. He was well aware of Miss Fairfax's temper, having been on the receiving end of it once or twice. So she couldn't stand to be dominated. That was the problem. What had happened to his nimble brain? What had happened to his keen perception about people? He should have realized it before. That was one of things that had attracted him to her to begin with; the fact that she was no milksop miss. She was different and because she was different, she resented his having control over her. Blake could understand that. He often felt the same way about things beyond his control. Pleased with his revelation, Blake was prepared to be magnanimous. He glanced up at Mackie. ''Wait, Mackie.''

''Yes?''

''Ask my aunt to inform Miss Fairfax she can dine alone in her room if she wishes. For tonight.''

Leah successfully hid her smile. ''I think that's very generous of Your Lordship,'' she told him, and knowing Cristina's temper, very wise of him as well.

Blake blossomed under her praise. He seemed to have made everyone around him angry lately, and he was very pleased to have someone agree with him for a change.

''Come, Leah, we'll talk over dinner.'' He took Cristina's maid by the arm and led her into the dining room and pulled out the chair beside his at the long, mahogany dining table.

Leah was surprised by his breach of etiquette. She was a servant and servants didn't sit at the same table as their employers. She blushed. ''Your Lordship, I can't sit with you.''

''Why not? I like you. I want you to keep me company. I live in a world of formality. I work in a branch of the government chockful of rules and regulations and etiquette, so I'm not much on formality at home. I prefer to relax a bit and relax the rules governing the household. You haven't eaten this evening, have you?''

Leah shook her head.

''Then my aunt and I would be very pleased to have you

join us for dinner.'' He flashed her a smile and the dimple in his cheek gave him a boyish appearance. ''Besides, I hate sitting at one end of the table while my aunt sits at the other end. And as my aunt is rather hard of hearing, the seating arrangement makes for rather difficult conversation. But Perryman and Mackie insist that this formality preserves the order of the household, that my eating in the kitchen would make my employees uncomfortable. So . . .''

''I'm truly honored by your generous offer, Your Lordship. I've been a servant all my life and not one of my employers has ever asked me to sit down and eat with him, but it's like your housekeeper said—some rules about the household shouldn't be broken. ''Besides''—she leaned closer to him—''I'm afraid I'd be too uncomfortable havin' fellow staff members waitin' on me. I know you'll understand if I say that like you, I prefer the kitchen.''

Blake nodded and graciously allowed Leah to make her exit without further embarrassment. He sighed. Despite his initial reluctance to invite her to stay at Lawrence House and chaperon Cristina, Blake discovered he enjoyed Aunt Delia's company. Enjoyed having her in the house, and she enjoyed being there. But meal times were awkward with the two of them sitting at opposite ends of the table. She couldn't hear and because neither one of them wanted to shout across the vast expanse of the mahogany dining table, they were destined to eat in lonely silence once again.

THE BIG HOUSE was quiet except for the sounds of the two women who sat in the kitchen. The master of the house had long since retired to his room to bathe and to nurse his wounds with a full bottle of brandy and Cristina hadn't made a sound in hours. It was the perfect time for the two women to get acquainted—to share a pot of strong, sweet tea and a bit of household gossip.

''I'm not one to gossip about what goes on in the family to strangers, mind you, but seeing as how you're going to be here a while and seeing as how you're part of Miss Cristina's household, I think you ought to know some of our family history, so to speak,'' Mackie stated firmly, lest Leah think she indulged in common gossip.

"Please, Mistress MacKenzie, you don't need to give me any explanations. I've been in service to the gentry since I was thirteen years old and none of their goin's on surprises me at this stage of my life.'' Leah didn't want the kindly woman to think she regularly indulged in common gossip.

"I insist.'' Mackie silenced any further token protests and began to explain. It was so nice to have someone to talk to. Someone who had not been involved with the family and who knew nothing of the life Lord and Lady Lawrence had lived before her fatal accident. Mackie sensed the other woman's concern for Lord Lawrence and was glad of it. It was wonderful to be able to share her worries with another woman. Master Blake had been a source of concern for a very long time and Mackie felt she needed a fresh opinion to help her help him. And it was important to Mackie that Leah understand about him because she hadn't met him at his best. She wanted Leah to understand that Master Blake didn't make a habit of overindulging in brandy. He wasn't the worse for drink very often and when he was there was always a reason. And usually that reason had something to do with the memories of his late wife. A man needed a woman of his own. And that was something Master Blake had never had. Mackie wasn't blind. She knew Blake had sexual appetites just like any other man and those appetites didn't go away now that he was widowed. Nor had they gone away just because he had been unfortunate enough or unwise enough to marry a woman who would never be faithful to him. As far as she knew, Master Blake had never turned to his wife for companionship or solace. He sought his pleasure elsewhere. But he had always been very discreet. He rarely returned to Lawrence House after a night with a woman, preferring to stay at his club until the effects of the night wore off. He didn't think his employees should see him in a drunken state and he never brought a woman into his home. It was his private place. His sanctuary.

But now there was Miss Fairfax, and she was different. She was a lady and anyone with half an eye could see that Master Blake was crazy about her. He had been short-tempered and eaten up with jealousy whenever anyone dared to look at her. And he had broken his cardinal rules. He had gotten drunk in front of the staff and he had brought a woman into his home. Mackie was as moral as they come, but she was no fool. She knew something was going on. Master Blake's valet, Hudson, had shown her the bloodstained neckcloth and she had been the one to find the remains of the torn nightgown Miss Fairfax had stuffed between her mattress—a nightgown torn from behind, which bore the same reddish-brown stains as Master Blake's neckcloth.

There was a powerful attraction at work here and everyone in the house was aware of it except the two people involved.

Mackie needed advice. She needed guidance. She needed help dealing with Master Blake and the young miss, and so she decided to share everything she knew about Blake Ashford with Leah.

The lady doth protest too much, methinks.

—WILLIAM SHAKESPEARE 1564–1616

Eleven

"FEELING BETTER?" MACKIE cheerfully bustled into the master bedroom, and finding the occupant awake at last, placed her tray near the bed and hurried to open the drapes.

"No!" came the muffled shout. Too late, as the painful sunlight penetrated his eyelids, causing him to whiten beneath his tan. He impatiently raked his long lean fingers through his thick, black hair and muttered through tightly clenched teeth for Mackie to close the drapes.

"I've brought your breakfast."

The aroma assailed his sensitive nostrils and his queasy stomach threatened to turn over in revolt. "Take it away and leave me alone. Where is Hudson?"

"You gave him the day off last night. In fact, you gave everyone the day off. I thought I should check on you." She placed a plump hand against his forehead. "You feel positively clammy and you look a bit greenish despite that nasty black eye."

Blake slapped her hand away, irritably attempting to bury his aching head beneath the comfortable dark covers. "I don't need your cosseting, Mackie, and I certainly don't need that!"

He pointed a disparaging hand at the offending breakfast tray.

"But Master Blake, a man needs a nourishing breakfast to start the morning." Mackie removed the cover from the tray and the odor of bacon and kidneys filled the room.

Blake clamped a hand over his mouth and rolled to his stomach in a vain effort to escape from the smell. "Leave the juice and the coffee, then get out." He mumbled between clenched teeth.

She set a small glass of orange juice and a small pot of coffee and a cup and saucer on the bedside table. "But . . ."

"Leave, Mackie . . ." He stopped in mid-sentence to gain control of his roiling insides. "Now, please, and take that horrible smell with you."

"I still think you need a hearty breakfast," Mackie insisted.

Blake turned his head and pinned his housekeeper with a baleful glare. "I don't need anything except peace and quiet and a few more hours of uninterrupted sleep. Go on, now, and take that tray." Blake was trying to be patient with Mackie but it was next to impossible when he felt as if the Ascot races were being run right through the center of his head and that smell . . . if he survived this episode, he never wanted to see, smell, or taste another kidney as long as he lived.

"Are you sure you're all right?" Mackie sounded genuinely concerned. "You still look a little peaked."

"I'm fine. Now, go." He had reached the end of his patience and it was all Blake could do not to roar at his housekeeper. Only experience with the sort of damage shouting could do to his pickled brain kept Blake's tone of voice low and even.

Mackie hovered near the door. "I'll go if you're sure you're all right."

Blake waved a hand to shoo her out the door and Mackie took the offending tray and left the room seconds before Blake's quivering insides rebelled at the abuse they had taken.

Mackie stood outside the bedroom door listening as the violent retching began. She was torn between shame for deliberately causing Blake discomfort and pride at the subtle punishment she had inflicted on the unsuspecting man. She smiled to herself and whistled as she descended the stairs. Master Blake would think twice about staying up to all hours and drinking like that again.

She paused at the foot of the stairs long enough to wonder how Leah was managing Miss Cristina, then whistled her way into the kitchen where she fed the old tomcat his customary breakfast of bacon and kidney.

"I don't understand how you can be so disloyal to me. I don't understand how you can like him or how you can take his side when you know he's keeping me a prisoner in this house." Cristina sat on the side of the massive bed, looking down at her lap and toying a loose thread on the pleats of her nightgown.

Leah's face was impassive as she bore the brunt of her young mistress's anger. "I'm not bein' disloyal to you or takin' his side against you, missy, but I don't agree that he's keepin' you here with him just for spite. I think he has other reasons. I think he's doin' what he thinks is best for you. After all, your mother did run off and leave you without a guardian or a chaperon. What's got you so upset? Are you sure you told me everythin'?" Leah asked, knowing full well that Cristina had left something out.

"Of course I told you everything," Cristina replied softly, pulling at the string, avoiding Leah's knowing gaze. "What else is there to tell except that Lord Lawrence is keeping me here against my will? I've asked to leave and he refuses. I don't think that's what's best for me. And I think that whether you know it or not, you're taking his side and you're being disloyal to me in doing so."

"Well, I don't think I'm bein' disloyal to you at all and you can forget using that haughty tone of voice with me, 'cause it won't do you a bit of good. It might fool other folks, but it don't fool me. I may be a servant, but I happen to know how much my opinion means to you."

"It doesn't mean anything this time. I can't believe you think he's a good man when he's cruel and arrogant and overbearing. Why, he—" Her voice trailed off.

"He what?" Leah prompted, stiffening in her chair, preparing herself for Cristina's revelation.

"He took advantage of me. He kissed me against my will."

Leah almost smiled. "Are you sure it was against your will?"

"Of course, I'm sure," Cristina answered, continuing to pull at the loose thread on her nightgown. "Why do you persist in defending him?" Frustrated, she gave the thread a vicious yank and unraveled three delicately stitched pleats.

"Because nobody has ever taken advantage of you unless you allowed it," Leah told her. "Nobody except your mother, and Lord Lawrence didn't have anythin' to do with that sorry trick."

"How do you know he didn't?"

"He ain't that kind of man."

"How do you know what kind of man he is? You only just met him. You only arrived last night."

"Maybe so," Leah agreed. "But I've lived a long life and I've worked for the gentry a long time and last night was the first time a gentleman ever invited me to dine with him."

"You used to have breakfast with my father all the time," Cristina reminded her.

"In the kitchen," Leah pointed out. "I always ate breakfast with your father in the kitchen. Lord Lawrence is the only gentleman I've ever known who invited me to sit down beside him *at the table in the dinin' room.* And that tells me a lot about the kind of man he is," Leah concluded.

"It tells me you've been taken in by his charm just like everyone else in this house," Cristina replied.

"Includin' yourself?"

Cristina didn't answer.

"You don't have to worry about it," Leah told her. "He is a charmin' man. A nice man. And I just know he wouldn't be taken in by a schemin' woman like your mother."

Cristina abandoned her haughty pretense, got up from the bed, and knelt before Leah's chair, placing her head in the older woman's lap as she had done when she was a child. "Leah, the night at Marlborough House was awful. I didn't know what to do except try to escape, and then Lord Lawrence showed up. He helped me, and yet I woke up in his bed. I'm so confused. A part of me wants to believe he's the kind of man you believe him to be. But another part of me is afraid. What if I'm wrong about him? What if I believe in him and find out he has the same morals as my mother or her friends and lovers?''

"Did anything happen while you were in Lord Lawrence's bed?" Leah asked.

"He says it didn't. He says all he did was rescue me, that I was too sotted for anything else."

Leah raised an eyebrow at that.

Cristina blushed. "I do remember drinking a bottle of wine."

"On top of the laudanum I gave you?"

Cristina nodded.

"Lord Lawrence was right. You were sotted and probably sleeping like a baby. But that wouldn't have stopped any of your mother's friends from taking advantage of you. The fact that Lord Lawrence didn't is proof of his character. It's all over now," Leah soothed. "The best thing you can do is to forget about what happened at Marlborough House. You're safe here, away from Claude and your mother now, and a man like Lord Lawrence ain't gonna let anythin' bad happen to you from now on."

"I'm not so sure," Cristina murmured as she leaned back on her knees so she could look Leah in the eyes.

"Why not?" Leah demanded.

"He thinks I'm a liar and a thief."

Leah eyed Cristina suspiciously. "What gave 'im that idea?"

Cristina buried her face in Leah's lap and refused to answer.

"Come on, missy, out with it, and I want the truth."

Cristina hesitated for a moment longer, then spoke in a rush. "I tried to break into his desk."

"You did what?" Leah was outraged.

"He had the necklace and I wanted it back. I thought he

might have put it in his study for safekeeping, so I went looking for it.''

''And then what 'appened?'' Leah prompted when Cristina finished speaking.

''He caught me going through his desk drawers.'' Cristina met Leah's gaze.

''And?''

''That's it. That's all that happened.'' Cristina turned away from Leah as she got to her feet and walked to the bedroom window.

''Missy, this is Leah you're talking to. Now look me in the eye and tell me what 'appened.'' Leah followed her young mistress to the window and placed her hand on Cristina's shoulder, urging her to turn around.

''All right,'' Cristina let out a deep sigh as she turned her back to the window and faced Leah. ''He kissed me.''

''Only once?'' Leah asked.

''More than once,'' Cristina answered.

''And tore your nightgown in the process?''

''He didn't mean to,'' Cristina defended Blake. ''The gown was old and fragile—one of the ones Mackie loaned me— one of the gowns that belonged to Blake's mother. He just reached out for me and the nightgown seemed to come apart in his hands.'' She stopped and studied the expression on Leah's face. ''How did you know about that?''

Leah chuckled at the question. ''Mrs. MacKenzie told me.''

''How did *she* know?''

''She's the 'ousekeeper.''

''So?''

''So if you're tryin' to keep secrets from servants you can't stuff the remains of a torn nightgown between your mattress. One of the maids is bound to find it.''

Cristina stared at Leah for a moment, registering the fact that she'd been baring her soul when the whole household probably knew. She sucked in a breath, her anger gathering steam like a boiling kettle as she headed out the door. ''Oooooh!''

Leah knew where she was going and what would happen

when she got there, but it was too late to stop her.

"They know!" Cristina slammed the door to Blake's bedroom so hard it shook in its frame. Blake bolted upright in the huge four-poster, the noise and the movement causing him such agony that he could barely reply and when he did, it was a mere whisper. "Who are *they* and what do *they* know?" He forced open eyelids that weighed a ton to fix his blurred vision on the magnificent spectacle standing in front of the door she had just tried to slam off its hinges. He focused on the vision and a smile that came close to being a leer transformed his frown of annoyance.

She stood there in complete disarray, clearly interrupting her toilette to barge in on him, for she was wearing a lacy corset, a thin lawn chemise, and little else. Her magnificent coppery-colored hair curled like a living thing around the curve of her rounded hips. She looked more beautiful and desirable than he had ever seen her look before, especially flushed with anger that seemed to be emanating from her satiny smooth body.

Blake raised himself up on the pillows. He leaned nonchalantly against the headboard, ignoring the insistent pounding in his temples in order to indulge his senses with a better view of the heady vision filling his room.

"Stop that grinning, damn you, they know!" She stamped her foot on the shiny oak floor, giving vent to some of the rage she felt for the smiling fool lying so unconcerned in his bed.

"Don't stamp your foot and shout at me," Blake shouted back. "This is my house and my hearing happens to be very acute!" More acute than usual.

"Well, Lord Lawrence, what are you going to do about it?"

"Do about what? Good God, Cris, I don't even know what you're talking about!" The shouting was killing him, and after being rudely awakened by Mackie, puking his guts out then bathing and managing to choke down a glass of juice and a cup of coffee before finally returning to bed, Blake was in danger of losing the small amount of control he had managed to regain. "Why don't you explain yourself?"

Cristina rolled her emerald green eyes upward to stare at the mural on the ceiling. Oh, the stupidity of the man! "Your staff, your housekeeper, Leah, and probably the whole neighborhood know about us!"

He arched one finely drawn black eyebrow, his grin deepening at the sight of her frustrated anger. "What exactly do they know? It must be fairly obvious to any of the household staff that you're a guest here and since it is my home, it would be fairly obvious for them to assume you're are my guest. What else can they know?"

Was he being deliberately obtuse? Or was he simply enjoying her difficult situation? The very thought that he might be gaining amusement from her anger made her blood boil. "W-w-what can they know? They know my reputation is in shreds! They know you tore off my nightdress! And I don't doubt that they know about the night we spent at Marlborough House in the same bed. They know that I've become your m-m-mistress!"

"That's news to me," Blake muttered.

"What did you say?" Cristina demanded.

"I said, are you? I wasn't aware."

Those softly sarcastic words sent Cristina flying into action. She launched herself at him. "Do you deny it? Do you deny that we spent the night together? Let go of my arms, I want to scratch out your eyes. Let go and stop laughing! Stop laughing at me!"

Blake couldn't help laughing, because despite his throbbing head, Cristina's wriggling was having an effect on him that was sure to make her angrier once she stopped wiggling long enough to notice. And being a man, he couldn't help but enjoy the marvelous effect she had on his senses or that special surge of adrenaline that made him forget everything but the exquisite thrill of battle with her. He had to fight to keep his wits about him as he struggled to hold her hands away from his face, and keep her teeth away from his vulnerable arms.

Far from angry, Blake was enjoying the duel of wit and strength.

But if he was enjoying it, Cristina was not. And seeing the glint of desire in his eyes was like rubbing salt into a wound. She turned her head from side to side to evade his lips.

Blake took no notice. He let go of her hands and framed her face with his palms on either cheek, holding her still while he fastened his lips on hers.

She bit down on his soft lower lip and he tasted the metallic taste of blood. His blood.

Blake's black eyes glowed with pain and for one long moment Cristina was afraid he might retaliate in kind. Instead, his eyes crinkled at the corners as he began to chuckle. "I knew you could be bloodthirsty. I just didn't know how bloodthirsty. Don't they feed you? Do you have to try to take pieces out of me each time we meet? Not that I mind that you find me so appetizing, but there are better ways to satisfy that hunger. . . ."

"Oooooh!" She took the bait. "You are without a doubt the . . . the—"

"Handsomest? Cleverest? Best?" He interrupted her with an offer of suitable adjectives.

"—most arrogant, conceited, vilest . . . man it has ever been my misfortune to meet. I wish—"

"That I would take you in my arms and kiss you again." He followed his words with action. His kiss was demanding at first, but gradually became softer and more giving, until she responded by wrapping her arms around his neck.

He kissed her to his satisfaction, then finally drew away from her upturned mouth and stared down at the desire etched on her face until she became aware of his studied gaze and jerked out of his grasp.

"You had no right. I—"

"I had every right. You gave it to me by marching into my bedroom half-dressed and throwing yourself in my arms. You were begging for my attention. You demanded it. And my kisses as well."

"I didn't."

"Didn't you? You had every intention of making me want you or you wouldn't be here now. You can call me a villain if it makes you feel better, but the fact remains that you sought me out and not the other way around. I took only what you wanted to give to me, what you flaunted before me.''

''You are the most arrogant, conceited, most vile—''

Blake interrupted her flow of abuse, ''You've said all that before and it's beginning to bore me to tears. Can't you come up with anything else?''

''Bastard!''

''There now,'' he grinned at her. ''Don't you feel better? It's not exactly correct or original, but I knew you could come up with something else. Not very ladylike, either, but then we both know you were born to the position and that it's strictly honorary.''

''If I'm no longer a lady in fact, it's because of you. You've ruined my chances of making a good marriage.''

''Indeed?'' His expression was full of scathing disbelief. ''Tell me how I managed that.''

''By abducting me from a public carriage in broad daylight, by taking me to your home and by keeping me here against my will, thereby forcing me to become your mistress.''

''I can be persuasive and even demanding on occasion, but I never use force,'' he told her. ''I'm too much of a gentleman. And I don't remember you objecting to my methods.''

Cristina stuttered with impotent fury, ''B-b-but—''

He continued as if he hadn't heard her. ''And my dear, as I've explained to you before, you're laboring under an obvious misconception. I don't consider you my mistress—only a houseguest. Although we spent the night together sharing a bed, we passed the time *sleeping*. There's a lot more to being a mistress than sharing a pillow. Of course, you could remedy that situation. . . .'' He finished his speech, his voice husky and filled with suggestion.

''I-I—''

''Speechless? That's something new for you. I thought you'd be only too willing to comply with my suggestion as it's all you've talked about since you stormed in here.''

Cristina suddenly found her tongue. ''That isn't why I came in here and you know it.''

"Really? Then why did you come?" He arched his brows in feigned innocence.

"I came to let you know your staff has a mistaken idea about my reason for being here," she informed him haughtily.

His mouth turned up a tiny bit at the corner, and what began as a smile soon turned into a chuckle and then into hearty laughter. "If they were mistaken, my dear, I'm relieved to know you've set them straight. I'll bet they have the right idea now!"

Cristina turned on her heel and exited the room with as much dignity as she could muster. She didn't stop until she reached the safety of her own room where she slammed the door with all her might, trying unsuccessfully to drown out the sound of his deep laughter echoing through the house.

"I guess you told him," Leah commented when Cristina flung herself down on the bed. "And the rest of house, too."

A drowning man will clutch at a straw.

——PROVERB

Twelve

THE WAR HAD to end. It couldn't go on. The tension in Lawrence House hung as thick and stifling as smoke caught between the layers of the early-morning fog. The staff tiptoed around the master and his guest and did their best to remain unnoticed. It was the only way to weather the storm.

Blake entered his home and started up the stairs. He met Cristina coming down them, her arms full of embroidered linens.

He halted in his tracks and stared at her. He had spent the last couple of weeks purposely avoiding her, throwing himself into his work until he was too tired to think of anything except sleep. He had left Cristina to stew in her own juices since the morning she had stormed into his room demanding he salvage her reputation. Blake had hoped his absence would reduce the unbearable tension between them and improve her disposition, but if anything, it had compounded the problem.

She was proud and she was angry, but enough was enough and Blake had reached the limit of his endurance.

Mackie had spent the better part of the morning begging him to do something about Cristina. According to the house-

keeper, Miss Cristina was working herself to the bone, burning off excess energy. She had asked to help plan the menus,
balance accounts, even polish his mother's silver and mono-
gram the linens. Miss Cristina meant well, Mackie explained,
she was trying to help, but she was driving the staff crazy
with requests for more tasks to keep her busy and Mackie
told him, she'd even cajoled his valet into parting with some
of Blake's shirts and handkerchiefs. Then his housekeeper had
demanded to know why he hadn't noticed the fancy mono-
gramming on his garments.

Blake decided to see for himself if what Mackie said was
true. So he had set out to find Cristina and the truth.

"Cristina?"

She peeked around her armload of what appeared to be his
shirts and looked down at him. He was taken aback by her
haphazard appearance. She was pale and thin and there were
dark smudges under the eyes that calmly returned his stare.

"What in God's name have you been doing? I almost mistook you for a maid."

Cristina glanced down at her dress. She did resemble one
of the staff in her plain, gray dress and with her hair hidden
beneath a cap. She knew she must look terrible. Cristina
blinked at him in surprise. "I spent the afternoon polishing a
collection of silver salt cellars and I was returning some of
the shirts I've—" She stopped. "I was taking these to Hudson
for Mrs. MacKenzie."

"You look as if you've been doing hard labor," he said,
uncharacteristically undiplomatic. "How long has it been
since you were out in the fresh air?"

"I don't know. A week or so," she answered him.

"You don't know? Don't you care how you look? Don't
you keep up with those things? I didn't hire you as a maid,
Cristina. You're a guest. And where's Aunt Delia?"

Cristina's temper flared. "Of course I care how I look, Lord
Lawrence, when there is someplace for me to go or someone
to see me. Since I've been at Lawrence House I haven't seen
anyone except the staff, your aunt, and Dr. Jameson. Why
should I care how I look? Who is there to see me? You left

orders that I was to stay inside—or have you forgotten? I didn't suppose I would be allowed to spend time out in the garden without your permission and I haven't had the opportunity to ask you. You haven't been here much. And what else is there for me to do but help out where I can. I've read half your library already and I'm not looking forward to tackling *The History of Anglo-Austro-Hungarian Relations and Diplomacy in the Balkans* or the rest of your books on diplomacy written in languages I don't speak or read. I was educated in a school whose headmistress thought ladies had to know how to perform the household tasks in order to supervise the staff . . ."

Blake grinned. "Sounds like a shrewd and inexpensive means of keeping a household staff for her school."

Cristina glanced up at him, surprised to find he shared her opinion. Their eyes met and something sparked between them. Suddenly nervous, she glanced down at his shirts. "Nevertheless, the fact remains that I'm not accustomed to being idle. As for your Aunt Delia's whereabouts, unlike me, Lady Wethering appears to have an active social life outside Lawrence House. She's busy making her morning calls. She invited me, of course, but since I'm supposed to be staying in the country, I didn't dare show my face in town."

"She's supposed to be here taking care of you."

"I'm not ill anymore. I don't need taking care of. But Lady Wethering spends her mornings with me just the same. We embroider in the parlor, in case you're interested, then she dresses for luncheon and after luncheon, she takes a carriage and makes her morning calls. She just returned and is upstairs changing for dinner. I wanted to finish this task." She nodded toward the stack of linen. "Before I dressed for dinner."

Blake watched her closely, relieved to find she still had her temper. He was appalled at the change in her and knew he was partly responsible. He'd been so involved in his work, and so determined to stay away from her, that he had almost forced himself to forget she was still a guest in his home. He could recall seeing her in passing only a few times since she had stormed into his bedroom spewing fire.

Cristina had underestimated the staff. There had been a few employees who believed she was or had been his mistress, but the household grapevine soon set them straight. Mackie, Leah, Perryman the butler, and Blake's valet, Hudson, had passed the word. The staff of Lawrence House understood that Miss Cristina Fairfax was his houseguest, not his mistress. He hadn't bothered to tell her, to ease her concerns about her reputation.

He'd allowed the seed of doubt about her reputation to remain planted in her mind, because he hadn't wanted her to risk leaving on her own. He'd meant for her to worry a bit, but he hadn't intended that she become a virtual prisoner in his home. Blake vaguely remembered Leah telling him that Cristina was proud and sensitive. She looked so fragile, so breakable and broken in spirit that his guilty conscience demanded he make amends for the pain he had caused.

"I'm returning to the city this evening and I thought you might enjoy dining out and maybe seeing a show. Aunt Delia will join us, of course. Would you care to accompany me, Cristina? I was just on my way upstairs to ask you."

Her head nodded "yes" of its own accord. She knew he was feeling the pangs of a guilty conscience and hadn't really intended to ask her to accompany him until he'd seen her standing on the stairs. She knew that he had asked her to come along simply to assuage his guilt and a part of her hated to accept his invitation. She hoped his conscience bothered him. He hadn't spared a thought for her in weeks while she had labored over his household linen and enjoyed it! Her pride told her she should refuse his invitation, but denying herself an evening out with Blake took more pride than she possessed.

Sensing her struggle, Blake smiled at her, "Go get ready and we'll make this night a night to remember."

It was the push Cristina needed. She turned and practically raced up the stairs in her excitement. It seemed like years since she had worn the regulation white gown and feathers for her presentation. She was so much older now than the girl who had danced with all the young men at the ball. So much had changed. She had changed overnight.

She bathed and dried herself and pulled on her underthings. When she finished she brought an evening dress of hunter green watered silk out of the depths of the armoire and called for Leah.

Leah buttoned the last of the tiny buttons and patted a stray hair into place before standing aside and allowing Cristina to view her reflection in the mirror.

Cristina couldn't believe her eyes. Leah had worked a miracle. The woman in the mirror was a stranger. "I don't believe it, Leah. Is that really me?"

"Well, it certainly ain't me," came Leah's honest reply.

"Do you think he'll approve?"

"Only a blind man would fail to notice and appreciate what's standing there."

And Blake wasn't a blind man. He stood at the bottom of the grand staircase as Cristina descended it. He registered the fact that she wasn't alone, that his aunt was by her side carefully negotiating the stairs. But he only had eyes for Cristina. Her transformation from housemaid to lady left him awestruck. With her thick hair coiled in a sleek chignon at the nape of her neck she seemed older and more poised and as untouchable as a piece of Dresden china until she smiled. Smiled, as she was smiling at him now, with warmth and just a hint of natural seductiveness. He was sure he had never seen any woman look quite as beautiful. The paleness he had complained of earlier complimented the dark green of the dress and emphasized the incredible green of her eyes. His breathing became labored as he gasped at the overwhelmingly lovely picture she presented.

Blake slowly realized she was waiting for his reaction and he spoke hoarsely, "I never dreamed anyone could be so lovely."

Cristina came to life under his warm praise. "Thank you, milord. And may I say that you and Lady Wethering make a very handsome couple?"

Blake smiled at her. "Then the three of us should make

quite a sensation, don't you think?'' He assisted the ladies with the wraps Perryman handed him, then offered his arm, first to his aunt and then to Cristina.

Cristina returned his smile and slipped her hand into the crook of his elbow.

She might have made the trip into London on a magic carpet for time seemed to float along in luxurious fashion. She remembered as if in a dream the magnificent restaurant where they feasted on food fit for the gods and the lavish theater where they saw the hit play of the season and the Prince of Wales who, it was rumored, was currently enamored of the leading lady. But Cristina couldn't remember a single line or the plot of the play. She forgot about it as soon as the lights dimmed, and concentrated on Blake—the way he smiled at the antics on stage, the line of his profile, the masculine scent of him sitting close to her, and the way his eyes sparkled with some inner light whenever he caught her looking at him under the cover of her lashes.

The sudden brightness of the lights at intermission startled Cristina after the intimacy of the darkened theater. Blake rose to his feet, stretched, helped his aunt to her feet, then took Cristina by the arm and led the ladies into the lobby for refreshment.

''Oh, no,'' Blake groaned as he secured two glasses of champagne for the ladies.

''What is it?'' Cristina asked.

Blake turned to his right and nodded. Cristina followed his gaze to the royal box where the Prince of Wales nodded in recognition.

''He's seen me,'' Blake explained. ''Drink up. We'll have to pay our respects.''

It was Cristina's turn to groan. She had wanted the night out with Blake so much that she hadn't given a single thought to the possibility of being seen and recognized when according to her mother's lie, she was supposed to be staying with friends in the country while Patricia was in Italy.

''It won't be so bad,'' Blake told her. ''Aunt Delia is here and she's a perfectly suitable chaperon. And I'll think of something to explain your presence." He took the ladies' empty glasses and placed them on a tray, then did his best to shield them from the crush as they pushed their way through the crowded lobby and headed for the royal box.

Cristina kept silent but her heart seemed to flutter at the knowledge that Blake was willingly assuming responsibility for her. She had never been so close to the Prince of Wales and at first she was surprised by the sheer size of him, but his renowned charm overcame her repulsion and she relaxed under the warm twinkle of his blue eyes. Blake bowed to the prince and stepped forward to present Cristina. "Your Highness, may I present Lady Wethering, my aunt, and Miss Cristina Fairfax?"

"By all means, Lord Lawrence, I am always happy to see friends like Lady Wethering and to welcome a new face, especially one as lovely as Miss Fairfax's."

"Thank you," Cristina murmured. "Your Highness is most gracious."

"Not at all, my dear lady." The Prince of Wales was thoughtful. "Fairfax? You must be Lady Fairfax's famous daughter." He studied Cristina. "I am well acquainted with your mother. I've spent many a lovely afternoon in her company." The look that passed between the two men did not go unnoticed by Lady Wethering or by Cristina.

She hesitated a moment before replying in a low voice, "Sir William Fairfax is my father, Highness, and Patricia is my mother."

"I see the resemblance," the prince commented with a tactful smile. "And now that I think about it, I remember you. . . ."

Cristina drew in a long breath, trying to still the hammering of her heart. He couldn't remember her from Marlborough House. He couldn't have seen her there. She waited for what seemed like hours without daring to breathe before the prince completed his sentence.

"From the last presentation. I pride myself on always remembering the prettiest girls. I didn't expect to see you again during the season. I understood that you were to be married and I heard your mother was on the Continent.''

Blake struggled to keep from wincing. Trust the Prince of Wales to remember Patricia Fairfax's infamous wager and the fact that Patricia had claimed her daughter would be auctioned to the highest bidder bearing a wedding band. Ignoring the consequences of his declaration, Blake answered for Cristina. ''Miss Fairfax has been staying at my parents' country house until quite recently and staying with Lady Wethering since her arrival. I agreed to escort her to the theater tonight.''

The Prince of Wales turned his attention to Blake. ''I see. I compliment you on your choice of companions, Lawrence. See that you show her a good time.''

''I will, sir,'' Blake promised.

The interview ended and the remainder of the evening passed in a romantic haze as Cristina ceased to be aware of anything except the look in Blake's onyx black eyes and the thrill it sent up and down her spine.

Neither of them spoke during the quiet ride to Lawrence House, both of them afraid of breaking the fragile spell the night had woven around them and of waking Lady Wethering. It was so quiet in the carriage, Cristina was certain Blake would hear the rapid pounding of her heart and know that she was as affected by him—by the nearness of him.

A sigh of longing escaped her lips as she remembered the way he had made her feel whenever he kissed her, wonderfully alive yet strangely content and at peace with the world.

The carriage slowed, then rolled to a stop beside the steps leading to Lawrence House. Cristina came out of her reverie to find Blake assisting his aunt out of the carriage. With Lady Wethering safely entrusted into the care of the footman, Blake turned to help her alight from the vehicle. Cristina gasped at the fire that ripped through her at his touch, then glanced up and met his gaze.

His dark eyes seemed to smolder with a depth of emotion that was almost painful to witness.

But Cristina couldn't look away.

His hands shook slightly as they lingered on her waist and

the feel of his long, strong fingers sent tiny sparks through her many layers of clothing.

"I've spent the last few weeks trying to convince myself to let you go wherever it is you want to go." Blake's voice was low and rough.

He lifted her out of the carriage but didn't release her. Cristina felt the tremor of his muscles and heard the dull thud of his heartbeat as he held her a hairbreadth away from his body. "I failed."

"I've no reason to leave," she whispered. "And no where else to go."

"I tried to stay away," he vowed.

"I know," she whispered.

"But I can't."

"It doesn't matter," she assured him, "because I don't want you to stay away."

Blake took a deep breath. "Are you certain?"

She heard the slight catch in his voice as he asked the question. "Yes."

"I won't be able to stop at kissing," Blake felt compelled to warn her. Cristina had to understand that this time, he wasn't playing at passion. It wasn't a game. And if he began making love to her, if she allowed him to make love to her, she had to be sure it was what she wanted—because his control was tenuous at best. If Cristina changed her mind, he wasn't at all sure he could walk away. He had waited too long—wanted too much—wanted her too much. "I might not be able to walk away."

"I won't ask you to."

"Good," Blake muttered seconds before he set her on her feet. He wanted to envelope her in his arms. He wanted to sweep her off her feet and carry her into Lawrence House, but propriety demanded that he keep his distance. They were standing in front of the house and in full view of his aunt, the driver, and the footman. The most he dared to do was hold her a moment longer than necessary and to allow himself the brush of her gown against his leg.

"I can't take this much longer. You've been driving me

mad all evening . . . ,'' he managed to whisper as he took hold of her elbow and escorted her up the steps to the front door. Blake dismissed the footman as Perryman opened the front door.

"If you'll see to my aunt," Blake directed, handing the butler his top hat and gloves, "I'll assist Miss Fairfax."

Perryman obliged by removing Lady Wethering's wrap, before reaching out to take Cristina's. They stood in the entrance hall and it was all Blake could do to keep from tapping his foot in frustration as he waited for his aunt to bid them good night.

Instead, she turned to Perryman and said, "I think we could use a nightcap in Lord Lawrence's study."

Perryman remained where he was, a quizzical expression on his face. "A nightcap, ma'am?"

"A drink, man," Lady Wethering told him. "Sherry for me and for Miss Fairfax and a nip of something stronger for Lord Lawrence. And some of those chocolate things left over from tea," she glanced at Blake and Cristina who both shook their heads, "*one* of those chocolate things left over from tea for me." She dismissed the butler with a wave of her hand and headed down the hall to Blake's study.

Perryman looked to his employer.

Blake nodded his assent and Perryman left to prepare the refreshments.

Blake glanced around the empty room then pulled Cristina closer, bent his head, and kissed her. He'd meant to kiss her gently, meant to take his time, but the unique taste of her—the champagne-flavored essence of Cristina—filled his senses until he couldn't seem to get enough. He moved his mouth over hers, kissing her deeply, hungrily as he clung to her like a drowning man clinging to flotsam in a raging sea. She had become his anchor in a world suddenly gone topsy-turvy. His only reality.

Cristina returned Blake's kiss with a fervor that matched his own, meeting the thrust of his questing tongue with her exploring one. She wound her arms around his neck as hot, fluid desire overwhelmed her. She kissed him as if he were the only thing on earth that mattered to her, as if he was the only sustenance she needed. Her knees weakened, and she shivered in reaction to the touch of his fingers against the bare flesh of her neck and shoulders.

"Perryman must still be looking for one of those chocolate things I had at tea," Lady Wethering's loud voice echoed through the hall. "Otherwise I'm sure he should've returned by now."

The sound of his aunt's voice brought Blake back to his senses and he suddenly realized that he'd spent several minutes kissing his houseguest in the front entryway of his home where any of his staff might witness it. He pulled his lips away from Cristina's and stepped away, forcing himself to put space between them when what he really wanted to do was eliminate it. He stared down at her. Her hair was mussed where he'd tangled his fingers in it and her eyes were dark with passion. Color stained her cheeks and her chin, from the flush of passion and the brush of his face against her baby-soft skin. And her mouth was swollen. Blake frowned. There was no disguising the fact that she looked exactly like a woman who had been well and truly kissed.

"Oh, my," Cristina breathed, looking up at him with eyes that seemed as deep as a Scottish loch. "I forgot about your aunt. To be perfectly honest, I forgot everything except you."

Her admission and the shy smile that accompanied it were nearly his undoing. "To be perfectly honest so did I."

Cristina reached up and smoothed her hair. "What will Lady Wethering think?"

Blake had no doubt what Lady Wethering would think. He braced himself for the setdown he knew he deserved as he escorted Cristina into the study.

"Well, boy, I see you made good use of your time. The gel looks as if she's been thoroughly kissed."

Blake's jaw dropped open.

Lady Delia was seated on the leather sofa facing the door and there was no escaping her sharp gaze. "I may be old," she announced, "but I'm not dead. I recognize flying sparks when I see them and I was positively singed by all the sparks flying about tonight. I thought you two might need a bit of privacy.'' She narrowed her gaze at Blake. ''Not too much, mind you, we can't have the servants gossiping. Nor can we have anyone casting aspersions on Miss Fairfax's good name, but I don't think there's anything wrong with a man and a woman sharing a few kisses—as long as she's willing.'' She turned to Cristina. ''Are you willing, gel?''

Cristina blushed.

''Very well,'' Aunt Delia continued. ''I'm willing to turn a blind eye upon occasion so you can indulge in a little romancing, but I'll not countenance even a breath of scandal. If anything happens to this gel, I'll hold you responsible.'' She reached out and tapped Blake on the knee with her cane as she directed her remarks at her nephew. ''And I'll expect you to do your duty by her. Do you understand?''

''I'm perfectly aware of my responsibilities,'' Blake replied warily. ''But I'm not so sure you understand yours. I asked you here in order to chaperon Miss Fairfax and I intended that you keep her safe from everyone—including me.''

''Especially you,'' Delia laughed. ''Did you think I was born yesterday, boy? For all that they choose cold-blooded careers, the Ashfords are a hot-blooded lot. Your uncle, God rest his soul, couldn't keep his hands off me before we were married and afterwards, after I'd learned a thing or two, I couldn't keep my hands off him. And although I'm not privy to what goes on in their bedchamber, I suspect it's the same for your mother and father.''

Blake had long suspected the same thing, but he didn't think it his place to comment on his parents' love life.

''And in our day, we understood passion. We understood that young men and young women need a little leeway to investigate the sparks. And I would have thought that our dear queen understood the need as well, but she and her dearly departed Albert have successfully snuffed out nearly every means of doing so—at least in public. Why, it's absurd when you think that as young girls, my contemporaries and I ran about with our muslins dampened to show off our figures. *We* didn't hide behind whalebone and bustles.''

"That must have been quite a sight, ma'am." Blake's respect and his admiration for his aunt was growing by leaps and bounds.

She acknowledged his compliment with a regal nod of her gray head. "The point is that while it's not my place to tell you how to live your lives, I insist on circumspect behavior in my presence at all times. I won't have you placing me in bad light but I see no point in sneaking around. I'm an old woman and while I'm perfectly capable of chaperoning a young girl, my eyesight is failing and my hearing is suspect. I won't be held accountable, nor will I condone servants' gossip or anyone questioning your morality. I'm expecting you to use the good judgment you were born with. Lord Wethering and I didn't cause a scandal and neither did your father and mother. We were smart and to this day, I'm certain no one has ever suspected that we might have anticipated our wedding vows. I'm not saying we did, mind you, I just saying that even if we did, no one would ever have suspected it. I expect no less from you." Leaning heavily on her malacca cane, Lady Wethering pushed herself to her feet, walked to the door, and peeked around the corner. "Now where is that blasted Perryman? I would like my nightcap before I retire and leave you young ones to yourself. He can't still be searching for those chocolate concoctions. Surely, he's realized that I polished them off at tea. Ah, here he is now."

"I couldn't find anymore chocolate bonbons," Perryman apologized to Lady Wethering as he entered the room carrying the tray of refreshments. "So I took the liberty of adding a few lemon meringues."

"That's fine," Lady Wethering said. She waited until Perryman bent to place her sherry on the table in front of the sofa to make her announcement, then winked at Blake and Cristina. "It was so thoughtful of you to go to all that trouble, Perryman, but I've decided to take my refreshments upstairs."

"I'll see you to your room," Blake offered.

"Oh, no, dear boy, you stay and keep Miss Fairfax company. Perryman will leave your drinks and some of the meringues before he accompanies me to my room. I'm sure Miss

Fairfax must be famished. She hardly ate a bite at dinner. It's all right, dear boy, Perryman is the soul of discretion. He wouldn't allow you to be alone with Miss Fairfax if it wasn't perfectly proper and so long as you don't indulge in spirits in her company,'' she picked up Blake's snifter of brandy and placed it on Perryman's tray, then set her glass of sherry on the table beside Cristina's. "I see no harm as long as you leave the door open and finish your refreshments, then go right upstairs to bed. Do you, Perryman?''

"No, ma'am.''

"Besides, I trust you. Good night, my dears, enjoy your desserts. I intend to enjoy mine.''

"Will you require anything else before I see Lady Wethering to her room and retire to my own bed, sir?''

"No, thank you, Perryman. We'll leave our dishes here. The maids can collect them in the morning. Hudson knows better than to wait up. I don't require his services at night.''

"Very good, sir. And shall I tell Leah that Miss Fairfax will be up directly?''

Cristina shook her head. "No, thank you, Perryman, but it isn't necessary. I'll wake Leah when I get there.''

Perryman nodded. "Very good, miss.''

"Come along, Perryman,'' Lady Wethering instructed. "I'm old and tired and eager to get into bed and sample my nephew's expensive brandy.'' She waved good-bye and Blake couldn't help but notice that despite her words to the contrary, his aunt took her own good time negotiating the stairs, Perryman hovering at her side.

"I thought they would never leave,'' Blake breathed, reaching out to pull Cristina to her feet. "Let's see if we remember where we left off.'' He tilted her face up to his and briefly covered her lips with his own, before moving from her lips to her cheekbones, then the tendrils of hair framing her flushed face. He pressed his lips against her temple and the corners of her eyes, gently closing her eyelids as he planted soft kisses there. Inhaling the sweet jasmine scent, he nuzzled her hair and kissed the pulse points behind her ears before working his way back to her mouth. He nipped at her bottom lip. He tangled his fingers in her hair and used the pads of his thumbs to massage her temples gently.

The motion of his thumbs and the feel of his mouth against her skin was hypnotic. Entranced, Cristina moaned low in her throat and pushed herself closer. He reciprocated by pressing his hips fully against her, allowing her to feel all of him. Cristina tightened her grip on him, surrounding herself with the feel and smell and taste of him as she deepened the kiss.

Her eagerness thrilled Blake, excited him, spurred him on as he used his tongue to blaze a trail of fire across her delicate collarbone, down the path between the firm young breasts to the smooth silk that hid the hard, tantalizing peaks of her firm young breasts.

She reveled in the delicious sensations, unaware that she was rubbing her body against his, shamelessly trying to ease her frustrations.

"Ah, sweetheart, you feel good," Blake murmured before he pulled away to turn out the lamps. He paused long enough to stuff two meringues in his pocket and down half a glass of sherry, then he swung Cristina up into his arms. He could hear his aunt in conversation with Perryman as he hurried past her room and past Cristina's room. He didn't pause until he reached the bedroom at the far end of the second floor hall—his bedroom. There he bent down and carefully placed Cristina in the center of the massive bed.

Blake fought to control his need. He struggled to go slowly. He didn't want to rush. He wanted to savor each sensation, to enjoy the moment, to make love to Cristina with style and grace and finesse, but his fingers worked feverishly at the fastenings of her dress and petticoats as he hurried to strip off her clothing that hid her from view. He kissed her as he worked at the laces and tapes and ties of the multitude of garments she wore and his hot, burning kisses seemed to blister her lips with its fire and to run unchecked throughout the length of her body. She answered his kisses as she pulled him down onto the bed beside her, begging him without words to quench the fire he ignited inside her.

"I've wanted this moment from the first time I saw you,"

he whispered against her lips as his kisses suddenly changed and became soft, gentle kisses that embedded themselves in her soul.

He touched her body with reverence and awe and a degree of tenderness that affected Cristina in a way nothing else could. She felt safe and secure and protected for the first time in years. She felt cherished, as if she were the most important person in all the world, and she wanted the feeling to last forever.

"What's happened to the ice maiden who's been living here for the past few weeks? Has she finally melted?" he teased, covering Cristina with those soul-stealing kisses. "Your hair and your temper give you away, my sweet. You make a rotten ice maiden. There is so much passion in you and I want to enjoy every bit of it. Now. Tonight."

She didn't care—so long as he continued to touch her. She sighed at the feel of his lips spreading a trail of moist heat along the column of her neck and down to the rosy peak of a breast. Logic escaped her and Cristina let herself be swept along on the crest of the intoxicating new emotions engulfing her. She was acutely aware of him—the rough feel of his evening clothes against to her uncovered flesh, the taste of sherry on his lips and the heat of his body, which penetrated his clothing and warmed her from without, while his kisses warmed her within. And suddenly she wanted to feel more. She wanted to feel his bare skin against hers. She wanted to caress his arms and neck and back and feel the heat of his flesh without the barrier of his clothes. She wanted him naked and pressed against her. She wanted him to fulfill the promises his mouth made to hers. She wanted him. And so Cristina let go of his hair, then twisted and turned, and bucked against him as she worked her hands between their bodies, clawed at his shirtfront, and pulled at the onyx studs on the front of his shirt.

"Cristina?" Blake ended the kiss. He looked down at her, studying the expression on her face, trying to gauge the depth of her passion. He caught her hands and held them gently within his grasp. "Sweetheart? What is it?"

"Want."

"What? What do you want?"

"You," she told him. "I want you."

Blake grinned. He let go of her hands, rolled off the bed, and began to undress. "Then you shall have me," he announced. "All of me."

Cristina stared up at him, her eyes widening in surprise as he bared himself to her. He stood tall and proud, broad-shouldered, and slim-hipped, like a Greek god come to life. No, Cristina thought dreamily, not Greek. He exhibited none of the effeminate qualities she remembered from paintings and Greek sculptures—he was completely masculine, all male. His flesh was hard-muscled from years of riding and mountain climbing and the sun had turned his skin a rich, golden brown. A thick mat of dark, curly hair covered his broad chest, snaking downward over his flat belly in an arrow that directed her attention to that mysterious member which stood firmly and undauntingly erect, proclaiming his desire for her. He was extremely attractive in clothes, but without them, Cristina found, he was devastating. He was a beautiful man and for the moment, he was all hers.

The possessive thought surprised Cristina, excited her, and pleased her enormously. She wanted him and she wanted this—this sensation that threatened to drown her. She wanted Blake beside her in his huge bed, holding her, loving her.

She didn't need to worry about a repeat of that other frightening episode. There would be no reason to bloody his nose. He had awakened her desire and only he could slake it.

"Satisfied?" His husky chuckle startled her, making Cristina keenly aware of the fact that she had spent the last few seconds admiring him.

She felt the red-hot rush of color flood her face and turned away from his intent gaze.

"Don't hide from me, my sweet. It's perfectly natural for you to be curious about a man's body, even though it isn't half as mysterious as yours." He leaned forward and traced the contours of her face, his fingers carrying tiny electric charges that sent shivers through her. "Look at me, Cristina.

Don't be afraid. There is nothing for you to be afraid or ashamed of. I'll be very gentle and I'll do my best to make it good for you. To make it right and beautiful. That's the way love should be for the first time. It should be beautiful and wondrous and it should mean something to the man and woman involved. I want you to enjoy this, Cristina, the way I'll enjoy it.'' Once again Blake surprised himself by speaking of love. What did he know of love? What did he remember of love? It had been so long since he had experienced it. Yet every time he opened his mouth he was talking of love and beauty and gentleness. What was it about Cristina Fairfax that made him think of love? And what made him yearn for the wistful, nostalgic, half-forgotten feelings she aroused?

Blake touched the rosy point of a breast and a shiver shot through them both. ''Feel, Cris, feel what we do to each other.''

Feel? She couldn't do anything except feel the lovely sensations sweeping through her as he touched her highly sensitive breast. All she could feel was his warm breath on the back of her neck as he placed tender kisses along her neck and shoulders. Her pulse raced through her body and her breath came in quick, little gasps. Feel? She wanted nothing more.

Blake gently pressed her back onto the warm mattress. His lips touched her skin and his mouth seemed to be everywhere at once—branding her with his own delicious kind of fire while his hands roamed over her body at will, lighting little brushfires along the way, completely melting any resistance she might have offered. She writhed under his experienced hands and moaned in mindless pleasure.

''Put your arms around me. Let me feel you next to me,'' Blake demanded huskily.

Cristina obliged, wrapping her arms around his waist, luxuriating in the feel of the dark, curly hair on his chest as it tickled and teased the excited tips of her breasts. She delighted in the feel of his warm body nestled so close to hers, the smooth feel of his back and the strong muscles rippling beneath her questing fingertips.

Cristina sighed and snuggled closer to the hard, male body and her wriggling closeness was almost Blake's undoing.

"Easy, sweetheart, I'm more than ready and we've got plenty of time. Let's enjoy it." Blake began to pay homage to her body in earnest, using all the skills of lovemaking he'd acquired over the years. And they had never been put to better use.

Cristina responded wholeheartedly, giving pleasure as well as receiving it. She learned quickly and she eagerly practiced her newfound skills on her willing tutor. She forgot everything except the exquisite joy of making love with Blake Lawrence.

He was in heaven. He had never dreamed she would respond to his touch in such a way. She was liquid passion flowing through his veins, teasing, coaxing, encouraging him to new heights of desire. He ran his hands over her rib cage, softly counting each rib until he reached the underside of her breasts. He caressed them, feeling the weight of each globe before journeying to the rosy tips and caressing them with the pads of his thumbs. He leaned over and kissed her lips once again, tasting the sweetness that was Cristina, fencing with the velvet roughness of her tongue as it followed his. She moaned and Blake surprised himself when he recognized his own deep baritone echoing her wonderment and pleasure. He tore his lips away from hers and blazed a trail down the hollow between her breasts, following the path to her beckoning navel. His hot tongue lavished attention on the small indentation in her stomach, exploring the shape, feeling the texture, before traveling still farther. His warm breath tickled the cluster of curls at the juncture of her thighs and Cristina's whole body jolted at the contact.

"What are you doing?" There was a note of alarm in her question and Blake forced himself to slow down. Go gently, he cautioned himself, one thing at a time. We don't have to do everything in one night. There will be other nights. He raised his head and caught the look of concern and puzzlement that crossed Cristina's face. "I'm not going to do anything that you're not ready to do, sweetheart," Blake promised, softly. And to prove his good intentions, he reversed his path and began to place hot kisses up her belly, back to her navel. His hands, however, continued their downward trail.

Cristina heard herself gasp with pleasure as Blake lightly ran the palm of his hand over one naked thigh. He teased the baby-soft flesh before allowing his fingers to journey upward over that wonderful skin to the tight, reddish-gold curls guarding her moist, throbbing center. He explored her with his fingers until her cries reached a fevered pitch.

Overwhelming pleasure washed over her and Cristina clutched at Blake's hair, lifting his head from her belly, pulling him to her mouth where she kissed him with a passion that took them both by surprise.

"Do you like this? Or this, sweetheart?" he asked anxiously, his fingers feverishly massaging the pulsating mound of feminine warmth. "Talk to me. Tell me what you like."

"I . . . don't . . ." The electric quiver took her breath away. "Oh, Blake, I . . ." Cristina felt another shudder well up deep inside, enveloping her until it was out of control. Her body shook violently again and again. Her heart hammered in her breast and her lungs seemed too small for her body. She breathed in short, panting gasps until all at once, her body relaxed. Her tense muscles turned to jelly and a warmth spread over her from head to toe. She cried out her tremendous satisfaction and her astonishment. She had never known anything could feel so wonderful.

"Relax and enjoy it, my sweet." Blake's deep voice sounded in her ear and Cristina opened her eyes to find him smiling tenderly down at her. He kissed the tip of her nose. "But don't go to sleep on me. It isn't over. The best is yet to come." Again his voice sounded in her ear, but this time Cristina recognized the excitement and barely controlled desire in his tender words.

She was much too relaxed and bemused by all that had happened to protest when Blake eased her thighs apart and positioned himself between them. "It's time, Cristina, I can't wait any longer." He brought himself against her, the hard male part of him probing the opening in her moist curls.

"Wrap your legs around me." Blake instructed softly as he nuzzled the valley between her breasts with infinite care. "I'll try not to hurt you, sweetheart, but if I do, I promise you it will only hurt this first time."

Cristina followed his instructions and slid her long legs over his outer thighs and buttocks and locked them tightly around his waist. She kissed the side of his neck to show that she was willing to accept a little pain along with the pleasure.

"Ready, sweetheart?" he groaned urgently.

She nodded her head and whispered, "Yes."

Blake moved closer. His placed his hands on her hips as he slowly entered her. The sensation was indescribable and Blake paused a moment to savor the exquisite feel of her.

Cristina braced herself but Blake had prepared her so well and entered her so gently that the pain she expected was a mere discomfort that disappeared almost as soon as he moved within her, inching his way inside her, filling her more deeply with each stroke. Probing . . . enticing . . . loving . . . until Cristina moved with him.

She held on, pulling his lean hips to hers, instinctively meeting him thrust for thrust until the darkness surrounding them exploded in a dazzling display of brilliant lights. They fell through time together, gasping out each other's names as Blake poured himself into her.

"Cristina, my lovely, lovely Cristina. . . ." His breathy whisper caressed her ears.

Cristina gently touched her lips to his, tasting the salt of lovemaking. "Always," she whispered.

Blake sighed contentedly then tightened his arms around her, pulled her close against him, and kissed the damp curls framing her face before he closed his eyes and drifted into a deep, dreamless sleep.

Thirteen

CRISTINA AWOKE TO the feel of Blake's gentle kisses. She stretched lazily, then slowly opened her eyes and smiled at him as he lowered himself onto the side of the bed.

"Good morning," she said shyly, fixing her gaze on his mouth, remembering the magic his mouth wrought.

"Good morning," he answered awkwardly, staring at an imaginary spot on the pillows at a point above her left shoulder. Her bare left shoulder.

Cristina glanced at the bedside clock, then turned her attention back to Blake. He was, she noted, completely dressed while she lay naked beneath the sheets. "You're up early," she said. "It's not even light yet."

"I've a train to catch," Blake told her.

"Oh."

There was a wealth of disappointment in the single word. Blake stabbed his fingers through his hair, looked down at Cristina, and nervously cleared his throat. "I didn't mean to wake you," he admitted, "but I wanted to say good-bye before I left."

"I'm glad you did," she told him. "I should have hated

to wake up alone without knowing . . . I mean, wondering if—''

"I hurt you," he blurted.

"What?"

"I was wondering if I hurt you," he said, his voice deep and laden with concern. "I didn't know if, perhaps, I was too rough?"

She shook her head. "You were perfect."

Blake's dark eyes crinkled at the corners and his face reddened slightly. "That shows how much you know." He gave into the impulse and kissed the tip of her nose. "Innocent," he teased.

"Not so innocent anymore," Cristina reminded him.

"Still much too innocent for the likes of me." The expression in his dark eyes only hinted at the deeper emotions he kept hidden from view.

Cristina reached up and grasped the lapel of his black morning coat. "Then teach me to please you."

"Teach you?" Blake chuckled at her absurd misconception. "Did you think you didn't please me?"

Cristina blushed and resolutely fastened her gaze on the center button of his waistcoat. "I thought I did, but now I'm not so sure."

Blake lifted her chin with the tip of his index finger, tilting her face so that he could see her expression. "My dear Cristina, if you had pleased me any more, you would have killed me!" He leaned forward and gently, briefly covered her lips with his own. "And I'm a damned poor excuse for a lover if you couldn't tell just how much you pleased me." He stared down at her, a quizzical expression on his face. " 'Please' is a horribly inadequate way of describing what you do to me. Awe, enchant, enthrall, overwhelm, maybe, but please . . .'' Blake couldn't keep himself from kissing her again—quickly—before he pulled away. A smile curled at the corner of his lips and a teasing light appeared in his eyes. "I don't think a mere 'please' will ever be sufficient."

"I do," Cristina disagreed.

"How's that?" he asked.

"Please," she whispered softly, entreatingly. "Please," she whispered, tilting her face up for his kiss.

"I stand corrected," Blake answered before he gave in to the overwhelming urge to kiss her once again.

~⦿~

"STAY," CRISTINA URGED, fiddling with the buttons of his waistcoat when Blake would have pulled away. "Stay with me."

"I have to go," he told her. "I'm due at Sandringham this evening, and if I don't hurry, I'll miss my morning train."

"Oh."

It was there again. The feeling of utter disappointment Cristina managed to convey in one single syllable. Blake caught his breath at the sound. He didn't have to catch the first train out of London. There would be another later in the day. So what if he arrived at Sandringham a few hours behind schedule? Who would miss him in the hubbub of the arrival of all the other weekend guests? Who would wonder at his delay? Whereas Cristina . . .

"I'll miss you," she said simply, eloquently.

Would miss him. Blake slipped his hands under hers and began unbuttoning the gold buttons of his waistcoat. "I can catch a later train."

"Are you sure?" she asked, leaving the unfastened waistcoat to him while she worked on the buttons of his shirt. "I don't want to detain you. I'd hate to make you miss something important."

"Please," Blake begged before grinning unashamedly. "Make me late."

~⦿~

IT WAS RAINING outside when Cristina awoke for the second time. She shivered in the cool morning air and automatically reached for Blake. She scooted over to his side of the bed, fitting her body into the curve of the mattress where he had lain, seeking his warmth. But he was gone. The indentation in the mattress and on his pillow and the fact that she lay in his bed were the only visible signs of the wonderful night and the exquisite morning they had shared. She let her gaze linger on the few stray black hairs that clung to the pillow slip, remembering the way she had run her fingers through his dark locks while she had eagerly returned his kisses. Cristina smiled at the memories and a blush crept over her face, staining it with color. She closed her eyes, sighing with pleasure as her mind replayed the events of the morning in glorious detail.

Blake had introduced her to the mysteries of her body and his own and had taught her the art of making love. He had been tender and caring and amazingly gentle as he worshipped her body. He had given her intense, mind-boggling pleasure and had taught her how to give that same intense delight to him. In his arms, she had come alive with passion. She had eagerly experienced the smell, taste, and feel of him with her lips and tongue and hands and eyes, adoring his body with the same single-minded determination Blake had used on her. They loved selfishly and unselfishly time and time again, exploring the realms of desire together—making love, sleeping, and waking to make love again until he left her in the first light of dawn, exhausted by their lovemaking yet supremely well-sated and happy.

She remembered protesting sleepily as Blake roused her from her delicious dreams to kiss her good-bye one last time after he had given in to her demands and made sweet love with her before leaving to catch his train for Sandringham. She had continued to protest as Blake tenderly washed away the remains of his lovemaking, then pulled the sheets up over her bare breasts and tucked her firmly into bed.

"I thought I'd find you in here." Leah opened the door and slipped inside the room without knocking.

Startled, Cristina looked up at her maid. "I can explain . . ."

"There's no need for explainin'," Leah said. "I don't want details. I can figure out for myself what happened." Leah liked Lord Lawrence and she hoped one day to welcome him into the family, but she loved Cristina and, despite everything Mackie had told her, she didn't like the idea of her precious charge sharing a bed with this man before she had a gold wedding ring on her finger any more than she liked the idea of Cristina sharing a bed with a man of her mother's choosing. "I also figured you'd be needin' this." She tossed a brown dressing gown across the foot of the bed.

"Thanks," Cristina answered automatically, pulling on the robe as she watched Leah retrieving articles of clothing that had been carelessly strewn around the foot of the bed.

"Don't that man ever take the time to undo anything?" The maid grumbled as she surveyed the damage the green silk gown had suffered under Blake's impatient hands and the assortment of buttons littering the floor.

Cristina shrugged her shoulders, deciding that the state of her clothing spoke for itself. "Where is he?"

"He left an hour or so ago. He said he had to catch a train for the Prince of Wales's country house in Norfolk."

"How did he look?" Cristina asked.

"Pleased with himself," Leah answered. "Very pleased. He was whistling when he came into the kitchen lookin' for me."

"Blake was looking for you?"

"Yes, ma'am," Leah told her. "He pulled me to the side, real quietlike, and told me where you were. He told me to let you sleep. Then, a few minutes later, when he was on his way out the door, I heard him ask Mrs. MacKenzie to keep the maids out of his room. He said he had work spread out everywhere and didn't want it disturbed." Leah glared meaningfully at Cristina.

Cristina smiled. "That was thoughtful of him."

Leah snorted.

"If Blake asked you not to disturb me, why did you?" Cristina asked pointedly as she snuggled back down into the covers to escape Leah's knowing eyes.

"The doctor is waitin' to see you."

Cristina sat up, instantly awake. "I don't need a doctor anymore. What's he doing here?"

"Well, I'm sure I don't know," came the sharp rejoinder from Leah. "And it wasn't my place to ask him. After all, I'm nobody special—just one of Lord Lawrence's many servants."

"Employees," Cristina corrected absentmindedly, knowing Blake disliked the term "servants." "And please save the lecture for later, Leah." She flipped back the covers, then stood up and glanced at the bedroom door before turning back to Leah. "Does anyone else know I'm in this room?"

"Nope," Leah answered. "As far as the rest of the household is concerned, you're sound asleep in your own bed. He waited until I was alone to issue his instructions." She draped Cristina's clothing over her arm, then crossed the room, opened the bedroom door, and surveyed the empty hallway. "If you keep this up, you won't be able to fool the 'employees' long," Leah warned. "And neither will he. But the coast is clear this morning. Come on. We'll sneak you into your room before anybody is the wiser."

Cristina nodded, then gripped the lapels of the dressing gown together against her body as she padded barefooted down the hallway and into the guest room. Cristina rushed through her morning ablution, wishing she had time for a full bath, wishing Nigel Jameson hadn't chosen to visit, wishing Leah hadn't barged into Blake's bedroom full of disapproval, but wishing most of all that Blake hadn't had to leave her alone. She finished bathing, dried off, and accepted the stack of linen Leah handed her. Cristina struggled into her undergarments, then crossed the room to stand in front of the armoire while Leah dropped a soft lavender morning gown over her head, settled it into place, and hurriedly fastened the buttons.

Leah finished with the dress and grabbed a silver-backed brush from the dresser where she proceeded to brush Cristina's unruly curls into a smooth knot at the back of her head, pinning it into place with sharp, jerky stabs of the hairpins.

"Ouch!" Cristina exclaimed. "Doctor Jameson will have

to sew up my scalp if you keep jabbing me with those hair-pins. I don't know what is bothering you this morning, Leah, but you don't have to take it out on me.''

"You know good and well what's botherin' me this mornin'," Leah reminded Cristina. "You are. You and Lord Lawrence.''

"Are you saying you don't like Lord Lawrence?'' Cristina asked haughtily.

"I like him,'' Leah told her. "I just don't like you endin' up in his bed without the benefit of marriage vows. In case you've forgotten, most young ladies don't sleep with men before they marry 'em.''

"Most young ladies aren't sold by their mothers as mistresses either. Most young ladies find husbands in the accepted fashion. I don't have that option. I have Blake instead and maybe one day soon—''

"You're dreamin', Cristina. He may want you now, but . . .'' Leah had to bite her tongue to keep from blurting out the reason for Lord Lawrence's present state of bachelorhood. She couldn't really give her blessing to the affair between Cristina and Lord Lawrence, but neither could she condemn them for it. From what Mackie had told her, Leah could see that Lord Lawrence had had as little happiness as Cristina. Who was she to tell his secret and burst Cristina's bubble? Who was she to destroy their moment of happiness? The love they were building? For Leah could look at her young mistress and see that Cristina was in love with Blake Ashford and she suspected he felt the same way, whether he knew it or not. Weren't all God's creatures entitled to a bit of love from someone? Leah felt in her heart that Lord Lawrence cared deeply for Cristina and that he would never hurt her intentionally, but the truth would hurt and despite her genuine liking for Blake Ashford, Leah felt she must do what she could to keep Cristina from pinning too much hope on the future. What they shared was in the present and Cristina must understand that her happiness would be fleeting. There could be no future in it. "I know you care for Lord Lawrence, child, but you mustn't put too much faith in what a man says in bed. Don't expect too much."

"I won't expect more than he can give."

Leah was merciless. "That's what you say now. What will you say when you're big with his child and he won't marry you?"

"That won't happen."

"It will if you continue to share the man's bed."

Cristina thought for a moment. "Well, I'm sure if it did happen, Blake would marry me."

"Don't be too sure," Leah warned. "The world is full of bastards whose mother believed the gent would marry her." Leah continued to raise obstacles. "Cristina, Lord Lawrence is a member of the queen's government. He's always travelin'. He don't have time for a family life. He don't need a wife or a family. What he wants is a mistress."

"You're wrong, Leah. He isn't like that."

"He's a man, ain't he? And he got what he wanted, didn't he?"

Angry at Leah for spoiling her beautiful morning, Cristina dismissed her maid. "You've had your say, Leah, so why don't you go tell the doctor to come on up?"

The doctor was a small man with curly red hair several shades brighter than Cristina's. He had sparkling blue eyes and an enormous red mustache that obscured the rest of his features. He was handsome in an unconventional way, and young. Cristina liked him instantly, although he certainly didn't resemble any doctor she could ever remember seeing. And he didn't sound like a doctor, either.

"You don't look ill." Nigel Jameson commented upon entering Cristina's bedroom. "From what Blake said this morning, I expected to find you at death's door. Instead I find you looking radiant and a bit like the cat who's been at the cream. But I suppose a good night's sleep does indeed work wonders." His voice trailed off into meaningless mumbles.

Cristina caught his meaning at once and blushed to the roots of her copper curls. "Blake sent you here? Why?"

"To see you, of course. Blake was afraid you might have

suffered a relapse." The doctor's smile widened. "He told me you'd been pale and listless for the past few days and not at all your charming self. I tried to assure him that it might be one of your 'off' times, but he was concerned about you, so he dragged me from my warm bed at an ungodly hour this morning so I could check on you."

"I've never felt better," Cristina assured him.

"I'm glad to hear it. Now let's get down to business, shall we?" The doctor offered his hand to her. "We haven't been formally introduced, Miss Fairfax. I'm Nigel Jameson and I'm happy to see you awake this morning. As I've already seen you asleep several times." His merry eyes twinkled in amusement and Cristina had the feeling that he was indeed pleased about something, though she wasn't altogether sure it had anything to do with the state of her health.

He stared down at her, studying every nuance of her appearance from head to toe, and Cristina had the feeling he saw a great deal more about her than she was ready to reveal. It was uncanny and a little frightening to know he found her so transparent, but it was impossible to be offended by those sparkling blue eyes.

Cristina returned his smile. "It's a pleasure to meet you, Dr. Jameson. Thank you for coming today and for taking care of me while I was ill. I understand I owe you a great deal."

"Who told you that nonsense? Mackie?" At Cristina's nod, he continued, "That's ridiculous. I did nothing any other brilliant, self-sacrificing, extraordinarily attractive young physician would have done to save such a lovely patient. And now that we have all the formalities out of the way, let's get down to business and have a look at you. If you would be so kind as to step behind the screen and undress."

Cristina reddened considerably. "Undress? But I thought . . ."

Nigel gritted his teeth. "You thought I would pull a female doll out of my medical bag and ask you to show me your aches and pains by pointing to the corresponding places on the doll. Right?"

Cristina nodded. It was the accepted practice among ladies

in Victorian society. Ladies, especially unmarried ladies, did not undress in the company of a doctor.

"I'm afraid I don't practice medicine according to the dictates of society. I'm considered to be a radical. You see, after my years at Oxford, I did practical training in Edinburgh and Paris, before becoming a fellow in the Royal College of Surgeons, so I tend to rely on knowledge, experience, skill, and my own observations for my diagnosis. I care more about the health and the life of my patients than I do about their 'delicate sensibilities.' I examined you thoroughly when you were brought here in an unconscious state. But if it will make you feel more comfortable, I'll welcome a chaperon. Shall I call your maid? Lady Wethering? Mackie?''

She stared at him. He was so perceptive. Could he tell? Would he know that she had spent the night making love with Blake Ashford? She had been too ill to be aware of the doctor's scrutiny when she first arrived at Lawrence House, but today she was conscious and had the memories of Blake's caresses, his exciting exploration of her most intimate body regions and the gentle, almost loving way he had bathed the perspiration and the scent of him from her body, washing each inch of her with a damp cloth after their impromptu morning bout of passionate lovemaking. Her memories and Nigel Jameson's too acute gaze made Cristina extremely self-conscious.

"Is there anybody there?" Nigel chuckled as Cristina turned an even brighter shade of embarrassed red and immediately ceased her romantic woolgathering. "Shall I send for Mackie?''

Cristina shook her head. "No. That won't be necessary. I'd rather this remain private.''

Nigel nodded his approval as Cristina walked over to the screen standing in the corner of bedchamber, stepped behind it, and began to remove her clothing.

When she reappeared, Cristina wore her chemise and corset. "I couldn't undo my laces," she explained, her face red with embarrassment.

"Quite so," Nigel replied matter-of-factly. "If you'll turn around and allow me."

Cristina did as the doctor asked and Nigel quickly unlaced the constricting corset and tossed it aside. He motioned for Cristina to sit on the bed and once she obliged, Nigel began his examination.

He slipped her chemise off her shoulders and listened to her rapid heartbeat and shallow breathing. "That's quite a collection of bruises you've got there," he commented and Cristina followed his gaze to the yellow-brown and greenish circles marring the flesh of her upper arms.

Cristina shrugged. "I bruise easily."

"You've added to them since I first examined you. Did Lord Lawrence do that to you?"

Cristina thought of the dozens of ways Blake had touched her while he made love with her—sometimes gently and sometimes not so gently. She was bound to have a few black and blue marks. "No, of course not. At least not intentionally."

"Care to tell me about it?" Nigel studied her closely, unfooled by her sudden interest in the lace of her shift. "Miss Fairfax?"

Cristina looked up to find his blue eyes serious and full of concern for her. She wanted to confide in someone who could be impartial and not judge and scold her as Leah often did. She wanted to trust this man who offered her compassion and friendship.

Nigel watched the play of emotions on her face and knew she was struggling to make a decision. "You can trust me, Miss Fairfax. My lips are sealed."

Cristina read the compassion in his eyes and the words suddenly came pouring out of her like water through a leaky dike. She told him everything.

"Maybe I should have let go of the sheets," Cristina concluded.

"If you had, I'd probably be tending your broken arms and legs, if not your neck." Nigel smiled at her. "So you spent the night at Marlborough House in Blake Ashford's bed."

Cristina nodded. "I woke up in the middle of the night and Lord Lawrence was in bed beside me. I tried to pull away but he held on to me. I fought him and hit him in the face. I think he bled a little. I hid until he went back to bed. I must have fallen asleep there, because I was on the floor and very ill when I awoke again. I dressed as best I could and sneaked away. But we shared a bed and well, now I worry about having a baby."

"Did Blake try to make love to you that night? Did he touch you intimately in any way?"

"No."

"Then there's nothing for you to worry about. You're still a virgin."

"But . . ." Cristina stopped abruptly and flushed red to the roots of her hair as she pierced the doctor with those great green eyes, pleading for him to understand.

"Have you shared a bed with Lord Lawrence since that night?" Nigel suddenly blushed as red as Cristina.

"Yes."

"When?" he asked.

"Last night," she admitted. "And this morning."

"You were bleeding quite heavily when Blake brought you here. Perhaps you'll be safe for now, but we must take preventive measures for the future, and plan for an eventual possibility."

"What kind of measures?" Cristina spoke quietly.

Nigel took several items out of his medical bag and began to explain the different methods of birth control. "I can't do anything about last night," he told her when he finished his explanations. "You might already be with child. We'll just have to wait and see. It doesn't always happen the first time you make love with a man, but it is a distinct possibility." Cristina's painfully innocent query angered Nigel. The girl had the best education money could buy, had spent the night with a man, and yet she was horribly ignorant of the workings of her own body. It was appalling that in these progressive times, society deemed it necessary to keep young women and even young men ignorant of the functions of their bodies, especially the sexual functions. Why, his grandmother had known more about sex as a young virgin than did many of the married females of his day! It was absolutely incredible and Nigel had made a solemn vow to educate as many young women as he possibly could. His gynecological and obstetrics hospital was dedicated to that purpose and his family and friends generously supported Nigel's charity.

He faced Cristina and reached for her hand as he lowered himself onto the edge of her bed. He sat beside her, and patted her hand comfortingly.

"What will happen if I am with child? What will I do? I have no place to go."

"Go? My dear young woman, you won't need to go anywhere. You'll stay right here at Lawrence House where Blake and Mackie and Lady Wethering and I can take care of you."

Cristina shuddered. After Lady Wethering's frank warning last night, there was no question of her causing a scandal by remaining at Lawrence House or in London. She would have to retire to the country, or better yet leave the country. If worse came to worst she would think of something, but unless Blake offered to marry her, there would be no question of her remaining. "I couldn't stay here. That would be impossible. I would be barred from society. No one would speak to me. And no one would receive me. Or Blake. We'd be outcast."

"London society is that important to you, Cristina?" Nigel's face hardened and his voice was stern.

"I don't care about London society for myself," Cristina replied. "But I do care about Blake and Lady Wethering and the opinions of the people in his household and I care about the welfare of an innocent child. I don't want to be responsible for ruining Blake's good name or damaging my child's future."

Nigel breathed a sigh of relief. "If you're concerned about the welfare of innocent children, then I know I can count on you to be sensible." He thought not only of an unborn child, but of Cristina herself, because despite her recent experiences and her mysterious relationship with Blake, Cristina Fairfax was still a babe in the woods. "I'll know that if you do discover you're with child, you won't be swallowing any more of your maid's concoctions or visiting any Seven Dials midwives or madams. Too many women in this country die from ignorance, poison, and botched surgeries because they're trying to conform to the standards of a hypocritical society.''

"Maybe I'm worrying for no reason."

"Maybe," Nigel agreed. "But you should know how to recognize the signs—just in case." He spent the next hour explaining the symptoms of pregnancy and touching on a few of the practices used to prevent conception. He spoke precisely and without embarrassment, patiently explaining the details and answering Cristina's hesitant questions.

Cristina listened and learned, aware of just how ignorant she had been. It was pathetic really to think that she had considered herself so well educated and so sophisticated when she faced her mother and her lover without batting an eye or the time she had called her mother a whore when talking to Leah. But she had been mouthing words she had overheard, pretending she was a sophisticate. It was embarrassing to learn just how much she didn't know, but at least she wasn't ignorant any longer. Now she understood. "Thank you for being honest with me, Dr. Jameson."

"Don't thank me, Cristina. It's part of my duty as a doctor." There was pain in those bright blue eyes when he looked at her. "And part of your duty as my patient is to heed my advice and notify me if your condition changes."

"If I exhibit any of the symptoms?"

"Yes," Nigel confirmed. "Send for me immediately. All right?"

"All right," she agreed.

"And what are you going to do in the meantime?" Nigel asked, wanting to remind her of the contraception device he had suggested.

"Follow Leah's advice and stay out of Lord Lawrence's bed."

Nigel Jameson chuckled. After learning the facts of life, no doubt Cristina Fairfax would try to ignore her attraction to Blake—to protect herself and Blake by staying out of his way.

And no doubt Blake would try even harder to stay away from her. But attraction was an overwhelming force and even the strongest people sometimes succumbed to their desires. "What if your best intentions fail?"

Cristina smiled shyly at the doctor. Her first impressions of Nigel Jameson had been right on the mark. He *did* see too much—*know* too much—about Blake and about her. "I'll remember to use the vinegar sponge or have Blake use one of those French letters."

Nigel nodded. "Good. Now is there anything else you wish to discuss with me?"

"How long will I have to wait until I know if—"

"Give yourself a few weeks," he told her.

He is mad past recovery, but yet he has lucid intervals.

—MIGUEL DE CERVANTES 1547–1616

Fourteen

BLAKE CALLED HIMSELF ten kinds of a fool as he paused in the cold morning rain outside the Gray's Inn solicitor's office. He was already late. He should be on the train headed for Sandringham, yet here he was standing outside the door to his solicitor's office about to make an irreversible, monumental mistake. He felt it in his bones, but there didn't seem to be anything he could do to stop himself. Blake knew he wasn't ready to get married again, had in fact resolved never to marry again, but he was about to do just that. Once he settled things with her father, he'd obtain a special license from the archbishop of Canterbury and talk to Cristina. Despite his best resolve not to touch her while she was living under his roof, he had touched her—seduced her, or allowed her to seduce him. He wasn't quite sure which. And he wasn't all that certain that it mattered. What did matter was the fact that he had allowed his desire to control his brain. And while the logical, rational part of him wished it had never happened, the fact remained that he had made love with Cristina—not once, but several times during the night and once this morning. He had made love with her and to her and enjoyed every moment of it and now it was time to do the honorable thing by her.

"I'm not that much of a reprobate." The phrase kept coming back to haunt him. Blake remembered saying those words to Nigel when Nigel had asked if he had seduced Cristina on the morning he'd brought her to Lawrence House—the morning Blake had relayed the details of Patricia Fairfax's wager at Lord Strathemore's midnight supper.

But it seemed he was. As much a reprobate as Strathemore and his friends or Patricia Fairfax or any other jaded aristocrat.

Blake Ashford, ninth earl of Lawrence, had never taken any young woman's virginity before—much less the virginity of a daughter of a member of the aristocracy. Cristina was a young woman of social standing and until she met him, she had been a young woman with a future and prospects ahead of her. Blake took a deep breath, then blew it out in a cloud. Well, he would see that she had the future and the prospects she deserved. He'd do the honorable thing, the right thing, the proper thing. He would grin and bear it as he stood up in front of the reverend and put a gold wedding band on her finger.

But first he had to find William Fairfax and get everything settled. He grabbed hold of the doorknob, opened the front door, and approached the first solicitor he found.

"Find him. Find out everything you can about him," Blake instructed.

"But, sir," Albert Mead, a thin, wiry, bespectacled young man, was having difficulty understanding his client's wishes. "Lord Lawrence, that might be difficult. William Fairfax left London over four years ago if my memory serves me correctly."

"I don't care how difficult it is. I'm paying you a substantial fee to find him and I expect results. I must see him. This matter is of the greatest importance to him and to me."

Mead was flabbergasted. The request was so unexpected. He rarely saw Lord Lawrence in the flesh. His normal duties consisted of tending to Lord Lawrence's monthly household accounts. The other business matters were handled by the senior partners of the firm and Albert Mead was only a junior partner.

"Lord Lawrence, I'm not sure I understand your request," he repeated nervously.

"It's very simple. I want you to locate Sir William Fairfax, late of Fairhall, and request a meeting with him as soon as possible. Tell him it concerns Cristina. That's all he needs to know for now. The rest I'll tell him in person."

"This could take weeks, even months."

Now that he had made up his mind about what to do with Cristina, Blake wanted everything arranged as quickly as possible and that meant talking to William Fairfax. Cristina was twenty, not twelve, and well over the legal age of consent. She didn't require her father's permission to marry, but Blake did.

He hadn't courted her, hadn't romanced her, hadn't treated her with the tenderness or the respect she deserved. Cristina had accused him of ruining her chances for a decent marriage. And she was right. But he was going to change all that. If she wanted marriage—and what young woman didn't—she was going to have it along with all the trimmings.

Starting with her father. Blake was going to get Cristina's father's consent to their marriage because he wanted it. He required William Fairfax's approval in a way he had never required George Brownlee's. Maybe it was because Blake no longer trusted himself, maybe he simply needed a man other than a lifelong friend like Nigel Jameson to approve of his decision to marry again. Maybe he needed William Fairfax's approval to release him from the burden of guilt he was feeling.

He stared at Albert Mead. "You don't have months. This is very important. I must see him. Contact me as soon as you find him." Blake drew on his coat, preparing to leave.

"And if I find him deceased—"

"You won't."

"How do you know that for sure?"

"I don't."

"But, sir . . ."

"It's just a hunch, Mr. Mead. If Sir William Fairfax was dead, his estate would have been probated. Lady Fairfax would have had her hands on her share of his property before he was cold in the ground. But as yet, none of his estate has been probated. I checked that myself, first thing this morning. So find him."

"I'll do my best, sir."

"I expect nothing less," Blake said. "I know I can rely on your firm to come through as it has in the past."

"Yes, sir, Lord Lawrence," Mead said. But he was speaking to an empty room. Lord Lawrence had already made his exit. He was gone within seconds, leaving a bewildered Mead to undertake the monumental task of finding a man who had been away from England for more than four years.

CRISTINA DECIDED TO give herself six weeks just to be sure. The crown prince was scheduled to leave in four weeks. And once he left, once Blake was no longer required to escort him all over the kingdom, things would surely settle down into a nice quiet routine. Blake would be able to spend his days and nights with her at Lawrence House. And if at the end of the six weeks she discovered she was going to have a baby, Cristina was certain she would find ample opportunity to approach him with the news.

He hadn't proposed yet. In fact, the subject of marriage had yet to come up between them. Cristina couldn't bring herself to mention it until she knew how he felt about her. But she wasn't really worried. After all, Blake hadn't had a moment to himself since returned from Sandringham. During the day, he escorted Crown Prince Rudolf's entourage on visits to the Bank of England, Smithfield and Billingsgate markets, the Corn Exchange, law courts, factories, old people's homes, military establishments, and the British Museum in London and attended private dinner parties given by peers of the realm; dinner parties at Marlborough House that were hosted by the Prince and Princess of Wales; and balls at the Austrian Embassy, Carlton House Terrace, the German Embassy, and the Belgian Embassy. He hadn't spent a single night at Lawrence House in the past two weeks. And while Cristina hoped Blake would ask her to attend some of the social functions with him, she understood when he didn't. She was, after all, supposed to be back in the country staying with her imaginary relatives. Cristina couldn't be upset when she rightfully suspected that Blake didn't invite her to attend those social gatherings because he wanted to keep her as far away from Rudolf—and scandal—as possible.

Blake was working hard and traveling continuously. There were more trips scheduled—weekends at country estates, visits to the industrial cities of Birmingham, Liverpool, Bradford, Manchester, and Sheffield and trips to Scotland, Wales, and Ireland.

Still, the days were passing and Cristina waited and hoped and prayed that Blake loved her. Because loving him meant she couldn't settle for anything less. She told herself that all she needed was for Crown Prince Rudolf to return to Austria so she and Blake could spend some time together. Blake cared for her. He had to. All she needed was a bit more time to prove it.

But time ran out one morning four weeks and two days after the doctor's last visit when she overheard Leah, Mackie, and Perryman the butler, discussing the "scandal."

"They say the queen is livid. This is the third scandal this year and the queen is demanding that everyone in her government be investigated," Perryman announced. "She says she'll have no more unsavory scandals in her government."

"He'll have to resign from the queen's government," Mackie said as the three of them savored a pot of morning tea at the kitchen table. "For an 'indiscretion' with a young woman residing under his roof."

Cristina drew in a quick breath. Had someone seen them

at Marlborough House? Had someone outside the household spoken of her relationship with Blake? Had their affair cost Blake his government career?

"Will the queen demand his resignation? Or will he be able to resign quietly?" Perryman asked.

"There's no keeping it quiet now." Mackie tapped the morning newspaper against the table. "The scandal's already become public knowledge. He can only hope to leave with as little outcry as possible. It says in the paper that the Lords have voted to censure him and are recommending he voluntarily step down from his post before the queen asks for his resignation."

"What if he refuses?" Leah asked.

"I don't see how he dare refuse," Mackie said. "His career would be ruined."

"But if he voluntarily resigns, he may be able to return to government service at a later date," Perryman added. "It's happened before."

"What about her?" Leah wanted to know. "What will happen to her?"

Mackie scanned the newspaper. "It doesn't name her. Nor does it say what will happen to her. But I'm sure she'll be asked to leave the house."

Cristina's heart seemed to stop beating. She couldn't leave Lawrence House. She had no place to go. She wouldn't go to Patricia and she had no money and no means of locating her father without it.

"It's such a shame," Leah commented. "If she's in the family way, the poor girl will need all the help she can get."

"She won't find it here," Perryman predicted. "She'll have to leave London. The gentry will cut her dead if she stays and there won't be anything Lord Ainsford can do to help her. Because he'll be disgraced as well."

Cristina couldn't keep from breathing a little prayer of thanks. She was safe for a while longer. Lord Ainsford was in disgrace. Lord Ainsford, not Lord Lawrence. But, Cristina reminded herself, it might be only a matter of time before she found herself in the same predicament as the unnamed girl in

Lord Ainsford's household. It was as if Leah, Mackie, and Perryman had described her worst nightmare.

"Perryman, you've met Lord Ainsford. I heard he was a widower. Is there no chance for a marriage between the lord and the young woman?" Mackie asked.

"Not at all," Perryman answered. "According to my sources, the young woman in question is a distant cousin—a poor relation who came to town as governess to his lordship's young children—"

"Surely he could marry the woman," Leah interrupted.

"Impossible," Perryman told them. "Because his lordship is no longer a widower. He remarried last year and I hear his new wife is anticipating an addition to the family any time now."

"Saints preserve us!" Mackie exclaimed. "He'll be having two additions to the family in the same year."

"Yes, indeed," Perryman said. "And only one will be born on the proper side of the blanket."

Cristina didn't stay to hear any more. Her breakfast suddenly seemed too much for her stomach to hold. She had to get to her room. She had to make plans.

She sent for Nigel Jameson seeking confirmation of her deepest fear a week later. Her monthly hadn't come yet and she had been sick upon rising for three days in a row. Unless Blake could see his way to admit to loving her, she would have to leave him—for her sake and for his.

Dr. Jameson arrived promptly and greeted her without preamble. "You sent for me, so I presume that you've missed your monthly."

Cristina nodded.

"Have you been ill upon rising? Unable to eat your breakfast? Tired?" He fired the questions at her one after the other until all Cristina could do was nod her head once again in affirmation.

Nigel smiled reassuringly. "I'll have to examine you to be sure, but I suspect we're going to have a baby."

Cristina had her confirmation. She and Blake were going to become parents in about eight months' time. "I don't know how I'll face him with news like this," Cristina said when Nigel finished his examination.

"You'll find a way. The opportunity will present itself. And you must face him, Cristina. It would be wrong to do otherwise." Nigel gave her his lopsided grin. "I wouldn't worry too much, my dear, Blake adores children. I think he'll be quite pleased. It isn't every day that a man becomes a father. Besides, Blake is responsible, too. He'll do what is best for you and the baby. You needn't worry that he will turn you away."

"Have you seen the morning papers, Dr. Jameson?" The investigation into scandal in the government was broadening and the newspapers were full of lurid details. Cristina held up the morning edition of *The Times* and read from the front page: "The scandal concerning Her Majesty's men in government widens and there appears to be no end in sight. Lords Barton, Griffith, and Ainsford have all resigned their posts and more secrets involving more scandalous lords are expected to follow. It appears there have been a number of fallen young debutantes as well as young governesses this year and one can't help but wonder which of Her Majesty's government men will be the next to resign."

She looked up at Nigel, then flipped to the gossip section of the paper to a column called "Ton Tidbits" and continued reading. "What's become of the lovely Miss————who was seen at the theater in the company of the handsome and elusive Earl of————recently? Has she been taken off the market? No one can say for sure, but Miss————who is reportedly staying with friends in the country hasn't been seen in weeks. Are wedding bells in the Earl of————and Miss————'s future? Has the earl who vowed never to taste matrimonial bliss changed his mind? No one seems to know for sure." Cristina folded the newspaper and stared at Nigel. "I shouldn't continue to stay here and allow Blake to take responsibility for me and a child."

"Why not?" Nigel wanted to know. "He is responsible for the child, if not for you. Besides, your going or staying isn't a decision for you to make alone. Tell him, Cristina. Share the joy. I've known Blake all my life, and believe me, there's nothing he would like better than to hear the sound of children playing in this house. He's always wanted a child and was bitterly disappointed when he and Meredith failed to have one.'' Nigel had been watching Cristina's face and was aware of his blunder almost as soon as the words left his mouth. She didn't know about Meredith—or hadn't known until he had foolishly blundered.

There were questions in her eyes that begged to be answered and Nigel could have kicked himself for letting Meredith's name slip out.

''Who is Meredith?'' Cristina whispered the name.

''Ask Blake. I'm sure he'll tell you all about it.'' Nigel didn't want to volunteer any more information. He'd said too much as it was.

Cristina recognized his hedging. ''I am asking you, Dr. Jameson,'' she persisted, ''and I want an answer.''

Nigel's expression was grim as he nodded his head in capitulation and told Cristina what she wanted to know. ''Meredith was Blake's wife.''

''His wife?'' Cristina echoed hollowly. ''Until I read this, I didn't know he had had a wife. Nobody has ever mentioned a wife.''

''She . . .'' Nigel cleared his throat. ''There was a riding accident several years ago and Meredith was crushed beneath her horse.''

As Cristina listened to the doctor tell about the tragic accident, her mind was busy assimilating the fact that Blake had been married. He had been married and he hadn't told her about it. She felt a twinge of some undefinable emotion that settled in the pit of her stomach. He had had a wife. Meredith. The name was etched in Cristina's brain. Every time she thought of Blake her mind conjured up the name like the missing part of a whole. Why hadn't he told her? Had his wife meant so much to him that he couldn't bear to speak of her? Cristina didn't know if most men spoke of their wives and families to their lovers, but she had thought that Blake would be honest with her. In her innocence, she had expected him to tell her if he had once been married. She pictured

Blake holding his wife in his arms, whispering the same words of love that he had whispered to her; working the same caressing magic that took her to the peaks of passion and that curious feeling in the pit of her stomach snaked through her, burning its way to her heart.

Nigel finished speaking and waited for Cristina to say something. He had to convince her to tell Blake about the coming child. "Listen to me, Cristina, you must think of what is best for you and the baby. Trust him. Tell Blake and let him help you through this. Let him help you decide the best way to handle things."

"He didn't tell me about Meredith," Cristina whispered, trying hard to conceal the hurt.

"I'm sure he had his reasons."

"And I have mine."

"Cristina, you must tell him about the baby," Nigel implored. "It's for the best."

"What about the scandal it will cause? Is that for the best, too?"

"A scandal might be damaging at first, but Blake won't be the first man in this town who wasn't married to his child's mother during conception and I'm sure he won't be the last. It happens. But everything will come right, Cristina, if you tell him. Please, think about it." Nigel advised as he said his good-byes, "I'll be back to check on you in a day or so."

Cristina didn't answer or look up as the doctor left the room. Alone, she continued to brood over her problem. As far as society was concerned, she was ruined. She was unmarried and carrying an illegitimate child. If the news got out, there would be a scandal like the one Lord Ainsford currently found himself in. But this time, it would be Blake. Blake. How it hurt to think of Blake in the arms of another woman. He had had a wife named Meredith who was killed in a riding accident—crushed beneath a horse. Cristina's romantic dreams died. He had had a wife. A wife he'd never mentioned, just as he had never breathed a word of loving her. Could she risk telling him about the baby? What if Blake decided to keep the baby but not her? Or worse, what if he

decided to marry her because of the baby? Could she stand
to live with the knowledge that he had married her to quell
gossip and not because he loved her. And what of her child?
Could he love the child without loving the mother? Would he
want his heir without wanting its mother?

⌘

TWO DAYS LATER, Blake was waiting for Albert Mead
when the office doors of Traherne, Carlisle, Jennings, and
Mead were unlocked. He followed Mead into the office, right
up to the junior partner's desk. "From your message, I assume you have good news for me."

"I do, sir." Mead was almost smiling. "You were quite
correct. Sir William is alive and living in the United States.
New York City, to be exact."

"That makes it difficult." Blake mentally counted the days
before he could reach New York.

"That's why I sent an urgent message. I contacted an office
on Wall Street and learned Sir William is president of one of
the city's most successful financial firms."

"And . . . ?" Blake prompted, eager for the excited solicitor to get to the point.

"He is currently in Paris on business and is scheduled to
arrive in London next week. I took the liberty of leaving a
message at his hotel in Paris and received a reply late last
night. He suggested you meet him at White's next Thursday
evening. Isn't that a stroke of luck? I was afraid you might
have to sail to the United States to discuss your business."
Mead was fairly bursting with pride at the success of his mission. He had tackled an almost impossible task and located
the man in only thirty-three days.

"You've done an excellent job, Mr. Mead." Blake was
quick to acknowledge the other man's skill at handling the
task assigned to him. "I've another task for you if you're of
a mind to take it. Of course, I'll see that you're amply rewarded for your services."

"Of course, Lord Lawrence, anything to be of help." Mead

was eager for another challenge. Being a junior partner in a law firm was not as mentally stimulating as he had hoped.

Blake removed a velvet pouch from inside his breast pocket and opened it to reveal the emerald and diamond necklace that had returned to Lawrence House by way of Cristina Fairfax's pocket.

Albert Mead gasped in awe.

"I want you to trace the history of this necklace, Mr. Mead. I'm aware of its origins, since I had it made especially for my wife, but it was taken from my home some time ago and only recently recovered. I want to know who took the necklace and how he disposed of it. This job will probably take a bit longer. I'll be traveling quite a bit, but you can reach me through the Foreign Office or our embassy. I think I know part of what you'll find, but I want to be certain. And no matter what you find, I want you to be completely truthful with me."

"You can be sure of that, sir."

Blake smiled at the solicitor and shook his hand. "Thank you, Mr. Mead, for everything."

"Thank you, Lord Lawrence," Mead replied sincerely, "for giving me the opportunity."

We heed no instincts but our own.

—JEAN DE LA FONTAINE 1621–1695

Fifteen

"CONGRATULATIONS, LAWRENCE."

"Don't know what to make of it, Lawrence."

"Best wishes, old man."

"Didn't think you'd be one of the ones to leg shackle yourself again so soon. Thought you'd wait until you were in your dotage. But a man must have an heir and at least you've chosen a deb. Pick 'em young, train 'em right, I always say."

Blake found himself surrounded by well wishers and empathizers as soon as he crossed the threshold of his gentleman's club in St. James. Having just spent the afternoon escorting Rudolf to various functions, he had sought the calm, quiet of his club before heading home to dress for another round of embassy parties. "What are you talking about?" he demanded of Lord Telsham, who had just slapped him on the back in a hearty greeting.

"Haven't you seen the paper, old man?" Telsham asked.

Blake shook his head. He'd read yesterday's paper. He had seen the item in the gossip column speculating about his trip to the theater with Cristina and had read the headlines touting the queen's displeasure with the scandals rocking her government. In truth, *The Times*'s lurid coverage of Lord Ainsford's affair had disgusted him so much that he hadn't bothered to read this morning's edition. But he didn't need to read the newspaper to know what was going on in the Foreign Office and the other branches of government. He understood politics. He knew who had the power and the influence to sway the investigation and who didn't. He knew whose reputations were at stake and whose were not. As a member of the government, Blake was privy to more details than the newspapers and he knew that while his behavior wasn't yet suspect, it was only a matter of time before someone connected his appearance at Lord Strathemore's midnight soiree with the item in the gossip column. He could only hope that his aunt's presence in his household and the fact that he had publicly introduced Cristina to the Prince of Wales and had already petitioned the archbishop of Canterbury for a special license would remain unnoticed a while longer. He may have decided on his next course of action but until he had an opportunity to speak with Sir William Fairfax to ask his permission and his blessing on his daughter's impending engagement, Blake didn't want his intentions toward Cristina splashed across the pages of the newspaper for everyone to read.

Telsham shoved a folded newspaper at him. "Page four. Center column."

He stood at Blake's side, grinning like an idiot, while Blake unfolded the paper, turned to page four, and read the announcement: "Blake Ashford, ninth earl of Lawrence, son of the marquess and marchioness of Everleigh, announces his impending nuptials to Miss Cristina Fairfax, daughter of Sir William and Lady Fairfax by special license. No date has yet been set. Invitations will be forthcoming." Blake carefully refolded the paper and turned to Telsham. "May I keep this?"

"Of course," Telsham replied. "Felicitations, old man. May I stand you a drink in honor of your engagement?"

"Another time," Blake answered. "Thanks, Telsham." Anger surged through Blake, singeing his veins. He clamped his jaw shut, struggling to maintain his composure as he left the club and hailed a cab that would take him home.

꧁꧂

"PLEASE INFORM MISS Fairfax and Lady Wethering that I wish to see them in my study immediately," Blake announced as soon as Perryman opened the front door.

"I believe Miss Fairfax is engaged in bathing, sir. She asked that hot water be brought up less than a quarter of an hour ago," Perryman replied.

"Very well," Blake said. "Please inform Lady Wethering that I wish to see her immediately and I wish to see Miss Fairfax as soon as she's completed her toilette."

"Very good, sir," Perryman answered.

"Was this your idea?" Blake waved a rolled-up newspaper in the air as his aunt breezed into his study in a flurry of satin and a cloud of perfume, her black malaaca cane clutched tightly in her hand. "Or hers?"

"Hello, dear boy, it's lovely to see you, too," she chided, sidling up to him and presenting her freshly powdered cheek for him to kiss. "Will you be joining us for dinner tonight, dear boy, or will you be dining out again?"

Blake dutifully kissed his aunt's cheek, but he refused to allow her to sidetrack him. He took her by the shoulder and gently turned her, so she could see his face and repeated his question, scowling to make certain she understood he meant business. "I asked you a question, Aunt Delia."

"What question was that, dear boy?"

Blake slapped the rolled newspaper against his thigh, then unrolled it, opened it to the announcement of his engagement, and held it up for his aunt to read. "Are you responsible for this bit of fiction or should the credit go to my alleged fiancée?"

Lady Wethering drew herself up to her full height and huffed. "I took the liberty of announcing your betrothal." She narrowed her gaze at him. "After you took a few too many liberties with Miss Fairfax's person."

Blake raised an eyebrow at that. "Cristina told you that?"

"My dear boy, she didn't have to," Lady Wethering informed him. "My eyes are aged, but they still work well enough. I spend every morning regaling Cristina with reminisces of you. She can't get enough, learn enough about you," she told him. "You've been gone so often of late and she misses you terribly."

Blake swallowed the lump in his throat and attempted to brazen it out. "That's understandable. She's a guest in my home and I've been a terrible host."

His aunt snorted. "She doesn't miss you the way a houseguest misses her host. She misses you the way a woman misses her lover. Don't play me for an old fool, dear boy. Don't insult my intelligence. Miss Fairfax isn't an innocent any longer. She hasn't been innocent since the trip to the theater." She pinned Blake with her gaze. "I gave you room to woo the girl, to romance her. I didn't give you carte blanche to seduce her."

He was angry, but he had the grace to blush as his aunt voiced her opinion.

"Since you saw fit to bed her without benefit of vows or even a promise of such, I saw fit to remind you of your duty as a gentleman. You *will* do right by her."

"I appreciate your concern for Cristina's reputation, Aunt, but I invited you to become part of my household in order to chaperon her, not to act as my conscience."

"You invited me into your household to prevent gossip and scandal and that's exactly what I intend to do."

"What gossip? What scandal?" Blake asked. "I've yet to hear a whisper of scandal. With the exception of Nigel Jameson, no one knows Cristina is here."

"You as much as told the Prince of Wales that Miss Fairfax was staying with you."

"Staying with you," Blake corrected. "And with my parents in the country. No one suspected anything until this hit the paper."

"Surely you aren't that naive?" Lady Wethering demanded. "What about Patricia Fairfax's little wager and her announcement at Lord Strathemore's midnight soiree?"

"How did—"

"I'm a member of society. I have friends and acquaintances who gossip. The ton has been buzzing about it since it happened. They've been wondering if anyone had taken Patricia Fairfax up on her offer for weeks now and your escorting us to the theater and presenting us to the Prince of Wales·did more to increase the speculation than to end it."

"Bloody hell." He ran his fingers through his hair in a show of frustration. "I've been so busy, I haven't had time to pay attention to the gossip."

"I have," Lady Wethering assured him. "That's why I took it upon myself to look out for your interests."

"You were premature, Aunt." He dropped the newspaper on the desk and began to pace. "You made a public announcement, and true or not, I'll be held legally liable. Now, everyone will think I bought her, that I took Patricia Fairfax up on her offer."

"Did you?"

"No." He shot his aunt a fierce look. "I didn't. But that's not going to matter to London society."

"Have you spoken to Cristina? Have you expressed your intentions?"

"No," he admitted.

"She doesn't know how you feel about her?"

"How could she?" Blake asked, plunging his fingers through his hair once again. "When I don't know how I feel? Or what I feel? Or why I should feel whatever it is about her? All I know is that you made a public announcement that's left me with no choice but to offer her marriage. I haven't spoken to her or her father and already I find myself in an untenable position once again." He turned on his heel. "How could you have done this without speaking to me first?"

"I did what needed to be done when it needed to be done. People talk, dear boy. Servants talk. You don't have the luxury of unlimited time. And although you've anticipated your vows, this way you've done the honorable thing by announcing your betrothal." She smiled at Blake. "Cristina is a lovely girl. You could do far worse. And you know you had to get married some time."

"I've been married. I know what a disaster it can be. And I've no wish to live through that again."

"Meredith has been dead for a while."

"Six years," Blake said. "And even that isn't long enough to make the idea of remarriage palatable to me."

Lady Wethering sucked in a breath. She'd suspected that her nephew had been unhappily married, but she'd hadn't known how unhappy until she heard the contempt in his voice. "I had no idea."

Blake shook his head. "My marriage was hell. And now—" He broke off. "I'm fond of Cristina. I didn't expect to be drawn to her in a physical way and I certainly didn't intend to . . ." He stopped his furious pacing and stood in front of his aunt. "You made a public announcement of our betrothal. I won't dispute it and I'll make sure that no one else does. I'll buy her a betrothal ring and pay for the wedding of the season if that's what she wants, but . . ." He turned his back on his aunt and toyed with a paperweight on his desk.

"But what, dear boy?" Lady Wethering moved closer to her nephew and placed her gnarled, beringed hand on Blake's shoulder.

He took so long to reply that Lady Wethering wasn't sure he'd heard her. "I made a mistake. I've been feeling sorry for poor Ainsford and look at me. At least Ainsford isn't going to have to face his mistake across a breakfast table every morning for the rest of his life."

"Then you needn't worry, my lord," Cristina replied from the doorway, "because I don't expect you to marry me or share my breakfast table."

The shocked expression on his face when he saw her spoke volumes.

She'd just assured him that she didn't expect anything from him. But she had. She'd missed him so much that her heart seemed to leap at the sight of him. And it shattered when she'd overheard him. Cristina drew her pride around her like protective shell. "I apologize for interrupting your conversation, but Perryman told Leah you wanted to see me as soon as I completed my bath."

"I can explain."

"You don't want to marry me," she said softly. "There's nothing else to explain."

"I think there is." He walked over to her, took her by the hand and led her into the study. "Something's happened. Something you should know."

"I already know, my lord. I saw this morning's paper." She turned to Lady Wethering. "You sent it?"

Lady Wethering nodded. "I did what I thought was best for both of you. I'm sorry," she said. "I seem to have meddled where I shouldn't have." She glanced at Blake. "You've much to discuss. I'll leave you two alone."

"No," Cristina nearly panicked. "Please stay."

Blake frowned, but nodded to show he was willing to allow his aunt to stay. "I'm sorry you overheard that, Cristina."

"Well"—she tried to sound bright and cheerful—"you know what they say about eavesdroppers. They never hear anything good about themselves." Unshed tears sparkled in her eyes.

"I apologize just the same," he said. "I was angry and speaking out of turn. I never meant for you to hear that."

"Yes, well, I suppose it's best that I did. Otherwise it would be an awkward way to start a marriage," Cristina told him. "Knowing that your husband dreaded the thought of facing you at breakfast every day for the rest of your lives. But you won't have to worry about that, my lord, since there isn't going to be a wedding." Cristina wore her pride like a cloak against the rain. "I knew when I read the notice that there had to have been some mistake because you'd never even hinted at the possibility of a marriage between us." Say it, Cristina silently begged, tell me the announcement wasn't your aunt's doing. Tell me you didn't mean what you said. Tell me you want to marry me. Tell me you want a family.

Blake wearily ran his fingers through his hair and rubbed at the pain in the bridge of his nose. "I owe you an explanation."

Cristina could see the tired lines around the corners of his mouth and her heart went out to him. She wanted to hold him and to kiss away those tired lines. She wanted to love him and have her love returned. She didn't want to hear him explain why that was impossible. She held up her hand. "Please," she said a little shakily, "I don't think I could stand it."

"I must," he told her. "I was hoping to have some time off when Rudolf leaves—time we could spend together—but I'm leaving for Balmoral in the morning and I don't know when I'll be able to return to London."

"It makes no difference to me," Cristina told him softly. "I won't be here when you return."

Blake froze in his tracks as if she had struck him. He stared at her for an eternity before he recovered his power of speech. "What do you mean you won't be here? Where do you intend to go?"

Cristina's stomach twisted in agony but she looked him in the eye without flinching. "I don't think that's your concern any longer."

"I can't allow you to leave," Blake said. "I'm responsible for you."

"Do you want to marry me?"

"What I want doesn't matter," Blake answered. "Nor what you want. The fact is that we are going to be married at the end of the season. We can work out the details when I return from Balmoral." He reached out and gently trailed his index finger against her cheek. "I knew better than to compromise an innocent. I knew the price I'd have to pay."

"And marriage to me is too high a price."

"Not marriage to you, Cristina," he said, trying to soften the blow. "Marriage to anyone. I was married once before."

"I heard," Cristina informed him. "To Meredith."

"Yes," he admitted. "And it's not something I care to repeat or recall."

"What about children?" she asked.

"I don't have any," he said. "There was a time I thought I wanted an heir, but now . . ." He shrugged his shoulders. "Now I'm not so sure."

"At least you're honest," Cristina said. Brutally, painfully honest.

"It's only fair that you should know the truth," Blake said. "Young women usually have romantic notions about love and marriage. But it's been my experience that love and marriage really don't have much in common. You should know where you stand before we're married."

"I have a fair idea," Cristina said. "I'm to be your penance for sinning. And in exchange for allowing you to do penance, I get a gold band and a title."

Blake shook his head and managed a wry half-smile. "Marriage is the penance, Cristina. Not you. You're the temptation I should have avoided."

"You were right, my lord." The tears that had sparkled in her eyes, slowly rolled down her face. "The price is too high."

"I don't understand."

"I'm refusing your offer," she said. "I'm crying off. I've seen the kind of marriage you're proposing and I want no part of it. You're absolved of your responsibility. You're free."

"Don't be ridiculous, Cristina. There could be consequences."

"There are always consequences," she said sadly.

"I meant a child."

"Not this time," she said.

The look of relief on his face pierced her heart like an arrow. "I never meant to hurt you," he said.

"I'm young," she told him. "I'll survive." She wanted to wound him, to draw blood, but she hadn't realized it would feel as if she were ripping her heart from her breast. "I was the belle of the ball, remember? I'm sure I'll find someone who won't object to facing me across a breakfast table."

Blake winced. "Be careful who you choose. Most men dislike buying damaged goods." He was all cynic again. The Blake Ashford Cristina had held in her arms was gone and the stranger in his place was cold and indifferent—his face an unreadable mask. "And once he knows, he won't give you his heart and promise happily ever after."

"Neither did you," she whispered, "when I wasn't damaged goods." Her voice broke.

"Touché," he replied softly.

Cristina took a moment to compose herself. She didn't look at him or triumphantly attempt to measure the amount of damage she'd inflicted. She couldn't. It hurt too much. "But as long as he's young and exciting and not some staid middle-aged diplomat who cares more for his job than he does for me, I don't think I'll have to worry."

"Spoken like a true courtesan, Cristina. You learn very fast." Blake laughed a short, mirthless laugh. "Thank you for reminding me of the facts of life in the nick of time."

Cristina sucked in a breath. "I only just learned them myself."

"Then we were both saved in the nick of time."

"You won't try to keep me from leaving?"

"Not this time, Cristina." He spoke with the voice of a patronizing uncle. "Maybe I'm feeling my age, but I think I've altered the course of your life too many times already. I don't think I have any more rescues left in me. I don't think I could manage to wrest you from anyone else's clutches. Luckily Rudolf never puts up too much of a fight. And I would be the last person to cast stones at you for choosing to leave."

"Because you're so *fond* of me?" Cristina asked. Blake believed she was running to Rudolf for help and protection and she let him believe it. She should tell him about her father. But it was better for him and easier for her if he believed the worst.

"It doesn't matter anymore, does it? I hope you find whatever it is you're seeking, but I don't think you'll find it with Rudolf. I admit he's a better catch than a middle-aged diplomat like myself, but he'll use you. He isn't a one-woman man any more than I am." Blake's voice had grown colder and harder as he distanced himself from her, and the patronizing note was gone. He sounded hurt and disillusioned. "You probably think there's something special about being Rudolf's mistress, but there isn't. One bed is very much like another—

even if it is located in a palace. The rank and the title may be different, but courtesan or mistress or whore are really one and the same. He'll expect you to decorate his bed. And you won't have a choice, Cris, because this time, you really will be bought and paid for.'' He turned away, dismissing her. ''Now, if you will excuse me, I think I'll get ready for dinner. If you want to join me, I'll see you in the dining room— otherwise, good-bye, Cristina.'' He walked away, leaving her standing in his study, choking back the sobs.

SHE DIDN'T APPEAR at dinner, nor did she make her way downstairs for breakfast the following morning.

''He's gone.''

Cristina looked up from the stack of undergarments she was helping Leah pack to find Lady Wethering standing in the doorway. ''May I come in?''

''Of course.'' Cristina reached up and self-consciously smoothed the tendrils of hair escaping from her chignon into place, then rubbed at the creases in her gown. It was the same one she'd worn the night before, the one she'd cried herself to sleep in.

''You look fine,'' Lady Wethering assured her.

Her eyes and nose were red and swollen from crying all night and the cold compresses she'd tried to rid herself of the terrible morning-after headache hadn't made the slightest difference. She looked like hell and they both knew it. But Cristina appreciated the fact that Lady Wethering had tried to reassure her that her looks hadn't vanished with her shattered dreams.

''My dear child, I'm so sorry. This is all my fault.'' Cristina noticed that Blake's aunt seemed older and more frail. Her powdered face showed new lines and she leaned heavily on her malacca cane. ''I should never have sent that announcement. He wasn't supposed to react so strongly or in such a negative manner. But then, I didn't know about . . .'' She broke off. ''And I never dreamed he'd be so vexed with me.

Or with you.'' She walked over to the bed and clasped Cristina to her ample bosom. ''Oh, my dear, dear child, what's to become of you? Where will you go? Surely you aren't contemplating going back your mother?''

Cristina shook her head. ''I thought I might stay with you,'' she said. ''In your town house.''

Lady Wethering was momentarily overjoyed—until reason reasserted itself. ''Oh, Cristina, I would be most happy to have you live with me, but you see I've only a small portion from my late husband's estate. Only enough to keep the town house staffed. The rest of my income comes from the daughter's portion my father left. It's quite sufficient. More than sufficient, but it's administered by my brother, the marquess of Everleigh. I can't offer you refuge in a household whose bills are paid by Blake's father. If Everleigh and Cecilia found out I sheltered you after you refused Blake's offer of marriage, they would never forgive me.''

Cristina's knees suddenly became too weak to support her weight. Gripping the surface of the dressing table, she gracefully sank down onto the matching stool. She'd counted on Lady Wethering's support, counted on her help. Cristina bit her bottom lip, carefully considering her options. She could go to Nigel Jameson for help, but it seemed wrong, somehow, to force the doctor to choose between his loyalty to his patient and his lifelong friendship with Blake. She shook her head. No, she couldn't go to Nigel. She'd would have to think of another way. She could go to her father if she could find him. But that prospect suddenly seemed more daunting than facing Blake again. She hadn't seen her father in years and to suddenly show up on his doorstep with the secret she was carrying . . . How much welcome would he extend to a disgraced daughter? Could she count on his love? He'd left her behind once before. Would he abandon her again? She shuddered at the thought, then felt a soft touch on her shoulder and looked up to find concern mirrored on Lady Wethering's face.

''I wouldn't normally consider it, but there is something I can do to help you,'' the older woman said. ''Freshen up and change your gown. You're going with me on my morning calls."

"I can't go with you. I'm not supposed to be seen."

"Wear a veil. No one will be able to tell who you are in the carriage and we're only going as far as my house."

"All right."

Lady Wethering patted her cheek. "That's a good girl. Now don't worry, everything is going to be all right. I'll see that you're taken care of."

THEY BARELY HAD time to arrive and settle down to refreshments in the parlor of Lady Wethering's town house when the front doorbell rang. The butler answered the door, then showed the visitor into the parlor. Lady Wethering recognized her guest, then sank into a deep curtsey. Cristina followed suit.

"A pleasure to see you again, Miss Fairfax." Crown Prince Rudolf bent low over Cristina's hand.

"Thank you, Your Royal Highness." Her voice quivered with tension and her stomach lurched at the sight of him.

"I was surprised to get your note, Lady Wethering." He nodded toward the older woman.

"Thank you for coming, Your Highness."

"I made a brief trip to Ireland. Your note was waiting when I returned last evening. I was under the impression Miss Fairfax was staying in the country with relatives."

"She was staying with me," Lady Wethering said. "I asked for this private meeting so that Miss Fairfax might have an opportunity to speak with you on an urgent matter and with your permission, Your Highness, I'll retire and allow you to speak privately."

Rudolf nodded and Lady Wethering curtseyed once again and exited the room. "Have you been with Lady Wethering in London all this time?" he asked.

"Yes," she answered.

"And now you suddenly want to see me."

"Yes."

Rudolf smiled. "If you had stayed in my bed that night in Marlborough House instead of creeping out of my room like a thief in the night, you would have seen a great deal more of me. And I would have seen a great deal more of you."

Cristina was surprised. Had he discovered what had happened that night at Marlborough House? Did he know she had climbed out the third-story window on a rope made from the Prince of Wales's bed linens? "I apologize for that, Your Highness, but I couldn't stay and face you in the daylight. Not after . . ."

"If the memory of the night with me is so shameful, why ask for this meeting?" Prince Rudolf's eyes were glacial, his voice clipped and regal, the German-accented English more pronounced. He was every inch a Hapsburg prince.

"Because I'm going to have a baby." The words were out before Cristina could stop them.

"Hmm." Rudolf was thoughtful. Ladies of his father's court had tried this trick on him since he was fifteen years old and he was no novice to accusations of paternity. Someone was always trying to use him for their own gain. "Am I to offer congratulations or condolences?"

"Congratulations," she answered. "And condolences because I'm an unmarried woman in love with a man whose reputation and career will be ruined if word of my disgrace gets out."

"I saw the notice in *The Times*," Rudolf said. "And I believe Lord Lawrence is a widower. What is the difficulty? Why are you here?"

"He doesn't want to marry me. He doesn't want to marry anyone. He believes marriage is the price he must pay for compromising an innocent. And I can't accept a marriage knowing that he sees it as a form of punishment. I thought he . . ." She bowed her head and covered her face with her hands.

"Loved you?" Rudolf smiled ruefully.

She jerked her face out of her hands and pinned Rudolf with her gaze. "Please help me. Help us."

"I'm sorry, Miss Fairfax, but I cannot offer you marriage."

"I don't expect marriage from you. I know that's impossible, but I can't remain in London. I need someplace to go until after . . ." she let her words trail off. Cristina closed her eyes, squeezing them shut to halt the flow of her brimming tears. She was angry at herself for using the crown prince this way, but she was fighting to protect herself, and Blake, and their unborn child.

The effect of her tears on Rudolf was startling. His eyes warmed and his voice softened. "I see." He reached out and caressed her face with the palm of his hand.

Cristina's relief was overwhelming. Her knees buckled beneath her and she would have fallen to the floor if Rudolf hadn't reached out to steady her. Cristina took a deep breath, steadied herself, and faced him. He saw too much. It frightened her and she tried to retreat. "I'm very sorry, Your Royal Highness. I shouldn't have bothered you. This is my problem after all, and I shouldn't have asked you to come here. Thank you for your time." She stiffened her spine and held out her hand.

"Don't be so hasty, Miss Fairfax." Rudolf patted her shoulder awkwardly, trying to offer comfort. "Of course you should have come to me. It takes two people to make a child and as a gentlemen, I can't allow you to go through this ordeal alone." Rudolf was caught in a dilemma. He knew the girl had been a virgin when he'd bought her because her mother had assured him of the fact, but in truth, beyond the fact that he had found the lovely red-haired Miss Fairfax in his bed at Marlborough House, he could not remember a single detail about that evening. But he had passed the night with her and he had to take that into consideration. "I may be responsible."

Cristina stared at him. He couldn't be responsible for her condition. She and Blake were responsible. But for some unknown reason, the crown prince seemed to think . . . She had to set him straight. "But Your Highness, I didn't mean to imply that you were to be held responsible for my condition. It's just that—"

Rudolf smiled at her. "Don't worry, Miss Fairfax. I'm a man of my word. I'll help you. I didn't expect this to happen. I assumed you knew how to protect yourself. Your mother assured me she would explain the necessary details."

The world seemed to spin on its axis as Cristina fought to maintain her balance. She heard Blake repeating those hateful words: *I think I've altered the course of your life too many times already. I don't think I have any more rescues left in me. I don't think I could manage to wrest you from anyone else's clutches. Luckily Rudolf never puts up too much of a fight.* "You spoke to my mother about me?"

"Of course I did," he said. "That's how you came to be in my bed at Marlborough House. That's the way things are done—the way romantic alliances are formed. I sent a gift—a necklace—to show my intention toward you. Expensive gifts are often used to seal the bargain. I thought you understood. After all, you accepted my gift."

Cristina's sank down onto a sofa. It hadn't been Blake, but the crown prince. Blake hadn't bargained with her mother. He hadn't bought her. He'd rescued her. Cristina began to cry in earnest. "I didn't accept your gift. My mother did. I knew nothing about it until it was too late." She shook her head. She had wrongly accused Blake of a despicable act, accused him of sending the necklace as payment for her and keeping it and all the time he had been innocent. He had known about Rudolf's bargain with her mother. Somehow, Blake had known. And never said a word—never defended himself against her accusations, never even hinted that she was mistaken. In his own way, Blake had been protecting her from the truth, accepting the blame for something he hadn't done to keep her from suffering more pain and humiliation at her mother's hands. Cristina took a deep, steadying breath. And what had Blake gotten for his trouble? Except for the one extraordinary night and morning they had spent making love—making the child she carried—she had brought Blake nothing but trouble and the very real threat of a career-destroying scandal. Now she would do what she had to do to protect him.

Rudolf was stunned. It was a shock for him to discover that she hadn't wanted to become his mistress; that her refusal the night of the ball hadn't been a coy invitation for him to persuade her. "If what you say is true, why did you come to my room? Why didn't you refuse?"

"I did refuse," Cristina replied bitterly. "I refused to dress and my mother sent her bodyguard in to persuade me. I refused to leave my room and she had him carry me to the front door where your coach collected me. I even tried to drink myself into a stupor and to escape. I wasn't given a choice."

Cristina's confession was another unpleasant shock for Rudolf. He had often negotiated with the relatives of young women, but he had never encountered this situation. He had never bargained for an unwilling woman. Usually his wealth and position in society were enough to persuade any reluctant girl. A prince's favor could open many doors for girls who might not have other means of advancing in society. But Rudolf suddenly realized the other side of the coin was also true. A prince's favor could also close doors to young women who were already society belles. While married women might advance in the stratum by having an affair with a prince, an unmarried girl fell from grace and swiftly landed in the nether region of a demimondaine. Not accepted in conventional society, yet far above a common prostitute. He realized that a girl in Cristina's position really had no choice. To refuse him meant disgrace and punishment in her mother's eyes and to accept him meant disgrace in society's eyes. And society, especially English society, could be very unforgiving. And when he tired of her, she had no choice but to become some other man's mistress.

"My God." Rudolf swore in German and muttered something to himself before he remembered Cristina's presence and switched to English. "You must think I'm a monster who habitually preys on unsuspecting virgins. It isn't that way, but in this case, I feel responsible for what has happened to you because I failed to consider that your mother might force her ambitions on you. I'm sorry for what cannot be undone. But I still want you for my mistress, Miss Fairfax, and I will accept responsibility for you and your child in order to have you.''

She looked up at the crown prince. ''You're not the father of my child, Your Highness, but I need a place to stay until my baby is born. I need protection. No gentleman will have me for a wife when I've borne another man's child. I don't want to be your mistress. I want only to go with you to Vienna until the baby is born. It will be impossible for me to remain in England. I need to go far away, someplace where I won't be recognized.'' She stated her terms in a businesslike manner. ''Hapsburg princes are expected to have illegitimate children, but not men like Lord Lawrence.''

''He doesn't know.'' Rudolf whistled beneath his breath. ''You haven't told him.''

''I don't intend to tell him,'' she said. ''And if you're his friend, you won't tell him, either. He already dreads the thought of facing me over the breakfast table every morning knowing he was forced, by convention, into a marriage he didn't want. How do you think he'd react if he knew about the baby?''

''He'd marry you.''

''Yes, he'd marry me to claim his son and heir and he'd suffer the gossip and the whispering when people began counting the days until the birth on their fingers. He'd see me on a daily basis and he'd be miserable. We'd all be miserable.''

''Queen Victoria's government is reeling from the Ainsford scandal. You're trying to protect him. Protect his career,'' he said.

''I'm protecting myself,'' Cristina corrected him. ''I'm protecting my child from growing up in a household with parents who dread the sight of one another.''

Rudolf smiled. For all her protestations of innocence, Cristina Fairfax could be tough when she chose to be. It wouldn't do to underestimate her. ''What sort of arrangement did you have in mind?''

''I want your protection and support until I'm able to support myself.''

"And what shall I get in return?" he asked. "I have already paid for your maidenhead. I paid with a necklace fit for a queen and with my signature on several letters of introduction throughout the Continent."

"You paid my mother, not me," Cristina informed him. "I have neither the necklace nor the letters of introduction." She forced herself to be firm. As much as she disliked the idea, Cristina realized that she must bargain for her future.

"Nevertheless, your guardian was well paid for you." Prince Rudolf was as implacable as Cristina. "If I take you to Vienna, you go as my mistress. That is my only condition."

"But, you can't ask that," Cristina sputtered angrily. "You said you would help me."

"And I will," he told her. "As long as you remain my mistress."

"You can't possibly want someone who doesn't return your affections."

"I'm not interested in your affections," Rudolf reminded her. "I am only interested in having your delectable body for my own."

Cristina stared at him. "But . . ."

"Those are my terms, *liebchen*. Do you come with me to Vienna or do you stay?"

"I'll come," Cristina capitulated. "But I won't sleep with you. I'll fight you if you even try to come to my bed," she warned.

"The nights in Vienna can get very lonely, especially for a young woman. I'm a crown prince." He smiled at her. "I'm accustomed to waiting for my heart's desire. I have patience. I know how to wait. Sooner or later, you will come to me willingly."

"Forever is a very long time, Your Royal Highness."

"I'll take my chances, *liebchen*. We are scheduled to leave in two days' time. Be ready." He pulled her up from the sofa and planted a kiss on her tightly closed mouth. "I will send a carriage for you here."

Cristina nodded.

Rudolf laughed. "Cheer up, *fraulein*, our relationship may

not be as horrible as you imagine. You may even learn to like me a little when you see all the things I am willing to do for you.'' He executed a perfect bow, then clicked his heels together in the Austrian military fashion and left her standing, amazed, in the parlor of Lady Wethering's town house.

Part Two

There is a smile of love,
And there is a smile of deceit,
And there is a smile of smiles
In which these two smiles meet.

—WILLIAM BLAKE 1757–1827

Sixteen

CRISTINA MADE HER way down the steps of her small house situated in the heart of Old Vienna. She stepped onto the walkway and began her daily stroll past St. Stephen's Cathedral, down the street several blocks and around the corner where numerous coffeehouses and pastry shops filled the morning air with the mouthwatering aroma of chocolate.

The city of Vienna fascinated her. It was a charming mixture of old and new that enthralled her. From the modern apartment buildings and government offices with their plaster edifices located on the fashionable Ringstrasse—which was currently under construction—to the ancient shops and coffeehouses in the older part of the city, Cristina delighted in discovering Vienna. It was a city where the majority of the inhabitants walked and Cristina eagerly adopted the tradition, strolling along at a leisurely pace. She followed the same path every morning, faithfully trailed by Leah, often stopping to chat with the *hausfraus* and shopkeepers in her halting and often incorrect schoolgirl German. She enjoyed the people and the pace of Vienna and the relatively peaceful existence she led. She needed the calm after the tumultuous weeks spent with Blake. She needed peace, an outward peace even if the inward peace eluded her. Her life in Vienna could be perfect if only she could learn to care for the crown prince—if only she could learn to feel something other than amicable companionship for Rudolf. No, it couldn't be perfect, she brutally reminded herself, not unless the crown prince was magically transformed into Blake Ashford, the ninth earl of Lawrence.

It was so frustrating. She had left London determined to forget Blake and arrived in Vienna only to admit to herself that forgetting him was impossible. She missed him terribly and she desired him more than ever, even though she knew he was thousands of miles away from her and that he hated her. She vividly recalled every detail of Lawrence House and its inhabitants and every moment she had spent with its arrogant, stubborn owner became a cherished memory to warm and comfort her during the long, lonely nights in Vienna.

There was so much she wanted to share with Blake; so many new sights to see and anecdotes to exchange, and then there was the ever-increasing size of her abdomen. She wanted desperately to share that with him. He was the father of her child and he didn't even know it. A part of her longed to tell him. But she was afraid. Afraid that his guilt would prompt him to propose marriage, and Cristina didn't want him on those terms.

She reminded herself that she was protecting the baby and saving Blake from political suicide—that it was better for the three of them if Blake never learned the truth. But it hurt to keep the secret—hurt to drive him away—so much more than she had ever dreamed.

And then there was Rudolf. He had tried repeatedly to persuade Cristina into his bed in the months since their arrival in Vienna, but Cristina couldn't be persuaded—couldn't be tempted. Her longing was for Blake, and the crown prince was a very poor substitute. Cristina was overwhelmed with shame and embarrassment each time she remembered how Rudolf had tried to take her in his arms and caress her on the first night of the journey to Vienna. She had instinctively recoiled. The crown prince had been very good to her in his way—generous and thoughtful. But Cristina could not make herself respond to him, no matter how hard she tried. She felt as if she was betraying her husband and in her heart she knew it was true. So she had been stiff and unresponsive to Rudolf and he had released her instantly, his angry words echoing in her ears.

"We made a bargain. Is this the way you intend to fulfill your part of it?"

Cristina had cringed at the angry question. "I am trying, Your Highness."

"Trying, Cristina? What is it you are trying to do?"

"I am trying to fulfill my part of the bargain," Cristina had blurted out, desperately ashamed of herself. "I wish I could respond to you, but I can't." She hung her head, knowing her words injured Rudolf's pride, knowing it hurt him to know she couldn't return his desire, but helpless to do anything except reply honestly.

Rudolf felt a surge of pity for her in spite of his wounded pride. "You are a passionate woman, Cristina. You will awaken one day and respond." His fingers grazed the underside of her jaw. "I can wait. I won't try to force or cajole you. I will be patient. You will come to me when the time is right."

He had left her then with a soft kiss on her cheek, and Cristina had been both relieved and depressed by his absence. She didn't want to share his bed, but she did enjoy his company. He could be quite charming and entertaining when he chose. Without Rudolf to entertain her, and with only Leah for company, Cristina's days became monotonous, her elegant house little more than a gilded cage. She heard, through Leah, that Rudolf was amusing himself with one of the numerous *horizontales* in the city and Cristina was awash with relief. He had found someone else to claim his attention, someone else to entertain him during the long, lonely nights. Loneliness plagued her. She longed for Blake and at the same time she missed Rudolf's companionship, his amusing tales of the people at his father's court, their serious political debates and chess matches and the way his warm, blue eyes sparkled with humor at her blunders as she mangled the German tongue. She looked forward to his infrequent visits and despite her best intentions to hate him, Cristina found herself liking the crown prince and enjoying the time he spent with her. She had even begun to think of him as a friend.

The idea that she was subtly being courted by the heir to the Austro-Hungarian Empire never occurred to her. Cristina failed to recognize the fact that Rudolf was exercising his considerable charm and showing an abundant amount of restraint.

He still desired her. His body quickened at the sight of her, but he spoke the truth when he told her he could wait until she no longer thought of him as the enemy. Rudolf was convinced that with enough time and charm he could win her over. Time was his ally. Given enough time, Cristina would forget the dreadful bargain he had made with her mother and remember only his charm and generosity and the companionship they shared. She could learn to love him. He would see to it.

Cristina breathed deeply of the morning air laced with the pungent scent of coffee and chocolate. She paused for a moment before taking a seat at one of the outdoor tables in front of a coffeehouse. Leah shook her head in disapproval, but she joined Cristina at the table anyway.

A stiffly uniformed waiter sprang forward to greet them and watched in utter fascination as Cristina lifted the heavy black veil Rudolf insisted she wear on her walks.

The waiter bowed before her and returned minutes later with a tray of mouthwatering pastries and two cups of steaming Viennese coffee. Cristina smiled her thanks and slowly sipped her coffee as she deliberated on the problems ahead of her.

It was important to plan carefully for the future. Except for Leah, she was alone in Vienna. The idea frightened her a little, but she had made the city her destiny and she must find a way to survive in it once her child was born. She had rejected the idea of becoming Rudolf's mistress, but now she understood why he had sounded so confident back in London.

Women had even less freedom in Vienna under Franz Josef than in London under Victoria. Cristina had realized very soon after her arrival that she would never be able to gain respectable employment. No Viennese would hire her to work in their coffeehouses or beer gardens or shops when there were so many unfortunate Hapsburg subjects flocking to Vienna seeking work. And who would hire a governess as young and attractive as she to live with their family under their roof, even if she could keep the birth of her child a secret? Rudolf had known from the beginning that Cristina would eventually become his mistress if she accompanied him, because in Vienna, no other option was available to her.

Most of Vienna already thought of her as a lady of the veil, the crown prince's mistress. It seemed certain that the rumors would become fact. She had been labeled by Viennese society. She was a mistress. Rudolf's or someone else's. It didn't matter that it wasn't the truth or that her heart was engaged elsewhere. She wasn't expected to love her protector. Love wasn't the primary concern. He was a crown prince and it was her duty to serve him. There were worse protectors than the young, attractive heir to the empire and a young, foreigner was lucky to catch his eye.

Cristina brought the coffee cup to her lips, surprised to find the liquid was cold. She had been so engrossed in her thoughts, she had lost all track of time. She tried not to think of London, but sometimes . . . If only she had told him. If only she had stayed. If only he had told her he loved her. If she continued to dwell on what might have been, she was sure to go out of her mind. She had to go forward. She couldn't go back. A longing sigh escaped her lips and she turned to see if Leah or anyone nearby had noticed. Leah was busy with thoughts of her own, but Cristina turned her head and looked directly into the clear, gray gaze of a man several tables down and knew he was aware of her slightest movement.

His malevolent stare chilled her to the core.

She tore her gaze away from his, quickly lowered her veil, and began fumbling with her belongings. She plucked up enough courage to glance back at him and met his thin, knowing smile. He stood up, nodded in her direction, paid his bill, and vanished in the blink of an eye.

He disappeared so suddenly, Cristina began to wonder if she had imagined him and the exchange that had taken place.

She rose from her chair and placed a few coins beside her plate. "Leah, I'm ready. Let's go." Cristina pulled on her fur-lined cape and rebuttoned her gloves.

Leah followed suit and they left the cafe tables and turned back the way they had come. Fear prickled at the tiny hairs at the back of Cristina's neck and ran unchecked through her body, forcing her to walk faster, driving her on like a living thing, until her breathing became so ragged she was forced to stop and rest. They leaned against the brick wall of a Jewish moneylender's shop, panting for breath.

"What's the great hurry?" Leah asked, "You were practically runnin' down the street."

Cristina glanced warily around and saw him across the street, following them at a discreet distance. "We are being followed."

Leah looked around, not seeing anything out of the ordinary. "Of course we're bein' followed."

Cristina was shocked by her bald statement. "I don't understand. Why?"

"This ain't London, missy," Leah explained. "Here the secret police follow the crown prince's every step. It seems likely to me that they follow his lady friends around, too. Especially foreign lady friends."

Cristina decided Leah was probably right. She was a stranger to Vienna and if the Emperor Franz Josef had his secret police spy on his own son, he wouldn't think anything of having the police spy on his son's friends. The man was probably secret police and totally harmless.

Nevertheless, Cristina breathed a sigh of relief when she and Leah reached the safety and privacy of the house. She collapsed on a chair as soon as she reached her sitting room.

"You need to change. You're soaked through."

"I'm fine, Leah, don't fuss."

"I've got eyes in my head an' I can see for myself." Leah

took Cristina's damp cape and draped it over a chair near the fire. ''I don't think you should be traipsin' about in the mornin' air. The damp and chill ain't good for you or the babe.''

''I'm fine, Leah. Don't fuss. Don't you think I know what's best for my baby?'' Cristina's fatigue and the fright the man in the cafe had given her made her reply sharper than she intended.

''No, I don't,'' Leah informed her bluntly. ''If you really knew what was best for you and this child, you would've stayed with its father.''

''And what about Lord Lawrence?'' Cristina's voice rose alarmingly.

''He's a grown man and well able to take care of himself.'' Leah clamped her lips shut and faced her headstrong mistress with a disapproving stare.

''Leah, I don't want to discuss Lord Lawrence. As far as the world and the baby are concerned, Crown Prince Rudolf will be its father,'' Cristina said, shakily.

''I know why you came here. I understand that you want to avoid havin' any scandal attached to Lord Lawrence's good name, but darlin', you should have told him the truth and let him help you decide what to do. You shouldn't have taken this all upon yourself.''

''But, Leah . . .''

''I know you plan to pass the baby off as Prince Rudolf's so it can have the things we couldn't give it. But you ain't bein' fair to yourself, Lord Lawrence, or your child. Cristina, my girl, no good can come from livin' a lie.''

''But Leah,'' Cristina's voice echoed dully in her ears, ''he never said he loved me. And I was afraid that a scandal and this''—she rubbed her expanding tummy—''I was afraid. I was afraid he would hate me for trapping him into a marriage he doesn't want. I was afraid he would hate me when he found out. I couldn't stay. I had to leave. Oh, God, what have I done?'' Her voice thickened and she covered her face with her hands and released a flood of anguished tears. She was unhappy and forced to live a lie of her own making because she had been too afraid to take a risk on love.

~~~⌒~~~

"HAVE YOU LOST your mind?" It was late and Lawrence House was quiet except for the crackling of the fire in the library grate and the escalating argument between the two men sitting in the cozy leather chairs sipping coffee laced with brandy. Blake was being obstinate and Nigel was finding it increasingly difficult to understand his best friend. The same question had been on his lips once too often during the past months.

"No, I haven't lost my mind," Blake informed him, raking his fingers through his hair in a gesture of irritability.

Nigel remained unimpressed by Blake's reply or his obvious show of irritation. "But Blake, you're turning down the chance of a lifetime. The queen asked for you personally."

"I don't want the post in Vienna and the title, however glorified, is only temporary. I'm tired of the Foreign Office and I'm tired of Franz Josef's stifling court. It's time I settled down to my own business interests and let the queen find someone else to tend to hers."

"Blake, you must reconsider. Think of all you'll lose if you turn her down. Think of your future."

"Must I? Oh, come on, Nigel, next you'll be handing me that rot about serving my country and doing my duty. Well, I consider, I've done my duty. I've served in the Foreign Office ranks for nearly ten years. Like the Ashford men before me, I've served my sovereign loyally and faithfully and it's time someone else took over. Don't talk to me of duty. Let someone else watchdog the crown in the name of diplomacy. I'm tired of the games. I'm tired of the whole damned thing." Blake paused to collect his thoughts. "My God, Nigel, I'm thirty-one years old, and what do I have to show for these years? No real home, no family of my own, no wife, no children. Nothing but ten years spent bowing and scraping to Her Majesty's royal brood all over the globe. I need a change. I can't do this any longer. I'm tired and I don't like the man I've become."

Nigel studied his friend closely. He did look tired. There were a few flecks of gray in his midnight hair and his eyes were dark-ringed, dull, and self-absorbed. There was nothing in those eyes to remind him of Blake Ashford's sparkling wit. Nigel found himself recounting the weeks since he had last seen a flash of the old brilliance. It had been a long time. Too long. "What's wrong with the man you've become?" Nigel demanded of the disillusioned man who stood before him. "You're tops in your field. Everyone admires your diplomatic acumen. You're well liked by the royal family and well respected by your colleagues. What in heaven's name is wrong with that?"

"What's wrong? You said yourself, I've been behaving like a first-rate bastard," Blake pointed out. "Be consistent, Dr. Jameson, or all your sermons will be worthless. I've become the kind of man I've always despised most—cold, callous, cynic, incapable of feeling."

"The only problem you've ever had with feeling is feeling things too deeply. There are a great many chinks in your cynical armor if one cares to look."

"And I suppose *she's* one of them?" Blake shot out.

"I don't know who you mean," Nigel retaliated.

"Cristina," Blake spat out the name.

"I haven't mentioned Cristina," Nigel said quietly, "but I was wondering how long it would be before you did."

"Me?" Blake sputtered in anger, "you've been implying she's the reason I'm turning down the post in Vienna. That's what this conversation is about, isn't it?"

"I don't know. Is it?" Nigel's face gave nothing away.

"It's none of your damned business and I don't know why the bloody hell I'm even discussing it with you." Blake's voice was intimidating.

But Nigel had known Blake too long to be put off by an intimidating manner. He waited patiently for Blake to approach the crux of the problem.

"Nigel, you've done nothing but reproach me for months, asking me over and over again how I could let her go. I don't know how I let her go. I don't know how it got to that. I never believed for one minute that she would actually go through with it. But she did. She left me for Rudolf—and after all I'd done to keep her out of his hands!''

"And that's what's eating away at you? The fact she chose someone else after you'd gone to such a bother to keep her all to yourself?'' Nigel was merciless.

"*Him*, Nigel! The man who purchased her at an auction. The man who conspired with her mother—the man who paid to relieve Cristina of her virginity. You saw the condition she was in when I found her. Rudolf is a prince and he's quite capable of letting someone hurt her for his own gain.''

"And you aren't?'' Nigel's words cut like a scalpel, opening old wounds. "I saw the bruises your hands made on her body. And I know the physical bruises you left weren't intentional. But what about the invisible bruises to her heart—to her soul? Did you treat her any better?''

"I . . .''

"Rudolf must have offered her something. What did you offer her besides anger and arrogance and jealousy? I'm only guessing, but I'd say Rudolf acted as if he wanted her. You acted as if you couldn't wait to be rid of her. He probably made her feel like a wanted mistress. You made her feel like an unwanted whore. You used her, Blake. Did you ever stop to consider her feelings outside the bedroom? Did you ever stop to think that going with Rudolf might not have been her first choice?''

"Then what was?''

Nigel was under no illusions. He knew exactly what had had prompted Cristina to leave Lawrence House so suddenly. To Nigel's way of thinking, there was a perfectly logical reason for Cristina to run from Blake's home in London to Rudolf's palace in Vienna. She was pregnant. And she hadn't been able to face Blake with the news. Not after the horrible scandal with Lord Ainsford and his children's governess. That bit of gossip had struck too close to home.

Nigel wasn't surprised by the fact that Cristina had refused to stay in London. She had no intention of enduring a public humiliation—or of subjecting Blake and his family to one.

Cristina refused to give Blake cause to blame her for the destruction of his career or his reputation. She had chosen to run to Rudolf instead. Nigel didn't believe for one minute that Cristina preferred Rudolf to Blake, not when she was head over heels in love with the latter. She was doing what she thought to be the right and honorable thing to do. She was trying to protect Blake and her unborn child even if she had to sacrifice herself in the process. It was so obvious when one looked at the situation objectively. Cristina had chosen the man least likely to hurt her. Nigel marveled at the fact that Blake could still believe the pile of half truths Cristina had told him when he should have figured this situation out months ago.

But then Blake didn't know about the baby. And knowing about her pregnancy made all the difference. Blake shouldn't be left in the dark, but Nigel couldn't bring himself to betray Cristina's confidence and tell Blake outright. He couldn't bring himself to add to Blake's torment. At least, not yet. "Staying with you."

Blake let out an exasperated breath. "You're making about as much sense as Cristina did. If she wanted to stay with me, why did she leave with Rudolf?"

Nigel was silent.

"Nigel." It was a demand. "I asked you why Cristina left me. Tell me what you know."

"I can't violate my patient's trust, Blake. You know that."

"Then help me figure it out."

"All right," Nigel agreed. "Think about Cristina's leaving."

"It's all I do think about," Blake admitted.

"And what have you decided?"

"I haven't decided a bloody thing! Except that we both said things in the heat of anger. Things that we shouldn't have said to one another."

"What was happening when she left?"

"I was squiring Rudolf all over England."

"Her leaving had nothing to do with Rudolf."

"The hell it didn't!" Blake nearly shouted his frustration. "She left with him."

"Use your brain, Blake. Vienna is a long way from London. Why would she run so far? What reason would she have for going when she really wanted to remain at Lawrence House? Think about what was happening here in London— the major events that might have influenced Cristina's behavior."

"Hell, Nigel, I wasn't in London enough to know what was going on." He paused a moment. "There were treaty talks regarding the Russo-Turkish war."

"What else?"

Blake thought back. "Nothing much else in the way of politics. The papers were full of reports of Rudolf's visit and . . ."

"And?" Nigel pushed himself to the edge of his chair in anticipation.

"Some gossip about my escorting Cristina to the theater. The announcement of our betrothal. There was that nasty bit of business with Ainsford and the governess."

Nigel sat back and grinned. "At last."

"Ainsford and the governess? What did that have to do with Cristina and me?" Blake demanded. "Other than the speculation and gossip? If Aunt Delia hadn't meddled in our business no one would ever have suspected Cristina and I anticipated our vows. Our situation was completely different."

Nigel sighed in exasperation. He'd never known Blake to be so damned dense. "Was it? Consider the similarities between Ainsford and his governess and you and Cristina."

"The governess was living under Ainsford's roof, they had a relationship and the governess wound up—" Blake stopped abruptly. "Bloody hell!" He looked at Nigel. "Cristina's pregnant?"

The doctor nodded. "Congratulations."

Blake shook his head. "Christ, Nigel, I have the ring and the bloody special license has been in my pocket for months.

I had them before Aunt Delia published the announcement. We could have gotten married immediately.''

"Why didn't you?''

"I was waiting to speak to her father.'' Blake raked his fingers through his hair. "I offered to marry her. Why didn't she just come out and tell me about the baby?''

"Maybe she felt she couldn't face you with news of your impending fatherhood after learning how you felt about marriage. I seem to recall hearing that you told her you were fond of her but not enough to want to marry her. And you said she accused you of marrying her in order to do penance for your sins.'' Nigel sighed. "Christ! Blake, haven't you learned anything about women? She didn't think you'd let her go. She thought you would ask her to stay.''

"She'd already made up her mind to leave.''

"Then Rudolf must have offered her an honorable arrangement.''

"You call that kind of life in Vienna honorable?'' Blake's temper skyrocketed.

"What did you offer her here that was more honorable?''

"I offered her . . .'' Blake began, then silently bit back the words that sprang to his defense. What had he offered her except a marriage he obviously didn't want? He wanted to say that he had offered Cristina his heart, but he was honest enough with himself to admit that he had never spoken to her of love and had never offered his heart into her keeping. If he were brutally honest with himself, he had to admit that he hadn't given her anything beyond shelter and food and a few hours in his arms. He had nursed her through her fever, had listened to her feverish ravings and had promised not to let any harm come to her. But he hadn't kept his promise. He had harmed her irreparably by taking her virginity and begrudgingly offering her his name. He hadn't offered her his heart or the words that would have kept her by his side. And until this moment, Blake hadn't understood just how much of his heart she claimed. "I offered her nothing,'' he admitted, bitterly. "I didn't realize I had anything left to give.''

Until now. . . .

*The joys of parents are secret, and
so are their griefs and fears.*

—FRANCIS BACON 1561–1626

Seventeen

WILLIAM FAIRFAX WAS a robust man with sparkling blue-green eyes and coarse, thick red hair. He was shorter than the man standing before him, but William knew his huge chest and powerful shoulders gave him the illusion of height.

Years ago, he'd worn lines of discontent and dissipation on his face like the mark of a martyr, but the lines had vanished during his years away from London, giving him the appearance of a man younger than his forty-eight years. He had been successful in his travels to India, had invested in diamond mines in Africa, and finally settled in New York. And the success of his business in New York had restored his faith in himself. William was proud of his accomplishments and did not regret leaving Britain behind. His only regret was Cristina.

William shook hands with Lord Lawrence, exchanged introductions, then sat down at a corner table. The young diplomat had arranged, then canceled a similar meeting with him months ago. Now he'd asked for another one, claiming it concerned Cristina. William wanted to know why, and he wasted no time getting right to the heart of the matter.

"What's so important and how does it concern my daughter, Cristina?"

"Well, Sir William, it's rather difficult to explain, but I would like your help in persuading Cristina to return to London," Blake began.

"My daughter is boarding at a ladies finishing school in Switzerland," Sir William said. "I intend to collect her, have her presented at court, and have her accompany me home to New York. I only stopped in London to conclude some business before I went to meet her. I wrote her mother of my intentions months ago."

"I'm afraid you've been misled, sir. Cristina left school immediately before the start of the London season. She made her debut and is now living in Vienna."

"Vienna? What's she doing in Vienna without her mother? My man in London assured me Patricia was vacationing in southern Italy."

"Your wife is in Italy, as far as I can ascertain, but Cristina is—"

"What is it?" William interrupted. "Is she all right?"

"As far as I know, Cristina is fine." Blake's features became impassive, betraying none of the emotions churning beneath the surface. "She's living in Vienna under the protection of Crown Prince Rudolf. She's been there for over three months."

"My God!" The words echoed through the quiet dining room. "Do you mean to tell me that my daughter is his mistress?"

Blake took a deep breath. "I don't know if she's the crown prince's mistress yet. I don't think so." He cleared his throat nervously. "At least, I pray that's not the case. But she is living in Vienna in a house purchased for her Rudolf."

"I don't believe it."

"Everything I've told you can be confirmed through our embassy. Wire them if you don't believe me," Blake said.

"I'll do that," William told him. "In the meantime, why don't you tell me why we're discussing my daughter and why the Foreign Office is keeping track of her.''

Blake's eyes widened in surprise.

''Oh, yes, Lord Lawrence,'' William confirmed. ''I still have a few contacts in London. I'm aware of your reputation and your position in the government. Why is a diplomat meeting me to talk about my daughter? You said she's in Vienna. Is she in some sort of trouble?''

There was no way to soften the blow, so Blake began at the beginning by telling William Fairfax everything he knew about Cristina and her reason for traveling with Crown Prince Rudolf to Vienna. He spared Sir William none of the details. Blake related the events the night of Cristina's presentation ball—told of Patricia's wager and of the part he had played in thwarting it. He confessed everything to William Fairfax, except the fact that he had originally arranged the meeting between them to ask formally for Cristina's hand in marriage after making love to her.

When he finished, Blake sat quietly and waited for William Fairfax's reaction.

The drawn, tense expression on the older man's face was cause for concern and Blake immediately responded. ''Would you care for a drink, Sir William? I know everything I've told you has come as a terrible shock.''

''I'm fine.'' William fixed his gaze on Blake. ''I gave up drinking when I left my wife. I found I could live without both. Now tell me why I should help you. You told me what happened to make Cristina leave school and Fairhall and you told me how she came to be a guest in your home for two months. Now tell me what you aren't telling me. Why did Cristina leave your home?''

''*The Times* ran an announcement proclaiming my betrothal to your daughter. I didn't know anything about it until I read it in the paper. And neither did Cristina. But I promised to marry her anyway. She refused me and two days later she left with the crown prince. That was nearly four months ago.''

''Why are you so anxious for her to return?'' William saw the sweep of emotions cross Lawrence's face at his shrewd comment and knew there was more to the story than what Lawrence had told him.

"There are several reasons." Blake recovered. "A scandal of any kind involving a British citizen could cause problems right now for our government. Relations between Austria and England are strained by the negotiations in the war with Turkey and Russia."

"I see," William said, and Blake was suddenly aware that he did see, probably too much. "Is there any other reason? Aside from the mistake in *The Times* and diplomatic problems?"

Blake cleared his throat. "I do have a personal interest in your daughter," he admitted. "After all, she was a guest in my home for two months."

"And the emir of India was a guest in my home for some time, but I don't have a personal interest in him. Is there anything else you can tell me?" William asked.

"No." The firm set of Blake's jaw and the grim expression in his eyes told Fairfax that, for the moment, further probing was useless.

"All right, now let me explain my point of view," William began. "You see, I'm not sure Cristina will return to London with you simply because I ask her to."

"Why shouldn't she?" It was Blake's turn to probe. "I know she doesn't want to join her mother and you were the only other logical choice."

"To you, but not necessarily to Cristina. She may feel I've relinquished my parental rights where she's concerned, especially in view of what you told me about her leaving school. I haven't seen her in years and my only contact with her has been through letters, school reports, and occasionally through her mother."

"That happens in many families with children in boarding school. It happened in my own. That doesn't mean Cristina will deny you."

"You don't understand. I denied Cristina. When she was fourteen, I learned she wasn't my daughter, not my natural daughter. I was devastated by the news. So I took her to boarding school and left her there before I went wandering around the globe, trying to come to grips with myself and the mess I'd made of my life.'' William drew a deep breath and expelled it slowly, letting the meaning of his guilty confession sink in.

Blake began to regard the man in a new light. ''You mean you abandoned her? Your only child?''

''Not my child!'' The naked pain in the older man's voice couldn't be ignored.

Blake recognized the pain and softened his tone of voice. He knew what it was like to lose Cristina. He had listened to Cristina's family history and pieced together the parts of the story William had whitewashed. It was a sordid little saga and a hard one for a proud man to tell, but William Fairfax did it. He had admitted a stranger into his private thoughts and feelings, exposed his own weaknesses and failings, and Blake felt a kinship with the man that had nothing to do with their mutual feelings for Cristina.

He could appreciate William's marital mess, for he had lived through one of his own and he understood William's solution because he had wanted to run from his own fiasco more times than he could count. And then there was Cristina. . . . ''Are you absolutely certain she's not your daughter?''

''As certain as I can be under the circumstances. Her mother told me. She taunted me with the knowledge. I've spent the last six years trying to prove her wrong. I've hired private detectives to follow her in hopes of discovering the identity of Cristina's natural father.''

Blake's laugh was mirthless. ''You've suffered needlessly. You wasted six years of your life in a futile search. What you want to know is written all over your face. Your money would have been better spent commissioning a portrait of Cristina. Anyone who knows her would recognize the resemblance between the two of you. It's quite remarkable. I saw it right away. Your wife must have been mistaken.''

''Patricia couldn't·mistake a thing like that and she had no reason to lie to me about it. Why, she even implied that the Prince of Wales was Cristina's father,'' William explained.

"That isn't possible," Blake told him.

"Why do you say that?"

"It doesn't fit with the facts. Cristina was born while the prince was still at Oxford and the prince was having an affair with the actress Nellie Clifden at the time. His first affair." Blake was sure of his facts because the Prince of Wales had often spoken fondly of losing his virginity to Nellie.

"If what you say is true, then Cristina could be my child."

"Cristina *is* your child," Blake told him. "And even if you weren't her natural father, you'd be the only father she's ever known—the only father she's ever loved."

"Patricia lied to me." William shook his head in disbelief. "Why would she do such a thing when she knew how much I loved Cristina? As a child, Cristina never resembled me at all. . . ." William continued to put the pieces of the puzzle together.

"Maybe not as a child," Blake told him. "But the resemblance is unmistakable now. At fourteen, Cristina hadn't matured," Blake pointed out, logically, wondering all the while how jealousy and despair could make a man so blind. "Were you arguing with your wife when she offered the information about Cristina's paternity?"

William nodded. "We were having a nasty row. I was furious," Fairfax admitted, "and more than a little bit drunk. I'd just discovered my wife's lover had come to my house. I was angry and jealous and drunk enough to believe anything."

Blake was thoughtful. "But you've never been able to prove Cristina is someone else's child?"

"No," William answered. "Patricia was more discreet in those days. Now she's openly living with a penniless Italian prince whose title is ancient but whose coffers are empty. She's always been fascinated with aristocracy, and royalty in particular. So it came as no surprise when she hinted of her involvement with the Prince of Wales. I couldn't prove it, but I convinced myself he was Cristina's father. . . ."

"Cristina suffered needlessly, and for something that was none of her doing."

"I am afraid so." At Blake's furious expression, William Fairfax hastened to explain or at least excuse his behavior. "I couldn't take her with me. I knew I was going to India and Africa and I didn't want her to have to endure those hardships. And when I finally settled in America, I simply couldn't bring myself to write to her as if nothing had happened. She witnessed the whole sorry episode, you see, and I wasn't sure she would understand why I left her behind or if she would forgive me for it. And why should she, when I can't seem to forgive myself?" William Fairfax looked Blake squarely in the eye, his gaze unwavering. "I don't know if my words or wishes will carry any weight with Cristina now. I've neglected her for too long, but you're welcome to use my name to try to persuade her if you think will help convince her to return home. I would go to Vienna myself, but I think it best I spare her that embarrassment." He shifted in his seat, preparing to leave, no longer interested in dinner.

"I love your daughter," Blake said suddenly. "I want to marry her. That was my reason for asking for our original meeting. I intended to ask permission to marry Cristina."

"Cristina is of age," Fairfax told him. "You don't need my permission to marry."

"I'm aware that she's of age, sir." Blake looked William Fairfax right in the eyes. "But you see, Cristina is pregnant and the child she's carrying is mine."

"What?" William Fairfax came halfway out of his seat and Blake thought for a moment that the older man was going to hit him. But Fairfax quickly regained control of himself. "Why did she leave you?"

"Because," Blake answered. "Because I was too damn stubborn and proud to admit that I loved her and that I wanted her to stay."

William digested the information, then studied Blake Ashford. "Fair enough."

Blake rose to shake the older man's hand.

Cristina's father managed a smile. "I thank you for coming to me. I intended to collect Cristina from her Swiss finishing school and take her to New York and even then I didn't really know whether she would want to return with me." William moved to leave the table, then turned with one last thought. "When you find Cristina, tell her she's always welcome in my home regardless of the circumstances that bring her. I won't ask questions. We're all entitled to our own secrets."

"I'll tell her."

"And, Lord Lawrence, if Cristina wants to marry you, I'll grant you my blessing," William added. "As I said before, she doesn't require my permission. But if you try to force her into something she doesn't want—into a marriage she doesn't want—just so you can lay claim to your child, I swear I'll cut your heart out and feed it to the dogs."

"Fair enough," Blake answered solemnly. Fairfax was right. Feeding his heart to the dogs was no less than he deserved for the pain he had inflicted on the man's daughter.

"Remember, Lawrence," William reminded. "If she wants to come home, my doors are open. No questions asked."

Blake nodded. "I'll do my best to keep you informed." William Fairfax had finally reclaimed his daughter. All Blake had to do was find her and convince her to return to London with him. Convince her that he loved her and couldn't live without her. And after all that had gone between them, Blake knew it wouldn't be an easy task.

CRISTINA REACHED FOR the thick, creamy white envelope on the silver tray, then stopped with her hand poised just inches from its destination. A courier had delivered the letter some ten minutes ago and still she hesitated to open it. It must be a message from Crown Prince Rudolf. The fine stationery resembled that used in the Hofburg. But why had it arrived by courier? Why hadn't it come hand delivered by the same footman who delivered the other messages from Rudolf? The idea puzzled her and made her wary.

"Why don't you open it?" Leah urged. "You've been starin' at it for ten minutes."

"I'm almost afraid to," Cristina said. "What if it isn't from

Rudolf? What if it's another of those horrid letters?'' Several days during the previous fortnight, Cristina had received a series of anonymous letters that spewed obscenities and threats at her and warned the lady of the veil to be careful. The notes and the secret policeman who followed her along Vienna's streets had frightened Cristina into giving up her morning excursions.

"The only way for you to find out is to open it. Go on." Leah stood looking over Cristina's shoulder, waiting for her to open the letter.

Cristina drew a deep breath and lifted the envelope from the tray. Her hand shook so badly she could barely make out the symbols on the wax impression. The message wasn't from Rudolf. The seal wasn't the familiar double-headed eagle of the House of Hapsburg, but something even more familiar—the lion and unicorn of England. It was a government seal, the kind used by the representatives of Her Majesty's government.

Almost giddy with relief, Cristina ripped open the envelope to reveal the card inside. "It's an invitation to our embassy to meet the new ambassador, Leah. Next Tuesday at four P.M." Her voice held a note of surprise mixed with curiosity. "I wonder why I was invited."

"You'll just have to go find out."

"Do you think I should?" Cristina glanced down at the swell of her stomach and nervously smoothed away a nonexistent wrinkle in her skirt.

"Why shouldn't you go?" Leah asked her. "You got invited."

Leah was right, Cristina reminded herself. She had been invited and an invitation from the British ambassador wasn't something she could refuse lightly. She was one of Queen Victoria's subjects and there must be a reason for her invitation. Perhaps there was news of her father, of maybe a note from Blake. No, Cristina told herself, the invitation was addressed to the comtesse di Rimaldi, and only Rudolf, Leah, and she knew Cristina Fairfax and the comtesse were one and the same. Rudolf must have secured the invitation to tea for her. He must have realized how much Cristina missed the sound of English voices. He had probably told the new ambassador the comtesse had relatives in England.

Cristina frowned. She was letting her imagination run on. The invitation was exactly that. An invitation to tea. Every British citizen in Vienna had probably received an invitation identical to the one she held in her hand.

She knew there was a certain amount of risk involved in socializing with her fellow countrymen in her present condition, but with any luck at all, no one would recognize her or connect her with Prince Rudolf. She had been at school before her presentation to the queen, and she hadn't finished her London season. An invitation to tea at the embassy would be a diversion from the routine of her everyday life in Vienna and the fear that had begun to plague her. She desperately needed a diversion. Besides, she could always pretend to speak very little English. The comtesse di Rimaldi was, after all, supposed to be Italian nobility. She would smile prettily, nod her head, and enjoy the afternoon.

Her mind made up, Cristina sat down and wrote her note of acceptance.

THE FOLLOWING TUESDAY dawned cold and clear. And Cristina took special care with her toilette, lingering in the scented bath water before finally selecting a dress of black velvet for warmth as well as the slenderizing qualities it offered. The effect was striking. The rich, black velvet complimented her creamy complexion and emphasized the only color in her outfit—the thick copper curls piled atop her head and the green of her shining cat's eyes. She smiled at her reflection as she added the pearl earrings and matching necklace to her ensemble before descending the stairs where Leah waited to inspect her.

"Leah, I'm ready."

"Aye, I can see that and you look lovely—a vision."

"Just as long as I'm not a vision in a nightmare," Cristina teased.

"Never," Leah stated firmly. "Now, stop fishin' for compliments before the carriage leaves you to walk to the embassy."

Cristina laughed at the mock severity she saw in Leah's expression. She felt young and pretty again for the first time in months and the feeling gave her the confidence she needed to brave the environs of the British embassy.

She was still smiling to herself when the fiacre drew to a halt in front of the embassy. Cristina handed the driver her invitation and waited inside the carriage until a footman came to escort her inside.

"Right this way, madam." A young man in a business suit she thought must be an aide of some sort led her through a foyer, up a flight of stairs, and into a sitting room decorated in muted tones of silver and blue.

"If you will please wait here, madam," he motioned toward a group of chairs, "the ambassador will be in to see you."

The light that lies
In a woman's eyes
Has been my heart's undoing.

—THOMAS MOORE 1779–1852

Eighteen

SHE STOOD WITH her back to him, gazing out the window at the busy Viennese scurrying along the Ringstrasse in search of their warm homes, but he recognized her immediately. He knew that form. He would know that slender back anywhere. He had dreamed about her until he knew every inch—the round, smooth breasts; the tiny line of her waist; the delicious curve of her hips; the long, slim legs hidden beneath the folds of her skirts; and the hair—the thick, coppery curls confined in her sleek hairstyle hung past her waist when free and felt like spun silk in his hands. Hair like that could only belong to one woman. Cristina. And he knew every bit of her. Every word she had ever spoken to him and every inch of that luscious body were permanently etched in his mind and on his heart.

He studied her for some minutes before moving to stand directly behind her. He had been surprised to receive her note of acceptance. He hadn't allowed himself to think about her acceptance. He hadn't allowed himself to believe she would really come. Disappointment was easier to bear if you didn't let yourself truly believe in miracles.

"Cristina," he whispered her name softly, waiting for her to turn and face him.

"You!" Her one-word response was an echo of another meeting in a ballroom months before.

Blake nodded slowly. He didn't realize he was holding his breath until he let it out in a rush. "I had to see you."

"Oh, no. . . ." Cristina turned back to the window.

"Don't you have anything else to say? After I've come to rescue you from the clutches of the handsome prince." He hadn't meant to be sarcastic, but her reaction stung him.

"I'm not a damsel in distress. I don't need rescuing, Blake. You're relieved of duty." Cristina blinked back tears. She had hoped . . . but she hadn't expected to see Blake again and the surprise and the incredible joy surrounded by pain was almost too much to bear. She thought she had learned to control her feelings for him, but now she knew she had failed.

"I can't go away. I've left you alone for too long already." Blake moved to place his arms around her waist and draw her back against him.

"Blake, please, don't . . ."

"I can't help myself, Cristina. This thing between us is stronger than I am. I need to touch you. I have to hold you."

"Blake. . . ."

"I didn't intend our meeting to be anything but business, but when I saw you standing there silhouetted against the light from the window, I had to hold you. You're so beautiful. The perfect Madonna."

Cristina whirled around to face him, a quick denial framed on her lips.

"I know about the baby, Cristina. We've got to talk."

"It's too late to talk. We said everything in London." She somehow managed to get the words out despite the lump forming in her throat.

"We said too much in London and neither of us meant a word of it."

"I meant every word."

"I don't doubt that you meant to hurt me and to make me angry," Blake corrected calmly. "And you did. I couldn't see beyond my anger for weeks—months—but I finally came to my senses and put the pieces of the puzzle together.''

"It doesn't matter any longer."

"Yes, it does," Blake answered. "I should have realized what was happening when you refused to let me marry you."

"You're talking in riddles," Cristina said softly.

"You wanted me to make a declaration of love for you so you could tell me about the baby. You wanted me to prevent you from leaving Lawrence House. I disappointed you."

"I wasn't disappointed," Cristina told him. "It's no more than what I expected from you."

"I was too angry to understand what you wanted—what you needed from me," Blake explained. "It was my fault. I had a ring and a special license in my pocket. I'd had them for weeks. I should have been happy about the announcement. I should have taken you upstairs and made love with you until you couldn't think of any reason to leave. I was too angry to see that I'd left you no choice but to leave—if for no other reason than to prove to me you would."

Cristina struggled to keep her voice from breaking. "That's ancient history, Blake. It's in the past and best forgotten. I don't need anything from you except an explanation for this elaborate ruse. Why did you invite me here?"

Blake smiled at her. "I had a strange yearning to see the mother of my child."

"You're mistaken, Lord Lawrence."

"I don't think so," he replied. "Not after the strong hints I got from Nigel and the very informative letter I received from Leah. Unlike you, she came right to me with the news."

Cristina's eyes flashed fire. "Of course she did. But she is also mistaken. This child belongs to Rudolf." She began to pace the floor.

"Bull! I know a virgin when I sleep with one. And you, my sweet, were definitely virginal."

"That's impossible." Cristina lifted her chin a notch. "If you don't believe me, ask Rudolf. He swears he spent the night with me at Marlborough House."

To her amazement, Blake laughed. "Before or after I pulled you from the end of your rope?"

"Before," she answered.

Blake shook his head. "No, sweetheart, he was playing cards with me."

"All right then, after."

Blake shook his head again.

"Before, after, I don't know," Cristina stopped her pacing and flung out her arms in exasperation. "What difference does it make? He swears it happened."

"It makes a great deal of difference," Blake told her. "Because I don't want anyone questioning my child's paternity—least of all his mother." He reached out and smoothed his palm down Cristina's cheek in a gesture so tender it brought tears to her eyes. "Rudolf was supposed to think he spent the night with you at Marlborough House. I paid fifty pounds to ensure he would."

"I don't understand."

"I paid a red-haired prostitute fifty pounds sterling to impersonate you. I sneaked her in the house, up the stairs, and into Rudolf's room—the room you'd escaped by making a rope of the Prince of Wales's bedsheets."

"Why?"

"If Rudolf believed he had you in his bed, he wasn't likely to go roaming the house looking for you while I was smuggling you out." Blake smiled at her. "I was trying to be a hero. I never dreamed you'd climb out a third-floor window or that you would later convince Rudolf and yourself that my child belonged to him."

"I didn't convince him," Cristina said. "I told him the truth. But he assumed responsibility anyway and he seemed so sure that he had spent the night with me and I—"

"Pretended it was true."

"It seemed better that way," Cristina told him.

"Better for whom?"

"For you, for me, for the baby."

"Nigel didn't think so, and neither did Leah."

"They had no right to tell you. They had no right to interfere with my life."

"Why shouldn't they interfere with your life when you're bound and determined—when *we're* both bound and determined—to make a mess of it?" Blake demanded. "That child you're carrying sure as hell doesn't belong to Rudolf and he doesn't just belong to you, he also belongs to me."

"*She*," Cristina corrected. "I intend to have a daughter. And now that you know of her existence, Lord Lawrence, have you come to claim her or are you going to try to take my baby away from me?" She cupped her arms protectively around the slight velvet-covered mound and fought down her sense of panic. "Because I won't let you."

Blake's jaws tensed and a muscle began to twitch as he clamped his teeth firmly together in an effort to control his rising temper. "Do you really think I would take *our* child away from you? Do you really think I could be so heartless?" It hurt to know she trusted him so little.

"I don't know," Cristina said, honestly. "I barely know you, your lordship."

"I didn't come to take the baby away from you, Cris, but I have a right to know he exists. I want to have a say in what happens to him and to you. I admit Nigel and Leah were wrong to betray your trust, but they're your friends, *our* friends, and they did it out of love and concern for you and the baby."

"But you were never supposed to know," Cristina whispered so softly Blake had to strain to hear her. "I never wanted you to know."

"And so you sold yourself. Why, Cristina?" He demanded an answer. "Why sell yourself to Rudolf?"

"Because"—Cristina burst out—"because I didn't think I had any choice. Because I was more afraid of having you hate me than I was of becoming his mistress. I knew you didn't want to marry me. I heard you talking to your aunt. And I was afraid that if you knew about the baby, you would hate me for saddling you with another unwanted responsibility. I know you didn't conspire with my mother. None of this is your fault. You didn't ask to get stuck with me as an indefinite houseguest. I've interfered with your life—with your comfortable routine. I've been nothing but a disruption for you, and now this . . .''

"Oh, Cristina.'' He reached out to her. ''Having you live in my house has been the greatest joy of my life.''

She gave him a wry look.

Blake held up his hand. ''All right, at times you've been a disruption and a royal pain, but I wouldn't change any of it. Not a thing. And this child you're carrying is no more of an unwanted responsibility than you've been. You've been a welcome addition to Lawrence House and our baby will be as well. He's not a burden, he's a joyous opportunity for both of us.''

''What about your career? Your name and reputation? I would hate for you to become another Lord Ainsford. I left London so I wouldn't cause you any more problems.'' Cristina felt the tears roll down her face.

Blake stopped dead in his tracks, unable to believe his ears. Could she really mean what she said? Had she tried to protect him by sacrificing her honor? ''Cristina, sweet, brave Cristina, you and this child mean more to me than my career.'' He touched a stray curl that had fallen against the soft skin of her neck.

His tender touch was her undoing. His fingers seemed to sear her flesh, marking her as his. She made a deep sound in the back of her throat and Blake recognized it for what it was—an unconscious echo of desire.

It was all he needed. His lips were cool and soft against the base of her throat before roaming upwards to meet hers in a fiery kiss that made her forget everything everything except her need for him.

''Cristina . . .'' His moan expressed the months of agonized longing. Then he was kissing her again, holding her close against him, allowing her to feel his passion.

''Stop, Blake, please, stop . . .'' Cristina fought the flood of emotions that threatened to drown her senses, trying desperately to regain her composure against overwhelming odds. "Please listen to me. We mustn't do this."

"Why not?" he murmured against her lips as he moved his hands to cup her full, sensitive breasts and used his thumbs to tease her taunt peaks through the soft velvet. "Don't you want me to do this, Cristina?"

"I don't want to be hurt. And you can hurt me, Blake, without even trying. Please don't hurt me again. Let me go."

"I'll do my best not to hurt you ever again, sweetheart." He tore his mouth away from the tempting spot at the base of her neck.

"But you will . . ."

Blake cupped her face in his hands and stared down at her watery green eyes. "I don't understand, Cristina. Tell me why you're so convinced I'll hurt you."

"Because you don't trust me. You didn't trust me enough even to tell me you'd been married. You never told me about Meredith."

Blake froze at the sound of Meredith's name on Cristina's lips. The color drained from his face and he grew so still that Cristina thought he might even have stopped breathing.

Blake stabbed his fingers through his hair, then turned from Cristina and began to pace the room.

His reaction frightened her. She'd never seen him so agitated. "I'm sorry, Blake. I wasn't prying—really, I wasn't. But I overheard some of what you said to your aunt. Forget I mentioned it. I was curious. It isn't important. The fact that you were once married has nothing to do with me. It's really none of my business. I'm sorry," she repeated. "I never meant to bring up unpleasant memories. She was your wife. I know you must have loved her very much."

Blake stopped pacing and turned and faced Cristina, and when he spoke this time, his words were all the more shocking for the depth of emotion in them. "No, Cristina, I didn't love her very much. I hated her."

"What?" Cristina stared at him, at his rigid posture and the way his hands were clenched into white-knuckled fists at his side.

Blake took a deep breath, then slowly expelled it as he forced himself to let go of the anger. Cristina watched as he slowly relaxed his frame, unclenched his hands, and sat down on one of the chairs. He leaned over, propped his elbows on his knees, and buried his face in his hands. "It's a long story."

Cristina walked over to him, knelt beside him, and rested her forehead against his thigh. "I'll listen if you want to talk."

Blake looked down at her shining hair and managed a crooked half-smile. "It's not a pretty tale—not something I'm proud of."

"We all have parts of our life we'd rather forget and things we wish we'd never done."

"Not innocents like you," Blake said.

"Me, too," she told him. "I wish I'd gone to you with news of the baby as Nigel had advised me to do. I wish I'd never met Rudolf. I wish I'd never come to Vienna. But most of all, I wish I could take back all the horrible things I said to you in London."

Blake leaned back in the chair, then reached out and began to stroke Cristina's soft, silky hair. "I met Meredith when I was twenty. I was just home from Oxford and about to take up a post as an aide to my father here in Vienna. . . ."

Cristina listened as he told her about his courtship and hasty marriage. He didn't go into great detail; instead he related the story as if it hadn't hurt so much—as if it had happened to someone he knew rather than to himself. But Cristina knew how it hurt to have a loved one betray your trust and she choked back tears as Blake told her how he had found Meredith making love with his first cousin only hours after repeating her marriage vows with him.

"I couldn't bring myself to touch her after that," Blake concluded.

"Why didn't you have the marriage annulled?" Cristina asked.

"I wanted to, I threatened to, but Meredith swore she'd go before the church board and testify that I'd been her lover before we married. And since she wasn't a virgin, the only alternative was divorce and the inherent scandal it would cause.'' Blake sighed. ''I wasn't willing to subject my family to that sort of notoriety, so we remained legally married.''

''I'm sorry, Blake. I'm so sorry.''

''Ssh,'' he soothed her. ''It's all right. It ended when she died.''

But Cristina knew it hadn't ended. Pain like that didn't go away simply because the person who caused it died. It lingered. It left scars—invisible scars that no one could see, and sometimes other, more visible signs. Cristina reached for Blake's hand. She smoothed his palm over her cheek, then brought it to her lips and covered it with fervent kisses.

''No, Cristina, don't.'' Blake didn't want her to grieve for him—for Meredith's sins. ''It's in the past. It's not worth your precious tears.''

''I'm not crying for you or because Meredith betrayed your trust,'' she told him. ''I'm crying because *I* did. Forgive me.''

''There's nothing to forgive. You left me because I didn't give you reason enough to stay. But you're here now, sweetheart, and that's all that matters to me.''

Cristina knew he meant it. She couldn't find any reproach in his eyes or his voice. But she also knew he wondered about her current relationship with Rudolf and that she could ease his mind. ''He hasn't touched me.''

''Oh, Cris, you don't have to—''

''I persuaded him to bring me to Vienna by telling him I was going to have a baby. He immediately accepted responsibility and promised to take care of us.''

''In return for what?'' Blake asked.

''Me,'' Cristina whispered. ''He wants me for his mistress after the baby is born.'' She looked up and met Blake's gaze, facing the painful look in his eyes without flinching.

Blake took Cristina's hand in his larger one. ''Do you want to be Rudolf's mistress?''

Cristina shook her head.

''Then would you consider becoming my wife?''

''Wife?''

Blake smiled at her blank look. "Yes, you know—as in husband and wife."

"Do you mean it?"

"I've never meant anything more," he vowed. "Lawrence House has been like a tomb since you left. I need you, Cristina, and I want you with me. You and our baby. I don't give a damn about damage to my career."

Cristina choked back a sob and fairly flew into Blake's waiting arms. She had waited three long months for him to come to her and say he wanted her with him. She had prayed every day that Blake would come to Vienna to get her and her prayers had finally been answered.

She closed her eyes and melted into his embrace.

Blake held her close to his heart, kissing her with months of pent-up passion. He wanted Cristina and no other woman would do. For three months he had felt as if he'd been punched in the gut. He had walked around in a daze, barely able to function because there was a huge gap in his chest where his heart should have been. He had been an empty shell of a man until he'd come to his senses and admitted how much Cristina meant to him and how much she had taken with her when she left.

He tightened his hold on her and kissed her face and the salty tears in the corners of her eyes, breathing in the unique fragrance of her hair. "Let me love you, Cristina."

Cristina went willingly, allowing him to take her hand and lead her to one of the blue and silver wall panels. She frowned at him, puzzled, until he pressed against the panel and a door swung open. Blake bowed before her.

"My secret chamber awaits, mademoiselle." He swung her up into his arms and carried her inside.

She gave herself up to his skilled hands as he undressed her tenderly, revealing the body he knew so well, finding himself amazed and fascinated by the changes that had occurred. Her waist had thickened to accommodate the child, her once-flat belly was rounded with the flesh stretched around her navel. Blake lightly traced the circle of her navel with his fingers, marveling at the increased sensitivity of her skin. She shivered with pleasure. His moved his fingers higher, teasing her full breasts, then roamed downward to peel the silk stockings from her long, slim legs. He completed his mission, kneeling on the carpet in front of her, his lips pressed against the soft reddish-gold curls covering the mound at the junction of her thighs.

Cristina reacted immediately, tangling her fingers in his hair, pressing him closer, groaning at the spark of fire that swept over her when his tongue penetrated the tangle of hair.

"Sit down, sweetheart," Blake nudged her backward until Cristina half sat, half lay on a tiny couch. "I want to taste all of you." He buried his face between her legs, continuing the wildly exciting probing of his tongue.

When he finished his exploration, Cristina lay panting with the force of emotions that had flamed within her. Blake raised his face and smiled when she reached out for him. He moved onto the couch and lay next to her, fondling the turgid peaks of her breasts with his hands before his mouth followed in their wake.

Cristina tried to pull him closer. She wanted to feel him above her, but Blake would have none of it.

"The baby," he murmured between kisses, "I don't want to harm the baby." He rolled away from her and stood beside the couch.

"Please . . . ," Cristina begged, reaching for the throbbing bulge inside his trousers.

"Oh, hell, sweetheart, I can't contain myself if you do that," he groaned.

"I don't want you to contain yourself. I want you to make love to me." She eagerly unfastened the buttons of his trousers while he divested himself of his shirt and coat.

When he stood naked Cristina reached for him once again, pulling him down on top of her.

Her eyes widened in surprise when Blake reversed their positions and carefully guided himself into her warmth. He helped her to move above him, lifting her with his hands, teaching her the motion. Cristina reveled in the new freedom. She rode him hard, rocking above him then sensuously gliding down his length, driving him to the limits of his endurance.

Blake watched her moving above him through passion-glazed eyes, biting his lips to muffle his groans of pleasure. She had become a wicked temptress, teasing and taunting him with her power over him. She reveled in the power as she set the rhythm and he followed obediently.

Cristina enjoyed knowing she could still arouse him so completely that he couldn't hold back his exclamations of pleasure. She leaned forward suddenly, letting the ends of her hair tickle his chest.

Her sudden movement was almost his undoing.

"Do you surrender?" she teased provocatively. "Or shall I continue my torture?"

"Torture away," he gasped. "I'll never surrender willingly."

Cristina threw back her head and laughed with the sheer joy of the heady new sensation of power. But Blake brought her attention back to him by firmly grasping her hips, holding immobile and impaled on his hardness.

"I allowed you some freedom and I see I've created a monster. I'll have to regain control," he gasped as he guided her up and down the pulsating length of him, forcing her to continue the rhythm when she would have teased him, until they both lost control and cried out in unison.

And when they floated gently back to earth, Blake carefully rolled away, then settled Cristina comfortably against the curve of his body before he drifted off into a contented sleep.

"SSH."

Cristina opened her eyes to find Blake bending over her, fully dressed in immaculate evening clothes. He held one finger to his lips, while he balanced a cup and saucer in his other hand. "We overslept," he confided. "But I managed to smuggle you some tea."

Cristina slowly became aware of the noise drifting up from the rooms beneath them. She sat up and gratefully accepted the cup of tea. "What's going on?" she asked.

"A reception." He made a wry face. "The ambassador and Mrs. Paget are giving a reception for the British citizens in Vienna. I hate these tedious affairs." He winked at her. "I'd much rather stay in bed with you. Unfortunately this tedious affair has been given in my honor."

Cristina turned a brilliant shade of crimson as the memories came flooding back. She vividly recalled Blake carrying her through the secret panel to this office-bedchamber. She stared down at the rumpled couch, remembering the mutual passion that had exploded as they lay entwined in the cramped bed. She pulled the wrinkled coverlet tighter around her. "I thought you were the ambassador."

"Ambassador-at-large is the correct title; sort of a roving do-gooder, and it's only temporary. Until I'm sent elsewhere."

"You'll be sent away? I thought you just arrived."

"Oh, I'll be here a while," Blake answered vaguely. "Now drink your tea. You must be thirsty after such an *energetic* afternoon."

Cristina did as he instructed, escaping the knowing look in his eyes.

"I tried to wake you earlier, but you refused to leave the warmth of the bed so I decided to let you sleep. I've been sneaking up here every few minutes or so, checking to see if you were still asleep. I didn't want you to go looking for me and stumble into a formal reception or any of the guests in the process."

"It was nice of you to bring me the tea."

He smiled again, a sight that tugged at Cristina's heart. "To tell the truth, the tea was for me. I slipped away from the boring conversation to find better company."

Cristina giggled. "Poor Blake, you gave me your drink and now you'll have to do without."

Blake was enchanted by her husky giggle and realized it was the first time he had ever heard her sound so carefree. He sat down on the edge of the bed. "That's a hardship I can stand. If I can't warm you, I'll enjoy watching my cup of tea do it for me.''

"I would rather you did it." Cristina spoke the thought aloud, then blushed when she met his expressive gaze and realized Blake had heard it. "It must be late. I've got to get dressed and get home. Leah will be frantic." She chattered to cover her embarrassment. Blake's intimate looks had a way of unsettling her and made her acutely aware that she was naked beneath the spread.

Cristina swept the room with a glance. Her black velvet dress was not in sight and she wondered where it had fallen.

"Relax," Blake instructed. "Leah knows where you are. She knows you're safe with me."

"Safe?" Cristina giggled again. "This is safe?" She set the cup and saucer aside, then looked up at him. "I'm never safe when I'm with you."

"Pardon me." He sounded sincere, but his eyes danced with amusement, their jet-black depths gleaming. "I assure you it was a slip of the tongue."

"I don't trust your assurances," she told him. "Kindly keep them to yourself. You know they're useless when you look at me like that."

Blake raised an eyebrow, feigning innocence. "You've done me a grave disservice, Cristina, and yourself as well. I didn't know my glances could arouse you this way. You should have told me sooner."

Cristina opened her mouth to respond, then bit back her retort. He was enjoying his play on words, enjoying the way his teasing affected her.

Blake studied her closely. He knew she felt unsure of herself and knew she enjoyed their intimacy in spite of her uncertainty. She was shy one moment and full of the confidence that accompanied sexual intimacy the next. He understood her feelings because he often shared them. He never knew what to expect and that somehow heightened their sexual awareness of one another.

"I'd love to continue our discussion concerning your current state of arousal," he whispered softly, seductively. "Unfortunately, I've got to return to my other guests. But," he added, when she would have protested, "I'll return later so we can further explore the topic." He winked at Cristina and walked to the door.

"Wait!" she commanded. "What do I do until you get back?"

"Close your eyes and dream of me," he replied conceitedly, just before a blue satin pillow bounced off his stomach.

～◦⊱⊰◦～

IT SEEMED LIKE hours before he returned. Cristina had long since given up on him and succumbed to the warmth of the daybed.

"Asleep again?" Blake asked as he entered the room and found it in darkness. He lit the gas lamp, then made his way over to the bed. He studied the even rise and fall of Cristina's breasts as she slept.

"I could use a bit of that myself," he said, aloud, "but first I have to get you out of here." He leaned down and kissed her soft lips. "Wake up, Sleeping Beauty, it's time to go home."

Cristina smiled drowsily and moved to one side to give him room on the bed. "I don't want to go. Why don't you come to bed?" She reached for him when a knock on the door interrupted them.

"Will there be anything else before I retire, sir?" A voice asked as Blake reached out to accept a black-wrapped parcel.

Cristina recognized the voice. It belonged to the man who had escorted her to Blake's sitting room.

"Yes, please see that my carriage is brought around, Cason. I'm in need of some fresh air after the stuffy reception rooms."

"Right away, sir. Good night, sir."

"Good night, Cason." Blake turned from the door to find Cristina watching him with an expression of alarm on her face. "Cason is my personal assistant and majordomo combined. He's the soul of discretion."

"I'm relieved to hear it," Cristina returned haughtily. "As are all your other ladies, I'm sure."

Blake watched her for a minute before he burst into laughter. "That's my girl. Haughtily clinging to her dignity whenever she's caught with her finger in the pie."

"You certainly enjoyed having your finger in the pie," came her waspish reply.

Blake continued to howl with mirth. "Woke up ill-tempered, eh?"

"Out!" Cristina ordered, her feelings injured by his insensitive laughter. "I'm leaving. I don't have to stay here and listen to you laugh at me." She pointed toward the door then glanced around, searching for her clothing. "Where is my dress?"

"I'm not laughing at you. I'm laughing with you."

"I'm not laughing," she informed him.

"You should be. Oh, come on, Cris, can't you see the humor in it? You're always misplacing your clothes and you're always trying to make the best of it by cloaking yourself in haughty disdain." He tried to explain and soothe her ruffled feathers.

"Where is my dress? I don't remember seeing it earlier." Still smarting from his laughter and his apparent insensitivity, Cristina ignored him.

"I asked Cason to have it pressed. He was returning it just now and you stared at him as if he had committed a crime."

Cristina smiled suddenly and a few giggles escaped. "I suppose you're right. My clothes do have a way of disappearing whenever you're around you."

"Making your clothes disappear is my mission in life," Blake replied solemnly.

"Leah says you're a menace to my closet."

"Leah knows what she's talking about," Blake agreed. "Now let's see about getting you home. If we wait much longer the sun will be rising and I'll have a harder time smuggling you out of here."

"You sound as if you've had plenty of experience at smug-

gling ladies in and out of buildings,'' Cristina couldn't completely conceal the jealous note in her voice.

"In my younger university days Nigel and I were quite
adept at it.'' Blake smiled in remembrance of those carefree,
youthful days before Meredith. "However, most of our experience consisted of smuggling in, not out. And not one of
those women could be called a lady or be compared to you.''
He placed a light kiss on her nose and pulled her out of bed.

With her vanity soothed and her curiosity satisfied for the
moment, Cristina relaxed under Blake's capable hands. He
handed her her lacy corset and chemise, helped her put them
on, then tied her corset strings, gently nudging her backward
until she sat on the makeshift bed.

He knelt at her feet, lifted her silk stockings, placed them
over her feet, and slid the sensuous fabric over her shapely
calves, ignoring the throbbing in his loin and the pounding of
his heart against his rib cage as he fastened the stockings to
the frilly garters attached to her corset.

He reminded himself that he was out of his mind to be
dressing her and sending her away when all he could think
of was tumbling her back into the mattress. But Blake forced
his rebellious thoughts aside and turned his attention to her
petticoat, then to the velvet gown which he lifted and dropped
over her head and into place.

When she was fully clothed, except for her shoes and hat,
Blake produced a brush and carefully brushed her hair off her
neck, twisting the mass into a knot on the top of her head
and pinning her small velvet hat down to secure it. He located
her slippers beneath the bed and held them for her while she
slipped them onto her feet.

Cristina stared at him in astonishment. He had dressed her
completely and correctly and as impersonally as a dressmaker's mannequin in less than half an hour. "I believe
you've done this before.''

"Once or twice,'' he admitted. "I've been told I make
quite a lady's maid.''

"Dressing or undressing?''

"Both.'' He suddenly grinned a boyish grin that made him

seem years younger and almost vulnerable. "But I prefer the latter."

"So do I," Cristina blurted, amazed at herself for admitting it aloud. Her forehead knitted into a frown.

"Don't look so worried, Countess," Blake whispered, "I'll keep your secret. I won't tell a soul." His teasing was gentle and natural, designed to put her at ease.

She dazzled him with a grateful smile. For tonight, at least, he seemed to understand and respect her feelings. She loved him for that.

Blake had amazed himself with his gentle teasing. He hadn't cared about a woman's feeling outside the bedroom for years. He had even convinced himself that women had no feelings outside the bedroom and some he knew lacked those. But he cared about Cristina's feelings. They mattered to him. Everything about her mattered. He wanted to take care of her and not just physically, but mentally as well. He wanted to care for her, protect her, and somehow earn her trust.

He had treated her shoddily in the beginning, but he would change. He would earn her regard somehow . . . even if it took the rest of his life.

Blake picked up her cloak and placed it on her shoulders. There was a new tenderness in his touch and in his voice. "The carriage is waiting, Cristina."

"I know." She moved with him to the door. Her face was pale, the tears stoically held in check.

Minutes later, Blake smuggled her out of the embassy and into his carriage. "I don't want to take you back to his house."

"Then don't." She turned to face him and their eyes locked in a moment of silent communication that spoke volumes.

"I must. For now." His black eyes pleaded with her. "I know it's asking a great deal, but I'm asking you to trust me, Cristina."

Cristina opened her mouth to tell him she did trust him, but he held up a hand to forestall her.

"I want you, Countess, and Rudolf wants you. That's a tricky situation even without the political tensions between our two empires. I don't intend to let Rudolf keep you. I think you know that and I think you prefer it that way.''

"I do prefer it." Cristina's voice was confident. "That's the one thing I knew all along. I tried to lie to you, but now I want you to know I want you, Blake. I have from the first night. I want to be with you as long as you want me.''

Blake stopped her flow of words with a demanding kiss. He plundered the depths of her mouth with his tongue, seeking a commitment. "Then trust me, Countess. Trust me to do this right. For all of us. I know I haven't given you any reason to trust me in the past, but all that is in the past. We're going to married.''

"When?"

"As soon as I can arrange it.''

"And then what?" Cristina wanted to know.

"Then we'll live one day at a time and let the rest of the world take care of itself. I promise.''

Cristina reached up to kiss him.

"You won't have to stay here much longer," Blake told her when he forced himself away from her lips. "Rudolf hasn't tried to seduce you yet, but that doesn't mean he won't. I don't want you in his house or under his protection any longer than necessary. God knows I can't stand the thought of him wanting you the way I do. Arranging everything to spare Rudolf, the Austro-Hungarian Empire and our own empire embarrassment is going to require a great deal of tact and all the diplomatic acumen I can muster.''

Cristina stiffened ever so slightly in his arms, aware she had lost his attention for the moment. "You don't honestly see this as a challenge—as if you're really taking me away from Rudolf.''

Blake's attention was centered on her once again. "Of course, I do," he said as he took in the compressed line of her lips and the angry tilt of her chin. He laughed softly before kissing her firmly on the mouth. "The best kind of challenge. And taking you away from him has been easy, Countess; it's keeping you that's proving to be so difficult.''

"You should have told me you had a gold ring and a special license in your pocket." Cristina smiled mischievously. "You know how I love jewelry, so it looks as if you're stuck with me now."

"I hope so."

"And I always assumed you couldn't wait to be rid of me. As I heard it, you tried to foster me off on Nigel when I didn't want to go," Cristina teased.

"I know better than that now." He smiled at her. "I think I'll keep you around for a while," he teased, "so long as you don't bore me. I detest boring women." Blake didn't notice the hurt look on Cristina's face because he was too busy enjoying his own thoughts. Whatever else she was, Cristina Fairfax was never boring. That knowledge made him happy.

Cristina sat silently beside him. He didn't want her forever, only until boredom set in. "I'll see what I can do to keep from boring you."

Blake looked down at her with a puzzled expression on his face, then watched in something akin to horror as her face crumpled and she fought to keep the tears from rolling down her cheeks. Suddenly understanding dawned. "Good God, Countess! You can't actually think that being assaulted with jewelry or having a beautiful half-naked woman turn up in my bedroom at odd hours of the morning spewing fire is boring? I'm afraid I'll bore you long before you learn the meaning of the word." Blake held out his arms to her and Cristina moved closer.

"But I've gotten so big. . . ." She gestured toward her ever-expanding stomach. "And I get so droopy and cry all the time."

"Is that all that's worrying you?" Blake was half amused by her display of self-pity. It was so unexpected coming from Cristina. "Haven't I just proven I find you irresistible? I've never seen a more beautiful woman. You'll get your figure back after you have the little viscount here and you'll forget all about crying all the time and be back to your normal, unpredictable self."

"Are you sure?" She sniffed in a childlike voice.

"I know all about these things," he lied, "trust me."

"Oh, Blake. . . ." She sounded relieved, but the tears continued to fall from her luminous green eyes. "I can't find my handkerchief."

"Take mine." He handed her a square of linen. "Now dry your eyes and blow your nose. You're home and we can't have Leah thinking I've upset you again."

Cristina hadn't noticed the stillness of the carriage, but he was right, they were parked in front of her house.

The carriage door opened and the coachman reached up a hand to help her out. Blake remained seated in the corner of the coach. Cristina turned a questioning gaze on him.

"No," Blake told her, pulling her black veil from in back of her hat, concealing her face. "I won't get out. I don't want anyone to see us together yet." He jerked his head toward the closed carriage parked across the narrow street several houses down from hers. "You understand why?" he asked urgently, hoping to avoid any further misunderstandings between them.

"I understand," she told him. "I'm being watched by the secret police. And he's probably in that carriage."

"That's right." Blake leaned toward the door and touched her face with his gloved hand. "Don't worry. I'll take care of everything."

Cristina frowned up at him. She had learned that allowing someone take care of you had its drawbacks as well as its rewards. She didn't love Crown Prince Rudolf but he had been kind to her in his own way and she didn't want to embarrass or hurt him any more than Blake did. But not for matters of state. She didn't want to be the bone of contention between two men that she sensed genuinely liked and respected one another. But she also knew that she couldn't stay with Rudolf now that she had learned there was no joy or triumph in being desired by a man she didn't desire in return.

Some of what she was thinking must have shown on her face because Blake took her chin in his hand and spoke to her. "Cristina, are you reconsidering my proposal?"

"No."

"Are you sure? Because this decision can't be halfhearted."

Blake was allowing her to make a choice regardless of the effort it cost him to say the words. ''If we marry, it's forever. The decision is yours.''

Cristina hesitated a moment while Blake held his breath and prayed. ''I've made my decision.'' She leaned back into the coach to kiss him. ''I've chosen you.''

''Then leave everything to me.''

All this and heaven too.

—MATTHEW HENRY 1662–1714

Nineteen

HIS IMPERIAL HIGHNESS, the crown prince Rudolf, left for Prague two days later after bidding Cristina a careful good-bye. Officially the emperor was sending him to review several of his army regiments, but he and all Vienna knew that this was the emperor's way of removing Rudolf from the arms of his mistress, the comtesse di Rimaldi.

Negotiations were stalemated and Austria-Hungary was caught in the middle. No hint of scandal would be allowed to reach the ears of England's Queen Victoria, especially when everyone knew that the crown prince had met his mistress in London and that she was rumored to be half English on her mother's side.

Cristina knew who was responsible for the hastily arranged trip to Prague. Hadn't he said he would take care of everything? She hadn't seen Blake in two days, but she knew he had been very busy carrying out his immediate plan for Rudolf's removal. She wondered how Blake had managed to gain an audience with the emperor in so short a time.

"How long will you be gone, Your Highness?" She hated

to pretend, but it was important that she sound heartbroken and sympathetic to Rudolf's ears.

"A minimum of three months, *liebchen*. I may not be able to return in time for the child's birth."

"You must do your duty, Your Highness. You mustn't worry about me or the baby. We'll be fine," she assured him.

"But you will be alone," he protested.

"I'll have Leah."

"She's a servant."

"She's my dearest companion. So, you see, there's nothing for you to worry about. You must go and attend to your regiments and not concern yourself about me."

"You're a rare gem, Cristina. I'll miss you more than I believed possible and I shall pray every day that my absence will make your heart grow more fond of me."

"Pray, Your Highness?" Cristina teased. "Surely, you don't intend to kneel to a higher god?"

The crown prince laughed as he made his way to the front door. His views on religion were well known in Vienna, much to the dismay of his staunchly Roman Catholic father and Holy Roman Emperor. "For you, Cristina, I will even do that."

"Then perhaps you should stay," Cristina ventured, taking a huge risk. "I don't want to be responsible for corrupting a perfectly good crown prince. . . ."

"Ah, *liebchen*, if only I could stay with you." He kissed her lightly on the lips and disappeared out the door and into the confines of his imperial carriage. There was a reason for the distinctive imperial carriage with its golden wheels. Soon the whole of Vienna would know that their handsome crown prince had taken official leave of the mysterious fraulein. And that would please the emperor.

BLAKE ARRIVED AT the little house the next afternoon. Cristina was tense and uncertain. She had been on tenterhooks since the crown prince's visit, waiting for Blake to come.

Blake recognized her nervousness for what it was and took the bull by the horns. "No greeting, Countess?"

She stood hovering near the door to the salon. "Did you think that I would fling myself into your arms whenever you decided to visit?"

"As a matter of fact, I did." He held out his arms and Cristina took a step toward them before she could stop herself. "Don't you want to? Even a tiny bit?"

She did. She let herself be held in his strong embrace. "I thought you would never come."

"I had to wait until Rudolf was out of Vienna. I couldn't follow immediately hot on his trail. This way it looks as if I'm paying a social call."

"Are you?"

"You know better than that." He bent his head to capture her lips.

Cristina melted against him. "I've missed you, Blake." She ached to feel him next to her. "Shall we go upstairs?"

Blake caught his breath at the open invitation—the first she had ever offered—then regretfully shook his head. "Not here. Not in Rudolf's house."

"Then where?" Cristina was anxious at the prospect of enforced celibacy when Blake was so near. "In your secret room?"

"No, I've arranged for you to move to an apartment on the Ringstrasse."

"The Ring? Oh, Blake, the Ring is terribly expensive. Can we afford an apartment on the Ring?" she protested.

"Spoken like a wife already." He chuckled. "And yes, my darling countess, we can afford an apartment on the Ring."

"When?"

"Tomorrow morning," Blake told her. "But we'll have to keep it quiet for a while."

At her crestfallen look, he hastened to explain, "It's these bloody negotiations. Everyone is so touchy, so damned afraid of being slighted or of slighting someone else."

"And?"

"There are still a few sticking points in the San Stefano

Treaty and the Berlin Congress. I feel as if I'm walking on
eggshells, trying hard not to exert too much pressure, for fear
they'll break. The relations between our two empires are
strained to the limits of endurance, not only by the treaty
negotiations but by the Empress Elisabeth's continued visits
to and support of Ireland.'' He massaged the tired muscles at
the back of his neck, stretched his shoulders, then rubbed his
eyes and pinched the bridge of his nose in a effort to ease the
strain of hours of negotiations. ''The emperor can't or won't
rein her in and she sees Ireland as an underdog to be cham-
pioned and protected from our government. I'm sorry, sweetheart, but I don't know how much more our governments can
stand. I informed my superior of my plans to marry you and
of our situation, but I've been advised by Ambassador Paget
that it would be best if we marry quietly and delay announcing it until these negotiations are resolved. We can't risk al-
ienating the emperor by embarrassing his son.''

''How would our marriage embarrass Rudolf?''

Blake took a deep breath and tried to explain a part of
diplomacy that was almost impossible to grasp. ''It's all about
appearances, Cristina. Rudolf bid you a very public farewell.
He visited you during the daylight in full view of the emperor's secret police and he used his imperial carriage so that
everyone would know who he was and where he was going.
But he did it only to appease his father. He agreed only to
review his regiments in Prague because his father ordered him
to go. He gave every appearance of ending his affair with his
mistress, but Rudolf has no intentions of giving you up yet.
He's simply waiting for the negotiations to end before he
resumes his courtship.''

''What does it all mean to us?'' Cristina asked.

Blake sighed. ''It means you'll be moving into my apartment on the Ring.''

''With you?''

He shook his head. ''Not at first. I'll be moving into bachelor's quarters in the embassy.''

''Why?''

''Because I'm an ambassador to Franz Josef's court and I

mustn't give the appearance of stealing the crown prince's mistress right from under his nose—especially since I intend to marry you. Unless he's released you from his protection, I can't accept you into mine. It's not considered gentlemanly or honorable. And to do so here in Vienna while I'm representing Her Majesty's government would be an unforgivable breach of royal etiquette.''

''That's barbaric.''

''That's the way these things are done, Cristina. In this case, I've no choice but to follow the rules. Normally these things are personal and don't involve the fate of nations. They're handled in a quiet, civilized manner. But Rudolf was required to make a public farewell in order to convince the emperor and that public act will work to our advantage because by the time he returns from maneuvers after leaving you alone for three months, he'll find you gone. There won't be anything he can do. The emperor will be informed that you've left Rudolf's house and most, if not all, of Vienna will know of the change in your status and accept the fact. And Rudolf will, too. Because he'll have no other choice.'' Blake explained his plan.

''Then why do we have to keep our marriage a secret?''

''Because,'' Blake told her, ''it's one thing to steal a man's mistress and quite another to marry her. We can't risk tweaking the crown prince's nose or the emperor's and if our marriage was made public, you, as the wife of an ambassador, would be expected to accompany me to certain diplomatic functions which would include the imperial family. And in light of your acknowledged relationship with Rudolf, that would be considered a slight.''

Cristina nervously bit her bottom lip. ''So I'll be a wife pretending to be a mistress.''

''Only until we can make an official announcement.''

''When will that be?''

''Hopefully by Christmas.''

''Oh.''

He looked at Cristina and recognized the disappointment in her face. ''I'm sorry, Cristina. I know it's not the way you wanted it. It's not what I wanted, either, but until these bloody negotiations are over it's the best I can offer. What do you say?''

''This isn't exactly what I had in mind.'' She tried to smile, but couldn't quite manage it.

Blake wasn't any happier about the situation than Cristina. He didn't like the idea of them living apart or the fact that most of Vienna would believe that she had, indeed, found a new protector instead of a husband. And although it wasn't the way he had wanted things to be, at least he had found a way to marry her with as few political repercussions as possible. ''You can always refuse to marry me again.''

''I don't want my child to be born a bastard,'' she said bluntly.

''Neither do I.''

''Is that why you're marrying me?''

''No.''

''But it is part of the reason,'' she persisted, hoping Blake would say the three little words that would make her feel so much better about the entire situation.

''Of course it is. It's also part of the reason you're marrying me.''

''But it would make everything easier for you if we didn't get married—if I simply became your mistress, wouldn't it, Blake?''

''You already are my mistress,'' Blake told her. ''And no, it wouldn't make anything easier, not when I want you to be my wife.''

Cristina sighed. He wasn't going to say it. He'd said he wanted her, had told her he needed her, but he hadn't said he loved her. Not yet. And after Meredith, who could blame him? At least he was showing her. ''What will happen once we let everyone in on our secret?''

''Nothing, I hope,'' Blake said. ''The negotiations should be completed by that time and everything should be back to normal.''

''What if someone should find out before we can make the

official announcement? Would that undermine your position here?''

''I don't know,'' he admitted. ''After the negotiations conclude, I don't think anyone will care—except maybe Rudolf. But it's a risk I'm willing to take.'' He paused for a moment and looked at her, almost afraid to breathe for fear she would change her mind and decide not to marry him after all. ''How about you, Countess?''

''I'll risk it.''

There was something in the way she answered him that made Blake offer her the other alternative—the one he'd been trying to avoid. ''There is another way,'' he said.

''What way?''

''You could stay here, Cristina. You could wait in this house until Rudolf returns and see if he really means to obey his father—if he really has taken his leave of you or if he's simply giving his father three months to cool off and forget about ordering him to stay away from you. The negotiations should be concluded by the time he returns.''

She wasn't about to consider that alternative, but she was curious. ''You don't think he intends to continue to try to see me, do you?''

''I would.''

''Will he?''

Blake turned and began to pace. ''I don't know. But I think he might.'' He let out the breath he'd been holding. ''I've known Rudolf for years. I've seen what happens when he tires of his mistresses. He presents them with a gift, Countess. A silver cigarette box engraved with his initial and his archducal crown and writes their name in his official ''Register of Conquests.'' Believe me, I've seen it many times before. Did he give you a cigarette box before he left?''

Cristina frowned. ''No. I don't smoke.''

''It doesn't matter,'' Blake told her. ''He gives one to each of his mistresses when he tires of them. But there's no reason for him to tire of you because he hasn't become your lover yet. I'd feel better about this if he'd given you a cigarette box. As it is, I think he's waiting for your child to be born, waiting for his opportunity." Blake shook his head. "Maybe I'm wrong. Maybe he'll have forgotten all about you once he returns from Prague and goes hunting for a suitable royal Catholic bride."

"I didn't know he was looking for a bride," Cristina said.

"Well he is and I'm happy to say your name isn't on his list."

"I never wanted to be on Rudolf's list," she said, softly. "I simply don't want to build my happiness at someone else's expense."

"Then make your decision."

"I've already made it, Lord Lawrence. I chose you. And I want you any way I can get you. Don't leave me here. Take me with you. I can live without Rudolf. But I don't want to live without you."

Blake crushed her to him. "Have Leah pack your things as quickly as possible. I'll send someone by later tonight to take them to the apartment. I don't think there's any reason to drag out the process. I'm going out of my mind thinking about you in this house. I want you where I know you'll be safe."

Cristina hugged Blake tighter, burrowing into his hard chest. "I'm so glad you cared enough to come for me."

Blake kissed her on the forehead. "I was a fool to let you go in the first place. I promise you it won't happen again. We belong together. We make a special kind of magic together that I've never experienced before and I don't want to lose you or it again."

He hadn't said he loved her but he was placing his career in jeopardy for her and it didn't seem to faze him at all. Maybe he didn't love her or couldn't love her; but he was giving her a part of himself and that was more than he had ever offered before. Cristina knew she would accept whatever part of himself he chose to share and make it enough. She had promised to trust him and she intended to keep that promise. There was no room for further doubts. He had shown her he cared. Perhaps one day he would tell her how much.

THE PACKING TOOK several hours. Blake had returned to the embassy to finish some work. Cristina didn't expect to see him again until after she was settled into the apartment, so it was an unexpected pleasure to find him standing beside the wagon issuing orders while their trunks were loaded.

"What are you doing here?"

"Helping to move my little family." He enjoyed the surprise and the look of pleasure on her face. "What sort of host would I be if I let you travel to my apartment alone at night?"

Cristina smiled at him. He had known she dreaded the thought of facing a strange empty apartment. "Leah would have been with me."

"That's not the same and you know it." Blake grinned at Leah. "Not that Leah isn't a marvel."

"Oh, you're quite right, Lord Lawrence," Leah encouraged, "I am a marvel but I'm not as young as I once was and I like havin' a strong man around the house myself. Just in case. . . ."

"You're both impossible," Cristina scolded playfully, happier than Leah at the prospect of having Blake around.

"I may be impossible, but you're glad to see me just the same," Blake told her.

"Whatever gave you that idea?"

"You did, Countess. Except for a kiss, your greeting couldn't have been any better. I like the warm light in your eyes. I don't know if the baby's responsible or if I am, but I like the change in you, Cris." His words were sincere, warm, and caressing.

"My feelings toward you haven't changed since this afternoon."

"The warm light was there this afternoon, Cristina. It's been there since our meeting in the embassy."

"Well at least there's something warm about me. I remember you once called me an ice maiden and your accusation is about to become fact."

"That was long ago, Countess, and all in the past—" he began.

"No, it isn't." She looked toward the heavens and Blake realized a light rain had begun to fall. He also realized Cristina was shivering.

"You should've told me you were freezing," Blake admonished. "Wait in the fiacre behind the wagon while I get you a cloak."

He helped her into the carriage, asked the driver to wait a few minutes longer, then left to find her a cloak.

The rain began to fall harder and Cristina could hear the driver grumbling about moving in the middle of the night, and in such weather, too. She sympathized but there was little she could do about his discomfort at the moment. She shivered again and pulled the lap robe as high as she could, tucking the ends beneath her.

Blake returned a few moments later with Leah and Cristina's velvet cloak. He handed Leah up into the fiacre and followed her inside, then took a seat beside Cristina where he began arranging her velvet cloak around her shoulders. "It won't take long to get there," he promised.

"Tell us what it's like," Cristina urged.

"It's an apartment in a very respectable building on the Ring opposite the site of the new Court Theater."

"Have you lived there long?"

"Not very." He shook his head, refusing to divulge any more details of his residence in Vienna.

"What's it like inside?" Cristina persisted, eager to know all about the new home Blake had provided for her and for their child.

"You'll see for yourself soon enough." Blake changed the subject by regaling her with the history of the Ringstrasse. "It's a wide boulevard built on the site of the ancient medieval wall that surrounded Vienna for centuries and provided protection from the Turks. The walls were razed and the Ring begun in honor of the birth of the crown prince. It has yet to be completed."

"You mean it's taken twenty years to build a street?" Leah blurted out.

Blake laughed. "Vienna can be a bit slow about things at times, but that's one of her charms. Everything changes and everything stays the same. Don't judge the engineers too harshly because this isn't just any street. The Ring is meant to be the center of all activity in Vienna. Everyone who is anyone will want to live on the Ring."

"And you have rooms here?" Cristina was surprised. "I thought you shunned polite society as much as possible."

"I do," Blake agreed. "But I like a new building as opposed to a four-hundred-year-old dwelling and the address is convenient."

The vehicle rolled to a stop before a modern, stone building, one of the newest on the Ring. Blake helped the ladies out of the fiacre and paid the driver. Cristina strained to see the exterior of the building but was unable to make out any details. The rain was heavier and the gaslights that lined the streets glowed eerily through the haze, giving off little light.

"Welcome home," Blake merrily announced, unlocking the door. He ushered Cristina into the first-floor apartment and lit the gas lamps.

Cristina looked around. "It's lovely," she breathed, "everything is perfect."

"I'm glad you like it. Cason has done his job well," Blake told her. "Now come see the rest of it. This is just the sitting room."

The apartment was larger than Cristina imagined. There were eight beautifully furnished rooms and a modern bath. Leah followed at a discreet distance as Blake took Cristina through the apartment. "There is a library through there"—he indicated a door—"a small kitchen, a guest room, a bedroom for Leah, and a master suite as well as the sitting room and dining room and bath."

"I don't know what to say!" Cristina exclaimed.

"Don't say anything until you see the rest of it," Blake told her.

"There's more?"

"A little." Blake took her hand in his and led her toward the master bedroom.

"Blake, you've already shown me the bedroom—" she began.

"You only saw a part of it," he explained, opening the door that connected the two rooms of the suite. "Surprise!"

Cristina couldn't believe her eyes. The second bedroom of the suite had been turned into a nursery with beige wallpaper printed with scenes of little girls hosting tea parties and little boys rolling hoops. A lace-canopied baby bed stood beside one wall and a matching cradle stood on the other. A rocking chair sat on a Turkish rug in the center of the room while a beautifully carved wooden hobbyhorse occupied a corner opposite the cradle.

Several porcelain dolls, a set of tin soldiers painted a vivid red, a toy drum, and a set of story books were placed about the room. It was a dream nursery.

"Oh, Blake, it's wonderful!" She hugged him impulsively. "You tricked me. You've never lived here. All this is brand new."

"Oh, but I did live here." Blake smiled at her.

"But a nursery?" Cristina's face dimmed the slightest bit as she wondered for a moment if this nursery had once been prepared for a child of Meredith's and abandoned after the death of their marriage.

"It was a bedroom. I've had decorators working around the clock for the past three days turning it into a nursery, painting and papering while I shopped. I knew you would want the baby close by. And I wanted to surprise you and make you happy."

"It's the best surprise I've ever had." The joy was back in her face. "It's wonderful! I can't believe you went to all this trouble for me."

"For us, Countess. I did it for us." The expression on his face was serious, his voice a little stern. "For you and me and our baby."

"Will you stay with me tonight?" Her eyes communicated her passion.

"I have to stay," he admitted. "I don't think I can force myself to leave."

"It will be all right," Cristina assured him, thinking of the problems their marriage could cause.

Blake nodded, "As long as we keep everything quiet. As long as we're discreet."

I know that's a secret, for it's
whispered every where.

—WILLIAM CONGREVE 1670–1729

Twenty

DISCREET. IT WAS impossible to be discreet in a city like
Vienna. The very walls had ears and the Austrian populace
loved nothing better than a romance. This new romance whet-
ted their appetites for gossip. It seemed the mysterious comtesse di Rimaldi had wasted very little time in finding a new
protector after the crown prince had broken her heart, but an
English ambassador? The coffeehouses were full of whispered
speculations concerning the real reason behind the absence of
the prince. It was common knowledge around Vienna that the
crown prince had bid farewell to his mistress at the request
of the emperor. There had to be a reason. And the city's most
enterprising gossips were hard at work producing embellished
stories and polishing rumors. The emperor didn't usually concern himself with his son's affairs of the heart; why this one?
And just how acquainted was the English ambassador with
the comtesse? The gossips had it on the best authority that
the lady in question was with child. Whose child? That question was on the lips of many who regularly patronized the
coffeehouses, and the Viennese were determined to find out.

Blake heard the whispered rumors and speculations and

ignored them. He had followed the rules as best he could. He had married Cristina in a small quiet ceremony in the tiny English church several blocks from the embassy with only Leah and Cason as witnesses, although he would have preferred the big formal wedding he had had with Meredith. And so far he had managed to follow his government's instructions and keep their marriage a secret when every fiber of his being urged him to have the church bells rung and to announce his good fortune from the spire of St. Stephen's.

Now his private life was his own. And if the Foreign Office couldn't accept that, then the Foreign Office be damned! He ignored the heated exchanges from London demanding that he cease his folly, as he ignored the lectures from his superiors regarding the gossip and the time he spent in Cristina's company and the possible consequences to his sterling career.

Let them wonder about the mysterious comtesse. Let them whisper about him at official functions. He could whisper a few things about some of their private lives if he chose to do so. For once, Blake Ashford, ninth earl of Lawrence, didn't give a damn what the British community thought of him. Being with Cristina and sharing the impending birth of his child was all that mattered to him.

He had meant to exercise restraint. To be discreet. But he couldn't stay away from Cristina. He didn't want to stay away. She was his wife even if the rest of the world thought otherwise, and Blake invented excuses to see her and spent every free moment in her company, taking her for carriage rides along the Ringstrasse, strolls in the Prater Amusement Park and the gardens of the Hofburg, and romantic carriage rides through the Vienna woods. He resented the diplomatic functions, receptions, and tedious court balls that kept him away from her. He preferred the quiet evenings in their apartment to anything the city had to offer. He stayed with her in spite of his better judgment and hadn't seen the inside of his bachelor's quarters for weeks. His nights were spent holding his bride in his arms. Blake knew he was behaving foolishly—throwing caution to the wind for the second time in his life. He felt once again like a youth caught in the maddening throes of first love, and while a part of him recognized the folly of his obsession, he was unwilling to control it.

Blake had always prided himself on his ability to detach himself from his emotions and even to perform distasteful duties with skill and certain aplomb. He enjoyed the company of generals, statesmen, and ruling monarchs and was stimulated by the conversation of brilliant men and the demanding task of dealing with problems in a logical manner. He had never dreamed he would risk it all for a woman. Any woman. The idea had been so repellent to him during his years with Meredith that he had plodded on in the marriage working to further himself in his career, loving his work when there was nothing else for him to love. His personal life had been a shambles for so long there had been no room for other involvements. Lovers had been expendable, easily acquired and just as easily discarded. And Blake had never doubted his way of life until he fell in love with Cristina.

No other woman challenged him quite like Cristina—not even Meredith. And he had certainly never gone to such lengths to be with one. He still found it hard to believe he had coerced Cristina into staying with him in London to keep her within his reach. He considered himself a gentleman. But he realized now that he was a gentleman only when it suited his purpose. Cristina brought out the explosive side of him that had always lurked beneath the cool, rational, gentlemanly surface as well as the protective, intimate part of his nature. His life had changed since meeting her. Now everything was secondary to his overwhelming need of her.

Blake watched her now, diligently sewing some small garment for the baby, her shining head bent over her work. He hated to spoil the Christmas holiday for her, but he had to tell her the truth. "Rudolf is back in Vienna."

She looked up and her gaze found his, searching. "Why?"

"It's the Christmas season, Countess. Rudolf's come home for the holidays. The Russian Embassy is hosting a Christmas ball tomorrow night and the entire Court will be in attendance."

"Does he know about us?" Cristina was anxious. "Does he know where to find me?"

"How could he not know? It was silly to think we could keep it a secret. The whole city knows about us, Cristina. We haven't exactly been discreet."

"Will he come here, do you think?"

"I know he will. I saw him at the embassy this morning. He thinks our government and the emperor pressured you into accepting me as your protector while he was away."

"But that's not true."

"Rudolf thinks it is. He's adamant about seeing you, talking to you," Blake told her grimly, clearly upset with the new turn of events.

"I'll have to see him," Cristina acknowledged. "I didn't like sneaking out of his house any more than I like the idea of keeping our marriage a secret. I think I owe him an explanation."

Blake exploded with a force of anger that made Cristina jump. "You don't owe him anything."

"In his own way, he was kind to me," Cristina reminded her husband.

"He used you, Cristina."

"He may have tried. But he didn't use me any more than I used him. It happens that we were both victims of greed. He was a victim of my mother's scheme as much as I was." Cristina spoke the bitter truth as she understood it.

"Rudolf wasn't a victim, Cristina. He was a willing participant in your mother's little plan to deflower you for profit."

"But he had no way of knowing that I wasn't just as willing as he was," Cristina insisted.

"I thought you made that quite clear on the dance floor. You practically spat in his face. I thought you made your position very clear. I understood it, even if he didn't."

"Your memory has become very one-sided, Blake. Even you accused me of enticing him. He thought I was willing. He had reason to believe I was when my mother accepted that necklace on my behalf."

"But if you hadn't escaped down the bedsheets and I hadn't intervened, he wouldn't have stopped long enough to find out," Blake insisted stubbornly. "He still used you."

"No more than I used him when I made him bring me to Vienna. And in its way, my deception is worse. I allowed him to think I might care for him one day. Rudolf and I are even. Why can't you see that?" Cristina was tired of the argument. It was pointless. They seemed to continue to beat the topic of Rudolf to death with no possible hope of resolution. She struggled to rise from her oversoft chair and find a more comfortable position for her aching back, but was hampered by the heaviness of her unborn child. She couldn't stand to argue with Blake after all the months of happiness. It made her sick inside.

Blake watched Cristina struggle with her burden and was filled with remorse for his jealous behavior. Because deep down, Blake knew Cristina considered Rudolf a friend. "Maybe it's because I came so close to losing you to him."

Cristina looked over at Blake with tears in her eyes.

"I didn't mean to upset you, Countess. I just wanted to prepare you for Rudolf's return."

Cristina's anger melted when he'd called her "Countess" in that particular tone of voice. It reminded her of all the sensuous whispers he used when he held her in his arms and made love to her. "Blake, we've been happy together these last months, haven't we? We haven't been living in fool's paradise, have we?"

"Yes . . . no." Blake raked his fingers through his hair. "I mean to say that yes I've been happy with you and if it's a fool's paradise, then I want to be a fool for the rest of my life."

"Have I given you any reason to distrust me since our marriage?"

"Of course not."

"Do you think I'm like my mother or Meredith?"

"Christ, no!" Blake snapped. "You're not like that at all and you know it."

"Then why do you feel threatened by Rudolf?" Her logic

was inescapable and Blake finally began to see things from her point of view.

Because I love you. He wanted to say the words aloud but something stopped him. It had been so long since he'd dared say them. And Blake was afraid to tempt fate. What if she couldn't say them back? "Countess, I never meant to argue about him again. I don't want him coming between us."

"Then don't let him, Blake. Please, just forget about Rudolf until the time comes for me to tie up loose ends and say good-bye to him in my own way. It's something I have to do. I don't want anything to spoil our first Christmas together. I want to be happy and I want to be with you."

Blake smiled then, remembering the remainder of his message. "Then I have a surprise for you, Countess."

Cristina's eyes sparkled with excitement. "What is it?"

"Our embassy is giving a Christmas ball next week, after the Russian and the French parties, and Ambassador Paget asked me today if I would like to use the ball as an occasion to announce our wedding."

"Oh, Blake!" Cristina clasped her hands together in delight. "This is the best Christmas gift you could give me!"

He grinned. "The negotiations ended early this morning. I telegraphed my parents in London to tell them the news, and although they can't be here for our announcement, they've agreed to make an announcement of their own at our traditional Christmas gathering at Everleigh tomorrow night."

Cristina pushed herself out of her chair and made her way over to Blake, then leaned over and covered his face with kisses. "You've known since early this morning and you waited all this time to tell me? How could you?"

"I've been keeping a major secret for months," he teased. "I didn't think one more would matter."

"Are we really going to go?" She couldn't believe it. She'd waited so long.

"Of course we're going, Cristina. I'm not foolish enough to pass up a golden opportunity to present my wife—my countess—to the world."

Cristina shrieked in glee, looking every bit like the twenty-year-old young woman she was. "Did you hear that, Leah?" she shouted. "I'm going to another ball!"

Leah came running from the kitchen. "It's about time," she proclaimed, knowing well the importance of the announcement. She studied the excited gleam in Cristina's shining eyes and the satisfied expression on Lord Lawrence's face and then she turned her attention to Cristina's burgeoning figure. "Merciful heavens," she muttered. "What are you going to wear?"

Cristina stopped, remembering her advanced pregnancy. "Oh, no."

She looked so mortified, so stricken that Blake's heart seemed to stop.

"Don't worry," he told them. "I stopped by the dressmaker's. Your dress will be delivered in two days' time."

THE FOLLOWING WEEK, the British embassy in Vienna was all decked out for the holiday season and the annual Christmas ball was just the beginning. After Christmas came New Year's and a new round of parties and on the day of Epiphany, January sixth, the most brilliant party of all began—Fasching, or carnival, a splendid citywide celebration that continued on until Lent. But Cristina didn't care about the rest of Vienna's glorious winter season. She only cared about the British Christmas ball. She wanted everything to be perfect and as if acquiescing to her wishes even the weather cooperated, taking part in the enchantment by dropping several inches of beautiful white powder snow on the city, turning the parks into a winter wonderland.

The entrance to the embassy was decorated with green garlands—pine boughs, holly, and mistletoe tied with red bows and draped with gold cord. And inside the vast marble foyer stood a huge fir tree decorated with glass ornaments, paper fans, cornucopias filled with holiday sweets and a multitude of tiny white beeswax candles, and topped with a pure white porcelain angel.

The holiday display enchanted Cristina as she collected the smells, sights, sounds, and impressions of her second ball like tiny treasures meant for Christmas stockings. She shivered with excitement. Her second ball was even more exciting than the first one because this time she arrived on the arm of her husband.

"Isn't it beautiful?" she asked Blake as they stood in the entrance of the embassy waiting to be announced. She stood transfixed, staring at the breathtaking sights around her.

"Yes," he replied sincerely, staring at Cristina, at the sparkling green of her eyes and the snowflakes melting on her hair and eyelashes.

Cristina giggled, a deep throaty giggle that caught Blake in the midsection with the force of a blow. "I meant the embassy—all the decorations."

Blake glanced around. "A fitting setting for a beautiful countess."

"Oh, Blake, I can't believe it's really about to happen. I can't believe the day has come when we can make our announcement and tell the whole world."

"At least this corner of it," Blake commented. He couldn't seem to keep his eyes off his wife. He had never seen her look so vibrant. Even her voice quivered with excitement.

"I'm so happy." She tightened her grip on Blake's arm as he handed his invitation to the doorman, then she looked up at her handsome husband who was formally dressed in white tie and tails.

"I'm glad," Blake told her simply. "Because I want to spend the remainder of my life making you happy."

Cristina shivered again involuntarily. "I keep thinking there must be a law against being this happy, that something must happen to change it."

"Never," Blake promised. "Not while I'm alive." He leaned down and brushed his lips against her forehead. "Don't worry, Countess. This is our night. Nothing will be allowed to spoil it."

"His Excellency Blake Ashford, ninth earl of Lawrence, Her Majesty's special envoy to Austria-Hungary," the doorman intoned, "and his guest, the comtesse di Rimaldi."

Cristina heard the gasps of surprise that came from the lips of the assembled guests as Blake proudly escorted her into the ballroom, but she ignored the outraged whispers. She had debated the issue of using her alias, the comtesse di Rimaldi, with Blake for hours before she decided it was better than using her true name—her father's name. The comtesse di Rimaldi already had a less-than-sterling reputation in Vienna. Cristina saw no reason to risk tarnishing her own name by showing up, obviously pregnant, at a British embassy ball. As far as Vienna and the British community in Vienna was concerned, Comtesse di Rimaldi was Lord Lawrence's mistress. And Cristina thought it best that she remain Comtesse di Rimaldi. Ambassador Paget knew the truth and that was all that mattered. She didn't care that some of the men in the group were loudly protesting the fact that Lord Lawrence had dared bring his mistress to an embassy gathering where wives were present. She ignored the protests and insults thrown their way, and resolutely refused to let anything spoil her lovely Christmas ball.

She had every right to accompany Blake, every right to stand at his side at an embassy function or any other. On her left hand, beneath the elbow-length gold kid gloves, she wore was a heavy gold band that bore a carved adaptation of climbing roses. It wasn't the traditional wedding band worn by all the Lawrence brides—the one Meredith had worn—but a new one, designed by Blake and engraved with their initials, the date of their wedding, and the words: *I choose thee*. It was elegant and precious and all hers.

Cristina glanced over at her husband and smiled. In an hour or so, after the announcement, everything would change. Their secret would be out and everyone would know she and Blake were legally married.

A part of her almost regretted letting the rest of the world into their lives. Keeping a secret—an extraordinary secret— amidst the gossip and speculation and talk sometimes seemed more romantic than the reality—and so intimate and cozy. But another part of her was sick of the subterfuge, sick of the need for it, and Cristina gloried in the idea that the truth would set them free to love in the sunlight, as well as the shadows. And she knew Blake was weary of the subterfuge as well. He was proud of her and of their unborn child and he wanted to show them off.

Blake had gone out of his way to make this night special for her—lavishing her with expensive presents and outrageous compliments to make her feel more at ease in the company of the wealthy, sophisticated diplomatists and statesmen and their wives. He hadn't given a thought to the cost of dressing her for this occasion—only of making her feel beautiful, pampered, and loved.

And it had worked. The dress she wore was an exquisite velvet creation the warm color of pure gold—a shade that complimented her fair complexion and her lustrous red hair. With it she wore the gold kid gloves and another of Blake's early Christmas gifts—an extravagant rope of perfectly matched pearls which sported a rare canary-yellow diamond pendant fashioned in the shape of a teardrop. A matching bracelet and dangling dropped-pearl earrings completed the ensemble.

Blake stared at his wife as she tightened her grip on his arm. He had given her a king's ransom in jewels, but the diamonds and pearls couldn't begin to compare with the beauty that was Cristina. She sparkled, she enchanted, she captured the attention of everyone in the room the way she had captivated him on the night of her first formal ball.

"Don't pay attention to the ugly remarks, Countess," Blake urged. "Keep your head up and your back straight, look everyone right in the eye. You have nothing to hide. Nothing of which to be ashamed." He lifted her chin with the tip of his finger. "And believe me, there aren't many of us in the room who can say the same."

"Blake," Cristina let out the breath she'd been holding. "What would I do without you?"

"You wouldn't be in this situation if it wasn't for me. You wouldn't be subjected to this gossip if it wasn't for me. But, believe me, Countess, no one has ever made me happier or more proud than you," he answered honestly. "You're intelligent, and you have determination, grace, and courage. You'd do very well all on your own. But, lucky for me, I'm by your side. So you won't be able to get by without me."

Cristina reached up and touched his cheek. "I never want to get by without you. You're the best thing that ever happened to me."

Blake shook his head. "No, my sweet, I'm the bastard who got you into all this mess."

She looked him right in the eyes, daring him to contradict her again. "Like I said," she repeated. "You're the best thing that ever happened to me. The day you burst into my life is the day my life began."

Blake couldn't speak. Tears glistened in his eyes and for a moment he simply stood there and gazed at her—at the marvel who was Cristina.

Cristina smiled up at him. "Well," she teased, "since you brought me to this party, the least you can do is ask me to dance."

Blake swallowed the lump in his throat and extended his arm in invitation. "Dance, Countess?"

And they did. Almost every dance. Right up until the time the orchestra stopped playing, a few minutes before the midnight buffet, so Ambassador Paget could make the announcement. "Ladies and gentleman," he addressed the crowd. "There have been a few whispers this evening and several of you have approached me to air your grievances concerning Lord Lawrence's appearance here tonight with the young lady who accompanied him."

There were further whispers and several loud protests regarding the lack of form Paget displayed by publicly airing the controversy. "Quiet, now." The ambassador raised his hands, gesturing for the guests to quiet so he could be heard. "As it so happens that tonight's Christmas ball is a closed affair. The invitations issued tonight went to members of the British community serving Her Majesty's government here in Vienna. No outside tickets were sold and no other invitations issued to any person not a member of our little community.

As you know from previous balls, this is highly unusual. The Austrian emperor and his representatives usually attend our gathering, but because of the sensitive nature of the negotiations we've just concluded in the San Stefano Treaty and the Berlin Congress, the emperor decided not to accept any invitations from the countries involved in the negotiations, for fear of slighting one or the other. Her Majesty agreed with the emperor's decision and, indeed, applauded it, for it gave us a chance to make most important announcement concerning Her Majesty's special envoy, Lord Lawrence and the young lady who accompanied him tonight.''

"What's he doing?" Cristina whispered to Blake.

"I don't know," Blake answered. "He told me not to worry—that he was going to make an announcement that would set everything to rights." He reached for Cristina's gloved hand and gripped it.

"Don't you have any idea?" she whispered again.

Blake shook his head. "We'll just have to trust him."

"Now," the ambassador continued, "I'm going to ask Lord Lawrence and his young lady to step up here." He motioned for Blake and Cristina to join him.

Blake escorted Cristina to the first landing of the staircase where Ambassador Paget waited, then stood next to her. The ambassador moved to stand on Cristina's other side, while Lady Paget the ambassador's wife, stepped forward to stand beside Blake in an indisputable show of acceptance and unity. "Ladies and gentlemen," Ambassador Paget addressed the guests once more. "Lord Lawrence and this young woman have made a tremendous personal sacrifice on behalf of Her Majesty's government. Those of you who were in London several months ago know of the visit of a certain member of the Austrian imperial court. What you don't know is that our government arranged for this young woman—known to you as the comtesse di Rimaldi—to accompany that most royal person from London to Vienna in order to avoid any complications in the delicate negotiations we've just completed.''

The ambassador's announcement was news to Blake and

to Cristina, but as they stood before the assembled guests, their faces didn't betray their surprise.

"Is our government acting as procurer now for members of foreign royalty?" came a question from the crowd.

Blake started. The voice sounded familiar. Very familiar. He scanned the crowd, but he couldn't locate the owner of the voice.

"No, indeed not," the ambassador replied. "But our government and His Imperial Majesty agreed that it would be a very good idea for someone like this young lady to accompany that most royal personage on the journey home from London in order to keep other less scrupulous members of other governments from trying to persuade that most royal person to intervene on their behalf."

The fictitious explanation the ambassador wove sounded completely legitimate to these men and women who had been a part of the royal machinery for years. They understood the way the government worked and that one of the major problems a ruling monarch had to face was how to rein in the heir to the crown effectively—how to govern the heir without undermining that heir's of their own position in government and in society.

"The woman known to you as the Comtesse di Rimaldi was in fact working for Her Majesty's government. She was accompanied by a most acceptable chaperon at all times and lived alone in a house belonging to that royal member of the Austrian imperial family. She was not and never has been his mistress."

"Then how do you account for that?" the same voice asked, bringing attention to Cristina's pregnant state.

"I can account for it," Blake stepped forward.

The crowd erupted into amused laughter. But the ambassador had had enough. "Ladies and gentleman, what Lord Lawrence means is—"

"We know what he means."

"The comtesse di Rimaldi, or as she was formerly known, Miss Cristina Fairfax, is Lord Lawrence's wife."

"What?" a collective gasp went up from the crowd.

"May I present to you the ninth earl and countess of Lawrence?" Ambassador Paget paused for effect, then continued his story. "As I said earlier, Lord and Lady Lawrence made a tremendous personal sacrifice when they agreed to keep their marriage a secret until after the sensitive negotiations were completed. Lord and Lady Lawrence have suffered the indignation of being labeled by Viennese society and members of our own community when all the while they were acting to protect the interests of Her Majesty's government. We owe them both a debt of thanks," the ambassador concluded, "and a heartfelt apology." He turned to Cristina, leaned forward, and kissed her on the cheek. "My dear Lady Lawrence, let me be the first to welcome you into our little community."

The guests stood in stunned silence for a moment, then began pressing forward to offer their felicitations to the happy couple. But a disturbance between the sergeant-at-arms and an apparent gate-crasher off to the right of the stairway at the first-level entrance interrupted the procession.

A lone person began to clap. "Bravo, Ambassador Paget, congratulations on a very credible explanation and an extremely touching gesture." The crowds parted as a beautiful black-haired woman in a stunning ballgown was wheeled toward the platform by a man who bore a striking resemblance to Lord Lawrence. "There's just one tiny detail you overlooked." The woman paused dramatically. "That woman can't be Lord Lawrence's wife." She stared at Cristina. "She can't be Countess Lawrence. Because, you see," she pointed to Blake, "he already has a wife. *I'm* the countess of Lawrence."

Cristina turned to Blake for confirmation.

He stared at his cousin, Jack, standing behind the wheelchair, then fixed his angry gaze on the triumphant face of the woman sitting in the wheelchair. "Meredith."

The serpent hath slithered into the garden.

—ANONYMOUS

Twenty-one

CHAOS ERUPTED IN the ballroom as the gong sounded announcing dinner.

Ambassador Paget leaned down and spoke to Lady Paget. "See that everyone goes into dinner. I'll join you in a moment." He waited while his wife ushered the curious group into the dining room, then shouted for a sergeant-at-arms. "Escort Lady Lawrence into Lord Lawrence's office."

The sergeant-at-arms stood between Cristina and Meredith and glanced from one to the other.

"The first Lady Lawrence," the ambassador snapped. "The dead one."

The sergeant-at-arms elbowed Jack Ashford aside, then grabbed hold of the back of the wheelchair and pushed Meredith to the stairs where two men-at-arms stood on either side of her wheelchair and lifted it, carrying her up the stairs to the privacy of Blake's office. Jack followed behind them.

Ambassador Paget turned to Blake. "Shall I retire to the antechamber?"

Knowing the ambassador could hear every word spoken in

his office from the tiny adjoining antechamber, Blake nodded. "Thank you, sir. I may need a witness."

"Agreed." The ambassador hurried up the stairs and down the hall to the secret entrance of the antechamber that connected Lord Lawrence's suite of office to his own.

Blake shouted for his assistant. "Cason, take Lady Lawrence back home."

Cason appeared almost immediately and gently took hold of Cristina's elbow.

"No, Blake," Cristina protested. "I don't want to go home. I want to say with you."

"I'll be home later," Blake promised. "Now please go with Cason while I find out what's going on."

"Blake . . ."

"Please, Countess," Blake leaned down and ignoring the others around them, kissed his wife tenderly. "I can't think straight if I'm worrying about you. Please go home. I don't want you or the baby in harm's way."

"I thought she was dead," Cristina murmured.

"So did I," Blake told her. "Dear God, so I did. Go home, Cristina, and wait for me."

"Blake," she reached out and grabbed hold of his arm. "There's just one more thing."

"What is it?"

"She's come back from the dead for a reason," Cristina warned. "I believe she could be dangerous."

"She's a viper in women's clothing," Blake answered.

"All the more reason for you to be careful."

"I will. Now go with Cason." He kissed her again.

"I'll wait up for you," Cristina told him.

"It may be very late."

"It doesn't matter," she said. "I'll still be waiting."

SHE SAT WITH pillows surrounding her slender frame, supporting her slight weight. Her skirts were meticulously arranged to camouflage the unnatural angle of one hip. Blake was forced to admire the illusion she presented. Even Victoria herself could not have done any better. But then, Meredith was a master of illusion—of always appearing to be something she was not.

Blake crossed half the length of the room and halted within inches of her. "All right," he said when he stood facing her, "you've come back from the dead. Do you mind explaining the reason for this dramatic resurrection after six years?"

"I think that's self-explanatory," Jack said.

Blake turned to Jack. "I warned you, Jack, years ago. Now get out before I throw you out." He pointed to door.

Jack glanced at Meredith. "It's all right, Jack darling. Blake won't hurt me. Not when there are witnesses."

Jack still hesitated.

"Get him out of here," Blake ordered the sergeant-at-arms.

The sergeant didn't hesitate. He grabbed Jack by the arm and forcibly escorted him to through the door.

"You were about to tell me why you reappeared after six years," Blake continued once Jack had been removed from the room.

"Was I?"

"Meredith, I'm in no mood for your taunting games. Either you tell me what you want with me or I walk out that door. I have better things to do than spend my time sparring with you."

"Ah, yes, little miss Fairfax is waiting with open arms at your little apartment on the Ringstrasse, no doubt."

"Leave Cristina out of this," Blake ordered. "Tell me what you want and be done with it."

"My, aren't we touchy?"

"Mer—e—dith." He bit out her name, holding his temper tightly in rein, forcing the words through his tightly clenched teeth. "I asked for an explanation."

"As Jack said, it's self-explanatory. I had to reappear in order to protect my interests."

"You have no interests where I'm concerned."

"My monetary interests."

The look in Blake's eyes hardened until his eyes resembled

two lumps of hard, polished onyx. "I wouldn't make the mistake of thinking you had interests that weren't monetary."

"Once you believed I had no interest in your money at all." She saw the immediate spark of emotion cross Blake's face and knew there was certain danger in taunting him with ancient memories.

"Once, I should have listened to the magistrate."

Meredith gasped. "I often wondered if you knew about that," she recovered, quickly remembering the look on the old pig's face when she triumphantly told him she was going to marry Blake.

"He confessed your sins shortly after we returned to England after my first posting to Vienna, but by then, I already knew you weren't the girl I thought you were. You should have married him, Meredith. He would've died a natural death soon enough and left you well off."

"I loathed the old buzzard." She shuddered in revulsion.

"And me? Didn't you loathe me as well?" Blake's face was an inscrutable mask.

"You were young and handsome and the heir to the oldest and richest titled family in the district. And you were Jack's first cousin. I planned to marry you the first time I saw you. I was seven or eight at the time. You were ten or eleven and the answer to a little girl's prayers." Meredith glanced at him through her lashes to hide the alarm she felt. He was different. Changed. He seemed the same, but something had affected him. Changed him. She knew because she knew him so well, much better than he liked to admit. In the years since she had married him, Meredith had made it her business to know him, to find his weaknesses and to exploit them—to torment him as he tormented her with his indifference. He had loved her when they married; loved her to the point of worship, and she had used that love to get the things she wanted out of life— a home of her own, a title, money, lots and lots of money, and a way of remaining close to Jack. She had had enough money to buy and sell most of her friends, but only as long as she stayed married to Blake. After her accident, Meredith had faked her own death and gone to ground like the foxes she loved to hunt—gone to ground so she could recover from the devastating injury. He might have done away with her while she lay ill and vulnerable, so she had pretended to be dead. And she had managed to fool everyone—including Blake, as she manipulated him from afar—while she pulled strings like a master puppeteer. Meredith had waited patiently, secure in the knowledge that one day she would have her revenge—secure in the knowledge that one day Blake would want to marry again and give her the ultimate in revenge.

During their marriage, Meredith had lived in fear that one day Blake would risk scandal and divorce her. The certainty of it haunted her during her recuperation from her accident. She was crippled and unable to bear children. He needed an heir. The courts might listen to his plea. He was a popular member of government and wealthy enough to pay for a parliamentary divorce without the risk of scandal. He might emerge from his marriage to her unscathed—able to marry legally and father a legitimate heir. In a desperate act to retain control over Blake's future, Meredith had decided to orchestrate her own death. Her accident had taken away her mobility, but it had been a strange sort of blessing in disguise. Her death had given her a certain amount of security that she hadn't had before she lost the use of her legs. Now she sat back and pulled the strings and watched her puppet dance. It gave her great pleasure to know Blake continued to support her beggarly family and to have them dance attendance to her, to come when she summoned them and carry out her bidding for the promise of money to pay gaming debts or to buy thoroughbreds. And it gave her enormous satisfaction to use Blake's money to pay spies to follow him and report his movements to her.

He was changed. The weeks with the Fairfax girl had changed him. And to think she had been worried about his having an affair with the girl's mother. She should have known Patricia Fairfax was too jaded for Blake's tastes. He believed in honesty and integrity and was drawn to innocence. It had been the girl he'd wanted, not the mother.

Meredith had never valued her virginity except as a means

of getting the material things she desired. Maybe she had sold her virginity too cheaply after all—to Jack instead of to Blake. Blake might have continued to worship her if she had been the innocent girl she'd pretended to be. His utter rejection of her still rankled. She simply couldn't understand it. It never occurred to her that he might be repulsed by her lack of innocence or her affair with Jack. As long as they kept it in the family, what did it matter who she slept with? Blake had had no right to dismiss her. So he felt foolish and betrayed. So what? He had married her. Besides, Jack hadn't been repulsed. He had been eager to trade favor for favor. Why didn't Blake understand that that was the way the world worked? She hadn't asked for his love, just his name and the power he could give her. Power was what she needed from him, not love. She wondered if he knew how stupid he had seemed to her before the wedding—a lovesick schoolboy mooning about making calf's eyes at her. Refusing to bed her before the wedding, unwilling to compromise the reputation of his intended. Well, the joke had been on him! The whole village had been laughing at his ignorance. Blake hadn't known that Jack was already her lover, had been her lover since she was fourteen. Hadn't he known that the only reason Jack hadn't married her was because he had to marry money and her family had none? Blake hadn't understood that she had always planned to marry him and keep Jack as her lover. She had very nearly run out of time. Her family had decided she had to marry for money and the old magistrate had offered for her. Her parents would have accepted him, too, because he was well off. Old, disgusting, and fat, but the richest man in the district next to Blake's father. Meredith had held out for Blake, refusing to marry the old pig, even though he threatened to expose her affair with Jack and even went so far as to blackmail her, and just when she thought she might have to reconsider the magistrate's offer, Blake had finally noticed her. The heir to Everleigh had finally stumbled into her web. She had married Blake and then she waited for the opportunity to rid herself of the blackmailing old magistrate.

She had been so confident. She had thought she had everything. But Blake was her ultimate mistake. She mistook his youth for weakness and his love for blind devotion and she had overplayed her hand. She had been so sure of him and her power over him that she failed to recognize the depth of his character. He had been young and full of ideals and the completeness of her deception abhorred him. He had believed her pure and above reproach, and he had found her dirty and soiled from overuse. They had badly misjudged each other and both had vowed never to repeat their mistake.

"If we keep sitting here reminiscing I'll begin to think you care about me, Blake, and that just won't do under the circumstances . . ."

"Just what are the circumstances?"

"Pretending to be dead has it limits. I'm bored by the lack of activity, so I've decided to reclaim my position as your wife." She said it so matter-of-factly, Blake was taken aback by her audacity.

"You've never been my wife."

"Legally I am," she said. "And that's all that counts. Will you really try to prevent me, a poor cripple, from reclaiming my position in society and the comforts my husband's wealth can provide? I don't think so."

Blake immediately recognized the threat. "There's a grave in a cemetery with your name on it, Meredith. It's been there for the past six years. Under the circumstances, I'm sure the courts will understand. Now that you've unexpectedly returned from the grave, I think a divorce is in order."

"You can't prove adultery," she said. "So you wouldn't dare go to the courts."

"Try me, my dear." He smiled grimly. "Please try me."

Flustered for the first time in years, Meredith tried to bluff. "Jack—"

"Owes a small fortune in gambling debts in nearly every club in London. Most of them to me. His father-in-law has been paying his bills and I've been buying up his markers for years." Blake found some satisfaction in Meredith's obvious surprise. "And I don't think Annalise's father would continue to support his son-in-law if he learned about you and Jack, do you?''

"My father—''

"Is also greatly indebted to me. Come now, Meredith, I know that doesn't come as a surprise to you. You had to have money to live on. And accomplices in your elaborate scheme.'' Suddenly the pieces of the puzzle fell into place. Suddenly Blake understood why he'd never been able to put his past with Meredith behind him. It had all been too neat. He'd never been able to believe the past was over because he hadn't seen her body, hadn't really believed it was possible for Meredith to die so quietly. "I'm sure if I dig deep enough, I'll find that a vast majority of the money I've been loaning to your father over the years has gone to your upkeep and to pay your spies. The courts might be interested in talking to you, your father, the other members of the family, and Jack as well for helping to perpetuate a hoax in order to extort money from me.''

"Why would the courts listen to you—an adulterer and a bigamist? Suppose I tell them you participated in the hoax? Suppose I convince them that you kept me locked away in a house in the country while you pretended I was dead? Who do you think they would believe then?''

"Suppose we dig up your grave and see who's really buried there?'' Blake shot back. "The village of Everleigh is without a magistrate—and has been for the last six years.''

Meredith blanched as Blake's barb hit it's mark.

"It's over, Meredith. You should have stayed dead. Because you don't have a choice. I won't let you get away with your blackmail this time. You won't be reclaiming your position, or your title, or moving into Lawrence House. That's my home. My sanctuary. The one place in England I can call home and where you have no claim.''

"But, I'm your legal wife. . . .''

"A mere technicality, like the one that protects Lawrence House from you.''

"I remember,'' she said. "Lawrence House is entailed. It belongs to mother of the heir. That brings us to Cristina Fairfax," she said smoothly. Too smoothly. "While you're in London petitioning the courts and parliament for your divorce, it might be a good idea if you make other arrangements to house your little doxy. It wouldn't do to have both of us under the same roof at the same time."

Blake saw the grim determination in the firm set of her jaw. She would not rest until she had her revenge against him, but he didn't fear for himself. He knew she would think twice before tampering with the controller of the purse strings. No, her revenge would be more subtle than an attempt on his life. It would be directed at someone else. Someone he cared about. He had to protect Cristina. He had to keep her safe. He would have to find a way to protect her and the other people he cared about. For the time being, he would have to find contentment in doing everything humanly possible to thwart Meredith and to frustrate her scheme to get her hands on his property or on Lawrence House.

"Leave Cristina out of this."

"She tried to usurp my place," Meredith said softly. "She tried to take my title and what rightfully belongs to me."

"She did nothing of the kind. She has nothing to do with what's gone between us." Blake clenched his fists at his side to keep from wrapping them around Meredith's slender neck. "For Christ's sake, Meredith, you're supposed to be dead. I've believed you were dead for six years!"

"I've been *crippled* for six years," Meredith spat at him. "I've been crippled—confined to a chair—unable to walk, unable to ride, unable to . . . for six long years. And all because of you."

"Me?" Blake was genuinely surprised. "How?"

"You gave me that damn horse."

"That horse was a gift—a birthday gift—if I remember correctly."

"He nearly killed me," she gasped.

"I thought he had," Blake said. "Unfortunately I was wrong."

Meredith felt his disgust like something tangible hanging

between them. She saw the contempt he didn't bother to hide. His smoldering glances flickered over her.

"Nevertheless"—she dismissed Blake's contempt and his angry glances—"I'm warning you, Lord Lawrence, to be very careful about the arrangements you make for Cristina."

"I won't let you have Lawrence House, or anything else that belongs to me."

"But that's the problem, isn't it, Blake? Lawrence House doesn't belong to you. It belongs to the mother of the heir. Currently it belongs to your mother, but in a few months"— Meredith shrugged her shoulders—"who knows?"

A cold chill ran up Blake's spine. "If you do anything, if you attempt to harm Cristina in any way, I'll—"

"I wouldn't dream of harming Cristina," Meredith assured him. "I'm sure she's a sweet young girl. I have nothing against Cristina Fairfax—except the fact that she's about to inherit everything I've ever wanted."

"All right, Meredith," Blake said. "I'll give you whatever you want. I'll give you Willow Wood and Lawrence House and any other property you name."

"You can't give me Lawrence House, it's entailed," Meredith reminded him.

"I'll telegraph my mother," Blake promised. "I'll have her give it to you."

"Nice try," Meredith congratulated him. "But your mother can't give it away, either. Nobody can give it away, remember? It has to be passed down from one mother of the heir to the next."

"Then name it, Meredith," Blake said. "I'll give you whatever you want."

Meredith smiled. "Will you give me your firstborn child, Blake?"

Blake recoiled as if she had slapped him. "What?"

"That's what I want. That's the only thing that will satisfy me."

"You're insane!"

"Perhaps," she agreed. "But I warned you years ago that you would regret not telling me about Lawrence House. How about it, Lord Lawrence? Do you regret it yet?''

"I heartily regret ever having set eyes on you."

"The feeling is mutual," Meredith assured him. "Now how much longer do I have to wait before I can claim my child. Two months? Three?"

"You'll never get your hands on my child," he told her. "And if you get within a foot of Cristina, I'll kill you," Blake swore.

"Poor Blake," Meredith clucked her tongue. "You don't seem to understand the situation. *I* will have your firstborn child. Or no one will." She smiled at him. "Pretend you're King Solomon. Give him to me or watch him die. And maybe his mother as well."

"Meredith, I'm warning you, if you attempt—"

"I don't have to attempt," Meredith said. "I've had ten long years to plan my revenge—four years of marriage to you and six long years of pretending to be dead. The die has already been cast. My revenge has already begun. Either you take your child from Cristina Fairfax and give it to me, or you watch them both die."

"I won't let you do this."

"You can't stop me. Even if you kill me, the plan will go forward. I'll have my revenge—from the grave if necessary."

"I will stop you," Blake vowed. "I'll find some way to stop you."

"I don't doubt you'll try," Meredith said. "In the meantime, we'll see how you enjoy the scandal of finding out the whole empire knows you're a bigamist."

"God damn you, Meredith!"

Meredith looked down at her chair. "He already has."

*No one delights more in vengeance
than a woman.*

—JUVENAL 60–130 A.D.

Twenty-two

AMBASSADOR PAGET ENTERED Blake's office through the
secret panel just after Blake called for the two sergeants-at-
arms to remove Meredith and Jack from the building and to
escort them to separate quarters on embassy grounds and to
remain there until a contingent of uniformed guards arrived.

"You heard?" Blake asked as the ambassador quietly entered the room. He didn't look up, but sat in a leather chair
near the fire with his face buried in his hands.

"Everything."

"Well?" Blake asked, softly. "Any suggestions?"

"We can't keep them under guard forever."

"More's the pity," Blake replied bitterly. "How long?"

"We have the right to hold them on charges of breaking
into the embassy, but as they are both the queen's subjects,
we won't be able to question them for more than forty-eight
hours."

Blake nodded.

"That should give you enough time to make a good start
on the journey to London."

"London?" Blake stared at the older man. "I can't go to

London. I can't leave Cristina. I can't protect her if I'm in London and at this stage of her confinement, I'm afraid for her to travel."

"You have no choice, Blake," the ambassador told him. "You must go to London. You must file a suit in Doctor's Commons and at a court of Common Law and have them grant you a divorce as soon as possible so you can sue Meredith on the grounds of adultery and petition Parliament for a divorce. And you must do so in person, before word of tonight's debacle reaches London—before she can reach sympathetic ears."

"It would be simpler just to kill her," Blake suggested half jokingly.

"Yes, it would," the ambassador agreed. "And as your friend, I'll pretend I didn't hear you suggest it. Go to London. Get your divorce."

"But, Cristina . . ."

"We'll protect Cristina." The ambassador placed his hand on Blake's shoulder. "As long as she stays in your apartment, she should be safe enough. We can put guards on the building and hire men to watch out for her. I'll even ask Franz Josef's secret police for help."

"For how long?"

"For as long as it takes."

"Protecting Cristina is only part of the problem," Blake said. "Once the baby is born, Meredith will try to take it."

"By the time the baby's born, you should have your divorce. I'll wire the queen. If I tell her everything, she may be able to expedite the proceedings. Ask for an audience as soon as you reach London."

"Meredith won't stop."

"But once you're granted a divorce, she'll have nothing to gain."

"Except her revenge. Good God, Paget, she's come back from the dead for revenge; a simple piece of paper dissolving our marriage isn't going to stop her."

The ambassador shook his head. "It's unbelievable."

"It's a damned nightmare," Blake lifted his face from his

hands and turned to look at his friend, the ambassador. "All these years I believed she was dead. I never questioned my good fortune in being released from the mockery of my marriage to her. I should have had them dig her up," Blake said. "I should have made sure."

Paget shuddered at the thought. "You believed the people around you. We all believed it."

"And now I'm a bigamist."

"Not intentionally," the ambassador pointed out.

"But a bigamist none the less."

"The irony of the story is that I stayed married to Meredith for four long years just to avoid a scandal that might damage my career—or my father's. I didn't want to hurt anyone. And now I've put Cristina and my child in jeopardy." He stood up and began to pace. "Cristina. How can I protect Cristina? How do I tell her the truth? How do I tell her what Meredith is after?" Blake turned to the ambassador. "Christ, Paget; you heard her. She wants our child!"

"She doesn't want your child, Blake. She wants revenge. She wants you to suffer the way she's suffered."

"Hell hath no fury . . ."

"I'll help in any way I can," the ambassador offered.

"Thank you, sir." Blake smiled his first smile since Meredith's appearance. "And for what you did earlier tonight. I can't thank you enough for sparing Cristina's reputation—for smoothing the way for her and for me."

"You were honest with me from the start, Blake. And I appreciate that. Besides, I think your wife is a remarkable young lady." Paget chuckled. "I can't believe she actually cut up the Prince of Wales's bed linens."

"She ripped them apart with her teeth." Blake grinned.

"Sure wish I could have seen that. Lady Paget and I had a good laugh over it."

Blake shivered. "I get chills every time I remember her hanging out of Marlborough House on nothing but courage and strong Irish linen." He extended his hand to the ambassador. "I apologize, sir, for having my personal troubles blow up in your face like this. And I thank you again for the white lies."

Ambassador Paget shook his hand warmly. "I didn't lie, exactly," he said. "Lady Paget and I discussed it. Whether she intended it or not, Cristina did our government a service when she ran away with Rudolf."

Blake raised a questioning eyebrow.

"She actually did your job by keeping him from seeking other, less reputable women for purposes of pleasure and running the risk of embarrassing both our governments. So you see, she *was* working for the Foreign Office."

Blake nodded. "Thanks again, sir." He stood up. "If it's all right with you, I'll take my leave now. I need to see Cristina . . ." he faltered. "I need to find some way to explain and say good-bye."

"Don't worry, Blake. We'll delay Meredith as long as possible and keep Cristina safe until the danger's over."

‹‹‹❦›››

CRISTINA WAS WAITING up with Cason and Leah when Blake arrived at their apartment on the Ringstrasse. He took Cristina in his arms, then turned to speak to his assistant. "I'll brief you tomorrow, Cason," he said. "Go home and get some rest. And thank you."

"My pleasure, sir."

Blake waited until Cason departed and Leah had said good night before he led Cristina to the sofa closest to the fire. Blake could see she had been crying and he cradled her close to him as he sat down on the sofa. "I'm sorry, Countess, I'm so sorry she spoiled our party."

Cristina placed her hands on Blake's chest and pushed away so she could see the expression on his face. "Tell me this is only a bad dream that will go away in the morning."

"I wish I could." Blake took a deep breath. "But it's worse than I could ever have imagine.

"I thought she was dead."

"So did I. So did everyone else in the room."

"Except the man who was with her," Cristina said. "He positively gloated."

"He would," Blake answered. "Because you see, my sweet, that was my cousin Jack." He closed his eyes and pinched the bridge of his nose to ward off the headache he could feel pounding just behind his eyelids.

"Jack," she repeated. "Meredith's lover. The man who betrayed you."

"The same."

"How did she find out about tonight? And what prompted her to rejoin the living?" she asked. Cristina recognized the similarities between Meredith and Jack and her mother and Claude. She understood that they never did anything without a motive or a plan and tonight's episode hadn't been a coincidence. It was timed too perfectly for that.

"I don't know how she found out," Blake said. "But it's possible she heard about our marriage from my mother and father's announcement at the Everleigh Christmas celebration. Or Jack told her. He would have been invited."

"I don't understand," Cristina said. "If she didn't want you to remarry, why did she let you think she was dead? What reason could she have?"

"Revenge." Blake looked at his wife. "'If you prick us do we not bleed? If you tickle us do we not laugh? If you poison us do we not die? And if you wrong us shall we not revenge?'"

"The Merchant of Venice," Cristina said.

"And Meredith wants her pound of flesh from me."

"Why?"

"Because she thinks I wronged her. She thinks I've taken what belonged to her and given it to you."

"She's insane!" Cristina breathed.

"Quite possibly. And all the more dangerous because of it."

"But Blake, you haven't given me anything that belonged to her except your name and the title." She looked up at him. "That's it, isn't it? She wants to keep the title. She wants to remain the countess of Lawrence."

"That's part of it," he admitted reluctantly. "But Cristina, she wants even more than that. She wants Lawrence House."

"Give it to her," Cristina ordered, an edge of panic in her

voice. "Give her whatever she wants, but make her go away. Make her leave us alone."

"I would if I could, Countess. But Lawrence House isn't mine to give. It belongs to my mother."

"Your mother? Well, then, if you explain about Meredith, surely your mother would—"

"Yes, she would. But she can't. It doesn't work that way. Lawrence House is entailed. It can only be passed down—it can't be bought, sold, or given away for any reason. If there is no legal heir or if the heir tries to sell it or give it away for any reason, the ownership reverts to the Crown."

"Doesn't Meredith know this? Doesn't she understand that you can't deed Lawrence House to her even if you inherit?"

Blake nodded. "She knows."

"Then what's the problem?"

Blake didn't want to tell her. He didn't want to hurt Cristina anymore. He didn't want her to know the full extent of Meredith's revenge, but he couldn't see a way *not* to tell her. He had to tell her the truth in order to protect her—and their unborn child. "In a couple of months, Lawrence House will change ownership, but I won't be the one inheriting it. You will."

"What?" Cristina was stunned.

"Lawrence House belongs to the mother of the recognized Lawrence heir," Blake told her. "And tonight, I publicly introduced you as my wife and recognized the child you carry as my own. And by doing so—" he stopped abruptly.

"Oh, my God!" Cristina reached for Blake and grabbed fistfuls of his shirt and clung to him. Her green eyes widened, seeming to grow larger as the blood rushed from her face, leaving it whiter than his snowy shirtfront. "She wants me out of the way. She wants my baby!"

Blake nodded.

"What are we going to do?" Cristina searched his face, looking for answers, for solutions.

"I'm going back to London."

"To London?" Cristina parroted numbly. "You can't. You can't leave. You're supposed to be here when the baby's born. You're supposed to stay with me."

"I can't stay, Cris. I have to return to London and I have to leave as soon as the Christmas holiday is over and the trains resume their schedule. I've got to file a petition for divorce. And I have to do it in person. I have to present my case to the courts before Meredith reaches London. I've got to get things well underway before our baby is born."

"Why?"

There was no gentle way to tell her. No gentle way to remind her that with Meredith's return from the grave, their marriage had become invalid in the eyes of the law. "Because I don't want my child to be born a bastard."

"Oh." Cristina fastened her gaze on the heavy gold wedding band on her left hand and burst into tears. "I didn't think about . . . I forgot that our marriage isn't real any longer."

Blake kissed her, tasting the salt of her tears, before he pulled away and forced Cristina to meet his gaze. "Our marriage is very real. What I had with Meredith wasn't real. But what we share . . . oh, Countess, how can you doubt that?"

Cristina blinked back more scalding tears and the lump of sand clogging her throat. "I don't doubt it. I'm just afraid. Afraid we're not ruthless enough. I'm afraid she'll win."

"I won't let her win," he vowed.

"You may not be able to prevent it."

"I promise you, Countess, that I will never let Meredith get our baby."

"Then take me with you. Don't leave me here alone."

"You know I can't. You can't travel as quickly as I'll need to travel and it would be too dangerous for you to try."

"I can ride a train."

Blake took a deep breath, raked his fingers through his hair, then gently took hold of Cristina's upper arms as she gripped his shirt. "Countess, I can't protect you on the journey and an armed guard would slow us down."

"An armed guard? Blake, she won't hurt me. Not as long as she wants the baby. Not as long as it's the only way to get Lawrence House, not while I'm still carrying."

"Listen to me, Cristina," he focused his gaze on hers. "Meredith doesn't care about keeping you alive long enough to have the baby. Do you understand? She'll take the baby if she gets a chance, but the baby isn't her primary concern. What she wants is revenge against me—any way she can get it. And if you or our child are hurt, so much the better. She doesn't want our child, she only wants to use him against me. She wants to take everything I care about away from me."

Cristina's teeth began to chatter and her body began to shake.

Blake held her closer, so close that her protruding belly came in contact with his firm, flat one. "You'll be safer here."

"With you in London?" Cristina's nerves were ragged and raw from the shocks she'd suffered. "I don't think so."

He couldn't know whether or not she'd be safe in Vienna, but he felt confident that she would be a lot safer in the apartment with guards to protect her than she would be exposed to the rigors of traveling and Meredith's treachery. "Meredith will follow me to London. She'll have to."

"How do you know she won't leave someone behind in Vienna to get rid of me or the Lawrence heir?"

"I don't," he admitted honestly. "I just have to pray I can provide enough protection for you. I have to pray that she won't hurt you."

"Not hurt me?" Tears rolled down Cristina's cheeks. "You think she hasn't hurt me already? She's taking you away from me. And she's after my child."

"Countess . . ." Blake's voice was soft and the look in his eyes was gentle.

Cristina pushed out of his grasp, struggled to her feet, and began to pace the carpet in front of the fireplace. The tears fell harder and faster and Cristina could do nothing to stop them. "Please, Blake, don't. Don't call me that. Not now. Not when I've just learned that Meredith is still your countess. Not when I've just learned that I'm your mistress and she's still your wife."

"*You're* my wife and the mother of my child."

"Then you've one wife too many." Cristina tried to smile through her tears. "The law frowns on this sort of thing. I don't think they allow you to have two at the same time."

"As far as I'm concerned, Meredith was never my wife. You are." He reached out for Cristina.

"But she was first."

Blake dropped his arms to his sides as Cristina's whispered words ripped at his heart. His expression was unreadable but his hands were clenched in tight fists as he sought to maintain some sort of control over his emotions. "I can't go back, Cristina," he said simply. "As much as I would like to, I can't change the facts. I can't undo the entailment on Lawrence House or do anything about the fact that I married Meredith before I married you."

"I know," Cristina couldn't stop the words she threw at him. She couldn't stop the hurt or the fear that drove her on. "But unfortunately for me, she's the only wife that counts— at the moment. And she wants my child."

"So do I," Blake said. "I want your child. And I want you. Tell me, Cristina, is that so terrible?"

"Not unless you only want me because I'm carrying the baby."

"I told you before, I don't want my child to be born a bastard and the only way to prevent that is to marry its mother." Blake hadn't meant to make it sound as if marrying her was like taking bitter medicine, but damn it, she was ripping his heart out, tearing the very life out of him with her fear and her doubt and her crazy accusations. "Countess, I'm sorry. I didn't mean that the way it sounded," he apologized. Blake wanted to tell her how much he loved her, but the words stuck in his throat. If she didn't know, if she could forget everything that had passed between them so quickly, if she didn't realize how he felt after all these months of living with him, sharing his life, then it was better for her to think the worst of him. And since he couldn't tell her the whole truth, he only told her part of it. "I don't think an innocent child ought to suffer for our mistakes. I don't want the child labeled a bastard when all I have to do to make things right is to marry you as soon as possible."

"Well, Lord Lawrence, you certainly have a way with

words.'' If only he would forget about the baby long enough to reassure her, if only he would tell her how he felt, how much she meant to him.

"Cristina," Blake began again, half placating her and half cautioning her. "I know that learning that Meredith is alive has been a nasty shock for you. It has been for me, too. I thought you wanted us to be married. I thought you liked being married."

"I did. I do."

"Then tell me what else I can do. Because I'm running out of options."

"Go to London, Blake. Go to London as fast as you can. Go do whatever it is you have to do, but keep her away from my baby."

"I can't leave for London yet," he told her. "I can stay with you if you want me to. Or I can return to the embassy."

She shook her head. She knew she was blaming Blake for something that wasn't his fault, knew she was punishing him for Meredith's sins, for the fact that he'd married Meredith first and brought this catastrophe down around their heads, but she couldn't help herself. She was angry and frustrated and very much afraid that if he stayed with her, his life might be in danger as well. "I think that, under the circumstances, it would be best if you stayed at the embassy. You've got a long trip ahead of you and the baby and I might as well get used to being without you for a while." Cristina walked to the front door and opened it for him. She paused in the doorway, then twisted the heavy gold wedding band off her finger and held it out to him.

Blake shook his head. "Please, Cristina, don't."

"I can't keep it. I can't wear it." She looked up at him, tears sparkling in her eyes. "Take it. Keep it until this is settled. Until I have the right to wear it again."

"Cris, I'm truly sorry." He reached out and caressed her cheek.

She rubbed her face against the palm of his hand, turning slightly so she could place a kiss in the center of it. "I know," she whispered. "I know."

Blake pocketed her wedding ring then stepped out into the cold night, flakes of snow settling on his midnight hair as he turned to look back at her. "You can reach me through the embassy. If you change your mind about tonight or if you need anything, anything at all . . ."

I love you, she thought. *I need you to hold me and tell me everything's going to be all right. I need you to make Meredith go away.* She stared at him, memorizing his features, knowing she would rely on those memories in the hours and days and weeks to come. She smiled at him sadly, but all she could say was, "Happy Christmas, Blake."

"Countess . . ."

"I know." She closed the door quickly, hiding his anguished face, before she turned and headed toward the bed they had shared on so many wonderful nights.

❧

CHRISTMAS PASSED WITHOUT a word from Blake, as did Boxing Day and four more days, but Cristina didn't shed a tear. She was far beyond tears. She was numb.

She had given up trying to sleep in the bed she had shared with Blake. Leah often found her asleep on the sofa in the sitting room or in the rocking chair in the nursery. Cristina told Leah the baby kept her awake at night, but Leah knew better.

"You've had a lover's quarrel," Leah said, firmly. "That's all it is, Cristina."

"You knew he had been married before, didn't you, Leah?" Cristina shot her friend an accusing look.

"Yes, I knew."

"And, that's why you tried to warn me about him in London."

"Yes," Leah admitted. "And I should have come right out and told you the minute I found out."

"Why didn't you?" Cristina asked, although she realized she probably wouldn't have listened. Even then, it was too late.

"I hoped it wouldn't matter. After all, she was dead and

buried. Besides, I thought Lord Lawrence would do it.'' Leah frowned.

"He did tell me he'd been married and widowed," Cristina admitted.

"How was he supposed to know she would come back from the grave to haunt him?" Leah asked.

"He didn't." Cristina was thoughtful. "But for some reason, I thought he should. I was scared and angry and I blamed him instead of blaming her."

Leah remained silent. "I should mind my own business, but I won't. You were wrong to blame him, but you don't have to keep blaming him. Your stubborn Fairfax pride ain't goin' to keep you warm at night. Lord Lawrence might not say what he feels, but he's tried to prove how much he cares in the only way he knows. He's a man and he's got his faults, but you have to love him for what he is or not at all. He has given you all he has to give and you can't expect more than that, especially when you ain't givin' in return. If all he wanted was a warm body, he could find that on any street corner. He made a mistake once by marryin' the wrong woman; don't make him think he's made the same mistake twice." She finished her lecture and left Cristina alone in the nursery to think about what she'd said.

And she did think about it. She sat for hours rocking in the rocking chair, thinking about it. The apartment felt so empty without him. She felt empty without him.

Was Leah right? Was he showing her how much he cared instead of telling her? Was he afraid his words would be thrown back in his face. Is that why he spent so much time trying to amuse her and keep her form becoming lonely and bored? Was she being selfish by not telling him how much she loved him? Had she been afraid her words would be thrown back in her face? Cristina battled with herself as the afternoon turned into evening, weighing the arguments in her mind against the pain in her heart.

The nursery had grown dark and cold with the waning of the winter sun, but Cristina resolutely refused to light the lamps or fire or seek the warmth of her bedroom. There were too many memories in that bedroom. Memories of the nights they had made love or lay quietly talking, thinking of names for the baby and trying to imagine the color of its eyes and hair while Blake felt the strong kicks in her belly against the palm of his hand or his soft lips; or the many times he gently massaged her aching back or rubbed cream into her itchy skin just like a thousand other expectant couples. *Couple.* Before she met Blake, Cristina had never thought of that word in relation to herself. When had her attitude begun to change? When she fell in love with him? Was that what love was all about?

She had never wanted any part of love until she'd met Blake. Oh, she had expected to marry one day, but she hadn't expected love. And here she was, a few short months later, afraid to marry without it. What had happened to her modern ideas? Hadn't she always said that love made you vulnerable and that she would never be vulnerable? Hadn't she seen what loving her mother had done to her father? Hadn't she always thought that marrying for security and companionship was preferable to love? Then, why had she found the idea of selling to the highest bidder so despicable? Why hadn't she simply agreed to go along with her mother's scheme and take whatever was offered? Was it because of Blake? Was it because the first time she met him he had managed to make the idea sound so sordid even though he professed not to believe in love?

She had never meant to love any man, and yet Cristina loved Blake Ashford with all her heart. But love was a new, powerful and frightening emotion and she had been afraid to tell him how she felt—afraid that he would use that knowledge as a weapon against her. Leah was right. She had been selfish—taking everything Blake had to offer without offering anything in return—even the trust she had promised him.

She told herself that she had been protecting Blake's reputation in London, but in reality she had been protecting herself. Running away from love because love could make her so vulnerable. And she was still running, blaming Blake for Meredith, using her as an excuse to drive Blake away because she was afraid that he might take her heart and break it into a thousand pieces.

But she had learned her lesson. Love did make you vulnerable, but it could also make you stronger. And life wasn't worth living without it.

Cristina slowly got up from the rocking chair and walked into the adjoining bedroom. She lit the lamp on the wall and carefully removed a wrapped package from the top drawer of the dresser. It was the Christmas present she had meant to give Blake on Boxing Day. Cristina quickly unwrapped the gaily colored paper and opened the box to reveal a small gold disk hanging from a sturdy gold chain. There was beauty in the simplicity of its design, but there was nothing feminine about this necklace. It was a medallion meant for a man. A medallion made especially for Blake. She removed it from its box and held it in her hand, allowing the heat of her body to warm the cold metal. She had meant to give it to him as a symbol of her love. She had pictured him wearing it and even now, when she closed her eyes, she could imagine it nestled in the thick hair covering his chest. Cristina reached out and traced the inscription with the tip of her finger. On one side was the single word, "Always," in elegant script and on the other side were the words "Cristina, 1878."

She wanted Blake to have it. She wanted him to think of her as he wore it above his heart—to have a part of her near him. *Always.*

Tomorrow she would find him, give him the medallion, and tell him she loved him. Tomorrow she would tell him she didn't care about Meredith or inheriting Lawrence House or a divorce or anything except loving him and the baby they'd created. Meredith could have the house and the title. Meredith could have everything except him and the baby. Because she wanted them. She loved them. They belonged to her.

Sighing, Cristina climbed into the large double bed and slept peacefully for the first time since Blake had walked out the door, the gold medallion clenched tightly in her fist.

Weeping may endure for a night,
but joy cometh in the morning.

—PSALMS 30:5

Twenty-three

CRISTINA AWOKE THE following morning feeling re-
freshed and optimistic. She dressed quickly without Leah's
help in a topaz-colored satin morning gown which fastened
down the front and allowed ample room for her burgeoning
belly. She finished dressing, and obeying the rumbling of her
empty stomach found her way to the kitchen where she at-
tacked a breakfast of cream-filled pastries and Viennese coffee.

She had just drained the last bit of cinnamon-flavored coffee from her cup when she heard Leah talking to someone in
the front hall of the apartment. Her heart raced at the sound
of the low voices. It was New Year's Eve and Blake hadn't
left for London without first seeing her. Cristina breathed a
prayer of thanks. She nervously patted a hair into place, licked
her dry lips, and headed in the direction of the sitting room.
She was halfway there before she remembered the medallion
and hurried back to her room to get it.

Minutes later she stood in the doorway of the sitting room
with the medallion in hand and a smile of greeting on her
lips. "Blake!"

"So sorry to disappoint you, Cristina." Crown Prince Rudolf rose gracefully from his chair as she entered the room and watched as her happy smile died on her lips.

"Your Imperial Highness," Cristina acknowledged him and managed a hasty curtsey.

"It appears the rumors circulating the city are true." Rudolf's usually warm blue eyes hardened perceptibly.

"I'm sorry," Cristina apologized. "I never meant to hurt or embarrass you in any way, Your Royal Highness." She bowed her head and studied the pattern on the rug.

"It was all a lie," Rudolf insisted. "You deceived me by pretending to care." His words struck a chord in Cristina. She had thrown a similar accusation at Blake only days ago.

"I made my feelings for you clear from the beginning, Your Royal Highness," she reminded him.

"I thought you were beginning to soften toward me, Cristina. I thought that you might even be learning to care for me as a man," Rudolf said solemnly.

"I value your friendship highly, Your Royal Highness."

"Friendship, Cristina? Is that all you think I feel for you?" the prince scoffed. "I want you, Cristina. I want you to give yourself to me of your own free will. I'll do anything to have you. Even marry you if there is no other way."

"You flatter me, Your Royal Highness, but you must know that's impossible. Even if the emperor allowed it, which I am certain he would not, a marriage between us would never work. I'm neither royal nor Catholic, and I happen to know my name wasn't on your list of prospective brides. And I'm married already."

"You were married," Rudolf said. "And you can be again. I'll renounce my rights."

"No, you won't," she said, shaking her head. "At least, not for me. I don't love you, Your Royal Highness, and you don't love me. You only want me because I'm different from the girls who fall into your arms and into your bed at a moment's notice. You've had to bargain with me and now you want me because I won't come to you willingly."

"I still want you."

"Only because you can't have me. You know I don't love you. You know I deceived you by letting you assume we might have—"

"You didn't deceive me, Cristina. I've always known I wasn't your child's father. I didn't make love to you, but to another lovely redhead—one someone paid, I suspect, to keep me entertained and far away from you. And when you came to me for help, I chose to let you take advantage of me," Rudolf told her.

"You knew?"

"Yes."

"You knew and still you helped me. Why?" Cristina wanted to know.

"I was curious. I wanted to know why you had suddenly changed your mind about me, so I played along. I decided to take advantage of the situation and see if I could to get what I wanted. I knew you were running away from someone. A lady doesn't cut up the Prince of Wales's bed linens and climb out the window to keep a man from taking her virginity and then run headlong into the same man's arms. At least not a lady like you, Cristina Fairfax."

"You knew all along." Cristina still couldn't believe he had fooled her so convincingly. "And I felt so guilty."

"I hoped you would." Rudolf had the grace to look away from her when he spoke. "I also hoped I might get another chance once your passion for Lord Lawrence burned out. I thought your coming to Vienna with me was a ruse to persuade him to follow you."

"No, Your Royal Highness," Cristina informed him. "I never intentionally pitted you against him. I didn't know how to tell Blake about the baby. And after hearing about Lord Ainsford's scandal, I was terrified that the same thing would happen to us. I had nowhere else to go, no one else to turn to. So I used you to get away from London."

"I've been wrong about you from the beginning, Cristina. I was wrong to assume you were interested in pursuing an affair with me. I was wrong to assume that you could be purchased for mere jewels. And I clearly misjudged your passion for Blake.'' The warmth returned to Rudolf's clear blue eyes when he smiled at her. ''You love him very much.''

''Yes.''

''Then I suggest you catch him before he leaves the embassy for London.''

Cristina's eyes sparkled with tears of gratitude. ''You've seen him?''

Rudolf shook his head. ''No, but I make it a point to know my rivals' whereabouts. It's one of the few advantages of being crown prince. He's taking the midmorning train out of Vienna.''

''Oh, no!'' Cristina breathed. ''I must get to the embassy. I must see him before he leaves.'' She searched the room for her muff and coat. ''Leah! Bring my coat and muff and call a fiacre. Hurry.''

''Take mine,'' Rudolf intervened.

''What?'' Cristina was too preoccupied to listen closely.

''Take my carriage, Cristina,'' Rudolf offered again. ''It's parked right outside and my driver knows the quickest route to the embassy. I can get a cab back to the palace.''

''Oh, thank you!'' Cristina flung her arms around his neck and kissed his cheek, then grabbed the muff Leah handed her and struggled into her coat.

''Godspeed, Cristina.'' The crown prince blew her a kiss as she raced out the door and into the waiting carriage. He would miss her, but he didn't love her. He wanted her, but there were other beautiful, more willing women waiting for him to favor them with his affections. And there was a most charming young woman waiting for him back in Prague....

Yes, he would miss Cristina Fairfax, but he doubted it would be for long. His guilty conscience was at rest.

CRISTINA INSTRUCTED RUDOLF'S driver to take her to the British Embassy as fast as possible, but on a day like this speed seemed impossible. The Ring was crowded with holiday makers showing off their Christmas finery and enjoying the entertainments provided by the emperor and the court musicians. It was carnival time in Vienna and the air was filled with delicious aromas and the music of Herr Strauss.

On any other day the excitement in the air and the frenzy of activity going on around her would have thrilled her, but today the carriage ride a few short blocks down the Ringstrasse seemed to take an eternity. Cristina sat on the edge of her seat, impatiently urging the driver forward through the jammed boulevard. She glanced out the window in a futile attempt to gauge the flow of traffic head of them, and met the hard gaze of the passenger in the cab next to hers.

Cristina sucked in her breath, suddenly and inexplicably afraid. That face was no stranger to her. She knew those fanatical gray eyes. She had first seen them that long ago morning in the coffeehouse. And she had seen them many times since that morning. They belonged to the man who had dogged her every step for months.

The man she had thought was a member of the secret police.

She watched in horrible fascination as he opened the door of his cab and hurled a plain brown-wrapped package in her direction. Warning bells sounded in her brain. She screamed for the driver to stop while she frantically snatched at the door handle on the opposite side of the vehicle, trying desperately to escape the confines of the cab. The brown-wrapped package bounced off the side of the imperial carriage and rolled under the gold, painted wheels.

The explosion was deafening. The carriage door came free at the moment of the blast and Cristina was hurled onto sidewalk by the force of the explosion. She instinctively reached out to break her fall and screamed in pain as a bone in her arm snapped and she thudded to the pavement.

Fragments of wood and glass rained down on her as she huddled, helpless, on the slushy, cold cobblestones. Somewhere nearby a horse screamed in agony, its tortured cries echoing her own suffering against a backdrop of lively Vienna.

She opened her eyes. Thick smoke stung her eyes and the

acrid smell of gunpowder mingled with the stench of blood and scorched horseflesh made her gag. She tried to raise herself on one arm and failed. She fell back to the cobblestones as her body protested the additional abuse. She was covered by a mass of cuts and bruises that throbbed and bled and her whole body ached. She fought the pain and the nausea that threatened to choke her, willing herself to stay awake until help arrived.

The crunch of footsteps on the broken glass penetrated the ringing in Cristina's ears and she focused her gaze on a pair of black boots just inches from her face. Bright spots of blood stained the toes of the shiny boots and the white slush on the pavement. Cristina turned her head to follow the path of the dripping blood and found herself staring into the barrel of an Austrian Cavalry Service revolver. The man leaning over her dripped blood onto her velvet muff and tiny crimson dots of it splattered the sidewalk. Cristina could see his wound. A fragment of black metal had ripped through his coat and pierced his left side. Forcing herself to ignore her pain, Cristina stared past the gun so that she might look into the face of the man behind it. She knew him. He had followed her around for months and he had looked her in the eyes before throwing a bomb beneath the wheels of the crown prince's beautiful imperial carriage and causing the devastating carnage around her. She watched as he pulled the hammer of the revolver back with his thumb and heard the sound of the chamber clicking into place. The quiet click seemed deafening to her as she focused all of her remaining energy on the man who would be her murderer. And there was no doubt that he intended to kill her. His fanatical gray eyes sparkled with an inner light as he smiled a grim smile and spoke to her for the first time. *"Auf Wiedersehen Fraulein Comtesse di Rimaldi."*

"Von Retterling!" A name rang out over the horrible chaos and the man standing over Cristina whirled to face a fellow cavalry officer. "You are wounded."

Von Retterling stared at the man in amazement, then realized he held his revolver pointed at Cristina's head.

"The horses," he lied as someone mercifully ended the

painful screams of the mortally wounded horses with two quick gunshots. "I was going to shoot the poor horses when I saw the young woman lying here. So young, so beautiful, and so badly injured . . ."

"It's all right, von Retterling. We will take care of the young woman, but first let us take you to the ambulance. That wound must be attended. You can do nothing for the woman."

Retterling fastened his gaze on Cristina's face, then allowed himself to be led toward the ambulance inching its way through the hysterical masses. From the looks of her, she would soon die; he might as well take care of himself.

There was confusion all around Cristina as the emperor's police and mounted regiments questioned the witnesses and removed the wreckage of the carriages, carcasses of the horses, and the bodies of the dead and wounded. Cries of "anarchist" rang through the city as word of the tragedy spread. Mounted soldiers patrolled the streets trying to calm the people who feared for the life of their crown prince. The strains of the Strauss waltzes ended abruptly as the maestro ended his concert and the bells of St. Stephen's Cathedral began their mournful toll for the dead.

Cristina tried to raise herself on her good arm, to scream at the police and tell them they had helped the man who had tried to murder her and had left her lying on the street—the man who had caused this destruction—but found she didn't have the strength to do more than lift her head.

"Try to lie still, frau." A kindly gentleman leaned over her, trying to comfort her when she screamed in pain and clutched at her belly. "I am Herr Doktor Kraus. We will be taking you to a hospital as soon as the ambulance wagon arrives."

"Retterling," Cristina whispered in a croaking voice as the abdominal cramps ripped through her, warning her that the precious life she carried was in danger.

"Ssh." Herr Doktor Kraus placed a finger to her lips. "We will do the best we can and try not to injure you further."

"Retterling," Cristina mumbled again. Her pain-filled

brain screamed the name at her, warning her to remember the name of her would-be assassin while several pairs of strong hands lifted her onto a canvas stretcher. She cried out at the jarring motion as they shifted her from the frozen ground to the stretcher until the pain became so intense she fainted, forgetting everything except the name embedded in her brain.

"WHAT THE BLOODY hell is going on outside?" Blake demanded of Cason, his assistant, as he hurried down the wide stairs of the embassy, valise in hand.

"There's been some sort of bombing, sir," Cason answered, stepping away from his observation point at the large window facing the Ring. "The crown prince's carriage was involved. The people are saying an anarchist made an attempt on the crown prince's life. The soldiers believe the anarchist escaped with injuries."

"How is Rudolf?" Blake asked. "There will be hell to pay if he was injured."

"The crown prince wasn't in the carriage, sir," Cason informed him. "The soldiers have been patrolling the street announcing that the crown prince was not in the carriage at the time of the explosion and that he is safe at the Imperial Palace."

Blake stepped to the window Cason had vacated. "Well, they'll soon have this mess cleared out of the way. They'll find an anarchist somewhere, hang him, and sweep the whole incident under the rug as if it never happened. Nothing must interfere with the routine of Gay Vienna during carnival," Blake commented cynically.

"You're probably right, sir. There are plenty of Serbs and Croats to choose from. Still, it's sad that such a tragedy occurs on the eve of a new year."

Blake frowned and started to turn away from his view of the carnage when a length of copper-colored hair hanging over the side of a stretcher caught his eye.

The hair on the back of his neck stood on end and gooseflesh pimpled his arms at the sight. "Oh, no," he groaned in agony, "it can't be. Merciful God! Cristina!" Blake dropped his valise where he stood by the window and was out of the embassy in second, running down the Ringstrasse like a man possessed.

"Wait!" Blake came to a halt beside the stretcher and seized the arm of the short, plump man standing next to it.

The man jumped as his arm was roughly seized from behind and quickly turned to face his assailant. "Herr, I beg you to let go of my arm. I am a doctor."

Blake studied the sympathetic face and the genuine look of surprise, then released his tight hold on the doctor's arm.

Freed from his hold, the doctor turned away from Blake and began supervising the loading of the ambulance.

"Where are you taking her?" Blake demanded roughly, unable to tear his eyes away from the bruised and battered face of the woman lying so still against the canvas.

"To the hospital. She needs immediate care."

"No!" Blake's objection was instantaneous. "No, she can get much better care at home. The hospital will be too busy to give her the care she needs." He didn't like the idea of Cristina lying in a dingy hospital ward with nothing but strangers to care for her. "We have an apartment just down the street and someone to give her the constant care she needs. Take her there."

The doctor hesitated. "We cannot take the ambulance. You will have to find some other means of transportation—and very soon, because I fear the child is coming."

Blake drew in a sharp breath, aware that the early arrival of the baby could endanger both the child and the mother's lives. "I'll find a carriage or wagon or something and find a specialist for her as soon as possible."

"There is no need to find a specialist."

"Yes, there is." Blake's tone of voice brooked no argument. "The child shouldn't be born for another month. I want her to have a specialist in childbirth cases."

"I am such a specialist," the doctor assured Blake. "I am Herr Doktor Manfred Kraus and I will accompany you and

your wife.'' He stepped away from Blake and gave the ambulance driver instructions in rapid German before turning
back to Blake. ''I told the driver to take the other patients to
the hospital. I asked the others to stay and help with your
wife.''

''I don't know how to thank you . . . ,'' Blake began.

''There is no need to thank me.'' The doctor understood
that the man before him was a strong man unused to express-
ing his deepest emotions. ''The driver of the carriage and the
footman were killed. It's a miracle your wife survived the
blast,'' he explained. ''I was down the street. I had just delivered a child and was walking home when the explosion
knocked me to my knees. I got up and down the street where
I found your wife lying in the snow on the sidewalk.''

''Thank God you found her.''

''I am afraid it may be too soon to thank the All Highest. . . .'' The doctor's voice drifted into nothingness when he
realized he had spoken his thoughts aloud.

Blake read the meaning behind the doctor's words and what
he read filled him with terror and galvanized him into action.

''I'll see about a vehicle.'' He spoke brusquely to keep the
fear out of his voice.

''Sir!''

Blake whirled around and spotted his assistant seated next
to the driver of the embassy-supply wagon.

''Cason.'' Blake breathed softly as relief swept through
him in the form of perspiration dotting his brow. He clenched
his fists tightly by his side and said a prayer as the wagon
inched its way through the remaining debris and rolled to a
stop beside him.

''I realized it was the countess as soon as you bolted from
the embassy, so I brought a wagon. I knew you wouldn't want
her taken to a hospital,'' Cason explained. ''We've put the
stableboy's mattress and several blankets in back for her.''

''Ever efficient, Cason.'' Blake struggled with his brimming emotions before he suddenly thrust out his hand to clasp
the other man's in friendship.

Cason smiled in reply, then got down to business. ''We

had better get her home, sir, it's beginning to snow again.''

Blake glanced up at the heavens and saw that Cason spoke the truth. He barked instructions to the men bearing Cristina's stretcher and they began to load her onto the wagon. She moaned with each movement and Blake gritted his teeth in helpless frustration as the men carefully settled the stretcher on top of the mattress, gently tucking the blankets around her as they completed their task. He thanked them for their time and effort, removed his wallet to pay them a generous sum, then climbed into the wagon and stationed himself next to the inert form on the mattress.

''Go slowly and carefully,'' he ordered the driver.

The wagon rolled away from the sidewalk and rumbled over the rough cobblestones. Cristina groaned as the wheels jolted her about; she finally opened her mouth to scream as pain sliced through her. Blake shouted a curse at the driver who hung his head dejectedly and apologized profusely in the flowery Viennese manner for causing the frau pain.

Blake looked anxiously from Cristina to the doctor. ''Can't you do anything?''

''I am sorry, Herr, but I dare not give her anything for the pain until I can gauge the child's condition.'' He shook his head sadly. ''She has fainted again. Perhaps nature will be merciful and not allow her to feel the rest of the journey.''

Blake found the short distance to the apartment unbearably long. He began to question the wisdom of taking her there when there were perfectly good hospitals in Vienna, but was glad Cristina couldn't read the doubt in his eyes. He cursed Nigel Jameson soundly for not being there when he needed him and prayed that this doctor would be as good as he claimed to be. Unable to keep from touching her, Blake reached his hand under the blanket to find Cristina's. He meant to squeeze her hand reassuringly but found it still covered by her velvet muff. He tugged the bloody muff from her hand and discovered that she had her hand clenched into a tight fist; almost as if she was holding something. Blake gently pried her fingers open. A glimmer of gold fell from her grasp and landed on the mattress in front of him. He bent to retrieve it and discovered a medallion of some sort. Blake removed his gloves and fingered the gold disk, turning it over in his palm, studying it closely.

He found it hard to focus on the tiny script through the haze of tears that stung his eyelids. But he managed to read the words and realized Cristina's intent. This medallion was her gift to him. And it might be the last thing she ever gave him. Blake choked on a sob that lodged in his throat as he held the gold disk against his lips. He kissed it gently, reverently, as if he were kissing the woman instead of the cold metal, then fastened the chain about his neck. He let the disk fall beneath his starched, white collar where it was warmed by the heat of the flesh that covered his heart.

"Always," Blake promised, carefully leaning over to kiss each one of Cristina's fingers and the palm of her hand before gently tucking her hand back inside the warm blanket.

O! call back yesterday, bid time return.

—WILLIAM SHAKESPEARE 1564–1616

Twenty-four

THE UNBEARABLE PAIN ripping through her body made Cristina delirious. Her world became a nightmare of terror, suffering, and confusion. A world where the sounds of explosions deafened her and cries of unbearable agony mixed with the tune of Strauss waltzes played over and over in her brain and where a man named Retterling tried to kill her. Over and over again.

She awoke with a start, crying the horrible name. She tried to move, but fresh waves of pain made her helpless. She opened her mouth and screamed. She was dying. The barest movement was sheer agony. Breathing required effort and sharp pains knifed through her abdomen in uncontrollable spasms.

Cristina licked feebly at her dry, cracked lips and screamed again, but the sound that met her ears was a thin, mewling wail.

Someone took her hand and Cristina croaked a pitiful plea. "H-help me. I-I hurt and I-I can't see."

"Open your eyes, sweetheart," Blake softly urged.

Cristina recognized the voice and obeyed without question,

forcing her eyelids to remain open while she struggled to focus on the beloved face above her. Her vision cleared and as she grew accustomed to the dim light she realized she no longer lay on the cold sidewalk, but on a bed. A low flame burned in the gas lamp above her bed and a warm fire glowed in the hearth, illuminating the familiar bedroom she had shared with Blake.

"Blake . . ."

"I'm here, sweet," Blake assured her. "And Leah is in the kitchen preparing everything while Doctor Kraus washes up."

"It hurts." She gasped as another contraction tore through her.

"I know, sweetheart," Blake sympathized. "You've been injured. You've broken an arm and bruised several ribs and been nicked by flying debris in a dozen different places."

"Th-the baby? What about the baby?" She focused her gaze on her stomach and was comforted by the presence of the familiar mound under the covers.

"The baby is coming, Cristina," Blake said the words very carefully, not wanting to add to her fear yet knowing he had to tell her the truth. "Your labor has started. The trauma you've been through has probably brought it on earlier than normal."

Cristina understood. She understood what was happening to her body. She was having her baby. Another burning pain sliced through her. She arched her back and bit her lower lip, but she did not cry out.

Blake smiled at her tenderly. "Don't try to be too brave, my love." The endearment slipped off his tongue naturally. She seemed so small and frail lying on the bed splinted and bandaged, bravely trying to conceal her pain. "Cry out if it helps."

She nodded. "You'll stay?"

"As long as you need me," Blake promised.

It was a hard promise to keep. Blake thought he had been frightened when her fetal water burst as Cason and the driver carried her into the apartment, but now he knew there was worse to fear in what had become the longest night of his life.

The waiting was interminable and the watching was so difficult. Cristina's struggle to bear his infant tore at Blake's heart. He had never felt so utterly helpless as he did when he coaxed her to breathe, lifted her so she could bear down, and wiped the sweat from her face. He did those things automatically but he couldn't do the one thing he wanted most to do—he couldn't end the pain.

If she survived, Blake promised himself he would never put her through the agony again.

After nearly twenty hours of almost ceaseless effort, Blake wondered how much more she could stand. She was utterly exhausted and still the doctor instructed her to try harder to push. Blake was ready to scream himself at the suffering she was enduring when Cristina found the strength to give one last push.

He stared in wonderment as the small head appeared. His emotions threatened to choke him as he gazed lovingly at the exhausted young woman who had given him this gift. Her eyes were closed and sunken, her cheeks bruised and scratched from glass and debris and the scrape of the sidewalk and her lips were cracked and bitten. Her beautiful hair was wet and matted to her head, but to Blake, Cristina had never looked more lovely. But she was so weak and there had been so much blood . . .

"Is she all right?" Blake demanded of Leah who was busily kneading Cristina's stomach to help dislodge the afterbirth.

Leah noticed the tired rings under Blake's eyes and the unusual pallor of his bronzed face and took pity on him. Lord Lawrence had suffered almost as much as as Cristina. "She'll be fine as soon as she gets some rest."

Blake expelled a sigh of relief and relaxed a bit. If Leah said Cristina would recover, she would. She had to get well because she meant so much to him. They meant so much to him. Cristina and her child. His child. Their child.

Blake turned to view his child and found Dr. Kraus feverishly working over the infant.

"What is it?" The bluish tinge of the baby's skin frightened Blake.

"I'm sorry, Herr Lord Lawrence, but he will not breathe."

Blake watched, alarmed, as the doctor opened the baby's mouth, ran his finger around the inside, then turned the tiny babe upside down and shook him gently, hoping to clear the air passages of any mucus blocking the way.

Doctor Kraus pinched the tiny nostrils closed, then breathed his own breath into the baby.

Blake waited anxiously for the baby to breathe his first breath and watched hopefully for the gentle rise and fall of his chest as the doctor worked over him, but the movement he hoped for, the cry he hoped for, never came. Their beautiful child was dead. Stillborn and silent.

Doctor Kraus raised his head and looked at Blake. A sheen of unshed tears sparkled in the doctor's compassionate eyes. "I am very, very sorry, Herr Lord Lawrence. I have done all I know to do. I cannot make him breathe."

"You must." Blake knew it was an impossible task, yet he felt compelled to order the doctor to accomplish it. "You must make him live. He's my son. . . ." Blake reached out a finger and softly caressed the downy, black hair and the miniature shell of a perfectly formed ear. He bent his head over the baby, kissed the tiny forehead, and whispered brokenly, "You have to live, son. I've barely gotten to know you. You have to live. There are so many things I want to share with you. How can I tell your mother? How will she bear this? We want you so much. We love you so much. . . ."

The doctor placed his hand on Blake's shoulder, shook his tired gray head in sorrow, and taking the baby from Blake, wrapped the tiny, still form in a pale blue blanket and placed him in the cradle Leah had prepared for him. "Herr Lord Lawrence, the little one, is in the hands of the Lord. There is nothing we can do."

Blake sank into the nearest chair and covered his face with his hands. "All that torment for nothing. All that pain for nothing. It isn't fair. Oh, God, how can you do this to her? How am I going to tell her? How can I break her heart again?'' His words were lost in the hoarseness of his voice as his shoulders shook with grief. He suddenly felt very old and very weary.

"Blake?" Cristina's voice was soft and hesitant, barely audible. "Blake, what is it?"

Leah leaned over Cristina and smoothed her damp hair away from her face. "Ssh, missy, rest. You're tired and Lord Lawrence is just as tired as you. Rest for a while." She murmured to Cristina, buying time and allowing Blake precious moments to compose himself.

"The baby," Cristina whispered, making her wishes known. "I want to see my baby. I didn't hear him cry. I want to see him. It's a boy, isn't it?" Cristina followed the direction of Leah's gaze. She could barely see the top of Blake's bowed head from her place on the bed. "I want to see my baby." Her voice was louder this time, anxious. "I want to see my baby. Blake?"

"I'm here, Countess." Blake slowly raised himself from the chair and crossed over to the bed.

"Blake, the baby? A boy or a girl?"

Blake struggled with the lump in his throat. "A boy, Countess. A beautiful baby boy."

"Nicholas," Cristina sighed. During the past few months she'd changed her mind about wanting a baby girl and decided she wanted a boy with dark hair and eyes like his father. "His name is Nicholas Fairfax."

"Yes, Nicholas Fairfax Lawrence," he repeated softly. Nicholas was the name they had chosen. "Cristina . . ."

Cristina was suddenly afraid. She could tell by the way Blake said her name that something was wrong. Terribly wrong. She fought to sit up against the pillows and failed. "My baby! Please give me my baby!"

"No, Cristina, please . . . ,'' Blake pleaded.

"What's wrong with him? What's wrong with my baby?" Her worried gaze darted from one face to the other, first Leah's then the doctor's, before finally settling on Blake. "Is he missing fingers or toes? Tell me! I have a right to know."

Blake moved closer to touch her hand. "Nicholas is dead, Cristina. Stillborn."

"No!" The anguished scream penetrated the deadly quiet of the house and ripped at the hearts and the souls of the three people who stood watching her, unable to ease her sorrow. "Oh, God, please, no!"

Blake glanced at Leah, then the doctor, then walked over to the cradle. He gently lifted Nicholas from his resting place and carried him to his mother, then sat on the edge of the bed next to Cristina and carefully unwrapped the blanket and allowed Cristina to see him.

Cristina stared at her son. He was perfect and beautiful from the top of his little head with its cap of downy, black hair to the tips of his perfectly formed toes.

He was all she had imagined he'd be; all she had hoped for in her firstborn son. He couldn't be dead. He couldn't. She had felt him turning and kicking within her womb during the carriage ride, so eager to see the world, and now he lay so still.

"Nicholas, my sweet baby, Nicholas," Cristina crooned before turning to Blake. "Wrap him back up, Blake. He's cold."

"Cris . . ."

"Babies shouldn't be exposed to the cold air."

The doctor looked at Cristina, then stepped to the bed to take Nicholas from his father's arms. Blake waved him away with a quick shake of his head and continued to hold his son.

Doctor Kraus spoke to Cristina. "I am very sorry, Frau Cristina. I couldn't save your little one. He is in God's care now."

"No," Cristina said, firmly. "You're mistaken. He's just sleeping. Tell him, Blake. Tell him our baby's fine."

"I wish I could, sweetheart," Blake said, gently. "I wish with all my heart I could make Nicholas breathe for you, but I can't, Cristina. I can't."

"Don't worry about it, Blake," Cristina repeated. "Nicholas will breathe when he's ready to."

"No, my darling, he won't. Our son is never going to breathe."

"Then, make him," she insisted. "You're his father, tell him to. You've always been able to make him do what you want. You can make him breathe."

"No, sweetheart, I can't."

"Yes you can," she said. "You have to. You can make anything right. You can, Blake, I know it. Please do something. I'm begging you. Please, please make my baby breathe." Tears rolled silently down Cristina's face as she pleaded for Blake to do the impossible, to turn back the clock and give her a healthy, living child. "Please, Blake, I'll do anything. Anything. Please make him listen to you."

Blake shook his head, afraid to speak for fear his own tears would choke him.

"You must! Don't you remember? You promised to protect us! You can't let our baby die! You promised!" Cristina screamed the words in a voice raw with naked grief.

"I'm sorry, love," Blake whispered roughly. "I'm so sorry." It was all he could say. All he could do.

Cristina stared at him with her huge, emerald eyes shimmering with tears, then collapsed back on the pillows, completely spent. She turned her face to the wall and cried softly, hardly making a sound.

Doctor Kraus filled a glass with water and stirred several drops of brown liquid into the water. He lifted Cristina's head and coaxed her to swallow the bitter drink. "This is laudanum, my dear. It will help you rest."

Cristina swallowed the drug without protest, but the tears continued to roll down her face long after she slept.

Blake sat next to Cristina until she fell asleep, then walked to the door on the other side of the room.

Leah stopped Blake at the door. "Where are you goin'?"

"Arrangements must be made." He walked on through the doorway and into the nursery. He placed Nicholas in the crib and covered him with another blanket.

"The arrangements can wait a while. You're tired and you need some rest," Leah said.

"We're all tired," Blake admitted. "But I can't rest. I have to see to the arrangements for Nicholas and return to the embassy."

"Why?" Leah demanded.

"Because I'm sending you and Cristina to New York as soon as she's able to travel. And I have to make sure everything is set before I leave for London."

"You're still goin' to London after what's happened?"

"I must, Leah. You see, I'm taking my son home to be buried. I don't want him left alone here in Vienna. I'm taking home to Everleigh where my parents live. They'll look after him." He saw the look of concern in Leah's eyes and held up a hand to forestall her argument. "I'm going to do this, Leah. I owe it to Nicholas and to myself. Please don't argue. Just send someone for a cab."

"There's no need." Leah placed her hand on Blake's arm. "Mister Cason is waitin' in the sittin' room. Has been all night."

"Thank you, Leah. And one more favor . . ."

"Anythin'."

"Dress Nicholas in that thing Cristina made him at Christmas. I want to remember my son in something his mother made for him."

"Yes, Lord Blake." It was the first time Leah had ever addressed him by his given name. It made Blake smile a little in spite of his grief.

"Ah, Leah." Blake leaned over and kissed her soft cheek. "I doubt I'll see you again before I leave for London. I'll have a coffin here later this afternoon and someone to take it to the station. Try to get some rest. Cristina will need you when she wakes up. Be strong for her, Leah, and love her for me." Blake's baritone voice cracked and he quickly turned away and headed for the salon where Cason waited patiently.

It took most of the morning, but Blake was finally able to locate a suitable coffin for Nicholas and obtain rail passage on a train out of Vienna. By the time he had finished his arrangements, he was so tired his body ached for sleep.

He wanted to crawl into bed and sob out the anger and

grief welling up inside of him, but he forced himself to go on. He felt old and weary. Bone-weary.

He needed a deep, dreamless sleep that would allow him to forget the horror of the past twenty-four hours.

But by the time he and Cason returned to the embassy, Blake knew there would be no opportunity for him to sleep. A letter from Albert Mead, his solicitor in London, lay waiting on his desk.

Blake sat down behind the desk, picked up the letter, ripped it open, and read:

Lord Lawrence:

I regret that it has taken so long to secure the information you asked me to obtain. The route of the necklace was difficult to trace, but I finally managed the task.

I spent several weeks contacting jewelers and pawn shops in London asking for information leading to the recovery of the necklace stolen from your residence.

The jewelers and pawn shops owners didn't know, of course, that you had already recovered the necklace. It took quite a while but I finally hit upon a bit of luck. I found a jeweler, Monsieur Jureau, who claimed to have designed a necklace such as I described for you as a gift to your bride. He referred to the necklace and the matching earrings and bracelet as his finest achievement. He remembered it well and described it in detail. He also recalled another incident that happen several years later.

A woman calling herself Lady Lawrence brought the same necklace into his shop, wanting to sell it. Monsieur Jureau recognized your wife from her pictures but he refused to buy back the necklace without your permission. He didn't understand why a woman of her wealth would wish to sell a wedding gift from her husband and he admitted to being insulted by your wife's dislike of his creation. When he refused to buy the neck-

lace, Lady Lawrence became furious and left his shop.

Monsieur Jureau followed her onto the sidewalk, try-ing to explain his position. She refused to listen and pushed past him to climb into a carriage.

There was a man waiting for her in the cab. He was dressed in a uniform and spoke with a German accent. He began arguing with Lady Lawrence over her failure to sell the necklace. After a few moments, Lady Lawrence shoved the necklace at the gentleman saying: "Take it, Oskar. It means nothing to me and I suppose it's a small price to pay for your loyalty." He an-swered: "A necklace is no good to me. I need money on which to live. I need the money you promised me for watching your husband." She answered in return: "Idiot! Sell it in Vienna. It's worth a fortune, much more than I owe you, but take it and keep it as payment on account in case I need your services again some day."

They stopped arguing and began to laugh as the car-riage rolled away. Monsieur Jureau attempted to con-tact you to tell you of this, but you were away and by the time you returned to London he had forgotten the incident. He only recalled it again while we were dis-cussing the necklace. After I spoke to Monsieur Jureau I took the liberty of searching through copies of the society pages until I discovered that one of Lady Lawrence's escorts during that London season was an Austrian cavalry officer, Captain Oskar von Retterling. He was a member of the Horse Guards attached to the Austro-Hungarian Embassy.

I regret that you must learn of your wife's indiscre-tions in this way and I can only hope that this infor-mation is what you require.

I remain . . .

Your Servant,
Albert Mead

Blake carefully refolded the letter. He had known in his heart that Meredith was responsible for the theft of the necklace. It was the only logical explanation. Who else could it have been? And he had known that Meredith was desperate, known that she was capable of exacting a terrible revenge. But that didn't make the proof any easier to bear. She had warned him. But dear God . . . It came as shock to know she had paid someone deliberately to murder his child! But there could be no mistake. Cristina had awakened after the bombing crying the name "Retterling."

Blake placed the letter in the pocket of his coat and called for his assistant. "Cason!"

"Yes, sir?" Cason hurried into the office.

"Find copies of yesterday's papers. All of them. I want to see the lists of the casualties from the explosion. The dead and the wounded."

"Your wife's name wasn't among them," Cason ventured. "I sent a request to the crown prince in your name asking that the name of Cristina Fairfax and the alias of Comtesse di Rimaldi be kept out of the newspapers."

"Thank goodness for that," Blake said. "Nevertheless, I need to see the papers. It's urgent."

"Right away, sir."

A quarter of an hour passed before Cason returned with the papers. Blake scanned the front page articles rapidly, going through each paper until he found what he wanted. A name in the lists of the wounded. Captain Oskar von Retterling.

It was simply too much of a coincidence to suit Blake. He knew the truth. Meredith had promised revenge and she had gotten it. There was no anarchist. The imperial guard could rest easy. The attack hadn't been aimed at Rudolf, but at Cristina. Oskar von Retterling was a henchman hired by Meredith to exact her revenge on him and Cristina and Nicholas had paid the price.

It was too horrible to be believed and yet Blake knew it was true—knew it had to be true. He had suspected Meredith on another occasion and had put it out of his mind. He had never wanted to think that a woman he had once believed himself in love with could murder in cold blood. He hadn't wanted to believe his judgment of human nature could be so faulty. Until tonight . . .

"Oh, God, Nicholas! Cristina!" Blake put his head down on the papers in front of him and wept. He cried for the son he would never know and for the agony he had unwittingly brought on Cristina in desiring her. He wept until his eyes burned from the salty tears and the hoarse, shoulder-racking sobs died in his throat. Then he slowly composed himself.

He had a great deal to do before sunrise. He had to devise a plan.

Blake cleared his desk and set out his pens and paper. He wrote out a cable to Cristina's father and a message to Rudolf asking him for one last favor while he thanked him for keeping Cristina's name out of the newspapers. Lastly he wrote a letter to Cristina. He finished his correspondence and called once again for Cason.

The young man came almost at once—almost as if he had been hovering outside the door waiting for Blake to call him.

Blake stated his instructions explicitly. "Send this cable to William Fairfax in New York City first thing in the morning. I'm sending Cristina to him as soon as she's able to travel."

"I thought you were returning to London."

"I am. And when my wife is able to travel, you're to make the travel arrangements for her and Leah in Leah's name. Leah Porter. Remember that, Cason. No one is to suspect that Cristina is on that ship. Veil her, lock her in her cabin if you have to, tell Leah to do anything, but keep Cristina's name a secret. When everything is arranged, cable William Fairfax and ask him to meet a Mrs. Porter, a prospective client, at the docks on the date of their arrival. I'll leave you money to cover the expenses. And when I've gone, I want you to give this letter to Cristina. It will answer her questions and encourage her to leave," Blake explained. "And Cason, send this message to Crown Prince Rudolf as soon as possible."

"Yes, Lord Lawrence," Cason responded automatically. "Is there anything else you require?"

"Please bring me a bottle of brandy and a glass. That will be all I require for the remainder of the night. Go to bed as soon as you're through, Cason. You need sleep just as much as I do." Blake suddenly realized that Cason had been without sleep for as many hours as he had. "You've been an invaluable friend through all of this and I thank you from the bottom of my heart."

Lord Lawrence's heartfelt thanks embarrassed the younger man. He nodded to Blake. "Thank you, Lord Lawrence. I'll get your brandy and take care of these letters before I retire." He hurried away before Blake could say anything more.

When Cason returned some minutes later, he entered the office quietly and placed the brandy decanter and glass on the desk. Lord Lawrence looked up from the letter he was re-reading and Cason was chilled by the expression of guilty anguish in those black eyes. He turned and left the room without uttering a word, leaving Lord Lawrence alone to drown his grief with his assault on the brandy bottle.

*The villainy you teach me I will execute, and it shall
go hard but I will better the instruction.*

—WILLIAM SHAKESPEARE 1564–1616

Twenty-five

BLAKE HAD BEEN in residence at Lawrence House for
nearly a week before he received the summons he was expecting from Meredith. It came in the form of a brief note
demanding his immediate presence in the country. It was a
command and not an unexpected one, for Meredith's spies
had been at work since Blake's return to England. Blake was
aware of their presence. He had been under surveillance from
the moment he'd left Vienna. There had been several attempts
to frighten him since he had returned from Everleigh and the
burial of his son.

Blake reread the note then crumpled it and flung it into the
fireplace. Meredith was very insistent in demanding his immediate presence at Willow Wood. Her spies had probably
reported the news about Nicholas and now she calmly expected him to dance to her tune.

Well he wasn't ready to make his appearance, regardless
of the threats and attempts on his life. He was making the
rules and this time he intended to prepare for his meeting with
Meredith very carefully. A delay would infuriate her and her
anger might prove to be his ally. It might make her reckless

and boastful and it might just keep her off-balance while he planned his course of action. He would answer her summons in good time and until then he planned to wait and give Meredith's temper time to simmer.

In the end, he waited a full fortnight and by the time Blake reached Willow Wood, Meredith's fury had reached its peak.

She began her attack the moment he walked calmly into her bedroom without knocking. "What do you think you're doing?" she hissed at him.

"I'm here at your request," he replied smoothly. It took every bit of Blake's self-control to stay in the same room with her and to carry on a reasonably civilized conversation. Every time he looked at Meredith, he saw Nicholas's tiny, stillborn face.

"I sent for you two weeks ago!"

"And now I've arrived."

"You certainly took your own sweet time about it," Meredith commented acidly.

"I assure you, Meredith, I came as soon as I could. I do have other things to do. I can't come running every time I receive a note from you." He spoke as if he were accustomed to receiving notes from her, as if it were commonplace for the wife he'd believed dead these past six years to begin sending him notes that demanded his presence. "If you had been seriously ill your lawyers would have notified me."

"I suppose you were hoping they would notify you that I was on my deathbed," Meredith taunted.

"Actually I'd rather hoped you'd be off your deathbed and six feet under the ground," Blake told her. "But I'm not foolish enough to think you'd do anything to suit me."

"You're absolutely right," Meredith confirmed. "And you must know that I'll never agree to divorce you. You married me for better or worse and I won't be shoved away at your convenience. The very idea! I am surprised at you, Blake, to even think of divorcing an invalid wife. Imagine what the scandal would do to your precious career. It would be a pity to lose everything you've worked for all these years."

"I'm sure my career would survive." Blake politely seated

himself on the chaise longue near the fire and nonchalantly lit a thin cigar. "After all, it survived my marriage to you."

"And your very public affair with Cristina Fairfax," Meredith charged.

Blake carelessly blew a ring of smoke before turning to Meredith. "What I had with Cristina wasn't an affair. It was a marriage."

Meredith wheeled herself within inches of him, her lovely face horribly contorted as she mimicked him. " *What I had with Cristina wasn't an affair. It was a marriage.*' How sweet! Too bad it wasn't legal. Too bad you married me first." Her voice rose an octave, taking on the characteristics of a shrieking harpy.

Blake nodded. "I suppose you're right, Meredith. I suppose there are some mistakes for which we never stop paying. What do you think? Have you paid for the mistake you made in marrying me? Have you sat in that chair long enough to repent?"

"Don't you dare try that on me! Don't you dare pity me!"

Blake's sharp laughter echoed across the room. "Pity? Good God, Meredith, there are vipers more in need of pity. I don't pity you. In fact, I don't believe it's possible for anyone to pity you."

"I despise you!" Meredith spat at him, whirling around in her chair with her back to him.

"Then there's no need for this pointless discussion. You despise me and I don't particularly care for you—a divorce should settle everything." Blake flung the remainder of his cigar into the fire.

"There will be no divorce."

"Why not? It would seem to be what we both want."

"Don't patronize me," Meredith warned. "And don't play games with me. A divorce is not what I want and you know it." She faced him again. "Oh, you thought you were clever sending your whore to Vienna under an assumed name and in the company of the crown prince, but I wasn't fooled. I knew better. I knew she wasn't in Italy with her mother because my sources informed me that she was at Lawrence

House with you. I knew she was your mistress. I make it my business to know everything about you—including the fact that you're in mourning for your infant son.''

"You must be mistaken, Meredith.'' Blake pretended ignorance. "I have no son, or daughter either, yet. My child isn't due to arrive until later this month.''

"Don't play dumb with me. I know about the coffin you brought from Vienna. I know about the trip you made to Everleigh.''

"I visited my mother. I usually do whenever I return to England.''

"Don't toy with me,'' she warned again. "I'm not a fool, Blake. My sources are very reliable. I know, for instance, that Cristina Fairfax was injured in the Vienna bombing and that shortly after the bombing you returned to London with the body of a male infant—your son, whom you buried at your parents' home.''

"You must be mistaken, Meredith. I heard about the bombing in Vienna, of course. Everyone has. But I can assure you that Cristina wasn't involved.''

"Don't be ridiculous! Of course she was. I knew about it. . . .'' Meredith faltered for a split second.

"Really? How was that possible? How did you learn about a bombing a half a continent away from London?'' Blake asked pointedly.

"The papers, of course. It was in all the London papers. Such a tragedy,'' Meredith told him.

Blake's eyes narrowed until they were dark slits in his dangerous face. "Cristina Fairfax's name was never in any papers.''

Meredith realized her blunder at once and attempted to brazen it out. "Well,'' she waved a dismissing hand, "someone must have mentioned it. You know how embassy gossip travels. I know I heard it from someone. . . .''

"Someone who was there, perhaps?'' Blake suggested helpfully. "The man who hurled the bomb? Someone named Oskar von Retterling?''

Meredith paled slightly. "I'm not acquainted with anyone

named Oskar von Retterling. You know how I detest Austrians.''

''You didn't detest him when you employed him. Surely you remember one of your most ardent admirers?'' Blake jeered. ''You know the one. You gifted him with the emerald and diamond necklace you took from the safe at Lawrence House. Remember the Austrian cavalry officer? You see, Meredith, I know a great deal about you, too. I know, for instance, that you were living in Jack's hunting lodge in Ireland during the time you were supposed to be dead. You spent the winters there and the summers in a schloss in the Tyrols— a schloss owned by one Oskar von Retterling''

''I don't know what you're talking about, Blake, or why you insist on accusing me.''

''Oh, yes, you do,'' Blake grabbed her by the shoulders and shook her viciously. ''I'm talking about revenge, Meredith. The petty sort of revenge you extracted on an innocent baby for things you imagined I did. I'm talking about the revenge you tried to extract on me because I committed the unpardonable sin of failing to go along with your grand scheme by falling out of love with you faster than I fell in into it. You wanted to marry the heir to the marquess of Everleigh and you did. You wanted a title and you got one. You wanted money and position and power and you got it. You could have had everything, Meredith, but you got a little too greedy when you decided to keep Jack. You wanted Jack and you thought I'd share you with him. You overplayed your hand when you thought you could have us both.''

''I love Jack,'' she said. ''I always have. And Jack has always loved me.''

''Then God help him,'' Blake told her. ''Because wanting has cost you dearly. It's cost you my fortune and your chance to own Lawrence House.''

''The mansion that belongs to the mother of the Lawrence heir,'' Meredith said. ''Only now there is no heir. And if you persist with this idea of divorce, there will be no more Cristina Fairfax.''

"You aren't in any position to make threats, Meredith." Blake shook her again.

"Try me," Meredith challenged. "I'll do anything to keep what's rightfully mine and I stand to lose a great deal if you divorce me in favor of Cristina Fairfax or Comtesse di Rimaldi or whatever name you've given her this time."

"Meredith, you can't win."

"Maybe not," Meredith agreed. "But either way, Cristina Fairfax won't be alive to witness it. If you make any attempt to see her I'll arrange another accident. I'll find her no matter where you've hidden her."

"The world is a very large place, Meredith, and you will have to do a great deal of traveling in that wheelchair if you hope to find her," Blake informed her.

"I have my methods. And I know you too well, Blake. You won't be able to stay away from her. One day you'll lead me to her. This wheelchair has taught me infinite patience. I can just sit back and let someone else dispatch Miss Fairfax."

"And how do you intend to pay them?" Blake asked bluntly. "You can't barter with your body any longer and from this moment on, you are without funds. Willow Wood's household bills will be sent to my solicitor to be paid and any goods purchased for Willow Wood will have to meet my approval. In other words, the generous allowance allotted to this estate is at an end. I intend to make sure you never have the money to pay your spies and henchmen again."

"Don't be so sure, Blake," Meredith purred. "There are other ways to obtain money to pay my henchmen, as you call them, and I would like nothing better than to be a rich widow. You're not indestructible. . . ."

"I expected something like that from you," Blake replied cryptically, then turned on his heel and left Meredith alone to speculate on his next move.

She didn't need to speculate long.

By early morning, Willow Wood was in total turmoil.

The sounds of busy feet scurrying throughout the large house woke Meredith long before her accustomed hour.

Unable to contain her curiosity, she levered herself out of bed and into her chair. She wheeled herself out the bedroom door and down the hall to the landing.

Below her, the main hall of Willow Wood was a beehive of activity. And Blake was at the center of it all, issuing orders.

"What is going on here?" Meredith demanded of the crowd beneath her.

Blake tilted his head to look up at her. "Ah, Meredith, I see you're awake. As you can see, I've decided to make a few changes. I apologize if the noise woke you." He somehow managed to sound sincere and concerned for her well-being, but there was an edge to his voice. An edge of utter contempt.

"What sort of changes?" Meredith asked suspiciously.

"Oh, a few pieces of furniture, a few paintings I think would look much better at Lawrence House, and some staff changes," came the bored reply from Blake.

"I don't want any staff changes!" Meredith shouted. "I want things left the way they are."

"I'm afraid that's impossible. I've already interviewed the staff and decided who will remain here and who will be forced to seek other employment."

"You can't do that!" Meredith gasped, her voice trembling with rage.

"I can," Blake answered scathingly. "And I have. Although I'm sure you and Jack probably used this house while I was out of the country, the fact remains that Willow Wood is mine and my money pays the salaries of the staff. I'll hire and fire whomever I please." The expression in his dark eyes and the stern look on his face issued a warning to all present. "My employees will answer only to me or they will look for other jobs."

"What about me? Don't I have some say in all of this?" Meredith demanded.

"No, you don't. Unfortunately for you and fortunately for me, England has yet to reform its antiquated laws regarding wives and property. I grew careless during the time I thought you were dead. I didn't pay enough attention to my property. But I've decided to remedy that unfortunate situation." Blake's insinuations were crystal clear to Meredith.

"You won't get away with this. I won't let you treat me this way."

"At the moment, you have no choice. I'm tired of having my money used against me. Oh, I know you'll find some way to pay your spies, but it won't be with my money any longer and it won't be with my family treasures. I'm taking everything of value that I don't want to see sold or pawned back to London with me. And that includes the Lawrence family jewelry."

"You're taking my jewelry?"

"I'm taking *my* jewelry," Blake corrected. "You may keep the jewelry I gave you, including the wedding and betrothal rings. They were family heirlooms, but I don't think anyone will care if you pawn those. You see, I don't wish to have any reminders of you and I know the future Lady Lawrence won't mind the loss." He smiled. "By the way, the pawnshops in London won't be accepting anything from you or Jack or any of your family members. Neither will anyone around here or at Everleigh. If you want to pawn the jewels you have left, you'll have to go farther afield. Unfortunately my influence only extends so far."

"I'll still find some way to fight you. And I'll never consent to divorce."

"You'll agree to anything when I've finished with you," Blake predicted. "And you'll do it on my terms. You see, Meredith, I have sources of information as well as you and by the time I've finished collecting my evidence to present to the courts, you'll sign anything just to keep your lovely neck out of the hangman's noose. Murder and attempted murder happen to be against the law." Blake turned away from the staircase and began giving instructions to two of the footmen standing nearby. "Take the former Lady Lawrence to her room. Help her back to bed and place her wheelchair outside her door on the landing when you've finished. Her supervision is no longer required."

"I won't allow this!" Meredith screamed at Blake as the footmen approached her. "I'll see you dead and buried for this!" she promised.

"I'm sure you'll try," Blake agreed. "But I've fired your esteemed footmen, your cook, and everyone else I thought was too loyal to you. You'll have to find your allies elsewhere."

"That might be true," Meredith conceded as the footmen reached for her chair, "but you won't stop me, Blake. I won't quit until one of us is dead."

"I never thought you would," Blake replied before turning his attention back to the employees gathered around him listening to the angry exchange. He appeared able to ignore the threats and insults that rained down on him from overhead, but he heard them. And later, alone in his bedroom, Blake worried. He no longer had any illusions concerning Meredith. She was capable of murder and she had made her threats against him known. He believed everything she had promised him. She wouldn't stop until one of them was dead. He was absolutely certain of that. Hell hath no fury like a woman scorned, he remembered, and now he realized that he had scorned Meredith in the worst possible way. He had withdrawn his blind adoration and become indifferent to her charms.

Blake knew he had to execute his plan very carefully. He must not make a single mistake and he must not leave any room for Meredith to maneuver or he wouldn't live to see Cristina again. His plan required precise execution, all the self-restraint and self-sacrifice he could muster, and a great deal of time.

Part Three

Was ever a woman in this humor woo'd?
Was ever a woman in this humor won?

—WILLIAM SHAKESPEARE 1564–1616

Twenty-six

April 1880
New York City

THE LATE ARRIVAL stood for a moment on the sidewalk listening as the melodic strains of violins drifted through the open terrace doors of the glittering Fifth Avenue mansion. Inside the house, William Fairfax played host to the cream of New York society which had turned out on this cool spring night to help his daughter Cristina celebrate her twenty-second birthday.

William had spared no expense on this special occasion. The immense marble ballroom was decorated with a profusion of red roses, white orchids, and lush greenery imported from hothouses all over the world especially for Cristina's birthday. Unfortunately the heady scent of the blooms mingled with the heavy, expensive perfume of overdressed society matrons to fill the ballroom with a too-sweet, almost nauseating fragrance.

Cristina sniffed the air, idly wondered how the musicians in the orchestra managed to breathe. The only breeze circulating the room was generated by the swishing of skirts during the dancing and that wasn't nearly enough to cool the crush of people.

Cristina longed to escape to the cool, fresh air on the terrace, but as the guest of honor she was obliged to dance at least one dance with the men who had signed her dance card.

But she didn't want to dance any longer. She was tired of dancing. Her slippers were new and tight and she was reminded of another dance when her dancing slippers had been too tight. Her feet ached and she wanted to be left alone to prop them up on the railing of the terrace and to fill her lungs with fresh air. But that wasn't possible any more than it was possible for her to skip the rest of the dances.

The musicians were already beginning to tune their instruments in preparation for another dance and Roderick was on his way to claim her.

"He's too good for her," complained one young lady as the tall, slightly built man took Cristina in his arms and led off the waltz.

"Anyone can see that," agreed her companion.

"Mother says that she's spoiled rotten," continued the first girl. "She says Cristina's father indulges her every whim because she was injured in a fall from a horse on the Continent when she lived with her mother. She nearly died. That's why she came to live with her father. Mother says Cristina's mother's affairs are common knowledge in Europe. You know Sir William"—she whispered this last bit of information—"*divorced* Cristina's mother almost a year ago."

"Really?" the second girl's eyes lit up. "And Cristina pretends to be a lady. With that background, it's a wonder she's accepted in our society. Imagine her snatching Roderick from right under your nose."

"Mother says Roderick must be mad to consort with baggage like Cristina. I can't imagine what he sees in her."

"I can." The resonant baritone came as a complete surprise to the gossiping young ladies.

They gasped in unison and turned to face the eavesdropper. He had obviously just arrived for he still wore his overcoat, and his silk top hat and cane were held in one white-gloved hand. He stood several inches taller than Roderick and his black hair was interspersed with strands of silver at the temples. His handsome mouth was curved into a mocking smile and he made no secret of his displeasure with the whispers of the gossip he had overheard.

"Sir, it is extremely rude to eavesdrop on conversations without making your presence known." The first girl delivered the setdown.

This statement increased his displeasure. "It's even more rude to gossip about one's host or the daughter of one's host while you're enjoying their hospitality, no matter how jealous of her you might be. And that's especially true when you're in a position to be overheard." His British accent was clipped and cutting. "Didn't your mothers teach you that ladies never gossip?" His icy sarcasm sent the two girls on their way, hiding their reddened faces behind lacy fans.

He bowed mockingly to the retreating girls, then focused his attention on the red-haired vision dancing around the room. He lounged against the doorjamb, enjoying the view.

"Please, Cristina . . ." Roderick Baker pleaded. "Have pity on me. Don't keep me waiting. Say you'll consider my offer of marriage."

"I can't, Roderick. I don't love you and I'm not interested in marriage," Cristina told him.

"You mean to say you're not interested in marrying me."

"I mean exactly what I said. I'm not interested in marrying anyone right now. I've only been in New York a year. I've barely had a chance to get reacquainted with my father. And I'm not ready to leave him. It wouldn't be fair."

"Fair to whom?"

"To me or you or any other man. And it wouldn't be fair to my father."

"It isn't fair to keep me waiting."

"I'm not keeping you waiting," Cristina said. "There are a dozen young ladies here that would be happy to marry you. Go ask one of them."

"I sometimes think you're too devoted to your father."

"Oh, Rod, that's ridiculous and you know it. Besides, I never asked for your attention or your affection. If you don't like my answer, then quit asking me. I'm only twenty-two. I have several more good years left before I even need to think about marrying a—" Cristina stopped. She had almost said "again." "At all," she amended quickly. "And I promised my father I would wait awhile."

"What kind of promise is that for a daughter to make to her father? Most fathers are thrilled to see their daughters married and settled down with families of their own. But from the way your father acts, I'd swear he wanted to keep you all to himself. I don't think he wants you to marry at all."

"Yes, he does," she said. "But he wants me to wait for the right man to come along."

"Don't wait too long," Roderick comment snidely. "Or no one will want you."

Cristina looked up at Roderick. Her green eyes sparkled angrily, but her smile was angelic. She lifted one white gloved hand from its resting place on his shoulder and patted him the way one would pet an overeager puppy. "I wouldn't worry about that if I were you, Rod, because I'm fairly certain that the fact that I'm sole heiress to my father's millions will guarantee there will be plenty of men waiting in line to marry me when I'm ready."

"I may not be available when you're ready."

Cristina stared at Roderick, almost dumbfounded by the young man's arrogance. What made him think he was such a catch? He came from a prominent New York family, but so did nearly everyone else in the room. She managed a laugh. "Then I guess I'll just have to suffer." *And you'll just have to miss out on my inheritance.*

Roderick stiffened. "You know, Cristina, your father has spoiled you. You need a man who will lay down the law to you—a husband who will curb your impulsive ways and keep you in line. You're headstrong and like Mother says, far too independent for any normal man's liking."

Cristina's full mouth thinned into a tight, angry line. "Including yours?" She issued the challenge coolly, wondering if Roderick would respond with an opinion of his own or if he would simply espouse his mother's. She was amazed by his sheer tenacity and his stupidity. Didn't he realize she saw through him? Didn't he realize she knew he wanted access to her father's bank accounts much more than he wanted her?

Roderick averted his gaze and avoided the anger he read in the depths of Cristina's eyes. "I didn't mean it like that and you know it. I love you, Cristina, but I'm not blind to your faults. Mother and I simply want what's best for you. And I'm afraid the longer you wait to marry, the harder it will be for you to settle down and become a proper wife and mother."

Cristina barely kept from laughing as she glanced at Roderick's boyishly handsome face. His expression was totally earnest. He meant what he said. He actually believed she needed to be molded into a suitable wife. Well, she thought sadly, he was probably right. She would require a great deal of molding in order to make him a suitable wife. That didn't bother her. What bothered her was the fact that she would probably require the same amount of molding for any man. Any man who wasn't—

Cristina squeezed her eyes shut, hoping to forestall the rush of memories. "I'm very tired, Roderick," she said suddenly. "And I really don't feel like discussing this subject any longer."

Roderick studied her face and noted the angry lines. He wasn't as smart as some men, but he knew better than to push Cristina when she was in a mood. He smiled down at her and his demeanor changed immediately. "You do look tired. The party arrangements have probably been too much for you. After all, it's only been a few months since your injury. I'm a brute not to have realized sooner. I shouldn't have pushed you so. Can you forgive me, Cristina?" The look in his clear gray eyes begged forgiveness. "You know it's only because I love you so much and want you so badly, don't you, Cristina?"

"Of course," she agreed automatically.

Roderick reminded her of his feelings for her at every op-

portunity. He vowed his love every time she saw him and
Cristina was heartily sick of hearing it. She had made no
pretense of the fact that she didn't return his feelings. And
she'd done nothing to encourage his continued devotion. She
treated Roderick in exactly the same way she treated all her
would-be suitors. She had been completely honest about her
feelings for him—or lack of them—but Roderick continued
to press his suit, continued to hope she'd change her mind
about agreeing to marry him.

And that made Cristina uncomfortable. She wouldn't
change her mind. She couldn't return Roderick's feelings,
shallow though they might be, because she didn't have any
feelings left. Blake Ashford had captured them all.

Blake. Cristina glanced around the room and a vision of
him swam before her eyes. She could almost swear that the
tall form leaning carelessly against the door was real. The
idea unnerved her. Cristina missed a step in the dance, stepped
on the hem of her gown, and stumbled heavily into Roderick.
She closed her eyes to combat her sudden light-headedness
and when she opened her eyes once again and glanced back
over her shoulder, the apparition had vanished.

Roderick grabbed Cristina by the shoulders to steady her.
The color had drained from her face and her eyes seemed
feverishly bright against the stark pallor of her face.

"Cristina, are you all right?" Roderick's anxious question
mirrored the concern on his face.

"Just a little faint," she lied. "I need some air. It's so hot
and stuffy in here."

"Should I find your father?"

"No," Cristina shook her head. "Just get me out of here."

Roderick wrapped an arm around Cristina's waist and
pushed his way through the crush of guests to the French
doors that led to the terrace.

"Will you be all right alone here for a moment while I
fetch you a cool drink, dearest?"

Cristina nodded in reply, opened the French doors, and
stepped outside onto the terrace. Standing alone in the darkness, she inhaled the cool, crisp air gratefully. It revived her,

cleared her head, and helped her regain her composure.

But the steely-soft voice coming from the shadowed corner of the terrace destroyed it. "Hello, Countess, it's been a long time." He raised himself from the marble bench and moved with the fluid Italianate grace Cristina remembered all too well, and came to stand beside her.

Cristina shivered at his nearness. Her senses reeled as she recalled the taste and touch and scent of him. She clutched tightly at the balustrade to keep from crumpling to the ground. She had dreamed of meeting him again. She'd imagined the scene in her mind thousands of times and now that he was close enough for her to touch, Cristina was angered by the sudden, casual, almost effortless way he had reentered her life.

"W-w-what are you doing here?" she demanded, angrily stumbling over her words.

"I came outside for a breath of fresh air."

"Isn't there fresh air in England?" she hissed. "What are you doing here? In New York? In my home?"

"Your father invited me," Blake replied guardedly. "I had some business with him while I was in New York and naturally he invited me to your birthday party."

"You should have refused."

Blake sighed. "What if I told you I had to come? That I had to see you again, if only to satisfy my curiosity?"

"And what do you see? Has your curiosity been satisfied?" Cristina asked, wanting him to be as aware of her as she was of him.

"I see that the lovely half-grown girl I knew has disappeared," Blake fixed his dark gaze on her, appraising every detail of her appearance from the top of her artfully arranged curls down the length of her shimmering champagne-colored dress to the tips of her matching slippers. And he was anything but disappointed. "You've become a beautiful woman, Countess." His black eyes burned through her as he delivered his verdict. Then he smiled rather wistfully. "But I can't help regretting the loss of the girl."

"Too bad," Cristina told him. "Girls do grow up, you

know. I did. I grew up the day you took Nicholas and left Vienna without me.'' The seductive gleam in Blake's eyes affected Cristina more than she liked to admit and she took refuge in bitter memories.

"I know you did,'' Blake acknowledged thoughtfully.

Cristina's eyes suddenly brimmed with burning, accusing tears. "I thought you'd come for me. I waited for over a year before I realized you wouldn't.'' She barely managed to choke out the confession.

"I'm here, Cristina. Now,'' Blake reminded her urgently.

The hot tears spilled over the barrier of her lashes. "And you've come too late, Blake. One year and three miserable months too late.''

"Countess . . .'' His rich, caressing whisper reached out to her. It was achingly familiar. Too familiar. . . .

"Blake, don't,'' she ordered. "Don't make me remember things it's best I forget. It can't be the way it was. Too much has happened. Do you know how much it hurt to wake up and find you were gone? I grieved for my baby, Blake, but I grieved more for you. Do you know how I felt when I read that curt note informing me you were off to London and that you had asked Rudolf and Cason to look out for me? Was there a problem with Meredith? Were you suddenly afraid the divorce might be granted? Were you afraid I would make you marry me after Nicholas died? Is that why you abandoned me?'' Cristina's words tumbled out—cries from the heart that had to be answered.

Blake reached out to brush away her tears but Cristina deliberately jerked her head out of the reach of his gentle touch.

"I know you won't believe me, Cris, but I never abandoned you. I was trying to ease your burden, not add to it. I wanted you to know that you and Leah would be taken care of while I was away and I wanted to make certain you were reunited with your father as soon as possible. It was important to me. I meant to reassure you.''

"You succeeded in assuring me that you could resume your life without me. It's a lesson I haven't forgotten, Blake.'' Cristina spat the words at him and spinning on her heel, marched back into the crowded ballroom in search of Roderick.

Blake remained standing where Cristina had left him on the terrace, staring into the night. Things had gone so wrong between them. She was bitter. And she had reason to be. She believed he had abandoned her and the evidence was overwhelmingly against him. The fragile strand of trust that had begun to grow in Vienna had snapped under the strain of separation and had been blown into the wind like cobwebs.

He reached into his coat and removed a thin cigar from the pocket, lit it, and began to inhale deeply. He had miscalculated. And badly. It had taken longer to petition the court for a legal separation from Meredith than he expected and longer still to conclude his mission for the queen. He had spent months struggling with the problems associated with the eastern question and the formation of the alliance between Germany and Austria. He hadn't wanted to be bothered mediating diplomatic maneuvers between Austria and Germany, but Blake had had no choice. England needed his expertise and the queen had a way of getting what she wanted from her civil servants. Blake's personal life had had to wait. The long weeks of work and travel had become months and the months had grown in to a year by the time he was able to return to London and resign his post in the Foreign Office.

He couldn't blame Cristina for the doubt she felt. Their fragile understanding had been ripped apart by Meredith's reappearance and Nicholas's death and he knew he had to repair the damage or lose everything.

Blake was grateful to William Fairfax for writing to invite him to Cristina's birthday party and for providing him with the opportunity to win her over again. He had two months before he had to return to London for the final divorce hearing and he intended to use any means necessary to prove to his love. Smiling to himself, Blake impatiently tossed the cigar aside and stepped back into the ballroom just as Cristina took the arm of Roderick, her wet-behind-the-ears would-be suitor.

Blake crossed the floor and bowed in front of her. ''Miss Fairfax, I believe you promised me this waltz.''

"I-I . . ." Cristina was astonished by Blake's blatant intrusion.

"Sorry, old man," Blake turned toward Roderick and calmly removed Cristina's hand from its resting place on the younger man's arm. "This dance belongs to me."

Cristina pleaded silently with Roderick to rescue her from Blake's unwanted attention, but Rod didn't seem to understand the look in her eyes. He yielded to Blake's superior authority without a word and allowed him to lead Cristina away.

"How dare you bully Roderick that way?" Cristina gave vent to her anger once she and Blake were out of earshot.

"I've told you before, I dare many things," Blake responded to her anger by pulling her closer. "I believe the fact he's easy to bully is one of his attractions. Don't you think?"

"You know nothing about Roderick. He's nice and considerate and—"

"Easy to manipulate?" Blake supplied helpfully. "And I do know something about him, Countess. I know he didn't care enough about you to make even a token protest when I snatched you away from him. He yielded to a stronger person. Something I suspect he does quite a bit. And I'll bet he tells you he loves you morning, noon, and night, but never shows you. Because he doesn't love you. He's the type of man who loves himself more than anything else. He values appearances more than feelings. I also know that you're angry, angry enough to chose deliberately a suitor you don't even like."

"I did not," Cristina denied. "He chose me. But I can tell you from personal experience that he's everything a woman could want in a husband. And don't hold me so close. It's indecent."

Blake ignored her order and continued to hold her close, his lean fingers pressed against one sensitive breast. "I used to hold you a lot closer than this and you never found it indecent." His warm breath caressed her ear as his lips brushed against the soft flesh of her neck.

"Stop that. What we had is in the past. I have a new life here in New York and I'm not going to run the risk of having you ruin it. Let me go. I don't want to cause any talk." Cristina pushed against his chest in a feeble attempt to put some distance between herself and his disturbing presence.

"Is that why you're allowing nice, safe Roderick to squire you about?" Blake demanded. "To squash any rumors that might have followed you from Europe? To insure your reputation in New York society?"

"Not at all. I see Roderick because he's a nice, dependable, respectable, single man, and—"

"Yes, I know, you've said all that before," Blake reminded her. "That's a very sound basis for a nice, dull, marriage. I wonder what happened to your 'I won't marry without love' ideal?"

"I married you."

Blake sucked in a breath, his face paled, and he stopped dancing so suddenly that he and Cristina barely avoided causing a collision among the remaining dancers. "You *have* grown up, Countess. Now you don't merely spit and scratch, you go straight for the jugular." He quickly regained his composure and led her back into the dance.

"I told you I'd changed," she said. "And in any case, Roderick loves me."

"I doubt that. And so do you. But even if it were true, you'd trample his heart to bits within a week because you don't love him."

"Yes, I do," Cristina insisted.

"Really?" Blake wanted to know. "Does he make you tremble with desire? Does he excite you? Make you burn with passion?" He lowered his voice to a husky, seductive whisper. "Can you really ignore all that's happened between us? Can you honestly tell me you don't want me? Shall I kiss you and prove you want me?" Blake lowered his head toward her upturned face.

Cristina waited breathlessly for the feel of his cool, firm mouth.

It never came. And when she reluctantly opened her eyes to find him staring down at her eager face, she felt like a fool.

"I could kiss you right now and make you forget everything except me and the passion we share, Countess, but I'm not going to.'' His words amazed and dismayed her at the same time. ''You see, I've also changed. It occurred to me that I've never been much of a gentleman where you're concerned. And I was brought up to be a perfect gentleman at all times. So I'm going to accept your word that Roderick is everything you want in a husband. From now on, I'll be a perfect gentleman in your presence. New York society will never suspect you were ever anything to me except the daughter of a business associate, and I promise not to trouble you with my unwanted attentions.''

Cristina was hard-pressed to believe the words he had just uttered. She had expected Blake to try to persuade her to forget all about allowing Roderick to court her and then, when his vast powers of persuasion failed, to use threats. He surprised her by doing neither and the shock must have shown on her face because he hurried to reassure her.

''I mean it, Cristina. I've treated you badly in the past, but no longer. I'll respect your wishes and treat you in the way you wish to be treated.''

It was what she wanted to hear, yet she couldn't ignore the rush of disappointment that spread through her as the dance ended and true to his word, Blake acted like a perfect gentleman. He took her back to Roderick and smiled a banal smile as he thanked her for the dance.

''It's been a pleasure, Miss Fairfax. My felicitations on your birthday.'' He held her hand for just a moment, then released it without so much as a kiss and left her standing with Roderick while he sought another partner.

Love and War are the same thing, and stratagems and policy are as allowable in the one as in the other.

—MIGUEL DE CERVANTES 1547–1616

Twenty-seven

"WHY ARE YOU following me?" Cristina demanded as soon as Blake Ashford stepped into the foyer of the Fifth Avenue mansion.

"I'm not following you." Blake appeared unperturbed.

"Then what do you call it?" Cristina stamped a satin-shod foot in vexation. "You turn up everywhere. I can't go anywhere in New York without running into you and Roderick and I haven't spent a single moment alone anywhere in town since you arrived. I can assure you that I don't need a chaperon. Especially you."

Blake shook his head from side to side. "I'm afraid you've jumped to conclusions, Cristina. I haven't been asked to chaperon."

"Then explain why you persist in following me," she directed.

Blake's eyes narrowed as all traces of amusement left his face. "I'm not following you." He was rapidly losing patience with her demands for explanations. "Did it ever occur to you, Miss Fairfax, that I might receive invitations to the same gatherings you and your illustrious suitor are so fond of attending? Did you ever stop to think that as your father's houseguest, my name is included on most of the invitations you receive?''

''Yes, it did occur to me. And it seemed too easy.'' Cristina remained undaunted by Blake's impatience. ''But knowing you, I suppose you've managed to pull off the coup of the century and become the instant darling of New York society.''

''Can I help it if I'm popular with your hostesses?'' Blake shrugged his shoulders. ''After all, I'm an English lord and I'm told titled lords are the current vogue in New York. And I can be quite charming to society matrons when I choose to be.''

''I'll bet,'' Cristina muttered.

''Why, Miss Fairfax, you sound put out,'' he chided softly.

''Not in the least,'' she informed him. ''I don't care how popular you are with society matrons, but if you think you can follow me all around New York City just to ignore me, you're sadly mistaken!''

''It's what you said you wanted, Cristina. Would you rather I follow you all around New York and press you with unwanted attentions? Would you rather I spirit you away from the crowds and your young suitor and make mad, passionate love to you? Is that what you want, Cristina?''

''What I want, Lord Lawrence, is for you to go to hell.'' Cristina smiled sweetly, then squared her shoulders, turned on her heel, and exited the hallway with all the dignity she could muster. Blake remained where he stood, but the sound of his rich, masculine laughter echoing off the marble followed her.

He was driving her mad! Stark, raving mad! He had upset everything by coming back after fifteen months and turning her calm, regimented existence upside down in a matter of days. She had spent nearly every waking hour in Roderick's company just to annoy Blake and if he didn't leave New York soon, Cristina was afraid she'd find herself accepting one of Roderick's daily proposals just to spite him. Or turn into a jealous shrew. Even shallow, vain Rod had noticed the sudden change in her behavior. She no longer bore any resemblance to the tranquil, secure society beauty she had been for the past few months. She had become an intensely emotional, hot-blooded, living, breathing woman almost overnight. And all because Blake Ashford, ninth earl of Lawrence, had finally come to claim her.

Cristina reached the safety of her room, slammed the door with all her might, and flung herself across the bed.

"Things are lookin' up," Leah commented, turning from the armoire to observe the unusual behavior of her charge. "You're showin' more spirit than I've seen since we came here. I don't have to guess who's responsible."

"That's nonsense, Leah. He has nothing to do with it."

"Don't he? You moped around this place for a whole year after we left Vienna. And you haven't shown a spark of real feelin' for anyone 'cept me and your father since we got here. Until Lord Blake showed up. He's the one that's got you in this fit of temper, all right. I guess he's bringin' you out of that icicle you been livin' in."

"I wasn't aware that I'd been living in a icicle," Cristina replied frostily.

"Well, you were. Oh, I know you threw yourself into your new surroundin's, goin' here and there, joinin' this and that to please your father. But you haven't been the same since Vienna. You haven't really cared about anythin'."

"That's an interesting theory, Leah, but if it's true, how do you explain Roderick's courtship of me?"

"Him!" Leah snorted. "Even that fancy Austrian prince was better than him. At least he had some backbone and he did have some real feelin's for you, even if they were mostly lustful."

"Roderick has feelings for me."

"How do you know?"

"He tells me. Every day."

"Huh! It's time you opened your eyes, missy, and come back to the real world. Roderick Baker has real feelin's for your papa's money. That's the only thing that puts a sparkle in his eyes. He wants your papa's business and the easiest way to get it is to marry you. That's all he cares about."

"You're talking about the man I'm thinking about marrying,'' Cristina addressed the older woman in her most superior tones.

Leah was unintimidated. ''More's the pity. You'll just make yourself miserable.''

Cristina pushed herself off the bed and wandered restlessly to the dressing table where she began removing the pins from her hair. ''What makes you such an authority on marriage? You've never been married.''

''I was in love once, same as you, and no man was ever good enough to follow in Tom's shoes after he was killed, just like no man will ever be good enough to follow in Lord Blake's shoes for you. I've spent sixty-six years observin' human nature and I've seen the mess folks make out of their lives when they ain't suited for one another. You ain't suited for Roderick Baker,'' explained Leah.

''I think we are,'' Cristina argued. ''Ideally suited.''

''Then you think wrong,'' Leah informed her mistress. ''There's only one man for you, missy, and that's Lord Blake. You'll never be happy with anybody else.''

''Maybe you should tell all of this to Blake instead of to me. Because you see, Leah, the great Blake Ashford, ninth earl of Lawrence, has forgotten I exist. He's forgotten I was once his wife and lover and the mother of his son. I've seen him nearly every day and he ignores me. Ignores me. He flirts with other women but he's been a complete gentleman to me.'' Sarcasm rolled off Cristina's tongue like thick maple syrup.

''You're jealous,'' Leah pronounced. ''And that's what's botherin' you.''

''I'm not bothered,'' Cristina insisted stubbornly. ''In fact, I'm rather amused by it all.''

''I can see for myself just how amused you are, so stop pretendin'.''

''I'm not pretending, Leah. I'm over Blake for good.''

''Then why're you so twisted up in knots over him?''

''I simply want him to leave so that I can get on with my life,'' Cristina answered.

''You don't have a life without Lord Blake.''

"Oh, yes, I do. Blake broke my heart fifteen months ago and it's taken me a while to put it back together, but now that it's back together I intend to keep it intact."

"What about Mister Roderick Baker? You seem to have forgotten all about him. Remember him—the man you're thinkin' about marryin'?" Leah pointed out.

"I'm not forgetting anything. It's just that nothing's been decided yet."

"I wonder . . . ," Leah mused aloud.

"Meaning?"

"Meanin' I think things were decided a long time ago—about two years ago—to be exact."

"You're wrong, Leah."

"I don't think so. You weren't interested in Roderick Baker before Lord Blake came to New York. I don't think you want young Mr. Baker at all except as a way to make Lord Blake jealous."

"That's not true."

Leah raised an eyebrow at Cristina's bald-faced lie.

Cristina sank down into the chair in front of the dresser and began idly pulling a brush through her curls. She glared at the mirror and her gaze locked with Leah's. "Believe me, Leah, I don't love Blake anymore."

"You can't make me believe somethin' you don't really believe yourself," Leah replied fiercely before she stepped through the doorway and closed the door behind her.

I don't love him anymore. Cristina repeated the statement over and over again in her mind after Leah left the room, trying to convince herself. I don't love him anymore. But it was an exercise in futility. She did love him. She always would. And she knew it.

Watching him casually flirting with the young debutantes at Mrs. Morgan's garden party during the afternoon had brought the fact home to Cristina like an arrow piercing her heart. She still loved him and more than that, she was jealous. She might deny it to Leah, but she didn't intend to deny it to herself any longer. She was jealous of the carefree debs who made Blake smile and laugh. She wanted to be the one to do that. And she wanted Blake to look at her with laughing, indulgent eyes, just as he had during those brief magical months in Vienna.

Cristina had been afraid really to look at him since her birthday, but at this afternoon's garden party she had given in to the unbearable urge and gorged herself on the sight of him. And what she saw surprised her. He looked different in the light of day—handsome still, but older, leaner, and harder than she remembered.

She hadn't noticed the difference in him that night on the terrace. She had been too stunned by his sudden appearance to notice the silver strands in his hair or the haunted, almost driven look that appeared in his eyes at times.

But at the afternoon garden party she had seen the subtle changes she'd failed to see before. And Cristina bled a little inside at the visible signs of his suffering. She suddenly realized how long she'd been fooling herself into believing she no longer cared what happened to him. And she realized how selfish she had been in assuming she had been the only one to suffer.

The death of their child had left as many scars on Blake's heart as it had left on hers. He had left her alone in Vienna in her hour of need, but he had been just as needy. And he had broken her heart by failing to come for her, but she had broken his, too, by failing to believe in him that night at the Christmas ball—that horrible night Meredith had come back from the dead to wreak havoc on their lives.

She didn't hate Blake. She never had, because she loved him too much. And Cristina knew that as long as she lived, she would continue to love him and forgive him anything.

He had suffered, too. For fifteen months Cristina had told herself that Blake hadn't really cared for her. He had taken Nicholas's tiny body and disappeared, leaving her alive and wounded in Vienna when she needed him most.

She had sworn she would never forgive him for leaving her behind. She had wanted to go with him. She had needed to be with him, to grieve with him over the loss of the baby

they had created, to comfort him and be comforted in return—
but Blake had left her bereft of all comfort.

Cristina's broken arm and bruised ribs had healed in weeks,
but her heart had never really mended. She had lain in the
bedroom in the Ringstrasse apartment for weeks after Blake
had left, dry-eyed and staring at the walls.

Nothing had touched her. Even Leah's sorrow failed to
make an impression on her as she pulled deeper and deeper
inside herself. Cristina had lost more than her baby and her
lover that New Year's Day in Vienna; she had lost her fire,
her sparkle—the thing inside her that made her fight to survive. She lay in bed for weeks wishing for death, hoping the
Almighty would be merciful and take her, too. Hadn't He
vengefully taken everything else?

She might have stayed in that bed forever if Cason hadn't
bullied her into journeying to New York. He and Leah had
made her leave her safe haven. Even Rudolf had aided them—
Rudolf, who had wanted her for a mistress, who had impulsively offered to marry her then had refused to give her use
of the little house near St. Stephen's. He had gently but firmly
told Cristina he had a new mistress and was content. He didn't
need a second mistress, even her. Their "bargain" had come
to an end and the best thing Cristina could do for herself was
to leave Austria and join her father in America. Rudolf had
told her there was no place for her in his father's empire. But
Cristina would have defied even the emperor and remained in
Vienna close to her baby—waiting for Blake to return.

She would have stayed, but Blake's note had forced her to
leave. She had read it so often she'd memorized it. *Cristina,*
he had written, *forgive me for the pain I've unwittingly
brought to you. You should have had more to show for your
suffering than this. I never meant to hurt you and I don't want
to hurt you now, but by the time you wake up I'll be on my
way to London. My presence will only bring you more pain.
So I ask that when you feel sufficiently able, you travel to
New York. Your father is waiting there for you with open
arms. Go to him, Cristina. Leave Vienna and all its memories
behind. Always, Blake.*

Three months after the bombing, Cristina and Leah had boarded the train for Paris and from there to LeHavre, where they caught a ship bound for New York.

And after fifteen interminable months, Blake had followed her to New York and turned her life upside down. He was here as a guest of her father's and residing under the same roof only one room away. She thought about that as she got up from the dressing table and began to pace. Blake was here and she still loved him. He was the only man who made her feel whole and alive.

She wanted Blake and she was willing to risk everything to have him back again. She was willing to swallow her stupid pride and try to win him back. She knew she might fail, but if she succeeded . . . if she succeeded, everything she did, every morsel of humble pie she ate would be worthwhile. And she would succeed. She had to. She would pull out all the stops and use every weapon in her arsenal to make her dream come true.

Once she had promised him always and she intended to keep her promise. From now on she planned to stick to Blake like glue and pretty soon the poor man wouldn't know what hit him. She was experienced. She knew Blake and she knew his weakness for her, that certain gleam in his dark eyes, and she would be damned if she forgot her promise again or allowed him to toss her aside for some garden-party virgin.

IN THE ROOM next to Cristina's, Blake lay on the bed, arms stacked beneath his head, listening to the sounds of her restless pacing. He smiled at the darkness as he imagined Cristina scantily clad in a thin, silk nightgown angrily measuring the length of her room while the rest of the house slept undisturbed. There was, he supposed, some consolation in knowing that she was unable to sleep, but he couldn't help wondering and worrying about the reason for her restlessness. What was she planning? She had refused to leave her room for dinner and he and William had spent the dinner hour exchanging theories concerning her odd behavior.

After enjoying brandy and cigars with her father, Blake had returned to his room and listened to Cristina's pacing for what seemed like hours. Although Blake enjoyed the images his mind conjured up of Cristina in various moods and states of undress, he wasn't sure how much more he could stand. He was only human, after all, and it was almost impossible to keep from breaking down her door, throwing her on the bed, and making passionate love to her. The waiting was agony.

The house grew silent and Blake gradually realized that Cristina had stopped her pacing. He wondered uneasily if she had decided to give him another chance. He had never known what to expect where she was concerned, but oh, how he loved her and oh, how he wanted her! It was hard to pretend he didn't. And getting more difficult by the moment. Pretending that Roderick Baker's squiring her about town didn't bother the bloody hell out of him was damned near impossible, but that's what he was doing. And Blake fervently prayed his whole scheme wouldn't blow up in his face.

He hadn't planned to ignore her, had in fact planned to court her as he should have courted her in London. But her resistance on the terrace on the night of her birthday party had come as a shock and her scathing remarks on the dance floor had cut him deep enough to make him bleed. But Blake had come too far to be daunted. He loved her too much to give up now when there was a chance for them to be together. And so he had suddenly found himself promising to treat her as she wished to be treated—even if that meant taking her at her word and leaving her alone.

It was a simple plan to make her jealous and Blake had reluctantly followed through. And during the past few weeks he'd been tempted more than once to give up and admit defeat, but the afternoon garden party had changed everything.

While he pretended to ignore her, he had been aware of Cristina's every move. He had felt her gaze following him all afternoon and once or twice he had looked around to find her emerald-green eyes shooting sparks at him and his female companions. Her attention was so completely focused on him that she was barely aware of Baker hovering at her side. Twice during the afternoon, Blake had noticed the two of them arguing and heard Cristina's curt, irritable replies. They had given him hope. And when Blake hurried to the Fifth Avenue mansion and found himself met at the door by an angry Cristina who was demanding explanations, the confrontation had increased his optimism.

And tonight, lying in bed listening to the quiet after the storm, he had begun to believe once more in the power of love.

Twenty-eight

"GOOD MORNING."

"You're up early this morning." William Fairfax greeted his daughter as she sat down to breakfast.

"I wanted to catch you before you left for work," Cristina responded, then looked around and noticed they were alone. "Where is Lord Lawrence? Still sleeping? I expected him to be breakfasting with you."

Cristina was ending her second week in the assault on Blake's senses and was effectively increasing her arsenal.

William scrutinized his daughter closely, noting the unusual care that had gone into her early-morning toilette. Things were definitely looking up.

"New dress?" he asked casually.

"Yes. Do you like it?" Cristina smiled, glad there was someone at the breakfast table to notice her, even if it was the wrong someone.

"It's charming, Cristy, brief but charming, and I'm afraid it's wasted on me. Lord Lawrence left earlier this morning."

"Left?" Cristina echoed in dismay.

William nodded an affirmative. "He packed up his things

and moved into a hotel at dawn this morning. He said he didn't dare risk seeing you and still be able to keep his word. The man has nearly drained this house of cold water these past two weeks,'' William commented with some amusement. ''This is the first time that a guest of mine has had to leave because he didn't trust himself not to molest my daughter.''

''I didn't want him to leave,'' Cristina admitted honestly. ''I just wanted him to notice me.''

''Oh, he noticed you all right. You haven't been exactly subtle. I've never seen so many daringly low-cut gowns. They must have cost me a fortune. And I think the dress you wore at dinner last night just about did him in.''

Cristina smiled. She had worn the same dress she had worn to her presentation two years earlier, but she had had the bodice cut much lower. The effect was as devastating as she had hoped it would be. Blake had remembered. She could see it in his eyes.

''By the way,'' William was saying, ''Blake left you a gift.'' He handed her a small wrapped box. ''He said it was something to go with the gown you wore last night. Something to remember him by.''

Cristina tore the paper off the box and quickly opened it. Pulling aside the silver tissue paper, she found that the box contained a white silk shawl embroidered with roses and bows. The word ''cover'' was scrawled across a white card in Blake's bold hand.

Cristina closed the box and hugged it to her chest. He had remembered. More than he liked, she bet.

''Cristy?''

''Yes, Papa.''

''I was saying that it's just as well Blake left the house. People are beginning to think you're an outrageous flirt or that you happen to fancy Lord Lawrence instead of your current suitor. And that's shocking in a young woman who's supposed to be considering a young man's proposal.'' William fought to keep the sparkle of suppressed laughter from showing in his blue eyes.

"I wanted to talk to you about that." Cristina cleared her dry throat.

"About what?"

"My current suitor. You see, Roderick is very upset with me."

"I think that's understandable. You haven't been exactly attentive to him these last two weeks. I imagine Roderick is jealous of your innocent flirtation with our guest. Don't worry, sweet, you'll patch things up. Roderick is itching to marry you."

"I'm not itching to marry Roderick," Cristina said. "There isn't anything to patch up. I'm not interested in marrying Roderick Baker. I never have been. And I don't care how angry it makes him. I don't love Roderick. I don't even like him, and I don't understand how he could think otherwise. Oh, he's asked me to marry him at least a dozen times, but I've always said no."

"Well, you have led the lad on a merry chase."

"I know. And I'm sorry for that. But the truth is, I thought that if I allowed Rod to escort me around town it would make Blake jealous."

"Oh?" William raised an eyebrow.

"I love Blake."

"I see," William commented after a moment's silence. "If Lord Lawrence is the man you want, why are you continuing to see Roderick?"

"I'm not."

"I thought you were planning to have lunch with him this afternoon."

"I am," Cristina confirmed. "I'm meeting him at the Victoria Hotel. I'm going to explain my feelings and tell him once more why I can't consider any of his proposals—why I don't wish to see him anymore." She glanced at her father. "I thought this was something I should do in person, not something I should write in a note."

"What a coincidence!" William remarked suddenly. "I recommended the Victoria Hotel to Lord Lawrence just this morning. I thought I might join him there for luncheon today, but unfortunately I have more pressing business.''

Cristina stared at her father, puzzled by his cheerfulness, until a sudden light dawned. . . . ''I believe you accomplished your mission, Papa.''

''My mission?'' The surprised question sounded genuine but Cristina knew better. ''What mission is that?''

Cristina beamed at the masculine features so similar to her own. ''I've heard it called matchmaking.'' She got up from the table and plopped a kiss on her father's head as she passed his chair, gathered up the box containing her precious embroidered white silk shawl, and left the breakfast room, humming.

⌘

SEVERAL HOURS LATER in the elegant dining room of the Victoria Hotel a bitter discussion was in progress.

''Are you out of your mind? You can't lead me on for weeks, then end everything with no consideration for my feelings,'' Roderick Baker exclaimed indignantly, his expression mottled.

''I haven't led you on. I told you from the beginning that I wasn't interested in marrying you,'' Cristina reminded him coolly.

''I've proposed to you every single day for the past month.''

''And I've said no each time.''

''I believed we had a future together.''

''I'm sorry, Roderick, but you'll have to exclude me from your future. I'm flattered that you asked me to marry you, but I never dreamed you were serious.''

''I was very serious.''

''Then I'm very sorry. I never meant to hurt you.''

''Hurt me? You haven't hurt me, you little bitch. I don't feel any more for you than you feel for me.'' Roderick laughed an ugly laugh. ''But you aren't going to make me the laughingstock of New York. All my friends and associates expect me to marry you and you have the nerve to turn me down.''

Cristina wasn't prepared for his vicious attack. ''Lower your voice, please, other people are listening.'' She was desperately aware of the curious stares of the other diners.

''I don't care if the whole damn restaurant knows what a slut you are. I knew all about you, Cristina. I never told you but I was in Vienna on my grand tour a year and a half ago. I never told you I once spent an afternoon watching the infamous comtesse di Rimaldi strolling through the Prater with a certain British ambassador. Or that it was apparent to anyone who cared to look that the comtesse was expecting a child.''

Cristina drew in a shocked breath, but Roderick continued his tirade. ''I almost didn't believe my eyes when the same girl showed up in New York as heiress to William Fairfax's millions. You certainly travel in exalted circles, Cristina—a crown prince, a British ambassador, and a New York millionaire. You seemed like such a lady and I liked that. I like my women to be whores in the bedrooms and perfect ladies everywhere else. It adds spice. And to be honest, you almost had me convinced I was mistaken about you until he turned up. That was too much of a coincidence for me. You never even let me touch you, never even let me kiss you, and all the time, you were whoring for Lord Lawrence. Do you deny it? Well, what have you got to say to me now, Cristina?''

Cristina sat perfectly still while huge tears rolled from her eyes slowly down her cheeks and dropped onto the linen tablecloth.

''You'll regret leading me on and throwing me over, Cristina,'' Roderick promised.

''I don't think she will.'' The words were deadly quiet and the man who spoke them was clearly struggling to contain his fury.

Roderick slunk back in his chair, conscious of the leashed rage in the man who stood rigidly behind Cristina's chair. Normally Roderick would have avoided confrontation, but the presence of an audience goaded him on. "So you've come to claim your slut."

Blake's face tightened visibly. "Shut up," he warned curtly, "or those will be the last words you utter."

The threat was genuine and Lord Lawrence looked eager to carry it out. Roderick recognized the fact and swallowed convulsively.

"Apologize," Blake ordered.

"What?" Roderick forgot his fear long enough to protest. "I won't apologize to that tramp!"

"You will apologize," Blake informed him, "or you'll pay dearly for the insult. The choice is yours."

The humiliation of a public scene was too much for Cristina. She made a move to rise from her chair and escape the horrible tableau in front of her, but Blake placed his hands on her shoulders and gently pressed her back onto her seat.

"Sit down, love." He spoke softly, but his words were laced with steel.

"I've had enough of this." Tears sparkled on the ends of her lashes and his face blurred as she looked up at him.

Blake's heart turned over in his chest and his anger at Roderick Baker rose. "Sit down, Cris, while this bastard apologizes to you. You may leave when he's done, but I won't let you run out of here as if the hounds of hell were chasing you. That would only encourage gossip and"—he smiled down at her—"it would absolutely crush my memories of a young woman who hacked the decorations off her presentation gown rather than face a second humiliation wearing it the way it was—the young woman who ripped up the Prince of Wales's bed linens and climbed down a palace wall. I won't let you run away, Cristina. I won't allow you to be a coward."

Cristina kept her seat.

Blake removed his hands from her shoulders and turned his attention back to Roderick. "I'm waiting."

Roderick muttered a quick apology, not daring to risk himself any further by delaying the inevitable.

Blake wasn't satisfied by the quickly muttered apology in the least, but he accepted it for Cristina's sake. His black eyes glittered dangerously at Roderick as he issued his next order. "Now, leave. But remember that if one word of this ugly scene reaches my ears or the scandal rags of this city, I'll hold you personally responsible."

"The other patrons in the restaurant heard everything," Roderick protested. "You can't hold me personally responsible—"

"But I do," Blake cut him off. "And if I were in your shoes, I would make certain I refuted any ugly rumors about the lady in question, as any gentleman would do."

"That's unfair," Roderick whined.

"Life often is," Blake reminded him brutally. "Cristina, if you've finished your luncheon with Mr. Baker, we can leave." Blake politely dismissed Roderick and stepped back to assist Cristina from the table.

Her legs trembled in reaction as she got to her feet. She wished she were anywhere in the world except the restaurant of the Victoria Hotel in New York City. She was mortified by what had taken place. She couldn't seem to stop shaking and she was afraid to take a step, afraid her legs wouldn't support her weight.

Blake sensed her sudden attack of nerves and apprehension and offered her his arm, whispering, "Chin up, Cristina, head high. Where is the girl who stood before me and declared that she wasn't afraid of any man who drew breath? Show these people the real Cristina Fairfax—the one I know so well. Or are you afraid to be yourself in polite New York society?"

That did it. Cristina stiffened her spine, held her head high, then she stood up, calmly lifted her wineglass, and poured the contents over Roderick's head. "I've made many mistakes in my life, Roderick, but I'm happy to say that accepting your marriage proposals so that you could get your greedy hands on my father's millions is one mistake I won't have to live with." With that, Cristina turned to Blake. "I'm ready to leave, Lord Lawrence. Would you be so kind as to escort me?"

"Delighted." Blake flashed her his gorgeous smile and led her out of the dining room.

Cristina paid no attention to where they were going until Blake stopped at the front desk to collect the key to his room.

"Where are we going?" she asked as they approached the stairs.

"My room."

"Why?" Cristina was suddenly wary.

Blake wanted to tell her that they were going to his room so that he could end his weeks of forced celibacy by touching her and tantalizing her the way she had teased and tantalized his senses these past weeks. But he knew better than to push her into a corner, so he said the first thing that came to his mind. "To talk." Then before she could protest, he added, "In private."

Cristina gave in gracefully, not because she feared another scene, but because she wanted to be alone with Blake and she was afraid any form of protest would scare him away. Cristina had recognized the gleam in Blake's dark eyes and her whole body began to tingle in anticipation. She followed him up the stairs, waiting patiently as he unlocked the door to his room.

She stepped into the room and walked to the center of it, waiting until the distinctive sound of the key turning in the lock signaled Blake's next move. She turned to face him and found him leaning with his back against the door.

They stared wordlessly at each other for a long moment. Both understood now that any talking would come after they had satisfied their urgent need to feel flesh against flesh. Blake moved from the door. He tossed the key on the night table as he walked toward Cristina.

When he stood before her, he cupped her face in his hand. "You're so beautiful, Countess." He groaned then and before he could stop himself he pulled Cristina into his arms and covered her lips with his own.

Blake half expected Cristina to pull away from him, but she was as eager for the kiss as he was. She surprised him by wrapping her arms around his neck to hold him closer. She melted into him and she kissed him back with a passion that sent their senses soaring.

She leaned back against Blake's arms as he stopped kissing

her lips long enough to explore the column of her neck. It had always been like this—a special brand of desire and tenderness that held them in its grasp, unable to escape. It had been there from the very first kiss.

"Sweetheart," Blake murmured between kisses, "it's been so long."

"Too long," Cristina told him, provocatively taking the initiative and running her hands up his ribs and around his back until his breath became a series of moans. She pressed her aching breasts against his chest and made her demand. "Make love with me, Blake. Now."

Blake hesitated for just a moment, remembering the consequences.

Cristina felt the hesitation. "What's wrong? Don't you want to?" There was the slightest hint of anxiety mixed with the indignation in her voice as she pressed closer, determined to tempt him.

"Yes, I want you. God, you must feel how I want you," Blake rasped, as the possibility of another pregnancy overshadowed his own needs. "There could be another baby. Cristina, we must be rational. . . ."

"I am rational but unless you have a pocket full of those sheepskin sheaths Nigel told me about, I don't think you're being very rational. Blake, I want you. Now," she whispered huskily. "And besides, I want another baby. Your baby. Are you going to disappoint me?"

Cristina cradled his face between her palms and pulled his face down to meet hers. She kissed him until he began to take command and plunged his tongue into the depths of her mouth.

She was right. He was beyond rational thought. This was what he craved—what he'd craved for weeks—for months—for fifteen long months. A willing, demanding Cristina. How could he deny himself the thing he wanted most in the world? And did he dare disappoint her now that she was making demands again?

Blake threaded his fingers in her hair, scattering hairpins, bending her back to deepen his kiss.

Cristina reveled in his kiss. She floated on a cloud of desire, feasting on the feel of his lips and his hands and the flaming passion that flowed through her and melted the months of ice. She caressed his shoulders, his arms, his chest, until she found the buttons of his waistcoat. She quickly unfastened the three gold buttons on his waistcoat and then the buttons of his shirt.

Blake drew a breath when she finally tugged his shirt from his trousers and began fumbling with the fastening at his waist. She located his trouser buttons at last, but she didn't rush to undo them. She took her time, unbuttoning them slowly, one agonizing button at the time. An eternity later, she pushed his pants and underwear over his lean hips, around his taut buttocks, and down the length of his legs where she let them fall in a heap at his feet.

Blake was intoxicated by her boldness and more than a little aroused. "A little eager, aren't you, my sweet?"

Cristina giggled wickedly, "A lot eager, my love. I've waited fifteen months. I'm not taking any more chances. You might have another attack of hesitation."

"Not bloody likely." Blake fell back on the bed, toed off his shoes, kicked free of his trousers, shrugged out of his jacket, and let his open waistcoat and shirt slide off his shoulders. When he was completely nude, he pulled Cristina between his legs and made short work of her clothes.

The rush of primitive desire was exquisite and they fell back onto the double bed eager to explore the depths of their passion.

Afterwards they lay together, legs entwined, lost in their own thoughts, resting while their labored breathing returned to normal. Cristina rested her hand on his chest. then foraged lazily through the thick, dark hair growing there, stopping abruptly as she encountered the warm, metal disk suspended on a gold chain around his neck. She traced her fingers across the surface of the gold medallion then raised herself on one elbow to stare down at it.

"Where did you get this?"

"You gave it to me." Seeing her puzzled frown, Blake explained. "You had it in your hand when you were thrown from the carriage after the bomb exploded. I pried open your fist and found it.''

"And you've worn it since then? All this time?''

"Yes,'' Blake confirmed quietly. "Having this meant everything to me, Cristina.'' He smiled sadly. "It was a re- minder of all that we shared. And it was a promise that kept me going after the baby died and I returned to London. It was always there to remind me that you were waiting for me safe and sound in New York.''

"How did you know I'd wait for you?''

Blake held the gold disk between his fingers and leaned closer to Cristina so she could see the engraving. "You prom- ised me you would. This promised me always.'' Blake rolled away from her, leaving the bed to walk over and stand at the window overlooking the street, his thoughts in turmoil. "Then I arrived in New York and you were . . .'' he let his words trail off. "I almost gave up hope.''

She sat up in bed, clutching the sheet across her breasts. "You didn't write me. I waited fifteen months for you, Blake, and I never received a single note,'' she reminded him, frus- tration evident in every softly spoken word. "Not one single line. . . .'' She left the accusation hanging between them.

"I left a note for Cason to give to you.''

"One page to tell me you were leaving me behind in Vi- enna. And not another word for fifteen months.''

"I couldn't write to you. I didn't dare.''

"Why not?''

"Meredith had spies waiting for me to contact you.'' He raked his fingers through his hair. "I was afraid for you. But I knew everything that was happening to you. I was trying to protect you, sweetheart. I didn't want to cause you any more grief. I didn't write because I didn't want Meredith to know where you were. I hired a firm who hired a firm who hired a firm who hired your father's firm to handle some investments for me so I would have some means of keeping in touch. I sent letters to your father that way and in diplomatic pouches. I wrote to him regularly under the guise of business. I asked about you in every letter. I'm sorry it took me so long to get here, Cristina. I'm sorry it took so long to come to you, but I couldn't risk you again. After Nicholas, I couldn't take the chance.'' Blake continued to gaze out the window as he recited the facts almost as if he had rehearsed the words many times. He made no attempt to convince her. He let the words speak for themselves and when she didn't say anything, he exhaled deeply and turned to face her in all his naked splendor. ''I don't expect you to believe me, Cristina. I don't know if I would even believe me in your place, but I wore the medallion because I loved you and I continue to wear it because I still do.'' Blake bowed his head and waited.

He had finally said the words that had haunted him for nearly two years and he couldn't help but wonder if he was two years too late. He turned back to the window, unable to bear the derision he was afraid he would find in her face.

Cristina's heart seemed to pound in her throat as she stealthily left the bed and moved to stand behind him. She encircled his waist from behind and pressed her cheek against his broad back, then she began to explore his body at will, lighting white-hot brushfires along the way. Blake's desire rose with every caress until he found it almost impossible to maintain control.

''My love,'' he managed between clenched teeth, ''you're playing with fire. You don't know what you're doing to me. . . .''

Cristina laughed softly as she let her hand snake lower to caress him. ''You silly, silly, man. I know exactly what I'm doing to you. I'm working very hard at seducing you again. I'm trying to tell you that I love you very much.''

''You what?'' Blake turned around, his dark eyes intently searching her face for the answer he required.

''I love you.''

''Are you certain?''

''Yes.'' She nodded and a wide grin spread across her face. ''I love you, Blake. I think I've loved you from the very beginning. But I was afraid to follow in my parents' footsteps. I wanted marriage, but I never wanted love until I met you and even then I didn't trust you not to use my love for you as a weapon against me the way my mother used my father's love against him. I sent you away in Vienna because I was hurt and so very afraid of losing you. I was wrong to blame you when I should have blamed Meredith. You were only trying to make the best of an impossible situation. But when I tried to tell you how wrong I was and that I'd realized you were as hurt and afraid of losing me as I was of losing you, I was caught up in the bombing. So I want you to know that I love you without strings. You don't have to marry me again. I don't care about the divorce. I'll be happy as long as I know you love me."

Blake enfolded her in his arms and held her there with her ear against his heart as he repeated the magical words. "I love you, Cristina. I don't know how it happened or why, but I love you with all my heart." He pressed his lips against her forehead and placed a kiss there. "I never thought I'd say those words again and mean them, but I do." His voice was low, husky with emotion and full of firm conviction, and the way he held her against his chest was every bit as gentle as his words and just as convincing.

Cristina listened to the steady beating of his heart, then gently pushed back to look up at him, teasing provocatively, "I love to hear you say it, but I'll be a complete failure as a seductress if you don't take me back to the bed and show me how much you love me."

Happy laughter rumbled from the depths of Blake's chest and echoed around the room. "You are eager. Well, never let it be said that I failed to help further the promising career of a budding, young seductress." And with those words he leaped back into bed and allowed Cristina to seduce him.

~~∽∾ℰ∾∽~~

THEY STAYED IN bed for two entire days, alternately making love and talking. They stopped only when the need for food or sleep overcame them. It was a wonderful two days, a time of learning and exploring new territory; of loving and trusting and finding that love and trust mirrored in the other's eyes. But it wasn't enough.

Blake awoke the morning of the third day with niggling doubts. He didn't want to feel them, but he knew that stolen kisses and rendezvous in hotel rooms would never be enough to satisfy him. He wanted Cristina by his side. He wanted what they had had in Vienna before Meredith reappeared. He wanted to marry her again. He had to marry her again. He couldn't settle for anything less.

Blake didn't want the gossip, the ugly whispering behind their backs, or the public scorn of Cristina being labeled a mistress to ruin the love they shared. He had witnessed the results of Roderick Baker's cruel sneers and Blake had promised himself that he would never let her be hurt like that again.

He slipped out of bed and began dressing, moving quietly to avoid waking Cristina. She stirred restlessly as his warmth left her side and Blake leaned over to kiss her hair and whisper, "It's early yet. Go back to sleep, Countess."

Her eyes fluttered open and Cristina gazed up at him sleepily. "Come back to bed with me. I miss you."

"I can't. I have some business to take care of today."

"What business?"

"Today's my last day in New York, Cristina. You knew I couldn't stay indefinitely without first returning to London. My court hearing is a fortnight away. I've got to go back to London."

"Can't you stay with me? Please, just one more day. . . ."

"I'd like to, sweetheart, you know that, but this can't wait any longer. I must be there. And if I stay with you today, I'll stay tomorrow, and the next day and the next and nothing will be done. I'm sorry, Cris, but it must be today."

Cristina bolted out of bed. Tears filled her eyes and threatened to spill out. "Weren't you going to tell me?"

He nodded.

"When?" she demanded. "On your way out the door?"

"When I figured out the best way."

"There is no best way, Blake. I don't want you to leave me again. I told you that I don't care about a divorce. I don't care if you're married to Meredith. It doesn't matter to me.''

"Well, my love, my dearest heart," Blake said, sadly, "it matters to me. It matters a great deal. I want you beside me, Cristina. And I don't want to watch you endure ugly whispers and slurs and vicious gossip. I want us to be together. I want the kind of marriage we had in Vienna before the nightmare with Meredith began.''

"We can be happy without being married.''

"For how long, love?" Blake asked her. "What if you should have another baby? Do you really want another child born out of wedlock? Is that what you would want for our children? To be bastards? To never quite fit into polite society no matter what you do? To never quite be good enough simply because their parents weren't married?''

"Damn society," Cristina muttered, "we would be together. We love each other, Blake. We can give our children enough love to make things good enough.''

"Oh, sweetheart, I wish we could. But you can't isolate them forever. And is it fair to them, Cristina?" Blake asked. "Would it really be fair to them? We're legitimate. We were born that way. Is it right for us to punish our children for our passion and our mistakes?''

"You could adopt them, Blake. You and Meredith have no children. You could adopt our children and make them legal.'' The fact that she offered to give any children she might have solely into Blake's keeping was a measure of her faith in him and of her love. "You're an earl, for godsakes, couldn't you do that?''

"What about you, Cristina?''

"I don't care about me.''

"I do, sweetheart. I love you very much. And I told you once before that I would never take a child of ours away from its mother.''

"Then they would live with me. That would be perfect.''

"Would it? Think, Cristina. Children of the earl of Lawrence living with his mistress?''

"But I'd be their mother. . . .''

"If I adopted them, the law would recognize Meredith as

their mother and so would everyone else. As they grew up, even the children—your children—would recognize Meredith. You'd be my mistress. Nothing more. Do you want Meredith to be the legal mother of our children, Cristina? Could you live in the background while someone else had control of your children?''

''I could if you were with me.''

''I won't live forever.''

''Please, my love, don't say things like that. Don't think like that.''

''We have to think like that, Cris, because Meredith is ruthless.''

''But it's all speculation, Blake. There aren't any children. There may never be any more children,'' Cristina reminded him.

Blake looked at the bed they had recently vacated and then turned back to Cristina with a wry expression on his face. ''After two days of mad, passionate love? It didn't take that much for you to get pregnant last time, Countess.''

''Blake, I don't want you to leave me again. I don't want you to go to London. I want you to stay here.''

''And I don't want to leave you, either, love.''

''Then don't.''

''I've got to. You know that. Cristina, I love you and I love what we have together. Together. I wish it were a simple matter of taking you to the nearest minister and making you my wife like we did before, but it isn't. There's Meredith and while I wish she'd stayed dead, she didn't. And while I wish with all my heart that I'd never married her, I did. I can't pretend she doesn't exist anymore. I can't sneak around, meeting you in hotel rooms all over the world, Cristina. What we share is good and clean and right. We love each other and we made promises to each other. I can't live a half life with you. I can't live with you in private and share my public life with Meredith. Some men might be able to do it, but I can't. I love you and I am proud of you and I want to share you with my friends and family and associates, openly. I want you to walk into a room on my arm and be Countess Lawrence with all the respect and privileges you're entitled to. I want that with all my heart, Cris, for both of us. And if I have to endure another painful separation now in order to have the rest of our lives together, I will, Cristina. And so will you. I've got to go back to London and I've got to see Meredith, but I'm coming back to you as soon as I can. In the meantime, I want you to stay here in New York, where you'll be safe."

"Blake, please. . . ." Cristina choked back the sobs that burned in her throat. "I'm afraid that if you leave something will happen and I'll never see you again."

"Ssh, Cris, don't. I promise I'll be back as soon as I can. Have faith in our love. Believe in it. Trust it. Trust me."

Cristina brushed away her tears, straightened her shoulders, and lifted her chin slightly. "How long will it take?"

"It shouldn't take more than two months at most," Blake assured her. "All I want is to get this over with and to come back to you."

"I'll give you exactly two months," she said.

"What?"

"Two months before I go to London and get you and we try it my way."

"Fair enough," he said. "Now give me a kiss and help me dress. This is for the best, my love."

"I know." Cristina nodded as she slowly helped Blake dress and pack.

Blake kissed her lips. "Don't be sad. This is our path to a future together. When I return, I'll be legally free of Meredith. We can be married. Remember that while I'm gone I'll be thinking of you every minute. No more misunderstandings. I am not now, nor will I ever abandon you."

"Just you remember that I'll be counting the days. No more delays."

"Understood," he said.

Cristina nearly choked on the word, but she managed to smile in spite of it. "Understood."

"Good. Now don't worry. I'll be back before you know it. Remember, Cristina, I love you. Always."

Twenty-nine

CRISTINA WAITED UNTIL the sound of his footsteps disappeared before she threw herself on the bed they had shared for the past two days and nights and allowed the flood of tears to escape. She cried until her eyes were swollen and dry, then walked to the adjoining bath and filled the tub.

She soaked in the hot, comforting water and thought about Blake and the woman back in England who bore his name. She knew Blake was going back to London to secure a future for the two of them, but she also understood that Meredith would fight it. Blake had never said it aloud, but that knowledge hung in the air between them. Cristina was positive that there was something more at stake than just a divorce petition; much more than Blake would admit aloud.

And she was just as sure that someone else in New York City knew exactly what it was.

She bathed quickly, stepped out of the tub, dried herself, and dressed in the same dress she had worn to the hotel for the luncheon with Roderick. She passed the front desk and was on her way to the front door of the hotel when the desk clerk called out to her.

"Madame."

"Yes?" Cristina turned and accepted the white envelope he held out to her.

"Your husband left this for you."

"Thank you." Cristina stared in amazement, then tore open the envelope and withdrew the message written on hotel stationery. There were three words: Love always, Blake. And the heavy gold wedding band engraved with climbing roses.

Cristina slipped the ring onto her finger, pocketed the precious message, and marched out the door filled with stubborn determination.

~~∞©∿~~

SHE DIDN'T STOP until she reached her father's Wall Street office. Cristina slipped past the clerk outside her father's door, knocked once, then entered before William could grant permission. He was busy at his desk and didn't look up.

Cristina slammed the door to gain his complete and undivided attention.

William jumped at the noise and looked up to find his daughter the culprit. "Good God, Cristina! Where did you get your penchant for slamming perfectly good doors off their hinges?"

His daughter ignored the question and asked one of her own. "Have you seen him?"

William took one look at the determination written all across her lovely face and didn't bother to pretend. "I haven't seen you in two days. But, yes, I did see Blake briefly this morning after he left the hotel."

"Then you know he's on his way back to England?"

"Yes."

"And you know why?"

"I'm sure he told you why," William answered.

"He told me part of it," Cristina admitted. "But he didn't tell me all of it. There's more at stake than his divorce. I feel it and I think you know what it is."

"I can't tell you, Cristina. I promised Blake I wouldn't."

"Then I'll have to book passage on the next ship to London and find out for myself."

"I can't let you do that, either, Cristy."

"Why not?"

"I promised Blake that I would keep you here with me where you'll be safe."

"Where I'll be safe?" Cristina's ears pricked up. "I am safe. Meredith doesn't want me. She wants Blake. Is he in danger? Tell me. I have to know what's going on."

"Cristina . . ." William had never seen his daughter truly angry, but he recognized all the traits.

"Tell me," Cristina demanded. "Or I'll leave on the next ship. You won't be able to stop me and how will you explain that to Blake?" It was blackmail, pure and simple, but it worked.

"Blake won't like it," William conceded reluctantly.

"I won't tell," Cristina smiled angelically.

"Sit down," William removed a stack of papers from the safe beside his desk and handed them over to Cristina. They were letters from Blake Ashford addressed to William Fairfax. "Those should explain everything."

Cristina sat in the chair her father indicated and began to read. Blake had left nothing out of his letters to her father. Each one consisted of several pages and the first one was dated nearly two years earlier. In the first letter Blake thanked William for agreeing to meet with him on such short notice and for being completely candid with him. He wrote that he had decided to accept the post in Vienna the queen had offered in order to be closer to Cristina. He wrote that he hoped to see her and promised to write William as soon as he arrived in Vienna and arranged a meeting with her.

The second letter was dated after Blake's arrival in Vienna. He had written to give William the news that he was going to be a grandfather. He apologized for not telling him in person, then went on to express his concern about Cristina's tenuous position in Vienna.

Cristina continued to read the letters and found that Blake had written to her father with vivid descriptions of the apartment on the Ring, each stage of her pregnancy, and Leah's gradual acceptance of him. He wrote of their plans for Christmas, and later, about the bombing and the subsequent birth and death of Nicholas. She wept softly as she read the tear-blotched letter that poignantly described her courage during her long, exhausting labor.

She knew instinctively that Blake had written it that same night. And she became furiously angry when Blake wrote his deepest suspicions concerning Meredith and the Austrian cavalry officer named Oskar von Retterling.

Oskar von Retterling. Cristina gasped aloud and the letter slipped from her trembling fingers. The name conjured up the imagine of the man in the shiny boots pointing the gun at her head as she lay injured and unable to move on the frozen Vienna sidewalk. And fifteen months later, the name still had the power to frighten her. She remembered the sound of each syllable as the other man shouted von Retterling's name and she remembered the look in von Retterling's eyes. That look would haunt her until the day she died. Von Retterling. Cristina hated the man and his name and everyone around him with a hatred that was frightening in its intensity. He had tried to kill her and he had succeeded in killing her baby. Her precious, innocent baby. And Meredith had hired him.

The very idea chilled Cristina to the bone.

She bent and picked the fallen page up from the floor of her father's office. She placed it on the stack beside her and continued to read as Blake poured out all of his feelings of anger and frustration and grief in the letters to William Fairfax. As Cristina read each one, she realized the reoccurring and underlying theme of every letter was his love and concern for her.

It took two hours to read all the correspondence and when she finally put down the most recent letter, Cristina turned to her father. ''Papa, Blake writes about his plan in every letter after the baby died, but he never explains it. Do you know what it is?''

''Yes, I know,'' William answered rather stiffly. ''That's part of the reason I invited Blake to come to New York. I didn't know what his plan was at the time, but I had the feeling it was something drastic and I hoped I could talk him out of taking any radical measures.''

"Is that the only reason you wrote him?" Cristina couldn't quite meet her father's knowing gaze.

"I confess that I wanted you to see him again before you found someone else you might want to marry. I knew all about your affair with Blake from his letters and it was perfectly plain to me that he was completely in love with you. I wanted to give you a chance to explore your feelings for him. I knew you didn't love anyone else, but I was afraid that you might not love Blake as much as he loved you.''

"And I thought I was sparing you by not telling you and all the time, you knew about our relationship." Cristina spoke in a voice barely above a whisper. "Papa, I never wanted to cause you any embarrassment. I never meant for you to find out that I planned to become the mistress of a crown prince or that I had had an affair with a married man, even if it was done in innocence. I didn't want you to think I had turned out just like Mother. I didn't want you to despise me. I couldn't stand that because I love you, Papa.''

William blinked at the sudden tears that blurred his vision. "I could never despise you, Cristy, for any reason. And certainly not for loving someone with all your heart. You are my flesh and blood, Cristina, all I really care about, and I was a fool to believe your mother's lies.''

"She did lie, didn't she, Papa?''

"Yes, she lied. She was jealous of my closeness to you and she wanted to destroy it. She wanted to hurt me. Did she destroy it, Cristina? Is that why you felt you couldn't tell me about your love for Blake? Do you still blame me for the things your mother did while I was away?'' He searched her face intently. She had every reason to blame him. He remembered the way his daughter had looked when she reached New York. He had met her at the harbor and after taking a good look at her, he knew Lawrence had done the right thing in sending her to him. The girl at the harbor was a mere shadow of the youthful Cristina he recalled so vividly, but she was still Cristina. His Cristina. His daughter. There wasn't a doubt in his mind about that. She was tall, only two or three inches under six feet and far too thin for her height, but he could see her beauty and something else he had failed to see all those years ago. Cristina was made in his image—a softer, more feminine image than the one he viewed in his shaving mirror, but with her bright copper tresses, green eyes, and too-firm chin, there was no doubt about her paternity. William saw it all so clearly and he could have kicked himself for all the wasted time. He was deeply indebted to Lawrence for having the wisdom to send Cristina to New York so that she might experience the depth of her father's love.

Lawrence had sent a pale ghost of the girl he had known in Vienna, but William had welcomed the challenge of bringing the real Cristina back to life, knowing he would have the opportunity to surround her with love and constant care and to make amends to his daughter for failing her years before in London. He had given Cristina's body time to heal, then he had begun to heal the rest of her by keeping her too busy to dwell on her tragedy. First there were shopping trips and dress fittings, gradually followed by afternoon teas and charity work at St. Michael's Orphanage and when he finally felt she was strong enough, he had introduced her to society and filled her world with endless rounds of soirees and balls. He lavished love and attention on Cristina and she couldn't help but respond to it all after having lost so much. She had begun to pull herself together and enjoy her life in New York. And it was almost as if he had arranged for her to have another debutante season. A second chance. And Cristina came close to forgetting about the first one. Almost, but not quite. She gave a very good imitation of being completely recovered, but William knew she hadn't gotten over the death of her baby or her heartbreak over Lawrence. One never got over the death of a child or the loss of a lover by pretending it had never happened.

Cristina kept her emotions tightly controlled. She was always nice, always polite, always above reproach and always carefully restrained with the people around her. And William understood, even if Cristina did not, that her healing process would never be complete unless she faced the past and allowed herself to feel again.

He decided then to give her a chance. He had written to Lawrence and invited him to Cristina's twenty-second birthday party.

The months of love and care he had given her since she had come to live with him could never make up for the months they had lost when he abandoned her at the boarding school, but William hoped that she would learn to forgive him—that she had forgiven him, or at least stopped blaming him for the pain Patricia had inflicted. But he had been too afraid to ask. Until now. . . .

"Do you still blame me?"

"I never blamed you, Papa," she said. "But after Nicholas—after I came to live with you, it hurt too much to think about Blake or the baby. I couldn't talk about it, so I waited for Blake to come and get me and when he didn't, I gave up hoping. I thought he had decided to live without me. I never knew, never guessed any of this." Cristina indicated the stack of letters beside her. "I never dreamed he was planning anything. Papa, couldn't you talk him out of it?" Cristina asked, hoping her father had accomplished an impossible task, yet knowing in her heart he had not.

"No," William answered slowly. "He presented me with the finished product as soon as he arrived. There wasn't anything I could do to stop him. I might as well have argued with a stone wall. He wouldn't change his mind. He's convinced this is the only way. But he isn't looking for revenge on Meredith, but protection for you. Protection for the both of you."

"I don't understand."

He smiled grimly and handed her another stack of papers. Not letters, this time, but legal documents. "You know everything else, Cristina, you might as well read these, too. I think you'll understand after you've read them."

Cristina pored over the papers, carefully studying the tiny script and the unfamiliar legal phrases. Blood rushed to her head as the meanings behind the Latin words sank into her brain and she realized exactly what the documents were.

The full implications of Blake's sacrifice cut deep into her heart and with tears welled up in her emerald eyes, she looked up at her father and whispered, "Papa, tell me this isn't what I think it is. Tell me he wasn't foolhardy enough to risk his life this way. Tell me Blake didn't do all this for me."

*Did you think the lion was sleeping
because he didn't roar?*

—JOHANN CHRISTOPH FRIEDRICH VON SCHILLER
1759–1805

Thirty

TWO MONTHS LATER Cristina's words were echoed in horror by a woman an ocean away from New York City.

"You must be out of your mind, Blake. You can't have done all this for that little slut!" Meredith, countess of Lawrence, screamed at the man who was her husband. "You can't have given everything to her. Your entire fortune!"

"I did." Blake faced the loathsome creature he had married in an impetuous moment so many years ago with a smile of satisfaction on his face. It was impossible for him to believe he had ever thought he had loved Meredith Brownlee. He hadn't known what love was until Cristina Fairfax had burst into his life and turned it upside down. He thought of Cristina with her fiery spirit and her loving nature and a gush of longing flowed through him.

He scowled at Meredith, eager to get through the ugly interview and be on his way back to Cristina, and the angry, jagged, red scar on his forehead contrasted sharply with the rest of his features.

That scar was one more reminder of Meredith's treachery. Her hired thugs had met him at the docks as he disembarked from his ship. They had beaten him senseless and left him lying in early-morning mist. Fortunately for Blake, Nigel had arrived at the dock to welcome Blake home and found him unconscious and hurt. A broken rib had punctured a lung and the deep gash over his eye had caused a slight concussion. He was bruised and badly beaten, and he was lucky to be alive.

His recovery had taken several weeks and the court hearing scheduled for the day after his arrival in London had had to be postponed and rescheduled for five weeks later.

Blake had presented his case to the court two days previously, then packed his bags and journeyed to Willow Wood to deliver the verdict to Meredith in person.

"I think I've been generous under the circumstances," Blake sneered contemptuously. "Had I known about the little surprise waiting for me at the docks, I would have signed everything over to Cristina."

"You *have* signed everything over to her!" Meredith declared angrily.

"Not everything, Meredith," Blake corrected. "You have Willow Wood for as long as you live."

"But you stripped it bare," Meredith complained. "And Willow Wood is a mere pittance compared to what you've given away. You gave her everything! You had no right! No right!"

"I had every right." Blake extended his arms to indicate the area surrounding him. "Be thankful I left you Willow Wood. It was mine to do with as I pleased just like everything else. And it pleased me greatly to give it to Cristina for her twenty-second birthday."

"I won't accept it!"

"You have a choice, Meredith. The hangman's noose, Bedlam, or Willow Wood and a divorce."

Meredith's face contorted with twisted rage. "I'll see you dead for this! I'll see you both dead!"

"You do and all of this will go to William Fairfax along with orders to evict you from Willow Wood and to prosecute you for murder," Blake retaliated, resting his hands on the arms of her wheelchair, forcing her to look at him.

"I'm your wife and you can't cheat me out of all I've worked so hard to gain. It can't be legal."

"It's very legal, Meredith," Blake's voice cracked like a whip through the quiet house. "You may still share my name, but you've never been a wife to me; not since the day we were married. You were ruthless in your ambition to have everything. You cheated me and stole from me to get what? Money? Power? You had all that and you would still have it if you hadn't let your twisted hatred of me control you. You've become too greedy, Meredith, and too brutal. You were willing to murder for money and power and finally for revenge."

Meredith wheeled her chair away from Blake's reach. For the first time since she had known him, Meredith was truly afraid of him—afraid of his next move. His face was a mask of cool contempt and she sensed that he felt absolutely nothing for her, not even pity.

Meredith's eyes widened for a split second before she veiled them with her thick lashes. She moistened her dry lips with her tongue and faced him. "I may have known about the bombing, but I did not murder your child. I didn't know anything about his death."

Blake's fists clenched at his sides. It took every ounce of his self-control to keep from choking the breath from her lying throat.

"I think you did," Blake told her sharply. "I know you did. And this time, I have proof."

"You have no proof," Meredith gloated. "Because there is no proof. I think you're bluffing."

"I have Oskar von Retterling."

Meredith paled.

"Retterling was arrested in Budapest last month. And I've been told that after a month in a Hungarian prison, he's willing to testify to anything. And implicate you." He backed away from her. "And then there's Jack."

"Jack loves me. He'll never betray me."

Blake shook his head. "He already has. He testified on my

behalf in court. He admitted to cuckolding me on our wedding day. He admitted to committing adultery with you.''

"You're lying!''

"No, I'm not. You see, Meredith, Jack loves his comforts more than he loves you.''

"That's not true!'' There was an edge of panic in Meredith's voice. "Jack won't leave me.''

"Then where is he? How long has it been since you've seen him?'' A small part of Blake wanted to feel sorry for her, but he ruthlessly forced that drop of pity aside. He couldn't let himself feel pity for her. Nicholas was dead because of her. "Jack's father-in-law has him on a very short leash. He won't be allowed to stray from home any longer. Not if he wants to keep a home.''

"But he has a home with me here at Willow Wood,'' Meredith said. "*We* still have Willow Wood.''

"That's true,'' Blake agreed. "But Jack doesn't want a bare Willow Wood any more than you do. He can't afford the upkeep on the place. And then, there are those fraud charges he's facing for helping you disappear.''

"There's no law against disappearing, Blake.''

"No, but there's a law against defrauding your creditors. And you and Jack and your family are all guilty of that.''

"You're legally responsible for my debts,'' Meredith reminded him.

"Not any longer,'' he answered truthfully. "So you see, Meredith, you've run out of options and allies.''

"And you're threatening me with a noose just to gain your freedom,'' Meredith said.

"I have my freedom,'' Blake said. "My divorce *a mensa et a thoro* has already been granted by a court of common law and since Parliament is in session, the House of Lords voted this morning to allow me to marry again.''

"That's impossible! What about my countersuit of adultery?'' Meredith was clearly surprised by the turn of events.

"What has happened to your very efficient spies?'' Blake asked sarcastically. "Surely they know I freely admitted to adultery with several women from several establishments around town during the years we were married—the years before your untimely death. And all of the ladies were willing to sign discretionary statements confirming it.''

''I don't care about whores from bawdy houses,'' Meredith fumed. ''What about your adultery with Cristina Fairfax and the illegitimate child she bore you?''

A muscle beside Blake's mouth began to twitch as he struggled to keep his anger in check and failed. ''There is no child. You murdered him, you bloody bitch. And by doing so, you destroyed your own evidence.'' Blake winced as he said those words and the pain in his voice was evident. ''Miss Cristina Fairfax's name was never mentioned in connection with adultery of any kind.'' Blake had told the panel of judges the entire story. He told of his suspicions concerning Lady Lawrence and presented his accumulated evidence. He told them how Meredith had faked her own death and coerced her relatives into helping her and stressed the fact that Meredith had become increasingly disturbed and violent since her return from the dead. He explained that although he was concerned for her ultimate welfare, he didn't love her and could not continue his marriage to her.

The judges had proven to be remarkably sympathetic to Blake's appeal and had voted unanimously in favor of the petition as long as certain provisions were made for the care of Meredith, Lady Lawrence.

Blake had considered the provisions to be fair and a small price to pay for his freedom. He had readily agreed to make them. ''I have your copy of the documents with me. The judges were extremely generous to you because of your condition. You'll be allowed to keep the title of 'countess of Lawrence' for as long as you wish.'' That irked him, but Blake hadn't argued the decision. ''And you will receive an annual allowance of thirty thousand pounds to provide for your care. Of course, Willow Wood is yours for as long as you live and all our dealings will be handled by solicitors because, after this, I never want to see you or Willow Wood again.'' Blake finished his discussion of the terms of the di-

vorce and handed Meredith a sealed envelope stuffed thick
with papers. "Do you understand?"

"You've taken everything away from me. Everything.
Even Jack." She looked up at Blake. "I love Jack. You've
ruined everything. All my plans. All my dreams. You've
taken away everything I ever wanted. Why should I do anything for you?" Meredith glared up at him and naked hatred
gleamed in the depths of her eyes. "Do you understand, Lord
Lawrence, that I will never sign any divorce documents?"

"The divorce has already been declared legal and valid
whether you sign the papers or not. The papers are simply a
formality." Blake walked to the door.

"If you walk out that door," Meredith promised, "I'll burn
your ridiculous divorce papers."

Blake smiled then, a beautiful smile that transformed the
stern mask he had worn into a handsome face. "Do whatever
you want with them, Meredith. I don't care anymore." He
turned his back on her and walked away, still smiling.

Meredith sat completely still for several moments after
Blake's footsteps sounded on the stairs and the front door
closed with a bang. She was raging inside at the injustice of
his actions. How could he give everything away to a someone
who wasn't even his wife? How could he trust her? Did he
love Cristina Fairfax that much? Or did he simply hate Meredith? Surely Blake was bluffing—trying to frighten her into
signing those papers. But he wasn't going to succeed. No one
would believe a poor, beautiful cripple capable of murder.
The court wouldn't believe she had killed a man and an unborn child because of an insatiable greed or the need to wound
Blake—to make him feel something for her besides his
damned indifference.

It wasn't plausible. Or was it? The doubt crept into Meredith's mind, unbidden. Blake had seemed completely confident. Perhaps he did have evidence. Should she risk her neck,
her very life, for the sake of a divorce? Was he bluffing, or
would he really go to the authorities or confine her to Bedlam? Meredith cursed aloud. She had never been plagued by
doubts before. She had always done what was necessary to

get what she wanted without doubting that she would succeed. She couldn't let everything she had worked for be ruined without a fight. If Blake wanted the scandal of going to the authorities and accusing his wife of murder, then he would get it. She was going to call his bluff. She wouldn't sign anything. She wouldn't take Blake's word about the legality of a divorce without her signature. She preferred to wait and see for herself.

Meredith made her decision and wheeled herself over to the huge fireplace. She smiled at the thick envelope, then flung it into the fire. The bright orange embers came to life and the yellow flames licked greedily at the edges of the envelope, curling their blue-tipped tongues around the parchment until the outside blackened and fell away into ashes, revealing the contents.

Meredith stared in stunned fascination as the yellow-orange flames turned brilliant blue and began to consume stacks of crisp new pound notes.

Her settlement. God damn him! What was it he'd said? Thirty thousand pounds a year as settlement. Money. Her money. Money she would need to win Jack back. Blake had given her the money in one lump sum. Thirty thousand pounds of her money. And it was burning.

Meredith reacted quickly, concern for the burning money her only thought. She leaned forward, thrust her hand into the fire, and closed her fist around the top stack of notes. Pain shot through her arm as the heat of the fire singed the hair from the back of her hand and arm and blistered the delicate skin beneath. She jerked her hand back and dropped the money into her lap.

One stack. And much of it burned beyond use. Meredith watched angrily as the flames continued to eat away at two other stacks of money. Thirty thousand pounds in three bundles. Ten thousand pounds apiece. It was too much to bear. It was all Blake's fault. He had let her burn her settlement. He had smiled at her, knowing what was in the envelope. He had let her toss it in the fire. It was his way of getting back at her. Damn him!

A determined rage filled her as Meredith seized the poker and desperately began to prod the bills. The flames burned brighter with each poke as the money crackled and dissolved in fragile brown ash. She had to get it. She had to.

Using her arms for support, she lifted herself to the edge of her wheelchair and leaning heavily on the brass poker, reached toward the fire in a last attempt to save the money.

The poker skidded across the smooth, polished marble. Meredith lost her precarious balance and fell headlong onto the hearth. Her useless feet struck her chair as she fell and sent it crashing backward into the writing table. The table toppled over and the oil lamp sitting on it crashed to the floor and exploded at her feet in a burst of hot oil and flame that splattered her clothes.

Meredith beat at the flames, unable to feel the heat yet knowing the fire and oil were burning her clothes and blistering her flesh. She tried desperately to drag herself from the hearth, but the pain from her blistered hand hampered her and the fire continued to snake up her skirts toward her loosened mass of black curls and to cling tenaciously to her dress until it spread across the floor in little orange rivers and began to feed upon new fuel in the form of carpets and drapes.

Meredith screamed then. Again and again until the smoke scorched her lungs and her screams became bitter moans lost in the noise of the hungry fire.

HER ANGRY SCREAMS carried across the lawn to the stables where Blake waited impatiently for a horse to be saddled. He smiled grimly. Meredith must have followed through on her threat to burn the envelope, discovering too late that it contained her first year's settlement. He supposed the angry screams meant that she was busy venting her wrath on the furnishings in her sitting room. And it didn't matter to him anymore. Willow Wood belonged to her. She was free to vent her spleen in any manner she chose.

Blake ignored the screams and climbed onto the back of

his horse. He whirled out of the stable and cantered toward the gates. He was almost through them when he heard someone shouting his name. He reined in his horse and turned back toward Willow Wood.

The stableboy was running down the drive, waving his arms and shouting to gain Blake's attention. Blake trotted his horse back to the breathless boy.

"What is it?" he demanded.

The young boy panted and bent forward in an effort to catch his breath. But his words came in unintelligible gasps and he finally pointed to the house.

Blake looked toward the house.

The stableyard was alive with activity as the household employees scurried from pump to pump, forming a bucket brigade that led to the window of Meredith's sitting room. Orange flames consumed the drapes and thick black smoke darkened the windowpanes, then spewed forth as the heat of the fire shattered the glass.

The fire roared brighter with the gust of oxygen from the shattered windows.

Blake heaved the boy onto the back of his horse and galloped back to the stable.

He dismounted at a run and dropped the reins in the dirt. "Where is Lady Lawrence?" he shouted to the butler who was busy organizing the firefighting effort.

"There, sir," the butler shouted back, directing Blake's attention back to the burning window. "I couldn't reach her."

Blake reacted without thinking. Dashing toward the house, he took the stairs leading to the burning floor two at a time. The door to the sitting room stood partially open, but it was impossible to enter. The room was a raging inferno, the heat unbearable. Blake stripped off his coat and held it over his face. He rushed through the doorway and returned coughing and choking as the wall of fire beat him back. He tried again and failed, then wrapped his coat tighter about his face for the third attempt.

"No, sir," the butler had grabbed his arm, "it's no use. You can't get in. It's too hot!"

Blake looked at the butler, and back at the room. Logic told him Meredith was dead. It was impossible for her to be alive, but decency demanded that he try to save her.

He took a deep breath of air and lunged for the door.

The butler held fast to his arm. "No, sir! Look!"

It was too late. The fire had spread too rapidly. There was nothing left alive and unburned in that room. Blake resigned himself to that fact, then accompanied the butler out of the burning house.

He worked tirelessly through the afternoon trying to save something of Willow Wood, but nightfall found the country house a smoldering ruin of ashes. Only the stables remained.

The exhausted crowd of employees stood in quiet groups awaiting instructions. Blake wearily rubbed at the taut muscles in the back of his neck. The employees filed around him to shake his hand and to offer their sympathies. He listened attentively to each one and when they had finished he stripped off his filthy tattered shirt and washed at the pump alongside the other men. He ruthlessly wiped the exhaustion from his fuzzy brain and made a mental list of the details that must be attended to before he could return to London. When he was reasonably clean, Blake pulled his sweat- and soot-stained shirt back on and instructed several of the men to hitch up the carriages. He resaddled his horse and mounted and walked it to the gates of Willow Wood—gates that guarded a simmering mound of ash. He waited until the carriages were loaded, then led an assortment of dirty, bone-weary employees, along with their few meager belongings, down the narrow road to the village and refuge.

Blake waited in the village until the ashes of Willow Wood cooled and the men were able to dig through the rubble and recover Meredith's pitiful remains. He ordered a coffin; notified the authorities, Meredith's family, and his own parents of the fire and of Meredith's death; and sent word to his aunt and to Mackie at Lawrence House before he followed the ugly black hearse back to London.

A STEADY STREAM of callers poured into Lawrence House on the day of the funeral. Blake's nerves were stretched to the limit as he acknowledged the offerings of food and flowers and sympathy cards filling the house. He had spent most of his time secluded in his study escaping from well-meaning friends and associates. He only wished that he could escape the whole charade. But that was impossible.

Blake absentmindedly picked through the sympathy cards on the silver tray someone had placed in his study. He paid little attention to the bereaved offerings, for his mind was several thousand miles away in New York City with Cristina. He wondered what she was doing and how she was taking his absence. He was late. He had promised the trip wouldn't take any longer than two months and he had missed that deadline by three weeks and four days. And Blake was worried. Had he broken her faith again? How many times could he leave her behind and still have her believe in him?

His mind had warred with his heart until he thought he would explode. God, how he wanted Cristina beside him! How he needed to hear her voice and to feel her arms around him! And how he wanted to tell her he loved her!

Blake impatiently flung out his arm and knocked the tray aside. He wasn't mourning Meredith and he didn't want sympathy cards from people who thought he was. Paper fluttered to the floor like snowflakes and Blake cursed aloud as he bent to pick them up. He scooped up a handful of cards and threw them back on the tray but one card slipped through his fingers and fell back to the floor.

He noticed it simply because it was different from the others. It was completely white, lacking the black mourning border of the others. Blake picked it up and discovered it wasn't a card at all, but a note folded over and written in a feminine hand. His heart seemed to somersault in his chest as he tore it open and read:

> *My darling Blake,*
>
> *Please don't be angry, but it has been over two months and I was very worried about you. I simply couldn't stand to wait any longer.*

Perspiration beaded Blake's upper lip, fear coiled in his belly, and his hand shook from the force of his emotions as he commanded his eyes to read on and learn the truth.

> *I made my decision weeks ago and stuck to it. Papa fought me every step of the way. But even he was forced to admit defeat and reluctantly saw us off at the docks when Leah and I left New York.*

Left? Where had she gone? Why hadn't she waited?

> *We docked yesterday morning and have reopened Fairhall. Everything is in an uproar, but I can live with a little discomfort. I can't live without you. Come to me, my love. I miss you terribly and I am waiting impatiently. Hurry, my love.*
>
> *Always, Cristina*

Blake read the note a second time and pure unadulterated joy shot through him. He hugged the letter to his chest and laughed aloud for the sheer pleasure of it. His wish had come true. She was in London waiting for him. She had come to him at last. His countess was waiting with open arms and the knowledge that she had traveled across an ocean to be with him made all the difference to Blake. His doubts about their future had been silenced forever and because of that, he could endure a few more final hours of hypocrisy.

Thirty-one

August 1880
London

IT WAS RAINING. Cristina stood near the window of her bedroom at Fairhall watching as thousands of raindrops hurried from the darkened skies to the cold, hard ground below. Wet droplets blew against the windowpanes, dotting the viewing area until the surface of the windowpane resembled a prism. Outside the window, brown stems emerged from the sodden garden like grotesque sculptures, all that remained of the summer's roses.

Cristina pressed her nose against the glass, her warm breath forming clouds on the cool surface. But she wasn't studying the garden. She was looking beyond it, peering out on the gray horizon searching longingly for the shape of a sleek, black carriage. Had he missed her message? Or had he received the note and decided not to come? Of course not. She chided herself for her moment of doubt. Blake would come when he could. He had promised "always" and he wouldn't fail her.

She was tired and nervous. She'd been waiting on pins and needles ever since her arrival from New York the day before. Her father hadn't wanted her to travel and he'd presented a number of sound, logical reasons against it. He had tried to persuade Cristina to be patient—to wait a little longer for Blake to return—but Cristina had been stubbornly determined to sail. And now, even though she knew she shouldn't doubt herself, Cristina couldn't help wondering if she had made the right decision. Would he understand? Would he be upset when he learned of the new wrinkle in their relationship?

She walked over to the mirror and examined herself critically, seeing herself the way Blake would see her, looking for signs of change. The white flannel nightgown concealed the growing fullness of her breasts and the added inches at her waistline. Would his knowing hands feel the difference when the rest of her looked the same? Cristina sighed and grimaced at the mirror. In a very few months she would be huge and distorted and would waddle like a duck when she tried to walk across a room, but today she felt beautiful. And she wanted to be beautiful for Blake a little while longer before the shape of her body caught up with the size of her long, narrow feet and Blake teased her unmercifully about her ungainly appearance.

"Missy, you'll catch your death of cold! It's freezin' in here."

Cristina turned to find Leah standing with arms akimbo in the doorway, gently scolding as usual. "I'm just watching it rain."

"Well, beggin' your pardon, missy, but it's the same as it's always been—cold and wet. And it looked to me like you were busy admirin' your figure in the mirror." Leah draped a shawl over Cristina's shoulders and directed her back to the warm bed. "You can see the window from here. And besides, it will probably be hours before he gets here. At least let the sun come up before you start worrying."

Cristina obediently climbed back into bed, partly out of habit and partly because she was too stubborn to admit she was cold. "You do think he'll come, don't you, Leah?"

"Don't doubt it a bit," Leah replied matter-of-factly. "I didn't come all this way for nothin' and neither did you."

"That's what I keep telling myself, but what if something has happened? What if he didn't get my note? What if she's done something to hurt him and he isn't able to come?" Cristina gave voice to her fears for Blake's safety.

"Try not to worry so much. It ain't good for you or the baby. He'll get here soon as he can."

"I can't help but worry, Leah, I know something terrible has happened," Cristina fretted.

"I think you're just anxious about Lord Blake and the new baby and you're lettin' the bad memories of Vienna worry you," Leah told her.

Cristina shook her mass of copper curls. "It's more than that. It's something I feel. Leah, I'm frightened but I'm not frightened for the baby or myself. I'm afraid for Blake." Cristina tried to block out her memories of the bombing, but Leah's words brought them back and there was nothing she could do except close her eyes and remember von Retterling and the night Nicholas was born. And Blake, with an incredibly gentle look in his eyes and a tender note in his voice talking to her, helping her through the agonizing labor. Blake, who had used those same incredibly gentle hands to place a cool cloth between her bitten and swollen lips and whose voice huskily commanded her to bite down and to push and who praised her while she did as he instructed. She had truly loved him then, more than any human being on earth. And she had continued to love him. Always.

"Missy? Cristina?"

The memories faded. Cristina opened her eyes as the sound of the worry in Leah's voice caught and held her attention.

"Yes?"

"I made your breakfast and brought the mornin' paper." Leah placed the tray on the table next to Cristina's bed and handed Cristina the newspaper.

Cristina took it from her and scanned the headlines. A black bordered column caught her eye and a familiar name leaped out at her.

"No!" Cristina cried out. Her hands trembled so hard, the newsprint danced before her eyes. She struggled to read the words. "A devastating fire destroyed Willow Wood, the country estate of the earl of Lawrence, on Wednesday last. Meredith, Lady Lawrence née Brownlee of the village of Everleigh in the county of Sussex died in the blaze. Though the stables and outbuilding were saved, all else was lost." Cristina recited the facts of the article in a clipped, cold tone of voice. "It doesn't say anything about anyone else being involved in the fire. Oh, wait, it says here that she is survived by her husband, Blake Ashford, Earl of Lawrence; her parents; and the marquess and marchioness of Everleigh." Cristina leaped from the bed, grabbed hold of Leah, and hugged her tightly. "Thank goodness! Oh, thank goodness he's all right!"

"That explains it," Leah said. "He won't be able to come right away. He'll have to wait until the funeral. You'll have to be patient a little longer."

Cristina nearly screamed in frustration. Meredith was dead once again and hopefully this time for good, but even in death, she had found another way to thwart them—to delay their marriage. If Blake was forced to endure the standard period of mourning before he could remarry, another Lawrence heir would be born out of wedlock.

THE EARL OF Lawrence stood apart from the mourners. Meredith was dead and he felt nothing beyond surprise—surprise that it was over. And surprise because Meredith had died the way she had lived—in an agony of hatred and bitterness, fighting him, hating him, thwarting him to the very end. And Blake didn't doubt that had she survived the fire, Meredith would have continued to fight him. She was truly dead this time. For good. He had seen the workmen recover her body and had been forced to help identify the pitiful remains. But in many ways, her death was hard for Blake to comprehend. It meant that she was harmless. Harmless. Funny that that particular word should apply to Meredith. She'd cheated death the first time, then used it to her advantage. She'd spent years confined to a wheelchair, constantly traveling, keeping herself hidden away from everyone except her family and Jack and Retterling and other hired henchmen, waiting, always waiting for her opportunity for revenge, feeding on her desire for revenge, and none of those hardships had rendered her harmless.

She had wanted him to hate her and she had done everything in her power to earn his hatred. And she had succeeded. Her attempted murder of Cristina and Nicholas's death had earned her his hatred. But the way Meredith had died had nullified that hatred. He had told her that he never wanted to see her again, but he had never wanted her to die the way she had died, unable to move while the flames and smoke burned and choked the life out of her. Blake had also wanted revenge and he had had it.

It left a bitter taste in his mouth.

The sound of metal scraping earth brought Blake back to the present. He stared dispassionately as the pallbearers lowered Meredith's charred remains into her grave. The mourners watched and waited silently for Blake to do something.

He turned and walked away from the open grave, leaving the crowd of mourners wondering at his unprecedented behavior.

Let them wonder. Let them think what they liked. Meredith was in the past. His future lay with Cristina and Blake didn't intend to waste any more time. Cristina was the important person in his life. Cristina loved him and needed him and he had been delayed by Meredith for far too long. He and Meredith had been tied together for more years than Blake cared to remember and they had finally been rewarded for their suffering. They were free of each other.

The early morning drizzle had given way to a cold, driving rain by the time the funeral ended. Blake ignored the rain and the biting chill and the dozen or so mourners who stood in the rain gaping at him as he hurried past them and leaped into the black-draped carriage. He ordered the driver to whip up the team and set out for Fairhall where he knew Cristina would be waiting.

London traffic was light on such a cold, rainy afternoon, but the rain made the cobblestones treacherous in the older part of the city and progress was frustratingly slow. The snail's pace of the carriage added to Blake's impatience. He shifted in his seat, cursed the weather that slowed him down, and ordered the driver to increase his speed at least a hundred times before he reached Fairhall.

He opened the door and jumped out of the carriage as it rolled to a stop. He ran the few steps from the sidewalk to the front door and descended upon the quiet house with the force of a gale wind. He shoved open the heavy front doors without knocking and began searching for Cristina.

He shouted her name over and over, his voice echoing dully through the empty rooms. "Cristina, where are you?"

Cristina recognized the impatient shout the moment it reached her ears and hurried from the kitchen, where she had spent the past hour sharing a pot of tea in companionable silence with Leah.

She collided with Blake in the dining room and began covering his face with warm, eager kisses.

"Blake, you came!" It was all she could think to say.

He held her at arm's length and studied her face. "I came as soon as the funeral ended. I suppose you know about Meredith."

Cristina nodded.

"I'm so glad to see you," he admitted. "So glad that I can't decide whether I should beat you for following me here or make love to you to show you how glad I am you did. Countess, why on earth did you come here when I asked you to wait for me in New York?" Blake tried to sound annoyed, but his smile ruined the effect.

"I had to come. I love you and I was worried about you. And with good reason, I see...." Cristina reached up and lightly touched the pattern of the ugly little scar that marred his perfect face. "It's been over two months. I knew something was wrong when you didn't return when you said you would. And I was right. You've been injured.''

"I'll be fine now that you're with me," Blake told her. "Don't worry. It's all over now. She can't hurt us anymore." He smoothed the worry lines from between her brows.

"But what . . ." The unanswered questions bubbled to the surface.

"Not now, Cris. I'll tell you all about it later, but right now I simply want to hold you." Blake wrapped his arms around her and held her close. "Cris, Cris, I wanted you to stay in New York. You were safe there. How could you risk your life by coming here?" Some of the urgent fear poured through Blake's voice as he demanded an answer.

"I didn't think about my life," she answered simply. "I only thought about yours."

"Didn't you think about the consequences?"

"Almost as much as you did," Cristina interrupted him. "I thought about the consequences of my actions about as much as you did when you wrote that ridiculous document. You took an awful risk yourself. And I'm not talking about Meredith. Blake, I nearly married Roderick just to spite you and then you'd have been a pauper!"

"You know about that?" Blake was surprised.

"I had to find out about it sometime, didn't I?" Cristina retorted. "And yes, I forced the information out of my father.''

Blake smiled down at her and began caressing her hair. "I can just imagine." He laughed. "What did you do? Threaten him with a letter opener? Ah, my fiery redheaded countess, what am I going to do with you?" He kissed her hair and sighed expressively, but Blake knew exactly what to do with her.

"Love me," she said.

And Blake needed no further prompting.

IT WAS A wildly exciting reunion for the both of them. Blake was pleased to notice that Cristina continued to meet him as an equal partner. She wasn't a shy girl any longer. She was a fully grown woman in love with her man and fully aware of the passion she aroused. She was demanding and eager in her lovemaking, but she was also generous and she returned in full measure the pleasure Blake gave to her. She held his happiness inside her heart just as he held hers and she accepted that as she accepted breathing; finally ready to face the heady responsibility of loving someone and being loved in return.

"I have something to tell you. A surprise," Cristina confided as she lay snuggled against Blake's shoulder.

"Hmmm," he breathed, sated and half-asleep.

"I'm going to have another baby."

Her calm announcement jolted him into complete wakefulness. He sat up in bed, stared at Cristina in the dim light as if seeing her for the first time, and began to laugh. "I should have known!"

Cristina bristled at his laughter and pulled away from him. "I don't see anything funny about this situation. I'm pregnant again and still not married and you have a year of mourning to honor. I don't find the situation funny at all." She regally tucked the covers around her body and turned her back on Blake.

"Sweetheart," Blake chuckled, softly in spite of her angry display, then kissed a bare shoulder blade. "Some women crave strange, exotic foods when they're expecting a baby, but not you. You're unique. Whenever you get pregnant, you hop a boat or a train and leave town. I suppose you crave new cities like other women crave sweets. And I suppose I'll have to tie you to the bed to keep you at home or we're going to have a house full of children with remarkably diverse citizenships," he teased.

"You don't understand," Cristina accused.

"No, my darling countess, *you* don't understand," Blake corrected patiently. "I don't intend to waste a year mourning Meredith. I don't intend to waste any time. I've decided that if I don't catch you between princes, I won't catch you at all. We'll telegraph your father in the morning and invite him to the wedding and I'll give him exactly three weeks to get here.''

Cristina turned back over to look at him. "And then?''

"And then after the wedding we're going on a long honeymoon.''

"Where?''

"Vienna, I think," Blake told her.

"Vienna? Why?''

"Because a certain friend of yours has a small castle he'll let us borrow. And now that he's engaged to a very proper Catholic princess, I think I can trust him. I really do like the royal rogue, except when he's around you.''

"He won't be around me. I'll have a husband to see that he isn't.'' She threw her arms around Blake's neck and kissed his lips. "I would like to go back to Vienna. It's a lovely city and I want to do all the things I couldn't do when I was a 'kept' woman.'' Cristina smiled angelically, then began an exploration of Blake's body that tested the limits of his control.

"You'll still be a kept woman," Blake reminded her. "I intend to keep you beside me for the next fifty or so years. And this time it will be very legal. No escaping.''

Cristina paused a moment and pretended to deliberate. "And what if I don't like being a legally married woman?''

"Then you can just go back to being my mistress. Any time you please," he added wickedly.

~⊙~

THEY WERE MARRIED in the chapel of the home of Blake's parents, the marquess and marchioness of Everleigh, exactly three weeks to the day of Meredith's funeral.

Cristina wore her presentation gown, altered yet again to allow for her slightly expanded waistline, the plunging décolletage modestly covered by an embroidered white silk shawl. Blake wore a formal morning suit with a single gaudy white satin rosette pinned to the lapel.

William Fairfax gave his daughter's hand into the keeping

of Blake Ashford, ninth earl of Lawrence, while Lord and Lady Everleigh, Lady Wethering, Ambassador and Lady Paget, Nigel Jameson, Stanley Cason, Leah Porter, Albert Mead, Sarah MacKenzie, George Perryman, Tom Hudson, and the staff of Lawrence House proudly looked on.

Blake's parents warmly welcomed Cristina into the family, completely laying to rest the worries Cristina had felt at meeting them for the first time the day before her wedding.

It was quite obvious to everyone at the wedding that the bride and groom were completely besotted with one another and that made a world of difference in Lord Geoffrey's and Lady Cecilia's opinion. Their son was happily married at last.

After the brief ceremony, Blake took Cristina by the hand and led her out of the chapel, a short distance down a narrow path behind it to a private graveyard.

"Where are you taking me?" Cristina asked.

"Here." Blake stopped suddenly and looked down.

The tiny mound was covered in etched marble and a miniature angel bowed its head in prayer at the base. Tears formed in Cristina's eyes and glided silently down her cheeks as she read the inscription:

NICHOLAS FAIRFAX LAWRENCE
JANUARY 1, 1879
BELOVED SON OF BLAKE AND CRISTINA,
EARL AND COUNTESS OF LAWRENCE

"This is why I left you behind in Vienna, Countess. I didn't want Nicholas buried all alone in a Viennese cemetery. I brought him home to be with his family." Blake paused to wipe away a tear and to gain control of his shaking voice. "I didn't want to leave you behind, but you couldn't travel and I had to do this for Nicholas. For my firstborn son."

Cristina held her husband's hand, squeezing it tightly before she brought it to her lips and kissed the palm. "Thank you."

Blake stared down at the little grave. "I wanted you to know he was buried here. I couldn't take you to Vienna and have you wonder where our baby lay. I couldn't let you go back to Vienna with too many unhappy memories. It's important to me.'' Blake embraced her, holding her next to his heart. ''I was attracted to you in London. I desired you in London. But I didn't fall head over heels in love with you until I saw you again in Vienna. I can't explain it, but it will always be a special place to me.''

''Oh, Blake,'' Cristina smiled through her tears. ''You've given me everything. I have you and our new child and a home and a family. I'm surrounded by love. I'm whole at last.''

''So am I, Cristina,'' Blake whispered. ''So am I.''

Look, how my ring encompasseth your finger,
Even so thy breast encloseth my poor heart;
Wear both of them, for both of them are thine.

—WILLIAM SHAKESPEARE 1564–1616

Epilogue

A CHORUS OF cheerful exclamations rang out as the ninth earl of Lawrence popped the cork on another bottle of champagne and filled the remaining glasses of the staff of Lawrence House. He emptied the bottle and raised his glass to make the toast.

"To my beautiful and beloved wife Cristina, and to all the wonderful things she has brought into my life—love, happiness, and now our daughter, Bethany."

"Hear, hear!" There were more cheers and the clapping of hands and the clink of crystal as the staff members drained their glasses in salute to the young woman who had touched their lives with love and laughter.

The birth of Bethany an hour earlier had been quick and easy and the staff of Lawrence House had thanked their lucky stars for that because the lord of the house had been raging like a wounded tiger during the last month of his lady's confinement. The staff of Lawrence House had survived three months of rule under an anxious, expectant father and in some ways that was reason enough to celebrate.

Blake smiled broadly at the cheers and laughter, accepting

it as his due for the stress and strain he had endured during the last month, then slipped away from the crowd and crept stealthily up the stairs to the master suite carefully balancing a tray containing three glasses of champagne and an intricately carved black box.

Blake quietly opened the bedroom door and tiptoed inside. He deposited the tray on the Queen Anne dresser, removed two glasses of champagne and handed one to the doctor.

"She's beautiful, isn't she, Nigel?" he said as he sipped his wine and watched the sleeping forms of his wife and newborn daughter.

"Cristina or the baby?" Nigel smiled indulgently.

"Both," Blake grinned proudly. He grinned a lot lately, and also smiled and laughed. The change in him was remarkable. Gone were the lines of disillusionment and bitterness that had once framed his mouth and the corners of his eyes, and in their place were laugh lines. Blake Ashford had become a happy, supremely contented man. Loving Cristina had done that to him. It had erased the harsh edges of his personality and the ugly, bitter memories of the years with Meredith.

Even Blake found it hard to believe that only six months earlier he had witnessed the destruction of Willow Wood and had impatiently endured the funeral of a woman he had married but had never truly loved. It seemed a million years ago. Another lifetime ago. He ran his long, lean fingers through his unruly hair and smiled crookedly, recalling the outraged whispers and the raised eyebrows of his associates when he married Cristina barely three weeks after the funeral.

Well, he thought, there would be a few more raised eyebrows and more gossip for the grist mill when Bethany's announcement appeared in the newspapers. Strange that he didn't mind a few raised eyebrows these days.

"What are you smiling about?"

Blake came back from his reverie and found Cristina studying him with an interested sparkle in her emerald eyes.

"I was just remembering my ride across London after Meredith's funeral. How my abrupt departure scandalized the mourners. And how glad I was to see you and how angry I was with you for leaving the safety of New York.''

Cristina's answering smile was slowly sensuous as she also recalled their reunion. "You have an interesting way of showing your anger, milord.''

"You have an interesting way of arousing it,'' Blake replied meaningfully.

"Uh-hmm . . .'' Nigel cleared his throat, pointedly reminding them they were not alone. "I think I'll go downstairs and celebrate little Bethany's birthday with the rest of the family. The atmosphere up here is positively indecent,'' Nigel teased. "I would never guess the two of you have been married six whole months.'' He smiled at the three of them and exited without another word.

"Well, milord, how do you like her?'' Cristina asked when they were alone.

"She's marvelous, Cristina.'' His chest seemed to puff out several inches. "And you were terrific. You came through with flying colors and so quickly, too.'' Blake was visibly relieved that her labor had been brief and easy. He didn't think he could have survived another twenty-hour ordeal. "I think I must be the luckiest man alive to have you and our daughter.''

"Except for her feet, she looks just like you.'' Cristina busied herself counting the tiny, red toes of the baby's long, narrow feet. "She has your black hair.''

The infant stirred restlessly at her mother's breast and eagerly began searching for nourishment.

"She's like me in other ways as well,'' Blake chuckled wickedly. "She seems to have a healthy appetite for two of the finest things in life.''

Cristina blushed at the hungry look in his eyes and turned her attention back to the baby.

Blake walked to the dresser and returned with the black box. He placed it on the bed beside Cristina. "I have something for you, sweetheart. A gift.''

Cristina stared at the carved box. She smiled at him as she read the inscription. "Blake, it's lovely.''

"Open it,'' he encouraged.

Cristina handed Blake the sleepy baby and picked up the box. She lifted the lid and was stunned to find the box full of emeralds and diamonds. "It's the necklace Rudolf sent to me. The one you accused me of stealing. Why are you giving it back to me now?"

"Because it's yours," Blake said simply. "I was wrong not to believe you. I'm sorry."

"Blake, you don't have to give me this jewelry. What happened in the past doesn't matter anymore."

"This matters. This necklace is part of our lives—part of what brought us together in the first place. An intricate part. When you left London with Rudolf, it was a reminder of you and what I thought was your betrayal. I was wrong. So now I want you to have it and remember everything we've shared and all the obstacles we've had to overcome to be where we are today."

"But there's more. . . ." Cristina lifted the necklace and discovered the matching pieces. "A bracelet and earrings. Blake, I don't understand. . . ."

"They go with the necklace."

"Someone did steal this necklace from you," Cristina replied matter-of-factly. "There's more to this than you're telling me."

Blake nodded his head in agreement. "I bought the necklace a long time ago as a gift for my bride. When I realized I'd married the wrong woman, I decided against giving it to her. It remained locked in the safe at Lawrence House for years until it was stolen and sold and somehow found its way into your pocket—the pocket of the right woman."

Cristina was completely quiet, waiting for him to continue the story.

"It's a very long story, my love, and someday I promise to tell you all of it, but right now I want you to say that you'll accept this gift for what it was meant to be—a gift from a loving husband."

Cristina couldn't doubt the sincerity in his voice, but there was something familiar about that certain gleam in his eyes that made her a little wary and more than a little suspicious.

"I'll accept the necklace and the matching pieces on the condition that you tell me the real reason you're so determined that I have it. We don't need symbols of our love. We already have living proof of that." She nodded toward the baby sleeping in her father's arms. "I believe what you say, my darling husband, but I suspect that your motives for giving me these aren't exactly noble. Tell me."

"You drive a hard bargain, milady."

"Tell me," Cristina demanded again.

"They match your eyes." Blake's handsome face was completely guileless as he walked around the bed and placed Bethany in her cradle.

Cristina relented and held out her arms to her husband. "You say the nicest things. I've always loved your way with women—especially me."

A wolfish grin replaced the innocent look on Blake's face. "And I've always had a burning desire to see a certain red-haired countess lying beneath me wearing nothing but diamonds and emeralds that match her enchanting eyes. . . ."

Cristina's leer matched his own. "I have remarkable healing powers, milord," she assured him.

"Promise?" Blake asked urgently.

"Always," Cristina answered firmly, pulling him down to lie beside her.

Author's Note

DURING QUEEN VICTORIA'S reign, presentations at court marked the formal entrance of a young woman into fashionable society. In 1878, ladies were presented to the queen at "drawing rooms" held at St. James's Palace. The court balls, which the queen did not attend during her years of mourning, were held elsewhere, usually at Buckingham Palace, and presided over by the Prince and Princess of Wales.

For the purpose of this story, I chose to keep Cristina's formal presentation to the queen and the court ball that followed at the same location.

Also for the purpose of this story, I chose to modify Crown Prince Rudolf's social calendar a bit. His actual visit to England in 1878 took place in January through February and he stayed in a hotel on Brook Street rather than at Marlborough House with the Prince of Wales. Otherwise, I left his agenda essentially the same.

The Ringstrasse in Vienna was begun in the year 1858 in celebration of the birth of Crown Prince Rudolf and was still under construction at the time of his death in January 1889. The Viennese citizens waited sixteen years for the grand opening of the New Court Theatre on the Ringstrasse. Begun in 1872, it opened on October 14, 1888 and was unfinished at the time this story took place.

For these historical manipulations and any mistakes or inaccuracies, I bear full responsibility and graciously beg your pardon.

—Rebecca Hagan Lee
   June 1999

Rebecca Hagan Lee

REBECCA HAGAN LEE set out to make her mark in the world of television journalism but somewhere along the way, decided she was a small-town girl at heart and settled in a town where the media consists of a weekly newspaper and an AM radio station. Seeking a creative outlet, she turned to writing romance stories far different from the world of television news, but not that far removed from the hundreds of episodes of *Bonanza, Big Valley, Gunsmoke*, and *The Virginian* she had watched growing up. She decided to create stories where good guys win, bad guys lose, prostitutes have hearts of gold, and the heroes and heroines who fall in love and perservere are richly rewarded with incredibly bright futures and happy endings. In her world, heroines don't die or get killed off to make way for the next episode's new love interest; they get their men and help them become ideal husbands, lovers, friends, and fathers.

Rebecca Hagan Lee is the author of five bestselling romances, and has won numerous awards including a Waldenbooks Award for Bestselling Original Long Historical Romance by a New Author. She lives in south Georgia with her hero husband, two miniature schnauzers, a rat terrier, a cat, and a host of imaginary heroes and heroines waiting to be introduced.

PENGUIN PUTNAM INC.
Online

Your Internet gateway to a virtual environment with
hundreds of entertaining and enlightening books from
Penguin Putnam Inc.

*While you're there, get the latest buzz on
the best authors and books around—*

Tom Clancy, Patricia Cornwell, W.E.B. Griffin,
Nora Roberts, William Gibson, Robin Cook,
Brian Jacques, Catherine Coulter, Stephen King,
Jacquelyn Mitchard, and many more!

Penguin Putnam Online is located at
http://www.penguinputnam.com

PENGUIN PUTNAM NEWS

Every month you'll get an inside look at our upcoming
books and new features on our site. This is an ongoing
effort to provide you with the most up-to-date
information about our books and authors.

Subscribe to Penguin Putnam News at
http://www.penguinputnam.com/ClubPPI